'*The Insult* is one of those rare, perfect, all-consuming books where you life takes on a new colour and texture for the days you are in its thrall.'

Julie Myerson, *Mail on Sunday*

'Strange and sexy . . . a story of rich, manic cunning.'

Maxim

'Thomson leaves you in no doubt that he's one of the best of an up-and-coming generation of writers. This is a wry, occasionally chilling tale about the catastrophic results of a random shooting. Arm yourself with a stiff whisky.'

Marie Claire

'Thomson is one of our finest exponents of the psychological thriller . . . Here is a world ruled by helpless paranoia and the shadowy recesses of the mind.'

Arena

'A vivid read which has both tempo and a string of surprises.'

Time Out

'An astonishing exploration into the blurred hinterland where fiction meets fantasy . . . Both crisply precise and extravagantly daring. *The Insult* is a remarkable achievement.'

Sunday Telegraph

'This novel, which begins with a random act of violence, ends in terrifyingly focused passion . . . Thomson has a pitiless humour about human confusion; his prose maintains a high tension between fragile polished ironies and Brando-esque spunkiness. *The Insult* is the most irresistible of his books.'

Times Literary Supplement

'Echoing the pschological confusion of Kafka's *The Trial*, Thomson's odyssey into the depths of isolated existence is absorbing and inspired.'

Elle

'Contemporary, original, inventive . . . New readers of Thomson's work should be prepared to have all their senses extended.'

The Australian

'The denouement might be worthy of Ruth Rendell, but until then Thomson's mischievously misleading methods ensure we keep bumping into the furniture while he creeps ahead in soft-soled shoes.'

Independent On Sunday

'When someone writes as well as Thomson does, it makes you wonder why other people bother.'

New Statesmen and Society

BY THE SAME AUTHOR

DREAMS OF LEAVING
THE FIVE GATES OF HELL
AIR AND FIRE

THE INSULT

RUPERT THOMSON

BLOOMSBURY

This book is for Dick and Marcia Wertime,
and for Michael Karbelnikoff,
Wolfgang Lackinger and Calvin Mitchell.

First published 1996

This paperback edition published 1996

Bloomsbury Publishing Plc, 38 Soho Square, London W1V 5DF

A CIP catalogue record for this book is available from the British Library

10 9 8

ISBN 0 7476 2601 X

Typeset by Hewer Text Composition Services, Edinburgh
Printed in Great Britain by Clays Limited, St Ives plc

'As the city grows bigger, it seems that people re-evolve, lose touch with their bodies, becoming disembodied almost, living only through their brains . . .'

– Shinya Tsukamoto

'I am afraid. One has to take action against fear, once one has it.'

– Rainer Maria Rilke

'. . . it is difficult to recover from illness precisely because we are unaware of it.'

– Seneca

CONTENTS

NIGHTLIFE

'You've been shot.'

I heard someone say it. I wouldn't have known otherwise; I wouldn't have realised. All I could remember was four tomatoes – three of them motionless, one still rolling. And a black shape, too. A shape that had a curve to it.

I've been shot.

Sirens circled me like ghosts.

I slipped away, the feeling of having fallen from a plane, of falling through dark air, and the plane flying on without me . . .

Each time I woke up, it was night.

Then voices spoke to me, out of nothing. Voices told me the rest. You'd been shopping, they said. You were in a supermarket car-park when it happened. It was a Thursday evening. You were walking towards your vehicle when you were fired upon, a single shot. The bullet took a horizontal path through the occipital cortex. One millimetre lower and you would've died instantaneously. You suffered no damage to adjacent structures; however, you have lost your vision and that loss is permanent. There were no witnesses to the shooting.

I lay in bed, my neck supported by a padded brace. My head had a strange deadness to it, as if it was an arm and I'd slept on it.

My mouth tasted of flowers.

The voices told me I was in a clinic in the northern suburbs. They told me how much time had passed, and how it had been spent: brain-scans, neuro-surgery, post-traumatic amnesia. They told me that my parents had visited. My fiancée, too. None of what they said surprised me. I could smell bandages and, behind the smell of bandages, methylated spirits, linoleum, dried blood. I imagined, for some reason, that the lino was pale-green with streaks of white in it, like certain kinds of soap or marble. It seemed to me that several people were positioned around my bed, though only one of them was speaking. I turned my face in his direction.

'Something I didn't understand. Occipital something.'

The same voice answered. 'Occipital cortex. It's located at the back of the head, the very base of the brain. It's responsible for visual interpretation. In your case, the damage is bilateral: both lobes are affected.'

'You said the loss of vision is permanent . . .'

'That's correct.'

'So there's no chance of recovery?'

'None.' The voice paused. 'I'm sorry.'

Somebody placed a hand on my shoulder. I wasn't sure which one of them it was – the man who'd been talking to me or one of the others. I couldn't have said what it communicated. Pity, maybe. Consolation. It reminded me of the feelings I'd had about churches when I was young. How I'd imagined an angel's touch might be.

I found that my eyes had filled with water.

Bits fly off me as I run.

The place is always the same. It's a city street, though not one I recognise. Sunlight everywhere. The buildings blaze with it.

I can see myself running. The bits flying off me. Two ribs, an ear. One of my arms. Some teeth. They come loose, drop silently away. It's like the way things happen in space. I watch a finger leave my hand, spin backwards through the bright gold air behind me. Soon there's just the running left.

You might think it would stop then, but it doesn't. I keep running, even though I don't have any legs. Even though the body's gone, the elbows too, the lungs.

It's hard to describe. It's like one kind of air passing through another. It's not a bad feeling. The flesh has gone. There's only the spirit left.

I wake up sweating . . .

The man who had talked to me before was sitting by my bed. This time he was alone.

'My name's Visser. Bruno Visser.'

'What do you look like?' I said.

'An understandable question.' He mentioned light-brown hair, pale-blue eyes. He was fairly tall, he said. Then he told me he was my neuro-surgeon, as if he thought that detail might complete the picture.

'And what about me?' I said. 'What do I look like?'

He paused, his silence awkward – or perhaps just curious, intrigued.

'I mean, am I disfigured?' I asked him. 'Would I recognise myself?'

'There's only one disfigurement, as you put it, and it's not really apparent.' He explained that I'd lost a small section of bone on the left side of my cranium, shattered by the stranger's bullet as it exited. The normal procedure was to wait until the tissues healed, and then to fit a titanium plate. It was a fairly simple operation, he assured me. There would be a scar, of course, but the hair would grow back over it. Nobody would know.

He continued, more earnest now (he had moved his chair closer to the bed, his voice was lower). I shouldn't underestimate the task that lay ahead, he said. When someone loses their vision suddenly, at least three stages can usually be distinguished. First there's shock, a numbness that may last for weeks – the body's own protective anaesthesia.

Then depression sets in. This stage could last longer. Months. Years even. Hopelessness, self-pity, suicidal thoughts – I had to be ready, he said, for any or all of these. Finally, when I'd finished mourning my loss of vision, there was the gradual rehabilitation: the development of a new personality, with different capacities, different potential.

'And now for the bad news,' I said.

'At this clinic, Martin,' Visser said, 'we don't believe you should be under any illusions about your condition.'

'I don't think there's much danger of that.'

There was a silence. 'Perhaps you should get some rest.' His chair creaked twice. He was gone.

I wake sweating, wait for my heart to settle. It always takes a while, after the dream, for my hands to join the smooth, glossy stumps of my wrists. For my body to piece itself together.

This is what must have happened after I was shot. I mean, that must have been the first time it happened. Only then it would have taken longer. Hours, probably. Maybe days. And there were parts of me that didn't reappear, of course. One small section of my skull, measuring, according to Visser, 2.75 cm. by 1.93 cm. My eyesight, too. That never came back either.

I lie here with my neck supported by the brace. I move my fingers against the coarse wool of the blanket that covers me. I move my feet against the undersheet. There will come a time, I think to myself, when this won't happen. When I don't wake up in a hospital bed – or any other bed, for that matter. When disintegration's pull can no longer be resisted. When the bits of my body continue to fly outwards, like the universe itself.

Visser returned. I knew him by his footsteps – or, to be more accurate, his shoes. They'd been repaired with metal, those steel crescents that prevent heels or toes from wearing out. I turned my head towards him. He wanted to explain something to me – I sensed his need – but he wasn't sure how to begin.

At last he leaned forwards, his clothes releasing a faint odour of carbolic. 'NPL,' he said.

'I'm sorry?'

'No perception of light. I'll give you a demonstration.' He reached into a trouser or a jacket pocket. 'I'm holding a torch. Now, can you tell me, is it on?'

I stared hard, but I had no awareness of a torch. I wasn't aware of anything.

'Is it off,' Visser said, 'or on?'

'I've no idea.'

'And yet your pupils still contract.' The torch clicked. 'What's interesting about cortical blindness is that it's absolute. Your eyes still see, they still respond to light. It's just that what they're seeing is not being recorded in the brain.' He shifted in his chair. 'Imagine a TV. A TV receives electromagnetic waves from a transmitter and it reconverts those waves into visual images. If the TV's faulty, the electromagnetic waves are not converted. Unfortunately, that's where the analogy ends. Unlike a TV, the occipital cortex cannot be replaced, or even repaired. We simply don't have the technology as yet. Do you understand?'

'I think so.'

'It's perhaps for this reason – the fact that the retina, the optic nerves and the anterior visual pathways are all still functioning as normal – that people who suffer from cortical blindness often believe, despite proof to the contrary, that they can see. This is a condition known as Anton's Syndrome. Rare, admittedly, but it exists.'

I didn't know what he meant by proof to the contrary.

'Oh, falling downstairs,' he said, 'bumping into furniture – that kind of thing.' Visser's tone was light, almost playful, and yet I wasn't offended. I saw what he was describing – it was slapstick, it was farce: policemen walking into lampposts, fat women slipping on banana-skins – and I, too, was entertained.

'You might also experience visual hallucinations,' Visser went on, 'flashes of light and so forth. It's quite common in cases like yours, where there has been a severe insult to the brain – '

'I think I know what you're trying to say, Doctor.'

Visser was silent, waiting.

'You're trying to say that I shouldn't fall into the trap of believing I can still see.'

'Well, yes. Precisely.'

He sounded so surprised, so pleased with me, that I couldn't help feeling proud of myself. In fact, I had the feeling that the pride was mutual, that we were, to some as yet unknown extent, dependent on each other.

Once or twice a year, when I was young, my parents would put me on a train to the city. My grandparents met me at the other end. From the station we caught a tram out to their small house in the suburbs (in my memory it's always the same ride, through streets that are sunlit, tree-lined, deadened by the heat, and my grandmother always offers me a pear, picked from a tree on their allotment). I usually stayed for two weeks, and was always sad when it was time to go.

Not far from where they lived was a big house that stood in a private park. I would ride there on my grandfather's bicycle, slow down as I passed the gates. Standing on the pedals, I'd turn in an unsteady circle, unwilling to stop, but wanting a second glimpse. There was a driveway leading up to the house between two rows of trees. On winter evenings their branches, black and gleaming, seemed to hoard the gold windows in their fingers. In spring, white blossoms lay scattered on the gravel, each petal curved and pale, eyelid-shaped. Otherwise there was nothing much to see. The house itself was a kilometre away, at least, a façade of dark bricks in the distance. Green drainpipes. Chimneys.

When I asked my grandparents about it, they told me it was a sanatorium. That means people who are sick, they said. I was never sure if they meant mad or just ill, and they were dead now, my grandparents; the last time I looked for the sanatorium, I was told it had been pulled down. If I'd been called upon to explain my fascination I don't know what I would have said. It wasn't so much what I saw as what I might see. Part of you recognises a potential. Thinking about it now, I found a cruel irony in it. It occurred to me that, if the boy on the bicycle had looked hard enough, if he'd looked really hard, he might have seen the man he would eventually become.

More than twenty years had passed since then, but just for a moment, lying in my bed in the clinic, I'm that boy again, turning circles on his grandfather's bicycle. And, looking up, I notice a man moving down the gravel drive towards me. I drop one foot to the ground and stand there, watching. The man's eyes are bandaged and yet he's walking in a straight line, as though he can see. And when he reaches the gates he stops and looks at me, right through the bandages, right between the black wrought-iron bars.

'Martin?' he says. 'Is that you?'

My hands tighten on the handlebars.

'It's you,' he says, 'isn't it.'

I start pedalling. There's a hill luckily, it's steep, the wind roars in my ears. But even when I'm back with my grandparents and everything's normal again, I can't be sure that I won't turn round and see him walk towards me through the house.

Knowing me, despite the bandages.

Knowing my name.

'Mr Blom?'

It was the nurse, Miss Janssen. She had two detectives with her. One of them, Slatnick, was making noises, strange little squeaks and splashes, which I finally identified as the sound of someone chewing gum. The other man's name was Munck. Munck did most of the talking. His voice was easy to listen to, almost soporific. I wanted to tell him he was in the wrong job; with a voice like that, he should have been a hypnotist.

He was shocked, he said – they both were – by what had happened. He could only express the deepest sympathy for me in my predicament. If there was anything that they could do . . .

'Thank you,' I said.

Munck talked on. The last ten years had seen a proliferation of firearms in the city. Incidents of the type it had been my misfortune to be involved in had increased a hundredfold. Random violence, seemingly senseless crimes. He had his theories, of course, but now was not the time. He paused. Wind rushed in the trees outside. A window further down the ward blew open; I felt cold air search the room. Munck leaned closer in his chair. The reason they'd come, he said, was to hear my version of the event.

'I'm sorry,' I said. 'I don't have a version.'

'You don't remember anything?'

'No, not really.'

'Did you see anything at all?'

I smiled. 'Tomatoes.'

Slatnick stopped chewing for a moment.

'They must've spilled out of my bag,' I said. 'I suppose I was going to make a salad that night.'

'I see.' I heard Munck stand up and start to pace about. 'Where do you work, Mr Blom?'

'A bookshop.' I mentioned the name of it.

'I know the place. I'm often in there myself.' Munck walked to the end of the bed. 'Do you have any enemies?'

I raised my eyebrows.

'It sounds dramatic, I know,' Munck said, 'but we have to ask.'

'None that I can think of.'

'You have no idea who might've shot at you?'

'I'm afraid not.'

Slatnick spoke next. 'Am I correct in assuming therefore that you would not be able to identify your assailant?'

I stared in his direction. What is it about policemen?

'Slatnick,' Munck said, 'I think the answer's yes.'

'Yes?' Slatnick hadn't understood.

'Yes, you'd be correct in that assumption.'

There was a silence.

'I'm sorry to have disturbed you, Mr Blom,' Munck said. 'I have to say that, in this case, it seems unlikely that justice will be done. All that remains is for us to wish you a speedy recovery. Once again, if there's anything we can do – '

'Thank you, Detective.'

I listened to the two men walk away, their footsteps mingling with those of other visitors. One of them sounded like a diver, the soles of his shoes slapping down like flippers on the floor . . .

Absolute blindness is rare. There's usually some suggestion of movement, some sense of light and shade. Not in my case. What I 'saw' was without texture or definition: it was constant, depthless and impenetrable. Sometimes I thought: *Your eyes are closed. Open them.* But they were already open. Wide open, seeing nothing. I could look straight into the sun and my pupils would contract, but I wouldn't know it was the sun that I was looking at. Or I could put my head inside a cardboard box. Same thing. There were no gradations in the blankness, no fluctuations of any kind. It was what depression would look like, I thought, if you had to externalise it.

Miss Janssen spent part of every morning at my bedside. It was her job to motivate me, though I found most of her efforts infantile and embarrassing. Take the rubber balls, for instance. She told me to hold one in each hand. I was supposed to 'squeeze and then relax, squeeze and then relax'.

'What's it for?' I asked.

'You'd be surprised,' she said, 'how quickly muscles atrophy.'

'Is that so?'

'Yes, it is. If you don't exercise, they just wither away.'

'Well, in that case,' I said, 'there's one muscle we definitely shouldn't overlook.'

She brought the session to an abrupt end.

The next morning she was back again, as usual. She made no reference to what I'd said the day before. In what was intended as a gesture of repentance, I asked her for the rubber balls. I lay there, one in each hand, squeezing and relaxing. I behaved. And, since her voice was all there was, I began to listen to it. Not the words in themselves, but the sound of the words. I tried to work out how old she was, what she did in her spare time, whether she was happy. There were moments when I thought I could picture her, the way you picture strangers on the phone, just from their voices: I saw the colour of her eyes, the shape of her mouth. It was like what happened when the dream I had was over: the gradual assembly of a physical presence. Some mornings I found that I could only see her breasts. Her voice seemed to be telling me that they were large. The curve from the rib-cage to the nipple, for example. That fullness, that wonderful convexity. Not unlike a fruit bowl. But I could never sustain it. Sooner or later the picture always broke up, fell apart, dissolved. And, anyway, they weren't her breasts. They were just breasts. They could have been anybody's.

I tried the same thing with the man in the next bed. His name was Smulders. He used to work for the national railways, first as a signalman and, later, as a station announcer. Then he got cataracts in both eyes. They'd operated during the summer, but the results had been disappointing. I asked him the obvious question, just to start him talking: 'Can you see anything at all?'

'Sometimes I see dancing girls. They move across in front of me, legs kicking, like they're on a stage.' Smulders took a breath. His lungs bubbled.

He must be a smoker, I thought. Forty a day, non-filter. The tips of two of his fingers appeared, stained yellow by the nicotine.

'Anything else?' I said.

'Dogs.'

'Dogs? What kind of dogs?'

'Poodles. With ribbons and bows all over them.'

'No trains?'

'Once.' Smulders chuckled. 'It was the 6.23, I think. Packed, it was.'

He talked on, about his work, his colleagues, his passion for all things connected with the railways; he talked for hours. But nothing came. Nothing except a pair of black spectacles, their lenses stained the same colour as the fingertips. Then I realised that they belonged to a friend of my father's, a man who used to work at the post office, in Sorting. I couldn't seem to picture Smulders at all. Somehow his breathing got in the way, like frosted glass.

These were, in any case, minor entertainments, scant moments of distraction. There were days, whole days, when I lay in bed without moving. Almost without thinking. The TV cackled and muttered, the way a caged bird might. Meals came and went on metal trolleys – hot, damp smells that were lurid, rotten, curiously tropical. My head felt as if it had been wrapped in cloth, layer upon layer of it. I often had to fight for breath. Once I tried to tear the covering from my face, but all I found beneath my fingernails was skin.

My skin.

There was no covering, of course.

Nurse Janssen sat with me each morning, her voice in the air beside me. It was still a kind of seed, yet I could grow nothing from it, no comfort, no desire. I'd lost all my wit, my ingenuity.

'How's your face?' she asked me.

'You tell me.'

'It's looking much better. How does it feel?'

'Feels all right.'

'You know, there are three trees outside your window,' she said, 'three beautiful trees. They're pines.'

If this was an attempt at consolation, it was misconceived, hopelessly naive. I stared straight ahead. 'Pines, you say?'

'Yes.'

'I can smell them.'

'It's a beautiful smell, isn't it?'

I scowled. 'If you like toilet cleaner.'

Later that day I picked up one of my rubber balls and threw it into the blankness in front of me. Now that *was* beautiful, the silence of the ball travelling through the air, an unseen arc, and then the splintering of glass. I hadn't realised there might be a window there. I saw the impact as a flower blooming, from tight green bud to petals in less than a second. It was like those programmes on TV where they speed a natural process up.

The next morning Visser put me on a course of medication. I took the drug in liquid form. It was acrid, syrupy in texture, but I didn't make any fuss. I drank it down and then lay back, waiting for the effect.

What happens is this:

The world shrinks. The world's a ball of dust. It rolls silently along the bottom of a wall, meaningless and round. You watch it go. You don't have to think about it any more. It's got nothing to do with you, nothing whatsoever.

You'd wave goodbye to it if you could lift your arm.

Not long after I surfaced from the anaesthetic, Visser visited me. He told me that he had replaced the missing bone with a piece of precision-engineered titanium. The fit was perfect; he'd checked it with a CT scan. There had been no complications, nor was there any trace of infection – at least not so far. The entire operation had taken less than four hours. The way he described it, he made my head sound like some kind of jigsaw, and there was a note of genuine pride in his voice, as if it had been clever of him to finish it.

'In short,' I said, rather drily, 'it was a success.'

I heard his lips part on his teeth. 'Oh yes. Most certainly. How do you feel?'

'Not bad.' I paused. 'It's a strange *idea*, though, a piece of metal in your head – '

'No stranger than a hip replacement,' he said.

I didn't agree. The point was, it was in my head. That's what made it squeamish.

But Visser would have none of it. 'You might experience some numbness where the cut nerves are,' he went on cheerfully, 'but there shouldn't be too much discomfort. You'll be up and about in no time.'

He was right about that. Within a week I'd recovered from the surgery and I was embarking on my rehabilitation. Every afternoon I was taken to the Mobility Training Centre, a special room in the east wing. It was laid out like a surreal, random version of the world outside. There were flights of stairs that stopped in mid-air. There were arbitrary brick walls – some knee-high, others reaching to the ceiling. There were kerbstones, but no roads. This was Dr Kukowski's domain. Kukowski had a patient, almost weary manner, and his skin smelled of vinegar. I sometimes speculated on the effect his work might have on him. I could imagine him pausing halfway up the stairs at home, for example, unwilling to go further. Or stepping off the pavement into the path of an oncoming car because he had completely forgotten about the possibility of traffic.

Kukowski gave me my first cane. It was lighter than I'd expected. Longer, too, almost shoulder-height. I was supposed to hold it at waist-level and then walk forwards, scanning, rather in the manner of someone with a metal detector. Tap, tap, tap went the toughened nylon tip. There was something ludicrous about the whole process; I wanted to pour scorn on it. But behind Kukowski's patience there lurked a threat: it was either the cane or it was back to tranquillisers, headaches, isolation. I took the cane.

In the mornings I was still seeing Nurse Janssen. During the afternoons I had to pick my way through the obstacle course that was Kukowski's world – a world that would be mine, he assured me, as soon as I was discharged. Towards evening Visser would pay me a visit. Sometimes he stayed just long enough to ask after my health. On other occasions we'd talk for an hour or more. He was almost always complimentary. *Bilateral cortical damage is so rare, Martin. It may sound tactless, but it's a privilege to have you here.* Whenever I was alone I was encouraged to work on what Kukowski called my 'long-cane technique'. There was the physical manipulation of the cane itself, of course, but there were also various mental skills and disciplines which had to be mastered. I had to learn how to use sound to determine distance and direction. I had to sensitise myself to echoes (a method known as echolocation). I had to be able to memorise a route. And so on. There seemed to be no end to it. It was the height of summer now, and I spent as much time as I could outdoors. Most days, after supper, I could be found in the clinic gardens, practising.

And that was when it happened.

One evening I was crossing the lawn, feeling as if I knew each mound, each root, each blade of grass by heart, when I realised that what lay in front of me – what I could 'see', as it were – was not the usual grey, featureless and empty. *It was green, and there were shapes in it*. You must be imagining it, I told myself. This is one of the illusions Visser warned you about. You think you're seeing, but you're not.

I stood quite still and looked around me.

The shapes in the green were trees. And I could see the lawn, too, reaching away from me, then sloping down. There was a smoothness at the end of it. A lake. I could see a stand of poplars, tapering like rockets as they lifted into the sky.

The sky!

For a moment I didn't dare to move in case it all cut out and I went blind again. Then I knew what I would do. I chose one tree and slowly began to walk towards it. The tree grew larger. At last I was close enough to touch it. I reached out. There was bark beneath my fingers, ridged and damp. I looked up. Leaves shifting in the evening wind.

This was no illusion. I was seeing the tree, the gardens – everything. *I was seeing*. I stood there with the tips of my fingers touching bark. Leaves turned and turned above my head – the rush of blood through arteries.

I couldn't move.

At last I set out across the lawn, my cane scanning the blades of grass in front of me, left and right, left and right. I climbed the steps to the entrance, feeling for dimensions, height and width, as I'd been taught. Inside the clinic I followed the corridor that led to my ward. My vision had faded slightly, but I could still make out the pipes massed on the ceiling, the plain wooden chairs against the wall in the visitors' waiting-room. I had to be careful to ignore the doctor who was walking towards me. I had to make sure I didn't move to one side. Suddenly it struck me – an exquisite moment, this – that I was only *pretending* I couldn't see.

I didn't say anything about it, though. It was partly excitement, partly disbelief. Partly fear of ridicule as well, no doubt; I didn't want people thinking I was mad. I felt I ought to explore what was happening for myself, to get the measure of it. I needed to be sure of what I had.

When I got into bed that night I still hadn't mentioned it to anyone. I lay there in the dark and stared at the ceiling. The paint had cracks in it. I saw the great rivers of the world – the Ganges, the Amazon, the Nile. I saw areas of nothing – the Russian Steppes, the Empty Quarter. My heart was jumping like something on a trampoline. It just kept jumping.

It was hours before I slept.

Bits flying off me.

This time it's my eyes. I watch them spring out of their sockets (somehow that's possible). I notice how they bounce on the road behind me. I see them burst.

But I run on.

Then it's my nose, my ears. Some teeth. The skin of my face peels off like a mask and flaps away into the bright gold distance. A bat, a leaf. A pricked balloon.

I'm still running.

A tiny section of my skull detaches and whirls backwards. Asymmetrical, off-white, it looks like broken china, part of a vase. That priceless missing piece.

As I run I can feel the sockets where my eyes once were. Hollow, smooth, picked clean. My skull's a flute. The air plays haunting music on it.

When I wake up, it's morning and I'm blind again.

That day passed more slowly than any day I can remember. To be given back my sight and then deprived of it again – I could imagine no greater cruelty; it seemed an act worthy of a torturer. Tears slid from the corners of my eyes on to the pillow. I wouldn't talk to anyone, least of all to Nurse Janssen; I couldn't bear her kindness, her concern, both of which seemed inexhaustible.

At last, towards evening, I willed myself to sleep.

I heard the clock strike ten. As I raised my head off the pillow I saw the same green that I'd seen the previous night. And there were shapes in it. Only this time they were beds, not trees. Rows of metal beds, each one painted the same colour. The eerie, shiny cream that institutions like so much.

I pushed the covers back and swung my legs on to the floor. I stood up. The lino was cool beneath my feet, and slightly sticky. I could see Smulders in the next bed, one solid curve from his shoulder to his knee; for the first time it occurred to me that Smulders might be fat. I moved out into the ward, stepping delicately through rectangles of moonlight. The night was thick with blind men's dreams.

Two doors separated the wash-room from the ward. Between the doors was a ventilation area, open to the air at either end. Placing my hands on the railing, I gazed out over the orchard and the vegetable patch. A smell lifted past my face, a smell that was like my childhood distilled: warm asphalt, grass clippings, the skin of plums. Beyond the clinic grounds the land rose up, a replica of Smulders' sleeping form. I saw lights dart across the sky. I couldn't tell if they were shooting-stars or aeroplanes. They were too far off.

I passed through the second door, closing it softly behind me. Though I was familiar with every feature of the wash-room, that very familiarity was strange, based as it was on discoveries I'd made while blind. Now I could make the same discoveries again, using my eyes: the tin basins, the window-catches, the spigots on the taps (as bulbous as murderers' thumbs) – nothing was too ordinary to escape my attention. I was shocked, though, by the dilapidation and neglect I saw around me. There were broken windows high up in the wall, draughts haunting the jagged gaps. There was paint peeling from the ceiling. There was damp. I don't know how long I'd been in there when I was startled by the sudden rattle of loose glass panes in the outer wash-room door. I stepped behind the wooden partition that hid the toilet, and waited. The inner door opened and somebody walked in. At first I wasn't sure who it was. Then I recognised the breathing. Smulders.

Peering round the edge of the partition, I watched intently as he stripped his nightshirt off and let it fall to the stone floor. He stood stark naked for a moment, listening. Then he reached out with both hands. He looked like a ghost – his arms horizontal, his fingers tickling the air. At last he found a tap. He turned it on, began to soap himself. His hands sucked and belched in the fleshy pockets of his armpits. The hair that grew there was matted, long and lank, identical to the hair you might pull from the plughole of a bath. It was like seeing a human being for the first time. We're ugly, aren't we? It's extraordinary how ugly we are. For a moment I was afraid I might vomit. (I hoped I wouldn't; apart from anything else, I didn't want Smulders knowing I was there.) I sank down, behind the partition. As I fought the nausea I had a curious thought: what a blessing blindness could be, what a respite from the frightful squalor of the world!

At last I turned back.

There he was, still soaping himself, his breath issuing in ragged gusts and the occasional grunt of satisfaction. I let my eyes course his ample contours. It looked as though handfuls of fat had been attached to him at random. There were creases and folds all over his body, places where one parcel of obesity had collided with another. And what would happen if you opened out those creases? You'd find a sort of melted butter there, mottled and rancid. The smell would be enough to burn out whole banks of olfactory cells. And then there was the ultimate crease, the most elaborate of folds: his foreskin. I balked at the idea of that.

Just then the panes in the outer door rattled for a second time. Smulders jumped, his flesh reverberating – a kind of visual echo. I shrank back into the corner of the toilet stall, between the cistern and the wall, and waited.

'That's enough, Smulders.'

It was Visser. His voice gentle but firm, with just a trace of amusement.

'Come on now. Back to bed.'

Smulders lumbered through the open doorway, his armpit hair still dripping. Visser followed. I saw him for a moment, over the top of the partition. All I got was an impression of his profile – his forehead, nose and chin – and a glimpse of a moustache.

As I lay in bed that night I had one further thought: among the blind there is no tact, no modesty; there doesn't need to be. It followed that, so long as I stayed in the clinic, I would constantly be assaulted by the most hideous visions. I didn't belong among the blind. I was in the wrong place. The sooner I got myself discharged, the better. The last image that appeared before I fell asleep was that of Smulders' penis, apprehensive, cowering beneath his belly, as if terrified that, at any moment, it might be crushed by the great burden of flesh that hung above it.

I sat on a bench outside Visser's office, waiting for someone to call my name. It was early evening; through the open window I could hear birds settling in the trees. Just before dawn, two of the night-staff had found me hiding (their word) in the broom cupboard. They assumed I was having another of my depressive episodes. They even suspected that I might be harbouring suicidal thoughts, that I might have been about to swallow bleach or some other convenient domestic poison.

The fools!

Almost a week had passed since the revelation in the gardens. I'd spent the time constructively, exploring my condition. In the washroom first, then in the broom cupboard. There were no windows in the broom cupboard. There was no gap at the bottom of the door. It was here, in absolute darkness, that I was able properly to test my theories. (I also believed – mistakenly, as it turned out – that I might have more privacy.) I would wait until everyone was asleep, then I'd tiptoe down the ward, out through the swing-doors, along the corridor and left, into the broom cupboard. Once inside, I carried out a series of simple experiments. I read the labels on bottles of disinfectant. I counted the strands on a mop. I tracked the progress of a spider as it crossed the cracked concrete floor and climbed the wall. It didn't take me long to reach a conclusion: night was my ally and my vision was in some way linked to it. In other words, I could see – *but only in the dark*.

My name was called. I tapped my way into Visser's office.

'Ah,' he said, 'Martin.'

He was most curious to learn more about what he referred to as my 'adventure in the cupboard'. He wanted to understand my motivation. What could I tell him, though? I couldn't think of anything. Also, I was distracted by his physical appearance. My brief glimpse of him in the wash-room had not been misleading. He *did* have a moustache. Thick and brown, it was. Lustrous. And yet, when I asked him to describe himself, he hadn't mentioned it. Why not? Could it be that he was sensitive about it? (Sometimes it hides a weak upper lip.) My God, a moustache – I'd never have guessed. I thought he looked a bit like a dictator. Not Hitler. It wasn't that kind of moustache. More like Stalin.

'Well?' Visser was still waiting.

Sweat began to accumulate on the inside of my elbows. Then, out of nowhere, inspiration: 'It must be something to do with not seeing anything.' I was making it up, but it sounded plausible.

'Yes?'

'Maybe,' I faltered, and then plunged on, 'maybe I was putting myself in a place where *nobody* could see anything. The kind of place where it doesn't matter who's blind and who isn't. I mean, in a broom cupboard everyone's blind, right?' I smiled. 'Maybe that's what I was after, the feeling of being the same as everybody else.'

'That's why you were in the broom cupboard?'

'Well, it's a thought.'

'See how this sounds.' Visser paused. 'You're finding it hard to deal with the world, to come to terms with it, so you turn your back on it. You isolate yourself. You hide.'

I leaned back. 'Mmm,' I said. 'Interesting.'

The whole premise was a fabrication – and yet Visser had swallowed it. How could I respect the man when I could so effortlessly steer him away from the truth?

And what is the truth? I asked myself later, as I walked out of his office. Each time the sun sets, I begin to see. Each sunrise I go blind.

As yet, I had no explanation for this.

Since becoming nocturnal, I'd learned something else about Smulders: he talked in his sleep. I stayed awake for hours, listening to his monologues. They were exactly like the announcements you hear on station platforms. This was Smulders being nostalgic, I decided. Smulders returning to happier days, when he still worked for the railways. He was particularly keen on departures and arrivals, the times, as always, strangely fastidious, almost neurotic: the 5.44 to somewhere, the 21.16 to somewhere else. And, every now and then, there were warnings, prevarications, excuses – especially excuses. A train had derailed. Points had failed. There was a cow on the line, or a child. Or a leaf.

I became addicted. Smulders sent me on journeys I had never thought of (once I even left the country!). Smulders offered me rail passes. Smulders marooned me on the platforms of obscure provincial stations, then told me that the next train wasn't due for three hours. I ate terrible food at stainless-steel kiosks. I got indigestion. Chilblains. Flu. Smulders apologised and I forgave him. His announcements took me out of the closed world of the clinic and put me somewhere else, somewhere real. They could often have the same effect as lullabies, long lists of destinations taking the place of sheep.

Then, one night, Smulders didn't talk. I waited in the darkness, ears cocked. Nothing. Not even a murmur. Somehow I resented it; this was a service I'd come to expect, rely on. How else was I going to get through the night? I wasn't going to risk another visit to the broom cupboard and I was tired of making maps out of the cracks on the ceiling. I wanted entertaining. I wanted *announcements*.

I decided to try something.

I crept across the gap between our beds. I paused. Smulders was asleep, his breathing coarse as someone tearing lettuce. I stooped over him. There was an intriguing shape to Smulders. It was as if his belly was the clumsy packaging for something else. Strip away the blubber and you'd come across it: a large cardboard box, containing some kind of domestic appliance. A TV, maybe. A Jumbo microwave. A tumble-dryer. I stooped lower. Ah yes. The reek. The stench. The butter trapped in trenches that were almost bottomless. I placed my lips as close to his ear as I dared. I composed myself. Then, softly, I began: 'Ch . . . . . Ch . . . . . Ch . . . . Ch . . . . Ch . . . Ch . . . Ch . . . Ch . . . Ch . . . Ch . . . Ch . . .'

A big round moan rose from Smulders' lips –

'*Ch*-Ch . . . *Ch*-Ch . . . *Ch*-Ch . . . *Ch*-Ch . . .'

– but he could not resist: 'The train now departing . . .'

I tiptoed back to bed.

He kept it up for more than an hour. There were the usual timetables. There were details of various connections. And there was something new – a convoluted explanation of the reason why a commuter train scheduled for an 18.04 departure had been cancelled, together with an appropriately long-winded apology. I lay there imagining the people massed in front of the departures board, their faces at angles of forty-five degrees. They'd be *fuming*. I smiled and turned on to my comfortable side.

The last thing I heard before I fell asleep that night was a reminder that smoking was forbidden on all platforms. I imagined that Smulders, with his great appetite for cigarettes and the freedom, presumably, to smoke them in his office, must always have relished that particular announcement.

'You have a visitor,' Nurse Janssen told me.

Visser stood beside her. I detected an exchange of glances that I didn't understand. The thick air of conspiracy hung around my bed.

'Someone to see you,' Nurse Janssen said.

I raised myself a little higher on my pillows. 'Oh?'

'It's your fiancée, Claudia.'

She'd visited before, apparently, while I was either medicated or unconscious. I'd been told how she would sit beside my bed with one of my hands in both of hers. A lovely girl, Claudia; that was the general consensus. It had even been suggested that her devotion had helped to pull me through.

I didn't say anything for a moment. I didn't like people gushing, I never had; I didn't like mindless sentimentality – and it surprised me to discover that not only Nurse Janssen (predictable, perhaps) but also Visser (Visser!) might be prone to it. And as for the idea of someone holding my hand without me knowing, it suddenly struck me as a violation, an obscenity – even if that someone was my fiancée.

'Aren't you pleased?' Nurse Janssen said.

'Where is she?' I said.

They led me to a room I'd never known was there. It didn't seem to belong with the draughty, antiseptic corridors and hallways of the clinic. Smelling of sponge cake, wood-polish and cut flowers, it was more like the drawing-room in a country house. I waited for Claudia in an armchair by the window.

Before too long she came quietly into the room and sat down in the chair next to mine.

'You look just the same,' she said.

I turned to face her. 'I can't see you.'

I was lying, of course. I'd asked them to dim the lamps in the room before they left. They probably thought it was for reasons of modesty or romance. It was nothing of the kind. It was so I could look at her.

She began to cry.

I studied her closely. Her narrow knees were pressed together and her head was bowed. She'd altered her hairstyle, drawing it sleekly back behind her ears. She'd fastened it with a piece of dark velvet. The colour was hard to make out against the light, but I imagined it was purple. She'd always liked purple.

Her shoulders shook inside her cardigan. I felt sorry for her, but in the way you might feel sorry for a stranger you saw crying in a public place – sitting beside a fountain, say, or standing at a bus-stop. There was nothing personal about it. On the contrary, I felt removed from her. Distanced. I felt so distant that I was almost curious to know the reason for her tears.

At last, she sat up straighter in her chair. She wiped her face with a hand that seemed clumsy; it was as if she'd lost the use of it, as if it had been broken at the wrist. That slender wrist. There was a time when it had meant something.

She apologised for not visiting me during the past few weeks. She'd had examinations. She reminded me that she was studying to be a lawyer.

'Did you pass?' I asked her.

'Yes.' She nodded.

I congratulated her.

Outside, it was September. The wasps on the windowsill were drowsy, and there were fires burning in the fields beyond the clinic wall. I saw Visser and Janssen walking through the orchard, among the pear trees, her dark head bent, his moustache mysterious in the half-light.

After a long silence, and so abruptly that I jumped, Claudia offered to come and live with me. She'd cook, she'd clean. She'd see to my every need. Her face tilted eagerly.

I tried to conceal my horror.

'What about your career?'

'I'd give it up.' She lowered her voice. 'For you.'

I found myself launching into a speech; it was completely unrehearsed, but the way it flowed from my lips without any prompting or effort, I might have been practising for months. I couldn't possibly ask such a sacrifice of her, I said. Since the shooting and the operations that followed it, I'd become erratic, demanding – even violent. In short, I'd changed. And I couldn't bear to burden her with such responsibility. She should leave me now, today, avoiding what would only be a far more painful parting in the future. I had, in any case, never been good enough for her – I held up a hand as she tried to interrupt – my father a post-office clerk in the provinces, now retired, hers a high-ranking official in the Ministry of Education. Leave me now, I told her, while our memories were unblemished, while we still had respect for one another and were free of bitterness and resentment, while we could still avoid recriminations. After all, she had her whole life in front of her (yes, I actually used that line!). She should find some young man who could provide her with the kind of future she deserved. I'd be better off with my doctors and nurses – people who understood my condition, and were trained to deal with it. As I was talking, I realised what an enormous relief it was to be able finally to put an end to our relationship. I'd just been waiting for a good opportunity, the right excuse. I wondered how long it would've taken if I hadn't been shot in the head. Years, probably.

'Forgive me,' I said, 'if I don't show you to the door.'

She began to cry again, her mouth crumpling, curving downwards, despite her efforts to straighten it, as if there were tiny weights attached to the corners.

I turned away from her, gazed vaguely into the room. I even wobbled my head a little, the way blind people often do. I heard her gather up her coat and rush out.

With Claudia gone, some kind of atmosphere or trance appeared to lift, its departure smooth, almost imperceptible – one level of reality shedding another. It reminded me of lying in bed at night when I was young. Sometimes a car passed and its headlamps entered the room. The way the block of light slid along the wall. It didn't seem to have anything to do with the car in the street outside or the sound of an engine. And yet the two were linked. That was the feeling I had suddenly. I was no longer sure why I'd acted the way I had. I hardly recognised myself. Was this the new personality they'd been talking about? If so, wasn't it rather early for it to be manifesting itself? Where was the numbness, the anaesthesia? Where were the suicidal thoughts?

I sat in my armchair, staring at the fireplace and breathing steadily.

At last Nurse Janssen came to fetch me. She was surprised that Claudia had left before visiting hours were over. She'd thought that every moment would be precious. No time goes faster, she told me, than the time that star-crossed lovers spend together.

'Ah,' I said. 'The voice of experience.'

I'd like to have heard her on the subject. I'd like to have known the truth about her and Visser. Were they involved? And, if not, what were they doing walking practically hand in hand among the pear trees? But she would not be sidetracked. All she was interested in was how I'd got on with Claudia. One or two of her nursing colleagues had joined us in the corridor. They were all clamouring to know.

In the end I gave them the substance of our conversation. I'd felt it only fair, I said, to bring the engagement to an end. I talked of selflessness (my own) and the need, at certain times, for sacrifice. By the time I'd finished, there wasn't a dry eye in the place. It was all I could do not to wind up with the words, 'And she was such a lovely girl . . .'

During the week that followed, Claudia wrote to me every day, sometimes more than once, catching both the morning and the afternoon post with an efficiency that seemed to augur well for her career in law. Nurse Janssen took it upon herself to read the letters to me. Terrible, heart-wrenching letters they were, too, full of pleading and regret. Fortunately, I'd never been much of a listener; within seconds of hearing the words *My dearest Martin*, my mind would be somewhere else entirely; there were times when I even drifted off to sleep, exhausted after having been awake for most of the night. I was only dimly aware of the tremble in Nurse Janssen's voice as Claudia reaffirmed her undying love for me or begged me to reconsider – though, once, Nurse Janssen had to break off altogether, and the rustle of starched cotton told me she was searching the pockets of her uniform for a tissue.

'Are you all right, Nurse?'

'Oh yes,' she said tearily. 'Yes, I'm fine.' A quick blast and then a sigh. 'Tell me, Martin, have you spoken to her?'

I told her that contact would only raise the poor girl's hopes. It was better to maintain a silence, no matter how punishing that might be – for everyone.

'I suppose you're right.'

'Trust me,' I said. 'I am.'

At the end of that week, just after midnight, the door to the ward swung open and, unexpectedly, Nurse Janssen appeared. My first reaction was one of dread; another letter had arrived – delivered by hand, no doubt – and she'd come in to read it to me. It must be something urgent – a threat of suicide, perhaps. I could think of no other reason for Nurse Janssen being there at midnight. I'd heard the hour strike and, like all regular staff, Nurse Janssen went off duty at nine. I peered at her as she approached, but I could see nothing resembling a letter in her hand.

Smulders was mumbling. 'All trains . . . delayed . . . signal failure . . .'

Nurse Janssen stopped at the foot of my bed. I didn't understand what she was doing, and she didn't seem about to offer an explanation. In fact, now I thought about it, her behaviour seemed strangely automatic, trance-like. Could it be that she was walking in her sleep?

As I stared at her, she removed her starched white hat and let it fall silently to the floor. Then she reached up and began to unpin her hair, her bare arms forming a pale diamond-shape against the darkness. Her hair tumbled on to her shoulders. She tilted her head to one side, so her hair hung down, vertical as a curtain, and bounced the tips of it on her upturned hand, as though testing its weight. It was an overwhelmingly erotic gesture. I propped myself higher on my pillows, but couldn't bring myself to speak.

She didn't seem to be aware of me at all. First she kicked off one shoe, then the other. Her hands lifted simultaneously to the top button of her cotton blouse, which slowly parted beneath her fingers. White lace showed underneath. She eased out of the blouse, her breasts pushing forwards, the points of her shoulders smooth and round. I watched the blouse float to the floor behind her.

'. . . delays of up to an hour . . . try the buffet . . . east side of the station . . . hot coffee and fresh rolls . . .'

Nurse Janssen casually leaned sideways, the skin creasing between her right hip and her bottom rib, and unfastened the catch on her skirt. The zipper's I became a V. She began to push the skirt down, over her hips. It was tight. She had to shift her weight from one foot to the other; she almost had to wriggle. The skirt dropped to her ankles and she stepped out of it.

Now she reached both hands behind her, her top teeth gripping her bottom lip. Her breasts rose in their lace cups, then toppled forwards as the bra came loose. They were much as I'd imagined them: a heavy curve up to the nipples, which were wide and dark. Bending over, she slipped her thumbs inside her knickers. Her hair drifted across her face, concealing it. Light caught her breasts as they swung out into the air and trembled. I came into my hand.

Smiling faintly, as if aware of her effect on me, she straightened up again.

'Nurse?' I whispered.

She wasn't looking at me. She was still smiling, though. Blissfully. Into the distance.

'I'm talking to you, Nurse.'

She knelt at the foot of the bed and began to gather up her clothes.

'Nurse?' I spoke more loudly now. 'Don't go yet.'

'. . . apologise for the delay . . . pleasant journey . . .' In the next bed, Smulders coughed. 'Do hope you'll travel with us again . . .'

Nurse Janssen wouldn't speak to me. Once she was dressed she simply turned away and walked off down the ward and out through the swing-doors. I lay in bed and stared up into the air. The darkness pulsed. I could feel the sperm drying on my stomach and my thighs. I could imagine the brittle, shiny crust, as delicate as flies' wings, or glue. I wondered at what I'd witnessed, tried to make sense of it. She had no way of knowing I could see her, so she couldn't have been doing it for my benefit. It had to have been some pleasure of her own, a private fantasy that she was acting out – unless . . .

It seemed far-fetched – laughable, really – but it was the only other explanation I could think of. I remembered how she'd cried when I told her I was breaking off my engagement. I knew how moved she'd been by that decision. Well, maybe this was her way of rewarding me. Some kind of symbolic tribute to my selflessness, performed in my honour, with no expectation of acknowledgement. Like the offerings people used to make to gods.

I began to stay awake at night, my eyes fixed on the doors at the far end of the ward. Would there be a repeat performance? And, if so, would she come up with a new routine, something more inventive, more exotic? (Not that I was complaining.) But I waited for a week and Nurse Janssen didn't reappear – at least, not when she wasn't supposed to. Her reward, if that was what it was, suddenly seemed a rather meagre one. I wished she'd thought of something more conventional. Flowers, for instance. Or even a brand-new pair of rubber balls. It was the beginning of a period of great restlessness.

One night I could stand it no longer. I decided to go for a walk. At two or three in the morning, there were hardly any staff on duty. I put on my dressing-gown and reached for my white cane. I carried it with me at all times now, like a disguise. After all, I didn't want to arouse suspicion. If I was caught, I was just a blind man who'd got lost on his way to the lavatory.

I moved down the ward and out into the hallway. To my left was the notorious broom cupboard. Ahead of me, I found another set of doors. I pushed through them. An empty corridor confronted me, all cream walls and gleaming linoleum. It stretched away into the distance. It stretched so far, I couldn't see an end to it.

I began to walk.

Silence. Only the trees shifting beyond the narrow windows and the tinkering of fluorescent lights. Something about the stillness unsettled me. It seemed to be constantly on the verge of becoming movement. It was like the stillness in horror films – stillness as anticipation, stillness as the prelude to a shock. I walked the length of the corridor, then turned left. Another corridor, almost identical. Shorter, though. With orange doors on both sides.

This corridor had different acoustics. For instance: the sound of my footsteps seemed to be coming not from where I actually was but from a point five metres behind me. I wondered what would happen if I used my voice.

'Hello?' I said.

Nothing odd about that. I tried again.

'Mr Blom?' I said. 'What are you doing, Mr Blom?'

No, it just sounded as if I was talking to myself. In the middle of the night. I didn't like the feeling.

I reached a flight of stairs and began to climb.

I remembered what Kukowski had taught me about the use of memory. It was a trick: you had to imagine walking into what you were leaving behind. The future was the same as the present, only backwards. So. I'd have to go down the stairs (keep count of the flights), turn right into the corridor with the acoustics, turn right again into the corridor that had cream walls. My ward would be somewhere at the end of it.

My breathing had thickened and I could taste blood. For the first time, I realised how much strength I'd lost. The operations, all those weeks in bed . . . *How quickly muscles atrophy*. There was a lop-sided sensation in my head, as if one half was heavier than the other. I had to steady myself, one hand braced against the wall.

I was lying halfway down a flight of stairs. Sweat had surfaced all over me; my hair hung in my eyes, a fringe of wet quills. I sat up and pressed my face against the cool plaster of the wall. First one cheek, then the other. Then my forehead. Outside, the wind had risen. There could have been an ocean in the garden.

I climbed slowly to my feet. Touched the place where the plate was. No feeling at all. It was as if my fingertips had entered another dimension. The deadness of titanium. Sometimes it seemed to count for more than all the sensate parts of me, and I could imagine my body rotting around it. Surely that was the end of the dream. The flesh and bone would fall away. The spirit, too. All that would remain of me was a piece of metal on an empty street, sun glancing off it. That single piece of metal. Perfect. Everlasting. Alien.

I took a deep breath and climbed back up the stairs. On the landing I rested. It was a landing like any other – a firehose reel fastened to the wall, a metal trolley piled high with towels. Out of the corner of my eye I saw a movement, something white and quick, but when I turned it was gone. A trapped bird, maybe, or dust in the moonlight. Not far beyond the firehose was a door. I tried the handle; it wasn't locked. When I opened it, fresh air pushed past me, like a crowd of people that had been waiting to get in.

I was on the roof – or part of it, at least. It was narrow where I was, the width of one person. There were metal handrails on both sides. What I was standing on was metal as well, the kind of perforated metal used for fire-escapes. To my left I could see the main body of the clinic, dark and turreted, a chimney releasing smoke that seemed casual until the wind took it, scattered it across the sky. Lower down, below me, was a row of lit windows. To my right, just darkness, trees. A sheer drop to the ground.

I moved along the walkway until I was opposite a window. I looked down into a small, square room that was almost bare: a steel table, two or three moulded plastic chairs, a water-dispenser – that was it. I moved on. In the next window I saw a man. I wasn't sure who it was at first because he had his back to me. But then he turned and walked across the room. *It was Visser.* I watched him pick up a file, then put it down again. He appeared to be deep in thought, the fingers of one hand pulling at the edge of his moustache. Only then did I realise what was written on the cover of the file: my name, MARTIN BLOM, and stamped across that, in red block capitals, the words HIGHLY CONFIDENTIAL. I leaned against the cold rail of the walkway. The trees below me tossed like furious black water. Highly confidential? What could be highly confidential about a patient at an eye clinic?

Turning back, I noticed the other files on his desk. They were marked with the same red capitals, but the names were different. On the far wall, pinned to a cork board, were at least a dozen X-rays. In each X-ray I could see the titanium plate, which showed as a white object lodged in the dappled, moon-like grey-and-white of the cranium. At first I assumed the X-rays were of me, but if I compared one with another I saw that each plate had a slightly different location. I'd been standing there for some time, pondering the X-rays, when I sensed something had changed. Visser had walked to the window. He seemed to be staring up at me. I held still, trying to slow the sudden pounding of my heart. Then I realised he couldn't see me. All he could see was his own reflection in the window. All he was staring at was the stream of his own consciousness.

The next morning, when he appeared on the ward, I said I wanted to ask him about my case. He wondered what aspect I was interested in particularly.

'Well,' I said, 'how unique is it?'

'In what sense?'

'The insertion of a titanium plate, for instance. Is that common?'

'Not common, no,' Visser replied. 'Though it does happen from time to time.'

I hesitated. 'So there aren't many people who've had it done?'

'The last plate I fitted was probably,' and he paused, 'three years ago.'

'There's nobody in the clinic then,' I said, 'apart from me?'

'Nobody.' I thought I could hear Visser smile. That faint, wet click of lips drawing back from teeth. 'In that sense, you're certainly unique.'

'Something else,' I said, in what I thought might be a cunning lateral shift in my approach. 'Are you engaged in any research at the moment, Doctor? Or is your time entirely taken up by your duties at the clinic?'

'If only there was money for research!' Visser said. 'Perhaps you'd like to dictate a letter to the government on my behalf.'

This was an extremely clever riposte, and I had no choice but to chuckle quietly and let the matter drop. After he'd gone, I thought back over what I'd seen the previous night. Had my eyes deceived me? Or was Visser lying? And, if so, why?

During the next week or two I tried on several occasions to return to the walkway in order to verify my findings. Kukowski's memory techniques proved worse than useless. One night I found myself outside, in the vegetable garden. In frustration, I pulled up half a dozen carrots, brushed the mud off them and ate them on a bench in the moonlight. Another night it was the laundry: washing-machines with drums the size of jet engines and huge cast-iron calendar-rolls for pressing sheets. Once I even mistakenly walked into the Reminiscence Room. It was while I was there, sitting on the therapist's chair, that I decided that I didn't have a past. I had a present, though, and it remained a mystery to me.

The summer faded, and the nights grew cooler. I started wearing socks for my clandestine expeditions. Visser toured the ward each day, the truth concealed beneath a white coat that seemed as crisp as the leaves that now lay strewn on the clinic lawn.

One evening I woke from a nap to see Nurse Janssen bending over me. She was wearing all her clothes, and gave no sign that she might be about to take any of them off. I'd referred to her performance once or twice – the references had to be oblique, of course – and she'd promptly accused me of being 'just like all the others'. I'd disappointed her, she said. She'd thought I was different. 'I *am* different,' I told her, though there was no way she could understand what I meant by that.

'You've got a visitor,' she said.

'What, again?' I said. 'I'm not here.'

'It's the police. The gentleman who came before, if you remember. Detective Munck.'

'Oh, well,' I said, sitting up, 'in that case. Yes, of course. What a relief.'

'It's not often you hear that, as a policeman,' Munck said.

He stepped out from behind Nurse Janssen, who turned and walked away, leaving us alone together. This was the first time I'd seen him. He was a tall, gangling man, with dark hair that was neatly parted and rather dry, and teeth that were ridged, like celery.

'No, I suppose not.' I laughed. 'I thought you were my fiancée. My ex-fiancée, I should say.'

'I'm sorry to hear that.' Munck drew up a chair.

'No, no. Don't be. It was over long before all this,' and I gestured to include the ward and all the blind men in it. 'This just made everything clear to me. Does that sound odd?'

'Paradoxical, perhaps. Not odd.'

I liked Munck. He was somebody I could talk to. He had a brain. And that sleepy voice, I now saw, was perfect for the work he did. It was an instrument for winning confidence. He could use it to coax information out of witnesses. Or lull criminals into confessions.

He opened his briefcase, took out a brown-paper bag and put it into my hands. 'I don't know whether you like pears,' he said.

'How kind.' I opened the bag. Inhaled.

'I was passing the market and, well – '

'Thank you.' I told Munck about my trips to the city as a child and how my grandmother always used to bring a pear for me to eat on the tram.

He was nodding. He seemed happy to have chosen the right fruit.

'But this is not a social visit, surely,' I said. 'Is there some news?'

'No, I'm afraid not. Not really.' He leaned his forearms on his knees, hands dangling. How old was he? Forty? Forty-five? 'There was something I didn't ask you before. I didn't think it was worth mentioning . . .'

'Oh?'

'The night you were attacked, a woman saw a youth running out of the car-park. He was wearing a T-shirt with a message on it. A slogan.

It said, THIS TIME IT'S FOR EVER.' He paused again, looked up. 'I don't suppose that rings any bells?'

I searched my memory, but there were no running youths in it, no T-shirts. 'No,' I said.

'Just the tomatoes?' he said.

I smiled.

'We checked with the manufacturers. They do a whole range. THIS TIME IT'S FOR EVER, YOU KILL ME, I LOVE YOU TO DEATH. They sell hundreds every month, apparently.' He sighed. 'And, anyway, the woman didn't think she could make a positive identification.'

I wanted to comfort him, but didn't know how.

'Sometimes you're looking for connections and they're just not there,' he said after a while. 'It's small things that you're looking for. Habits, for instance.'

'Habits?'

'Yes.' His voice had quickened. 'Take you, Mr Blom. You have an interesting habit.'

'I do?'

'Yes. You have this way of passing your hand across your head. Slowly, almost warily, from front to back. It's what some men do, men who are worried they might be going bald – '

'It must be the operation,' I said, 'the plate I had put in.' I was slightly disconcerted; he'd told me something about myself that I didn't know.

'There you are, you see? A connection.' The triumph in his voice didn't last. 'But this youth with the T-shirt – '

He sighed again and this time I sighed with him.

'As the victim of an unsolved felony you're in the majority, of course. I only wish it was otherwise. I'm afraid most crimes in this country go unpunished.'

I had the impression that he felt personally responsible for what had happened.

'You know,' he went on, 'I always wanted to be a policeman. Ever since I was a boy. I used to dream I'd solve some famous case and then I'd have a street named after me. Or a square – '

'Maybe you should've gone into politics,' I said.

He didn't answer for a moment. Then, dreamily, he said, 'Avenue Paul Munck.'

I smiled. 'Sounds good.'

'It'll never happen.'

'It might.' I was trying to encourage him, this seemingly doom-laden man.

'No,' he said, 'it's like I told you. Most criminals are never brought to justice. Not by me – not by anyone.'

'That's interesting, though,' I said, 'about the habits.'

'Yes.' He rose wearily to his feet. 'Well, it's time I was going.'

'It's been a pleasure, Detective. Do call in again. If you're ever in the area, that is.'

'Yes, I will.'

'And thanks again for the fruit.'

'Don't mention it.' Munck lifted a hand as he turned away, then lowered it as he remembered I was blind. 'Goodbye, Mr Blom.'

'Goodbye.'

I watched him move off down the ward, arms paddling in the air, feet slapping on the floor. So it was Munck who walked like somebody in flippers. This knowledge endeared him to me, and I hoped it wouldn't be too long before I saw him again.

Towards the end of September I made one final attempt to solve the mystery about the X-rays. As usual, the clinic fooled me and I was soon adrift in a maze of corridors and hallways. In some places, the ceilings were low and curved; I could touch bare brick if I reached up with one hand. There didn't seem to be any windows. It was damp too, a chill that I felt on the back of my neck but, curiously, nowhere else.

So far as I could tell, I was still at ground-level. I needed to be higher: three floors up, maybe four. As I walked, I was sure I could hear people behind me – the whisper of crepe soles on the lino, murmured words – but when I turned round, there was never anybody there. I wondered if this wing of the building could be haunted.

Certainly it was antiquated enough. Almost derelict. It was a disgrace, really, now I thought about it. Just because we, the patients, were blind, they felt they could keep us in conditions that were scarcely even fit for animals.

I found a stairwell and began to climb. Up and up it took me, opening at last on to a landing that was unfamiliar to me. The air was still, the floor littered with empty pill bottles, old magazines, bits of broken glass. I noticed a dandelion flower floating motionless above me, as though it had been there for centuries. Dead flies lay on the windowsill in heaps. At the far end of the landing was a door with a horizontal bar on it. I leaned on the bar and the door opened. A cool night wind. The roof. But which part of it?

I picked my way through heating-vents, fuel-gauges, pipes, my shoes sticking to the soft, tarred surface. There was a sudden rush of air above my head. Pigeons. I heard the clock strike three, each note blown out of shape by the wind and the cold. No walkway anywhere; no lit windows. I reached the edge of the roof and lifted my face towards the sky. I could smell salt now – no more than a trace element, but it was there. It was the sea that I could smell, pushing against low dunes some twenty kilometres to the west. The city lay south-east of where I stood, its skyline of domes and spires concealed behind a ridge.

I climbed on to the parapet, feeling like a swimmer at the beginning of a race. I bent from the waist and stretched my arms out past my ears. Then peered down. A drop of thirty metres, maybe more. I wasn't tempted. Those thoughts of suicide that Visser had predicted, they'd never be mine. I had to reshape my life, that was all. I would live the way people lived in primitive societies, only the other way round: I'd get up when the sun went down and go to bed when it came up again. I was glad it would be winter soon. What good was daylight to me? No good at all. It was an obstacle, a hindrance – the last thing I needed. I remembered Claudia's idea – how she wanted to look after me. I imagined her constant presence, her careful ministrations. I shuddered. It would have ruined everything.

'Martin?'

I jumped.

'What are you doing, Martin?'

I saw Nurse Janssen standing by the door to the roof.

'Nothing,' I called across to her. 'I couldn't sleep.'

I straightened up and watched her walk towards me, the wind flattening her thin cotton nightgown against her belly and thighs. Was this another of her routines?

'Aren't you cold?' I said.

'Don't worry about me.' She stepped up on to the parapet and stood beside me, looking out into the darkness.

'Careful,' I said. 'It's a long way down.'

She laughed, though somewhat breathlessly.

'I'm serious,' I said. 'You could fall.'

'And I suppose you couldn't?'

I turned to face her. The way she looked just then, I could have kissed her. Her eyes were so dark that I could only see the core of silver in the pupil. Her dark hair, which was usually pinned close to her head in a tight, sexless coil, now hung loose, touching her shoulders lightly, the way willow branches touch the ground. Her face, a little blurred, still held the memory of sleep. I wished I could ask her about the night she walked up to my bed and took off all her clothes. Did she do that kind of thing often? Or was it just for me? (For me, I hoped.) What was the pleasure she derived from it? I remembered how she smiled when I came; not gratified exactly, not merely amused either – a smile that was as enigmatic in its way as that moustache of Visser's. I had so many questions, but each and every one of them was dangerous. Because they weren't really questions at all. They were admissions. Confessions. They were keys turning in locks, nails in my coffin.

'What's your name?' I asked her.

'You know my name.'

'Your Christian name, I mean.'

'Maria.'

I smiled. It suited her.

'Do you think it's wise,' she said, 'coming up here?'

'Wise?' I said. 'I don't know.' I stepped down off the parapet and leaned on it. 'It's just, I've always been a private person. I don't like crowds.' The wind had dropped; I wondered how long it was till dawn. 'It's hard being on the ward sometimes. All that breathing, people talking in their sleep. I wanted some air.' I looked up at her. 'Are you going to report me?'

She thought about it.

'No,' she said at last. 'It can be our little secret.'

I looked at her sharply. Did she suspect? No, I didn't think so. She was just being light-hearted, conspiratorial.

'Shall we go back?' she said.

I took her arm in the correct manner and let her lead me across the roof. I glanced at her as we approached the door.

'You didn't think I was going to jump, did you?'

She didn't answer.

'I wouldn't do that,' I told her. 'I know the doctor sometimes thinks I'm depressed, but I'm not. Really, I'm not.'

I felt her squeeze my arm. I didn't think she believed me, though. And how could I convince her without giving anything away? It must have been disturbing, now I thought about it, for her to see me standing on that narrow parapet some thirty metres above the ground.

'I was only practising,' I said. 'You know, getting ready for the world outside.'

'I just hope it's ready for you,' she said, and we both laughed at that, and passed through the doorway, back into the building.

A Friday morning, ten o'clock. The moment had arrived. I could sense the autumn sun against my face as I moved down the clinic steps. There was hardly any warmth in it. It was October now, darkness eating into the day. My time of year.

My cane touched concrete, concrete, then touched gravel. The driveway. And, beyond it, the future. Excitement crackled through the lower layers of my skin. I felt as though I was playing poker and I'd just been dealt a hand that was unbeatable.

At the bottom of the steps, Maria greeted me. We'd grown used to one another, she and I; we'd spent so many hours together. I smiled past her shoulder, drew crisp air into my lungs.

'The pine trees are smelling particularly good this morning.'

'Oh, Mr Blom,' she said, 'I wish I'd never mentioned them.'

At first it surprised me, this use of my last name. Then I understood. It was actually more intimate, conveying precisely what it appeared to deny; it was like pretending that the night she took her clothes off never happened. I was sure that she was smiling, too. With her arms folded, probably, and one of her feet, the left one, pointing away from her body. I'd often seen her stand like that.

Visser stepped up and shook my hand. He was exhilarated by my progress, he told me, and full of confidence about my rehabilitation. He didn't think he'd ever seen a recovery quite like it. I told him that I couldn't have done it without him (not strictly true, of course, but I was building on that old feeling we had, of mutual congratulation and dependency). I thanked him profusely. There was nothing more to say.

I'd called on Visser about a month before and tried to explain what it was that I was experiencing. He listened to my description of the night in the gardens, my subsequent investigations. I admitted that I'd lied to him on a number of occasions. His eyebrows lifted. Lines appeared on his forehead, lines that echoed the venetian blinds behind him. When I finished, Visser didn't speak. He had his elbows on the table. His chin rested on his hands. I heard air rushing downwards from his nostrils into his moustache. I thought of the way wind moves a field of grass.

At last, he said, 'I did warn you, didn't I?'

'You mean it's some kind of hallucination?'

'I'm afraid so.' Visser shifted in his chair. 'What you're experiencing is a phase of denial. Temporary, I'm sure.'

'But it's so real, Doctor – '

'You see? You're denying your condition. You're blind, Martin. You always will be.'

'I really can make things out, though. Well, some things, anyway.' I paused. 'But only at night, of course.'

'Only at night.'

Visser allowed another silence to fill the room. Those silences of his were like people gazing at you with affection and shaking their heads. They were like gently mocking laughter. They were a bit like pity. And the lines were back, the ones that went with his venetian blinds.

Only at night.

Those silences were such fertile ground for reconsideration. If I'd had any doubts at that moment, they would have multiplied. But I didn't. Have any doubts.

'Maybe you're right,' I said.

Looking back on that meeting with Visser, I thought that maybe I didn't want him to understand. I wanted him to tell me that I was mistaken, deluded. Then I could go on secretly enjoying the power I had. It was as if, in attempting to explain it to him, I'd absolved myself of some of the responsibility.

So when Visser shook my hand outside the clinic and said he'd never seen such a positive response to sudden vision loss, I couldn't keep myself from grinning. I was grinning as I stepped into the waiting car. Grinning as it moved off down the drive and out through the gates. Still grinning as it passed the boy who stood there with one foot on the pedal of an ancient bicycle.

By the time we arrived at Central Station, the weather had changed. Climbing the steps into the train I could feel mist against my face, the rust of winter on my tongue. I followed my driver through the carriage. My cane touched rubber, then metal. Then someone's leg. I apologised.

The driver found me a seat in a second-class compartment and lifted my case on to the luggage rack. I thanked him, said goodbye. He gripped my shoulder for a moment, then he was gone. I felt for the catch on the window, slid it open. I leaned out. There was that coal-scuttle smell that stations always seem to have, a smell that's poignant, associated as it is with separations, tears, the end of love.

'Good luck, Mr Blom. Good luck.'

It was the driver, standing on the platform somewhere below. Thanking him again, I told him not to wait. I'd be fine, I said. The truth was, I was looking forward to being alone.

I sat down. Through the window I heard the PA system crackle into life, something to do with platform four. Whoever the announcer was, he wasn't in Smulders' league: he didn't have that imperturbable quality, the gift for making people feel that everything is running smoothly. The train lurched forwards, checked. A piece of luggage burst open on the floor. Five minutes passed; the train still hadn't left the station. One of my fellow passengers began to grumble about the state of the railways. Slowly he gathered momentum, his theme expanding to include inflation, the decline in morals, political incompetence. I sat back in my seat. I was thoroughly enjoying myself; this was the kind of thing I'd missed.

'What are you grinning about?'

I wasn't sure if it was me the man was talking to, not until another passenger, a woman, spoke up in my defence.

'Leave him alone. He's blind.'

I looked at the place where the woman's voice had come from.

'I just got out of the clinic this morning,' I told her. 'It's my first day of freedom.'

The train lurched forwards once again, and this time it kept going, stumbling over sets of points, following a long curve to the south. I knew the route by heart. Out of the station, past the grim, brick backs of warehouses and apartment blocks. Across the river on a narrow, cantilevered bridge. Green water below. White birds rising from pale spits of sand. On the marshy east bank, one or two men fishing. The suburbs next. More apartment blocks, with flower boxes on their balconies. A few shops selling car parts, fridges, tiles. The TV mast up on the hill, its red eye only visible at night. Then out into the countryside. Villages so still, they seemed uninhabited. Ponds reflecting the inevitable clouds. Copses, ditches – fields of sugar beet. I drew some comfort from this journey, which I'd undertaken so many times before.

My parents only came to see me once while I was in the clinic. (This was understandable; they lived some distance from the capital, and my father had a heart condition.) It was just a pity I was unconscious the whole time. In the months since their visit we'd talked on the phone and our conversations had been civil, at times even affectionate, if rather unspecific: the word 'blindness', for example, had never been mentioned. However, Visser still thought it best that I convalesce at home. I'd be in a place I knew, among people who cared for me. And as he pointed out, against any objections I might raise,

I'd already dismissed the only other candidate – namely, Claudia. But I didn't object. I'd been longing for freedom, freedom on any terms, so I eagerly embraced the idea.

As soon as I stepped down on to the station platform I knew the whole thing was a mistake. By then it was dusk, and I watched my parents appear in front of me like a Polaroid developing. There was a hollow, histrionic feel to my mother's embrace that I found unbearable (I felt sure she'd been reading self-help manuals: *How to Care for Your Disabled Son, In Three Easy Stages*, or *Be a Popular and Successful Mother of an Invalid*). As for my father, he scuffed his feet, smiling foolishly into the cheap fur collar of his coat. I knew what it was. The dark glasses, the white stick. I'd become extreme, theatrical, embarrassing – a travesty of something they hadn't even been comfortable with in the first place.

When we got home, I pleaded exhaustion. The journey, the excitement. I thought I should go upstairs, lie down for an hour. I couldn't help noticing that they seemed relieved.

That night we ate together in the dining-room. Flowers stood in a vase on the table and tall white candles burned in silver candelabras. My mother was wearing the necklace she always wore when she attended banquets or the theatre.

'What's the occasion?' I said.

'Oh, Martin.' Her voice was rich with mock reproach. 'Let's drink a toast to your return.'

Reaching for my wineglass, I knocked it over. Deliberately.

My mother rushed out to the kitchen for a cloth. My father gripped the arms of his chair like someone in an aeroplane expecting turbulence. I pretended not to notice the wine sliding towards me. I let it cascade on to my trousers, my eyes staring off into the corner of the room.

My mother had cooked some of my favourite dishes – a soup of white beans, braised lamb, marrow from the kitchen garden – and my father had selected a good bottle from his cellar, yet I had no sense of ease or familiarity. My father kept darting glances at me, surreptitious, sidelong glances, as if he was frightened I might catch him looking (which I did, of course). My mother plucked at her ropes of emeralds and pearls with insistent but strangely absent-minded fingers and gave me looks that were worthy of our country's most famous tragic actress. We talked about the weather, local politics, distant relations. My father entertained us with a story we must have heard at least half a dozen times before (the day a pig got into the post office and ate all the pay cheques). There was a tension in the air, as though, at any moment, somebody might burst through the french windows with a machine-gun and riddle us with bullets.

Then, during dessert, my mother broached the subject I'd been dreading.

'How's Claudia?'

I raised my napkin to my mouth, dabbed once and let it drop into my lap. I leaned back in my chair. 'Didn't she tell you?'

'Tell us what?'

'We've split up.'

My mother let out a contemptuous sound. 'To be honest, it doesn't surprise me. She's a pretty girl, of course, but I never thought she had quite what it takes. I always thought there was something missing somehow. Backbone, I suppose. And now, at the first sign of difficulty, well – '

This was my mother all over. She used to dote on Claudia (both my parents did). She used to say that Claudia would make the perfect wife – not just a wife either, but an example, too. Throughout my twenties I had drifted from job to job, never really settling, and my mother considered Claudia a good influence in that respect. Maybe, at last, I would start thinking in terms of a career. It was all Claudia, Claudia, Claudia. But my mother could never resist an opportunity to feel let down by somebody. *I always thought* – that was classic. There was nothing she relished more than being able to claim she'd known all along that something would go wrong, nothing she relished more than being dreadfully, dreadfully disappointed. I stifled a smile. It was almost enough to make me want to marry Claudia after all. I found myself in the highly amusing position of having to defend the girl.

'No, no,' I said, 'you don't understand. Claudia's blameless. She offered to live with me, look after me. Nothing would've made her happier. I was the one who said no. It was me who ended it.'

'But why?' Something about the way my father lurched forwards, over the table, reminded me of a cow. That numb weight, that clumsiness.

I tried to explain it to him. 'Everything's changed,' I said. 'Everything. Don't you see that? It's like when someone close to you dies. It draws a line through your life. Nothing's the same after that. The choices I made,' and I hesitated for a moment, 'the choices I made before I was shot no longer apply.'

A kind of shiver went through the room; even the heavy velvet curtains seemed to shift.

'Of course, you won't be working for a while,' my father hurried on, glancing anxiously at my mother, 'not in your condition.'

I lost patience suddenly.

'Oh, I don't know,' I said. 'I could always sell matches.'

My mother stood up. But then she didn't seem to know why she was standing. People look like that if they walk in their sleep and wake up in the middle. They're not quite where they thought they'd be. There has to be a moment of adjustment. At last she fell back on habit and began to clear the table. My father mentioned that the news would be starting soon. I wasn't sure which of us he was talking to. Perhaps, like Smulders, he was simply saying something that he always said, regardless.

We drank our coffee in the next room, watching television. The economy was in trouble again. Two children had been murdered. There was severe flooding in the north-west. I wondered if I'd been on the news when I was shot. Probably not. They like you to be famous. Or else you have to be a child, preferably under the age of ten. GIRL, 12, MURDERED – that sounds all right. But BABY MURDERED sounds much better.

'More coffee, Martin?' my father said.

I rested my head against the back of the sofa and closed my eyes.

I stayed awake that night and slept for most of the next day. I didn't appear downstairs until just after five in the afternoon. My parents thought I'd been avoiding them. That wasn't the reason for my behaviour, of course – it was simply one of the side-effects – but there was no persuading them of this and, in truth, I didn't really try. The mood in the house was awkward for the whole of that first week. I was still having dreams, too, dreams where my body came apart. I would wake up in the bed I'd slept in as a child, muddled, panic-stricken, sweating. I would hear my parents whispering about me in the room below.

Towards midnight, when they were asleep, I would go out for a walk. We lived on the outskirts of the town. At the end of our street there was a wooden stile and then just fields; in the distance the ground lifted to a ridge which was dense with firs and pines. I kept to the roads. I saw few people, even fewer cars. It was very quiet. I passed front gardens – waves of autumn roses breaking over fences, metal gates with rising-sun designs built into the wrought-iron. Not far from our house there was a restaurant that was open late. I used to go there when I was sixteen or seventeen. It had coloured light bulbs in the garden and a sign that said RESTAURANT – DANCING. I sometimes dropped in for a coffee or a schnapps. The place had changed hands recently and I didn't know the new owner. If he'd heard about me, he didn't let on; he just served me drinks and made the usual small talk. I appreciated that.

When I got home, the silence deepened. I spent hours at the window, watching the railway line that ran behind the house. Trains appeared from the left, one strip of yellow light, and slanted diagonally across the land towards me. At the last moment they seemed to speed up and, like some legend's sword of gold, plunged into the bank of trees that stood next to the cemetery. Though it was the same every time, I never tired of it. It reminded me of Smulders. And, by association, of Maria Janssen as well. There were no such consolations here. I'd never imagined that I might miss the clinic, but, sitting by the window, I would often think back to the night of the strip-tease. Claudia would never have done anything like that for me. She would have been too embarrassed, too ashamed. *No, I couldn't.* Or, *I'd feel silly.* Then, later, *I don't satisfy you, do I?* And my reply: a weary, *Yes. Yes, you do.* I was almost relieved when my mother woke me one morning with the news that Visser was on the phone. I took the call upstairs, in my parents' bedroom. He told me that he wanted to visit me the next day, if that was convenient. I asked him if we could meet outside somewhere, and mentioned the restaurant. He thought that was a good idea.

It was almost dark when I arrived the following afternoon. I bought myself a beer and took a seat by the window. The place was empty except for an old man who was wearing one of the green hats that used to be traditional in our part of the country.

I'd been sitting there for twenty minutes when Visser came up behind me. He held my elbow for a moment.

'Martin,' he said. 'How are you?'

He ordered tea, with lemon.

I was surprised he'd come so far and told him so, but he assured me it had been no trouble; he'd been in the area in any case, for a conference.

'Though it is a weakness of mine,' he admitted, sipping his tea. 'I can't seem to let go of my patients,' and he paused, 'especially the difficult ones.'

This was one of his rare attempts at humour. I dutifully chuckled.

We discussed my parents for a while and I conveyed a much greater degree of understanding than there actually was. He interrupted me. According to my mother, he said, I was sleeping during the day. Every day. I didn't deny it. Having known they'd go behind my back, I was prepared.

'Since I can't see the sun,' I said, 'it doesn't make much difference to me. And anyway, I prefer nights. They're more peaceful.' I smiled faintly. 'I had this conversation with Nurse Janssen once.'

'You're not hiding, then? This isn't another version of the broom cupboard?'

I laughed. 'Well, maybe a little.'

He liked the honesty of that.

I asked him, as casually as possible, how long a convalescence was supposed to last.

He fingered his moustache. 'That depends on you. Your progress and so forth.'

'So if I feel ready to strike out on my own – '

'It's a little early for that,' he said, 'don't you think? After all, you've only been home a week.'

'I know, I know. But still – '

I'd come a long way, I told him, since I'd been given my cane six months before. I recalled for him my first, tentative attempts at walking, the feeling that the ground was opening in front of me, the sudden sense of an abyss. I was convinced that if I took one step I would fall. And because I didn't know how far there was to fall, it would be like falling for ever. Like the game that children play with cracks in paving stones. I used to long to lie down on the floor and somehow wrap my arms around it and hold on.

'It seems so long ago.' I shook my head at the memory.

With Nurse Janssen's help – and his help, too, of course – I'd learned to employ my remaining senses to overcome my fear, to orient myself. And then there was old Kukowski, with his talk of tactile clocks and sonic spectacles. Touch, taste, hearing, smell – they all played a part; it was a vision that had to be worked on, practised – earned. Though I wasn't looking at Visser, I could sense him nodding. I was happy with my speech so far. The exaggerations seemed just right, as did the gratitude. Surely it would not be long, I went on, before I was ready for a challenge, before I wanted to explore my condition – its true limits, its possibilities. After all, I couldn't spend my whole life locked in darkened rooms!

Visser responded with one of his famous silences. He was delighted with my attitude, he said at last; it never failed to impress him. My optimism could only serve me well – provided, he added, with what I took to be a warning glance, provided I didn't once again lose touch with reality.

Once again? What did he mean, *once again*?

I'd always had the feeling, talking to Visser, that reality was something there was only one of. As if it was in some way responsive to testing, as if it could be proved to be constant in all its particulars and identical for everybody. When I had that feeling, I always thought of his moustache. I could hardly restrain myself, at times like that, from reaching out and giving it a good tweak. I'd find my hand wandering out into the air, and I'd have to rein it in. Make it pull at my earlobe instead, or probe my temple.

At last we rose from our table and walked out into the cool evening. Fog had drifted across the town; the light around the street-lamps was soft and round, the density of candy-floss. Across the road from the café was a wooded area. I suggested a stroll. To my surprise, Visser agreed.

We walked in silence for a while, pine needles snapping beneath our feet. Light flashed through the gloom in a flat, blue arc: a jay.

Still looking into the distance, I said, 'Sometimes I have the feeling that there's something you're not telling me.'

'Really? What kind of thing?' He turned to me, smiling.

'I don't know. Something to do with me.'

'If you don't mind me saying, Martin, that's a typical reaction.'

'Meaning what?'

'You're reacting to not being able to see. You feel excluded. It's only to be expected.'

Typical Visser, more like. Any question I asked, he always sidestepped or deflected it; he always turned it into a symptom of my condition. The substance of the question could be ignored. What he focused on was the fact that I'd asked it. I never got a straight answer. All I got were dull extrapolations from his diagnosis.

'Can I drive you back?' he said.

I nodded.

As we approached his car, he turned to me again. 'If you want me to tell you something,' he said, 'in my opinion, you're moving too fast. You're being a little *too* optimistic.' He reached into his coat pocket for the keys. 'However, I don't suppose it can hurt. Not so long as you're prepared for disappointments. Not so long as you're prepared to fail . . .'

Standing beside him, with one hand resting on my blind-man's cane, I laughed good-humouredly. 'Oh yes,' I said, 'I'm prepared for that.'

Fail? I thought. I'm not going to fail.

One evening not long afterwards I walked out into the garden. It had been raining when I woke up and water was still dripping from the trees. I turned and stared up at the house. Walls of pale-yellow shingles and a low slate roof. Shutters painted green. A terrace with a grape arbour to shield you from the sun. Nothing had changed in years. Even my sister's room on the top floor. I could see her ballet slippers in the window, shrimp-coloured, their plump toes crossed like fingers. A pointless exercise. There was no luck in our family; there never had been. I thought of her room with its pop-star posters and its shelves of sporting trophies and awards. A museum to her golden childhood. Anyone would think she was dead. I looked round quickly. I hadn't meant to laugh out loud.

I heard the french windows open behind me. My father joined me on the lawn. 'Bit damp out.' He stood there in his sheepskin coat, peering intently at the sky, half-smiling. I was sure that he'd been sent outside by my mother, to talk to me. He had the look of someone who had drawn the short straw.

He was a slow man, my father. Life was something he'd entered into reluctantly and withdrew from whenever possible. It came as no surprise to most people to discover that his hobby was collecting snails – though hobby was probably too weak a word for it: it was more of a passion, an obsession. When he worked at the post office, for example, he used to keep a photograph of his favourite snail on the desk in front of him (of his wife and family, there was no sign). The snails lived in a shed at the bottom of the garden. Their cages were fish tanks, which he'd bought second-hand and then converted. He'd built the environments himself: first a layer of sand, then one of earth and, lastly, various assorted pieces of bark, broken flower-pot and moss. Each cage had a pane of glass fitted over the top of it and weighed down with a stone to stop the snails escaping. He kept a notebook which was filled with observations about their ages, their distinguishing features, even the composition of their faeces. He gave them bizarre names, the kind of names that would have suited racehorses – Bronze Mantle, Lightning, Columella Girl. I remember asking him once if the names were supposed to be ironic. He gave me a blank look. He claimed they referred to individual characteristics.

'*Lightning*, though?' I said.

He led me to a cage and then bent down and pointed at the snail in the corner. 'See that flash,' he said, 'just there, below the suture . . .'

Do people really take on the appearance or character of their pets? Or do they choose a particular pet because they feel a kinship with it? I've never been sure. Either way, it was certainly true that there had been a narrowing of the difference between my father and his snails over the years, especially since he'd retired. He was constantly, as they say, retreating into his shell. He'd started eating the same food as they did, too. Most of it was fit for human consumption – potatoes, apples, carrots, etc. – but, over the weekend, I'd caught him in the kitchen after midnight, cramming leaves into his mouth. Not lettuce, though. Not spinach. Sycamore. And now, as we moved off down the garden, I noticed that he no longer picked his feet up when he walked. He didn't walk at all, in fact; he shuffled. I looked over my shoulder and it wasn't footsteps that I saw but one long, suspiciously continuous and slightly silver trail.

'I know how difficult it must be for you,' he said.

I turned and stared at him.

'Visser talked to us about it. How you believe you can see sometimes. How you can't accept what's happened . . .'

I shook my head. How could Visser do that? It was the last thing I needed, my parents pretending that they understood.

'You know, he's a good man, Visser. One of the best in his field.' My father's tone of voice was guarded, wary, as if Visser was actually a criminal, but a criminal he was defending, a criminal who might be capable of going straight.

'He's clever,' was all I was prepared to say.

'He's done a lot for you.'

We walked as far as the fence at the top of the garden. On the other side was a field. Everything was grey or brown or yellow, dulled by the rain. The brown horse that was standing there looked camouflaged, almost invisible. My father bent down to pluck a weed out of the flowerbed.

'It's a good clinic they've got up there,' he said. 'Excellent facilities, very up to date . . .'

I thought of the broken windows, the paint peeling off the ceiling, the narrow metal beds. I thought of the interminable corridors, the old linoleum. The chill.

'It was the best place for someone with your injuries. Everybody said so.'

He'd seen the place. Only once, admittedly, but he'd seen it. Obviously his faculties were going. Going, gone. All he was left with was the desperate stubbornness of old age. How long, I wondered, did the average snail live?

'I just wanted you to know. I just wanted to say that we did the best for you that we could . . .'

The space my father occupied was shrinking, tightening around him. Everything he said now mattered to him because there were so few words left. Let him believe what he wanted to believe. Let him be. It astonished me that I could be so charitable.

I walked several paces, my cane scanning the wet grass.

'How's Peristome?' I said. 'And Streak, how's Streak?'

The taxi dropped me by a public phone-box at one end of the shopping precinct. I waited until it had turned the corner, then I walked back along the main road that led east out of the town. The tarmac shone like black glass with the recent rain; trees boiled overhead. I remember a neon sign outside a bar and how it seemed to flicker on and off. I thought it was a faulty connection; the damp must have got into it. But then, when I was closer, I realised it was just a low branch dipping, blown sideways, so it kept covering the sign. Cars rushed past like gusts of wind. Once, a man stopped and offered me a lift, but I told him I didn't have far to go. It took me two hours to reach the station.

When I bought my ticket I disguised myself, replacing my white cane and my dark glasses with one of my father's gardening hats and a pair of his half-moon spectacles. I didn't want anyone in the station to remember seeing a blind man board the 9.03. I wanted my trail to go cold outside that phone-box, on that anonymous street-corner.

I chose the compartment that seemed the most dimly lit (one of the bulbs must have blown) and sat down by the window. Everything was blurred, of course; I hadn't realised his eyesight was quite so bad. No wonder I hadn't been able to find the right platform. After a while I had to take the glasses off. Alone in the compartment, I leaned back in my seat and peered at the photographs of national beauty spots which hung on the wall below the luggage-rack: woodland, river valleys, lakes. I wasn't sure how I felt. It was a mixture. Relieved, elated, edgy.

That afternoon I'd been for a drink in a place I used to go sometimes when I went home at weekends; they knew me there. I walked in through the door just after sunset and ordered a whisky and a beer. Suddenly it was as though all the voices and sounds in the bar had been poured into a jar and then a lid had been put on it. Everybody turned round. They were staring at me, and they all had the same look on their faces. I felt as if I was in a western. As if I was a stranger in town and I'd done what I'd just done: walked into a bar and ordered a drink. I spoke again, into the silence: 'A whisky and a beer, please.'

At last Andreas, the owner's son, responded. 'I heard about the accident.'

'It wasn't an accident, Andreas. They did it on purpose.'

This was meant to be a joke, but nobody laughed.

'I mean, the gun didn't go off by mistake,' I said. 'It wasn't someone who just happened to have a gun and their finger slipped or something and the gun went off. What happened was, they pointed the gun at me and then they fired.'

It wasn't getting any funnier.

And suddenly I knew what I had to do. I had to move away from everyone I'd ever met. Find somewhere different to live. I had to disappear. I knocked my whisky back and chased it with the beer. It couldn't be that difficult. All I had to do was leave and not tell anyone where I was going. Who were my friends? Robert, Daphne, Hermann, Paul. Max and Irene. Oh yes, and Patrice. Was that all? There were a few people from the bookstore, too, of course. The boss, Mr Schlamm. Iris, who I'd had a thing about. Another Robert. They'd sent flowers to the clinic. Cards as well. They'd done their bit. Most people were busy, or lazy. I knew what they'd think. *He'll get in touch sooner or later. When he's ready.* That suited me. Now I'd drawn up a list, I realised there weren't too many of them, anyway. It was a relief to me that I wasn't more popular. There was less likelihood of an uncomfortable coincidence. If I did run into someone on the street, someone I knew, I'd just pretend I hadn't seen them. Nothing personal. I simply wanted to start again, with no awkwardness and no comparisons – no past. I wanted my life to begin with the shooting, as though that stranger's bullet had given birth to me, as though the pain I felt in that split-second was the pain of a baby being catapulted from the womb.

When I returned from the bar, my parents were in the drawing-room. My father offered me a schnapps, which I accepted. I chose the moment to inform them of my decision.

'I'm leaving,' I said. 'Tonight, probably.'

I pressed my face to the cold glass as the train rushed north through endless fields of beet. I remembered something Visser had said about rebuilding the relationship between myself and my parents. It would take time, he said. We would have to be patient with one another. He was sure that, in the end, some kind of harmony could be achieved.

But there were things he didn't understand about my parents, things I hadn't told him. My sister had died as a result of misdiagnosed appendicitis when she was twelve. I couldn't honestly remember her at all – I was five at the time – but everybody said she was a bright, fun-loving girl without a care in the world. Her name was Gabriela. I wasn't like her – never had been – and I'd always had the feeling that, if my parents had been forced to choose between us, if they could have said which one of us they were prepared to lose, it would have been me, not her. Yet I was the one they were left with. And this knowledge, this frustration, was something they couldn't quite shake off. On my first evening home, it was my reference to the death of someone close that had so upset my mother. I also thought that what had happened to me in some way reminded my parents of what had happened to Gabriela. Their grief rebounded between the two terrible events; it had grown with time, rather than diminishing, as grief usually does. I doubted this was something they'd get over. Even our family name had a morbid, rather lugubrious ring to it. Blam would have been a gunshot (quite appropriate, actually), but Blom was a tolling bell, that gloomy m reverberating: Blommm . . . Blommm . . . Blommm . . . Blommm . . .

Yes, Visser was wrong.

I peered at the bleak, unyielding landscape. My parents would be sitting at the kitchen table, eating a supper of cold meat, pickles, soda bread. Upstairs, in Gabriela's room, the ice-skating trophies, ballet certificates, pictures of pop-stars who were also, mostly, dead. She would have been thirty-six next month.

Both my parents cried when I left. My mother first, her weeping so violent that I thought her body wouldn't stand it. My father later, just before the taxi came – silent, almost sacrificial tears. I didn't tell them where I was going. I didn't promise to write or phone either. There was nothing heartless about this; it was as much for their comfort and well-being as for mine. Though the more I thought about it, the more

I realised my plan demanded it. I now saw my visit for what it was. Not a convalescence, not a reunion at all, but a leavetaking – a goodbye.

It was late evening by the time the train pulled into Central Station. I stepped down on to the platform, my cane in one hand, my suitcase in the other. I could feel the money in my coat pocket, a roll of banknotes tightly bound with an elastic band; my father wouldn't let me leave until I'd taken it. *That should keep you going for a month or so. Until your disability allowance comes through.* I took a deep breath and then hesitated, uncertain which way to turn.

A dense fog had descended. The voices of travellers beneath the vaulted, wrought-iron roof had a reverential sound, the murmur of worshippers in churches, people speaking to people who are dead. My skin grew thin; a panic whirled inside my head. I suddenly had thoughts I'd never had before. Our century has taken all the things we relied on. Our century has stripped us naked. Religion's gone, the family, too. We're alone, among distractions, then it's over.

I wasn't sure how long I stood there for.

At last I forced myself to walk. My legs were made of bamboo, with string in the middle instead of muscle. The hand that held the suitcase didn't feel like mine. I gave my ticket to the man who asked for it and set out across the station concourse. The crowds parted before me. I passed along the tiled tunnel that led to the taxi-rank. A piece of paper fluttered over my face. I bent down, picked it up. There was handwriting on it. It was some kind of note, but the paper was torn; only a fragment was left. Five words were visible and my heart leapt because I knew they were intended specifically for me:

You were brilliant!
Well done!

The Hotel Kosminsky stood on the edge of the red-light district, behind the train station. I remembered it from before – the outside of it, at least. All flaky-grey, it had the look of cold roast pork. The windows were dusty, smoke-stained, often cracked. Above the entrance, a torn black canopy fluttered in the wind that always seemed to be tormenting that particular street-corner. Two brothers owned the place. I'd seen them once, climbing out of a foreign car. They had close-cropped hair and wore identical suits of grey silk. People said they had certain interests in the area – apart from the hotel, that is. I was banking on this reputation; the Kosminsky was dubious, and nobody I knew would think of looking for me there.

I found a bell on the reception desk and bounced my hand on it. A man appeared, his head and shoulders wrapped in cigarette smoke, his eyes filmy, blinder than mine. He looked me over.

'You're not planning on dying here, are you?'

'No,' I said. 'I'm not planning on that.'

'We had someone die on us last week.' He pulled on his cigarette and crushed it out in a tin-foil ashtray. 'Seems people only check in here to fucking die.' He opened a register, licked one finger. Turned the page. 'We've got a single on the eighth floor. How long do you want it for?'

'You got a monthly rate?'

'Two-fifty.'

I paid the money in advance.

When he asked for details, I gave him the name of a boy who'd been in my class at school and the address of a girl I'd been in love with when I was twenty-one.

'The lift's on your left, Mr Polyak.'

The lift had wood-veneer walls and a carpet that was brown and pale-orange with a kind of leaf design in it. There was a narrow glass panel in the door so you could see each floor as you passed it, but only for about two seconds. The bell sounded and the door slid open. My floor. I stepped out. There was a strong smell of very old fried chicken. It took me a while to find my room. There didn't seem to be any sequence to the numbers; they were arranged in the strangest manner, almost randomly.

The room was long and narrow, with a bathroom just inside the door, on the right. Beyond the bathroom door was a miniature fridge, a wooden table and a plastic chair that balanced precariously on slender metal legs. On the table, predictably, an ashtray, a bible and a telephone. A full-length mirror was bolted to the wall above the fridge. Along the left-hand side of the room there was a wardrobe and a single bed. A cheap oil painting hung above the headboard. Those oil paintings. Sometimes it's a gypsy, sometimes it's a kitten. This time it was a pierrot, a pathetic drooping creature, with one glass tear gleaming on his cheek. Between the bed and the table was a window. I pushed it open, leaned my elbows on the sill. I could hear the bells of a distant church, three notes endlessly repeating. The old city lay to the east. A glow arched over it, pale as the light that surrounds a galaxy. Below me I could see the humped back of the station roof, charcoal-grey and ribbed, a whale half-submerged. To my left, an abandoned warehouse, dark windows in a face of crumbling brick, and beyond it, concealed by the steeply slanting tiles, the river, thick as broth and garnished with weeds.

I turned back into the room. I picked up the telephone and

listened: a dialling tone. I replaced the receiver, sat down on the bed. The air smelled of other people. The image of Smulders' washing passed before me; I wasn't sure whether it was the staleness of the room or the proximity of the railway station. I lit a cigarette, smoked half of it.

After a while I got to my feet. I reached up to the centre light, unscrewed the bulb and put it in the drawer of the table. I found the piece of paper that had blown past my face in the station passageway and tucked it into the bracket that held one corner of the mirror to the wall. Then I took my shoes off, stretched out face-down on the bed. It was second nature to me now not to put weight on the back of my head, but sometimes, when I was lying in that position, I felt victimised, powerless. I thought of the police, and what they do with people they're arresting. I thought of soldiers, in a war.

A siren curled past the corner of the building eight floors below. It was a sound that seemed moulded, bent; somehow it reminded me of blown glass. But the sound died down and when it had gone, I heard church bells again, those three descending notes, repeating, endlessly repeating . . .

At one in the morning I unpacked the sandwiches my mother had prepared for me. As I ate I wondered whether Visser had heard about my disappearance yet. In a way, I hoped he had. I'd like to have seen his face. Was it part of a process described in those neurology textbooks of his? Or had I outwitted him once more? I thought back to our last conversation. He'd called me at my parents' house in the middle of the week.

'How are you, Martin?'

I remembered how my eyelids had burned. I couldn't have been asleep for more than an hour.

'Fine, Doctor. How are you?'

'You sound tired.'

'I was asleep. You woke me.'

'It's a beautiful morning. You should get up.'

He'd be sitting in his swivel chair, the black leather creaking. I could imagine the sunlight enhancing the chestnut tints in his moustache. I saw the man in all his vanity.

'Can I help you with anything, Doctor?'

'No, no. I was just ringing to find out how you are.'

'I'm fine. Really.' I had to be careful not to overstate it, though. 'I'm getting about a bit. You know, with my stick.'

'Good, good. Just because you're not at the clinic any more, it doesn't mean we're not concerned about you.'

'No – '

'I must say, I enjoyed our afternoon together, the walk and so on.' He paused. 'I hope you don't think I was too hard on you.'

'No. Not at all.'

'Perhaps we could do it again some time. It's important that we don't lose touch.'

I was having trouble sustaining the conversation. I wasn't sure what he wanted to hear.

Suddenly he was laughing. 'You're an extraordinary case, you see. Unique, in fact. We've never had anyone quite like you, Martin. As I'm sure you realise.'

Was I supposed to feel flattered?

'Well,' he said at last. 'I'll ring you again soon. In a week or two.'

'Thank you, Doctor. And thanks for calling.'

'Goodbye, Martin.'

A conversation that now seemed harmless, anodyne (certainly there was no suggestion that he suspected me of planning anything). A conversation that was supposed to take its place in a series of similar conversations. A conversation that would be instantly forgettable, in fact, were it not for my own preoccupations. On the afternoon he'd referred to, I'd had the feeling that there was something he wasn't telling me. I had the same feeling now, in the hotel. I lingered on certain of his words: *Important*. *Extraordinary*. *Unique*. I stared at the remains of my sandwich on its sheet of greaseproof paper. I thought of the night I'd found myself, as chance would have it, looking down into his office. Visser at three in the morning, with a file marked HIGHLY CONFIDENTIAL. X-rays of my skull pinned to the wall. What was it that was confidential? Why was I such a persistent source of fascination to him? It was as though, behind Bruno Visser, fifteen or twenty people were standing one behind the other. If I took a step sideways, I would see them right away. But I didn't know how to take that step. That was how it was with Visser. I was constantly probing his façade for an ulterior motive, some hidden design. I imagined what his reaction would be, if he knew. 'Martin,' he would say, and he'd be laughing, 'don't be so *suspicious*!'

I slept later than usual. By the time I'd washed and dressed, it was after rush-hour. I walked out into the corridor. The same smell of old chicken rose into my nostrils. I noticed the carpet. It was dark-pink and cream, a kind of meat-and-fat pattern I didn't think I'd ever seen before. Opposite the lift I discovered a lounge area: a sofa and two armchairs, all upholstered in black vinyl, and a tall ashtray that looked like part of a juggler's act – a silver dish balancing on a silver pole. I pressed the call button outside the lift, but there was no response; I decided to take the stairs instead. When I crossed the lobby, there was a different person on reception – younger, with slicked-back hair and a guitarist's fingernails. He was reading a comic-book. I asked him where the nearest restaurant or café was. He gave me directions without raising his eyes from the page.

I turned left out of the hotel. The traffic had thinned out, even on the main road. The night was cool and windless. And suddenly, as I stood on the pavement, I was back in the car-park and it was happening again. I felt a wide space open up behind me. Someone was there, someone I couldn't identify. The assailant? I started to walk away, but I stumbled, tripped. Someone was standing over me. The same someone? How was I to know? *Are you all right?* I couldn't answer for a moment. I was lying on the ground, that dark curve arching over me – it had to be the wheel of a parked car – and I could see the tomatoes I'd just bought, three of them, anyway, motionless and red and shiny.

There was still somebody standing over me. They pressed something into my hand. *Your cane. You dropped your cane.* The fourth tomato – where was it? And then, out of the corner of my eye, I saw it rolling silently away from me. *Do you need any help?* There was a look of concern on the person's face that mirrored that of people in the clinic. I sat up. Smiled. Dusted my left sleeve, even though it didn't need it. You have to do normal things or they don't go away. You have to reassure them. Or they just stand there staring at you, as if you're a car-crash, or pornography.

Back in my room I filled a glass with cold water from the tap. I sat on the edge of my bed and sipped the water. I could explain everything. I carried the memory of the shooting inside me; the shock of it still travelled in my blood. And if that memory was affecting me now, it was probably because I was alone for the first time, truly alone. My nervousness was only to be expected; it was rational, in fact, perfectly understandable and would ease with time. I thought of calling Visser. I even reached for the phone. But then his words came back to me and that soapstone voice of his was with me in the room. *So long as you're prepared to fail.* There was nothing he could tell me now. Our realities no longer overlapped. And besides, I didn't want him knowing where I was. I stood up. I placed the plastic chair in front of the mirror and then I sat on it, my feet propped on the fridge door. I sat there for more than an hour. I calmed myself by staring at my face.

The next day I took the lift to the ground floor as soon as darkness fell. The same youth was in reception, reading the same comic-book.

'I need an ironmonger's,' I said.

This time he looked up, his eyes dazed by the KA-THUNK and POW of mighty fists. 'Did you find the restaurant OK, sir?'

'Yes. Thank you.'

I told him to call me Martin. His name was Victor.

'Ironmonger's,' he said, half to himself. He thought there was one nearby, just west of the hotel.

I walked out on to the street and stood for a moment under the torn black canopy, then set off along the pavement. This time there was no panic, no hesitation. In fifteen minutes I was there, the door jangling as I entered. Tall plastic flip-top bins hung from the ceiling, twisting slowly on their ropes.

I couldn't see the shopkeeper to begin with. Then he rose up from behind a cash-register that somebody had lined with Astroturf.

'Can I help you?'

I looked up at the slowly twisting bins. 'There been some kind of lynching here?'

'I beg your pardon?'

'It's all right.' Not everybody has a sense of humour. 'I need a can of black paint.'

'Black paint, eh? What's it for?'

His eyes fidgeted behind a pair of spectacles. They could've been reptiles, the way they were kept behind glass like that. They could've been poisonous. Also, somehow, there seemed to be more than two of them.

'If you don't tell me what it's for,' he said, 'I won't know what kind of paint to recommend.'

'It's for glass.'

'Glass?' In his surprise, he gave the word more push. His breath had a bitter smell. Like saucepans.

'I want to paint my windows,' I said.

The shopkeeper gripped his chin with his forefinger and tucked his thumb underneath. 'For a darkroom, is it? No, it's obvious you're not a photographer – '

I interrupted him. 'What's your name?'

'My name? Sprankel. Walter Sprankel. Why?' He was stammering suddenly, which pleased me.

I leaned on the counter. Something cracked beneath my elbow, but I pretended not to notice. 'Sprankel,' I said, 'are you going to sell me any paint or not?'

'Yes,' he said. 'Yes, of course.' He reached behind him and a can appeared in his hand.

'That wasn't so difficult, was it?'

'No.' He was still holding the can. 'It's oil-based. Ideal for metal, plastic – and for glass.' He wrapped it up. 'Is there something else I can do for you?'

'I'd better have a paintbrush.'

'Certainly. Anything else?'

'A strip of felt one metre long. Preferably black, though brown would do. And some nails. Let's say two dozen.' I lifted a warning finger. 'And no guessing what they're for, Sprankel. All right?'

Just before dawn I had the dream again, only this time it wasn't me who was running down the sunlit street, it was Smulders. I looked on with a kind of disbelief. Smulders running – what a sight! Each stride he took, his body reverberated. And before the reverberation had time to die down, he took another stride. The reverberations merged, one into the next, a kind of crosshatching of the flesh. Some sections moved quite independently of others; or sometimes they collided, rebounded, collided once again. His armpit hair streamed horizontally behind him. Then bits started flying off. Sausage fingers, sausage toes. An earlobe the size of a dried apricot. One meaty arm, a tree-trunk of an ankle. I almost felt sorry for the road. I watched his tiny penis flee the threat posed by his overhanging belly. His scrotum, sheepish, followed it. Soon he was gone. Nothing left except a kind of after-image: fat air, thin air – one moving through the other. Essence of Smulders. I woke up smiling. It was a comic version of the dream, the dream mocking itself. I lay in bed, wondering if what I was seeing was the beginning of a new phase. Maybe the fear was burning off at last. Maybe the worst was over.

I sat up in bed. My smile widened as I saw the result of my night's work. The window next to me was black. The window in the bathroom, too. Three coats, just to be on the safe side. Strips of felt lined the edges of the windows and the bottom of the door. What I was trying to create was absolute, one hundred per cent darkness. In a city this wasn't easy. It surprised me how much light there was, and light seemed to breed light. It was like a headline I saw in the paper once: WOMAN MAKES SELF PREGNANT. I was close now, though; I was really close. The room was dark as a coffin with the lid screwed down. I could see every detail, even the dead insects on the floor, even the dust. When the maid came in to clean, which wasn't often in a place like the Kosminsky, she'd have to use a torch. I decided to pay her extra for her trouble.

On the same street as the Kosminsky was an all-night restaurant called Leon's. You walked in through a rickety glass-and-metal door, parting a curtain that was lined with vinyl to keep out the draughts. Once beyond the curtain you were hit by the smell of sweat and soup and cigarettes. Upstairs, there was a billiard hall. The restaurant lay to your left. It had yellow tiled walls and square Formica tables, and the windows always ran with condensation. On the ceiling, several white fluorescent tubes (I sometimes found Leon's a bit bright, but it was so close to the hotel, so convenient, that I was prepared to sacrifice a small percentage of my vision). You paid the woman at the cash-register and she gave you a receipt. It was self-service. There was a TV in the top corner of the room, its screen angled downwards, like some modern bird of prey. You ate with your eyes fixed on it, one arm curled protectively around your plate. Leon's clientele? Pretty much as you'd expect. Night-porters, taxi-drivers, hookers with their pimps. Junkies, divorcees. Insomniacs. These people were my people. Daylight? They could take it or leave it; it didn't do them any favours (in fact, in some cases, it did them a definite disservice). I quickly became a regular at Leon's. I always took a table by the wall and sat with my back to it (I imagined the Kosminsky brothers did the same – though for different reasons). I was in the restaurant every night, at midnight, to eat my lunch. Usually I ordered fried steak with onion rings (Leon cooked it just the way I liked it: juices seeping out of the meat, the onions slightly blackened). Or sometimes I had boiled beef.

Towards the end of my first week, on the Saturday, I asked for fried sweet cabbage with my steak (onion rings were off). A boxing match was on TV that night. Two heavyweights. Fff. Fff, fff. Blat. Fff. Blat, blat. BLAT. Over the din of people cheering I heard the legs of the chair opposite me scrape on the floor.

'Mind if I sit down?'

I looked up slowly from my plate. It was a man in a donkey jacket, maybe fifty-five years old. His bald head had the high shine of a dance-floor. What was left of his hair floated above it like dry ice.

'You live in the hotel, don't you.'

I put down my knife and fork and stared at him.

'The Kosminsky,' he said. 'Eighth floor.'

I was still staring at him. 'You following me or something?'

'Following you?' He paused. 'No. I live across the hall. Room eight-thirteen.'

'I haven't noticed you.'

He laughed. Or coughed. I couldn't tell which.

'The name's Gregory,' he said.

I stared at him for a moment longer, then reached across the table with my hand.

'Martin,' I said. 'Martin Blom.'

He took my hand in his and gripped it. His palms were dry, almost shiny, and one of his fingers was missing.

'You probably noticed the finger,' Gregory said. 'I lost it working on the trawlers.'

He told me how. Twenty years ago now, maybe more. Up in the Arctic, fishing for cod. His hand got caught in a rope as it whipped around a winch. The finger was too chewed up to sew back on. Funny thing was, he didn't remember feeling any pain. In fact, he'd never been calmer in his life. He just stood there, asked someone for a cigarette. Smoked it while they tied the tourniquet. After that they called him Smoke. People still called him Smoke today. Most of them didn't know the reason, though.

'What about you?' Gregory said. 'You always been blind?'

I hadn't talked to anyone for days – not across a table, anyway, not like this. There was a kind of warmth about it that made whoever you were talking to irrelevant. It occurred to me that I was about to tell my story for the first time. It was a strange feeling, releasing it.

'It happened in February,' I said. 'I was shot by someone. In the head.'

'Shot in the head? Jesus Christ!'

'I was coming home from work. Normal day. Stopped at a supermarket to pick up some groceries. Walked back to my car. All of a sudden – BAM!' I brought my hand down on the table. It caught the lip of a spoon and sent it somersaulting over Gregory's shoulder. He didn't even notice.

'Jesus Christ – ' he said again.

'Yeah, well. That's how it happened.' I decided not to mention the tomatoes; I didn't think he'd understand. Instead, I found myself making a confession. 'Sometimes it's scary. Not the blindness so much. More the memory. You know, of being shot. So sudden like that. Out of nowhere . . .' I paused. 'To tell you the truth, I don't much care for car-parks any more.'

'I bet you don't. Did they find out who did it?'

I shook my head. 'Nobody saw anything. Even I didn't see anything.'

It was such a relief to tell the story out loud, just those few disjointed sentences, to a complete stranger, that I did something I never normally do: I ordered dessert – a slice of apple strudel, with cream.

'No,' I said, 'he's still out there somewhere . . .'

Later, as I walked the red-light streets of the 14th district, I thought of how we'd traded, Gregory and I: his finger for a piece of my skull. That was what people did. They found something they had in common – an injury was always good; so was a disaster – then they traded. I suddenly saw my dream in a new light, not as fear but nostalgia. Returning to myself as I used to be, if only for a few moments. Revisiting a version of myself that no longer existed. The complete me.

Someone was pulling on my sleeve.

'Hey, blind man. I'm fucking beautiful and you can have me for twenty-five.'

I looked at her. 'You're not beautiful.'

The whore let go of me. 'What the fuck do you care?'

My life was simple, some might say monotonous. Most days I got up at four-thirty in the afternoon. Outside, dusk would be coming down. If I opened my window I could watch the street-lights fizz, then flicker on. People spilled from their office buildings, out into the orange gloom, all moving at the same speed, but in different directions, like cells under a microscope. At six o'clock I left my room. I walked along the west bank of the river, passing the rowing club, closed for the winter, and the outdoor swimming-pool, its blue floor strewn with leaves. Or else I followed the path that led through the park and round the artificial lake. Or sometimes I visited the zoo. In the street behind the hotel there was a café which was famous for the rudeness of its waiters. It was here that I ate my breakfast. They soon became accustomed to me, sitting at a table in the corner with my glass of *café au lait* and my slightly stale brioche. After breakfast I returned to the hotel. If it was Victor's shift, I'd stop for a chat. He had asked me about myself one night when I came in. I'd told him the story. Naturally, he wanted to know what it was like to be shot, right down to the last detail. I didn't mind his ghoulish enthusiasm. At least it was honest. If Arnold was on reception, however – morbid, chain-smoking Arnold – I'd walk straight past the desk; Arnold wasn't a man you could talk to easily. Back in my room I switched the TV on and pulled up a chair. For the next two hours I watched whatever they were showing: soap-operas, news programmes, dramas – anything. I'd been astonished when I realised I could actually watch TV. Since I'd established that my vision was linked to darkness, and since the light emitted by a TV screen is so intense, I'd automatically assumed that watching it would be impossible. But it was one of those vagaries of my condition – another mystery or miracle – that I could see the picture as clearly as I could see Victor's fingernails or Gregory's bald head.

Lunch at Leon's was the high point of my day. I always looked forward to my steak and onions, the bustle and clatter of the kitchen, the conversations I could listen to. I liked the plastic hoop ear-rings the cashier wore; I liked the way the cook's face hung in the steam above some boiling pot or pan. And it was Leon's that had provided me with my first real acquaintance. Gregory worked nights as a security guard at a bank, and he often dropped in halfway through his shift for a cup of coffee and a pastry. During my second week in the city, I ran into him again.

'I thought I'd find you here.' Gregory sat down at my table, without asking this time, and slumped over the Formica.

I could see that, before too long, I'd have to find somewhere else to eat. We were both lonely men, Gregory and I; the difference was, he hadn't chosen it. Still, by hearing me out the other night, he'd done me a favour (even if he wasn't aware of it), and that made me generous.

'Smoke,' I said, 'how's things?'

A grin split his face wide open. All you had to do was use his stupid name and he'd be happy.

For a while we talked generally, about the present – his job, his daughter's wedding, sport – then he narrowed it down, went back in time. He began to tell me about the factory he worked in for twenty years. He used to pack fish. This didn't surprise me. The first time I met him I thought I could smell fish, and now I realised that I hadn't been mistaken. It was as if the smell of cod had been preserved at some deep level of his skin, layers down, the way a tree's rings can record a bolt of lightning or a flood.

'Feel this,' Gregory said. 'Feel my hand.'

I reached out and felt it. I remembered it from the week before. It was smooth and shiny, like touching fibre glass. I told him so.

'That's twenty years of packing fish, that is.'

His hands were ruined. Where I had lines, he had cracks. And the cracks, he told me, often opened up and bled. There was nothing he could do about it. It was the price you paid, working in those factories. Before that, he'd sailed on trawlers, up into Arctic waters. 'But I already told you that . . .'

I nodded patiently. I was thinking about getting away, back to my room. I was thinking about turning on the TV. Maybe I'd drink a schnapps or two. Then, later, a walk through the red-light streets, peep-show neon silvering the puddles . . .

'You're a good fellow, Blom,' he said, and he stared at me, all watery-eyed and serious.

At first I wasn't sure why he had that look on his face. Then I realised what it was, and almost choked on my steak. The poor fool felt sorry for me!

'You're new to the city,' he said, 'aren't you.'

'I got here about a week ago.'

'You know anyone?'

'Only you.' I grinned. 'Sounds like a song, doesn't it.'

'You know, you should get out,' he said, 'meet some people.' His voice brightened suddenly. His daughter's wedding, he'd mentioned it already, it was in a few days' time. Maybe I should come along.

'That's very kind of you, Gregory, but – '

'Loots is coming.'

'Who?'

'Albert Loots. He's a friend of mine.' Gregory leaned forwards. 'He used to work in a circus. Works in a factory now. Cakes and biscuits.' Gregory sighed, but it was a sigh of deep satisfaction. He liked it when lives described a curve, as both ours did. He liked to have some kind of proof that fortune's wheel had turned. 'I see him on his bicycle sometimes. Usually it's when I'm going home, six or seven in the morning – ' Gregory yawned. 'Wish I could hit the hay. Ah well, no rest for the wicked.' He heaved himself to his feet, looked down at me. 'So,' he said, 'you think you'll come?'

'I'll try.'

I watched him leave with dread rising in me like a river whose history it is to burst its banks. Gregory's daughter's wedding. It was bound to be one of those interminable suburban functions. There'd be a band – some bunch of tone-deaf alcoholics playing folk tunes. There'd be dancing, which I'd always thought of as a kind of illness, like Parkinson's disease, or epilepsy (someone call an ambulance, for Christ's sake). There'd be displays of sentiment and bonhomie on every side. I was going to have to get out of it – but how? I walked through the 14th district for most of that night, trying to think up excuses.

Towards dawn I was on my way back to the Kosminsky when I saw a man riding a bicycle down the middle of a wide, deserted street. It was still very early, the trees loud with birds, light slowly beginning to ease into the sky. Because he was just about the only thing moving, I kept my eyes on him. He was some distance away, though; I couldn't see his face.

As I watched, the man swung himself up into the air. Suddenly he was upside-down, one hand on the handlebars, the other on the saddle. It was so deft, so effortless, that he appeared weightless, immune to the laws of gravity. And the bicycle was still travelling down the middle of the street; if you'd traced its progress with a piece of chalk, if you'd drawn a line on the tarmac, I doubt there would have been even a kink in it. The man wore tight-fitting, pale-yellow trousers and a glittering blue jersey with stars on it. It seemed to me that he was juggling what looked like oranges with his feet. Then, just before he disappeared from view, he dropped back down into the saddle, his feet synchronising with the pedals, the oranges vanishing, one by one, into his pockets. I found myself applauding.

'What happened?' asked a passer-by.

'It's over now,' I said. 'You missed it.'

As I prepared for bed I remembered something Gregory had told me. *Used to be in a circus. Sometimes I see him on his bicycle.* Surely it had to be the same man. That friend of his, the one he'd invited to his daughter's wedding. What was his name? Teats? Groot? Something like that. I felt my anxieties lift, my excuses fall away. I'd spent half the night in torment – and now? I realised I was actually looking forward to the event. All it had taken was a man on a bicycle and half a dozen oranges. I looked at my face in the bathroom mirror. I watched my mouth open wide, I saw my teeth. I was laughing.

That same week I noticed a disturbing phenomenon. It was after returning from Leon's one night. I pressed the call button outside the lift. Nothing happened. I must have waited five or ten minutes, first pressing the button, then leaning on it, but the lift never came. In the end I took the stairs.

I'd just reached the second floor when I saw something that brought me to a sudden standstill. Two people, having sex. They were lying on the carpet, half in and half out of the lift. One of the woman's arms trailed across the corridor, as if she was practising her backstroke, as if the whole thing was taking place in water and she was trying to swim away from it. Every now and then, the lift doors closed on her – then opened again. There were red marks where the stainless steel had bitten into her hips. It was like seeing one form of life caught in the jaws of another. This didn't seem to detract from her pleasure, though; in fact, it could well have been contributing. I smiled, murmured an apology and, stepping carefully over her outstretched arm, continued up the next flight of stairs. They didn't seem to notice me at all.

I might not have thought any more about it – after all, they were probably just business people: a company director and his secretary – but then, two days later, I saw another couple. They were sideways-on to me, at the far end of the corridor. The woman lay on her back, though her shoulders were taking most of the weight. She was folded almost double, her heels tucked into the old-fashioned radiator that stood under the window. Blue light flashed on the stretched backs of her thighs as a tram rumbled past outside. The man, dark-haired and muscular, half-stood, half-sat above her, knees slightly bent. As he pushed downwards, into her, he happened to glance round. A gold medallion swung across his chest, one stroke of a pendulum, and came to rest. Did he see me standing there in the shadows by the stairs? And, if so, was he reassured by my dark glasses and my white stick?

That was Saturday. As chance would have it, during the next week, the lift was either in use or out of order (for reasons I was now beginning to understand); most nights I was forced to climb the eight floors to my room. On Monday I saw the woman I'd last seen trapped in the lift doors. This time she was bent over the small table that had the hotel telephone on it. She was naked and a man was standing behind her, wearing a tuxedo and a pair of black socks. I didn't recognise him. The telephone was ringing underneath the woman. 'Don't you think someone ought to answer that?' I said. They looked at me, but didn't say anything. On Wednesday night, as I reached the second floor, I saw three girls in black leather sitting on the sofa. They were smoking. One of them wore a long metal ring that extended beyond her middle finger like a second, sharper nail. Halfway along the corridor I could see a short fat man on his hands and knees. He wore a black T-shirt, a black PVC mini-skirt and black high-heels. His legs were shaved. One of the girls stretched her thigh-length boot out as he crawled across the carpet towards her. He bent down and began to suck the toe. 'You got a problem?' one of the girls said suddenly (it was the girl with the ring). 'No, no,' I said. 'I'm fine.' I hurried on up the stairs. On Thursday I decided not to stop on the second floor, no matter what I saw, but as it turned out it was a quiet night. There was a girl in white-lace underwear standing in the doorway of a room. A man in a suit was talking to her. He had his hands in his pockets. The two of them were deep in some private negotiation, though they fell silent as soon as they noticed me. The girl didn't have the kind of face you'd associate with somebody who was almost naked; it was attentive, businesslike, as if she was in an office, or a bank. The man was probably a pimp, I thought, as I began to climb towards the third floor. At that moment he looked at me, over his shoulder. His face was entirely without expression.

That weekend I met Gregory in Leon's. I leaned over the table in a conspiratorial manner that I knew he liked and asked him if he had noticed anything strange about the second floor.

'You mean, at the Kosminsky?'

I nodded.

'No.'

'You haven't noticed anything at all?'

'Like what?'

I told him to go and have a look for himself. The second floor, I said. From midnight onwards.

That morning, close to dawn, I saw eight people doing it. They were standing in a circle at the top of the stairs, four women and four men. All the women had dildos strapped around their hips. Each person was being fucked and fucking at the same time (somehow it reminded me of a doughnut). You could charge for this, I was thinking. But, at the same time, I was wearied by it and I wished there was another way of getting to my room. I decided to have a word with the management. I wasn't going to complain, exactly. I'd just mention it. Discreetly.

I found Arnold on duty the next evening and, since he was the more senior of the two receptionists, I thought it was him I should speak to. It was raining outside; water tipped through the rips in the canopy, splashed on to the pavement below. I took him aside and told him of the recent goings-on.

'Goings-on?'

I leaned closer. 'On the second floor.'

Arnold lit a cigarette with a snap of his lighter.

'All right, I'll be blunt,' I said. 'People fucking.'

Arnold's eyebrows dipped towards the bridge of his nose. Just for a moment they resembled the logo of our national airline.

'Actually, sir, now you mention it, there have been a few complaints – '

'There. You see?'

'About you.'

'What?'

'About you loitering.'

'*Loitering?*' I couldn't believe what I was hearing.

'It's probably an over-reaction.' Arnold inhaled. Smoke poured upwards from his nostrils and his mouth. His whole head disappeared. 'You're blind. Blind people – well, you know. They frighten people.'

'I suppose – yes, that's true, but – '

'I'd stick to your own floor in future. I mean, we don't want to go round upsetting people, do we.' He smiled suddenly, disarmingly, then he inhaled again.

As I walked out into the rain I pondered Arnold's attitude. There was only one conclusion I could draw: that part of the hotel was being used as a whorehouse – clandestine, certainly, quite possibly illegal too – with all the rooms, even the corridors, reserved for hookers and their clients. No wonder he wouldn't admit to anything. He was probably being paid by the Kosminsky brothers to run the place. He probably got commission from the girls. After all, there had to be a reason why the hotel had such a dubious reputation. In retrospect, it had been naive of me to mention it to him.

That night, as I sat in Leon's, watching the football on TV and waiting for my pig's heart goulash, I suddenly thought of a name for the second floor. It could be a name known only to a privileged few (though I could also see it in slow-flashing, scarlet neon). THE LOVE STOREY. Should I suggest it to Arnold, who could pass it on to the brothers for me? No, maybe not. To pretend I knew nothing of their operation might be wiser. They weren't the kind of men who welcomed interference. If they thought you were poking your nose into their business, they'd probably pay someone to cut it off.

Towards one o'clock in the morning the door opened and the draught carried an unmistakable hint of fish. Gregory sank heavily into the chair beside me. He'd spent most of his night off on the second floor. He hadn't seen a thing.

'What?' I said. 'Nothing?'

'Nothing. Not a thing.'

'There's people fucking all over the place,' I said. 'There's couples, there's threesomes. There's people sucking shoes – '

'Keep your voice down.'

'It's a brothel, Gregory. Haven't you noticed?'

He began to stammer. 'Well, of course, sometimes – '

'You haven't noticed,' I said, 'have you.'

'Well, no,' he muttered, 'not – '

'You must be blind.'

History could be happening outside his window and he wouldn't know about it. He'd be too busy wondering what was for supper, which soap-opera to watch. I should never have mentioned it to him. I looked at his hair plastered to his forehead in a frieze of unintelligible hieroglyphics. I looked at his jutting lower lip, his hands fumbling on the table-top. Now I'd upset him. And we were supposed to be friends.

'Don't worry about it, Smoke,' I said wearily. 'I probably made the whole thing up.'

'You did?' He chuckled to himself. 'Sometimes I can't figure you out, Blom.'

Sometimes!

One further development, regarding the suspected involvement of the Kosminsky brothers. It was two nights later. I was in the hotel lift, going up. I'd pressed 8, but the lift stopped on 2. Nobody got in. As I reached out to press 8 again, a door directly opposite the lift swung open. The sight of one of the brothers emerging from a room full of laughing, half-naked girls at three-fifteen in the morning confirmed all my previous suspicions.

I was late for the wedding. It wasn't my fault. If they'd started at a sensible time, I would have been there – but one-thirty in the afternoon? The house was out in the suburbs, too, not far from the bleak square where the trams turn round. One dismal street after another, all of them identical. I don't know how long it took me, but it was dark when I arrived. I would have been even later if an old woman hadn't insisted on walking me right to the door.

It wasn't unlike the place where my grandparents used to live: small and grey, with a patch of grass for a front garden, a glass-house at the side and a wrought-iron fence that had been painted pale-green. The latch clinked as I opened the gate. The front door was just a few steps along a concrete path. I could hear music coming from somewhere. So there was dancing. If the old woman hadn't been watching me, I might have left there and then. Instead, I had to knock.

'Blom!' Gregory embraced me. Fish mingled uneasily with beer. 'We thought you weren't coming.'

He took me over to the bride and groom and introduced us. His daughter's name was Petra. She looked like Gregory, only she had hair. Her husband's name was Rolf. I offered them my congratulations.

'We're so glad you could come,' Petra said. 'We've heard all about you.'

How lonely I was, presumably. How terribly alone.

'And look,' Gregory said, 'here's Loots.'

I didn't recognise him at first, without his glittering, star-encrusted jersey and his bicycle. I saw a thin young man with reddish hair, his shoulders high and stiff inside his shirt as he bounced across the room towards me. His heels hardly seemed to touch the ground.

'I've seen you before.' Loots mentioned a street that ran parallel to the Kosminsky.

'I feel the same way,' I said, and smiled mysteriously.

Gregory laughed and put an arm around my shoulders. 'He's quite a character, is Blom.'

We drank chilled vodka from thimble glasses. A toast to the newlyweds, then down in one. Another toast, to happiness this time. And then another. Friendship. I wanted to question Loots about his acrobatics, but he'd already moved across the room to where the music was. I watched him dancing with the bride. He had a rather formal style, very correct, almost quaint. Their arms – his left, her right – curved up into the air like handles on a jug, their joined hands floating high above their heads.

I met the bride's mother, Gregory's ex-wife. She was drinking cheap champagne.

'No, I didn't throw him out,' she was telling me. 'He left.'

She had a hoarse, serrated voice; it seemed to come from further back in her throat than most people's. The skin beneath her eyes had broken up into a mass of tiny diamonds – the powdery, reptile skin that alcoholics sometimes have. Her name was Hedi.

'You may think you're blind,' she said, pressing up against me, 'but you're not half as blind as Gregory . . .'

'No?'

'I was going with Harold for a year before Gregory suspected anything. Harold's over there. We're married now.' She wrapped her hand around my wrist. 'I hope I didn't offend you.'

'No, no,' I said. 'I've come across adultery before.'

'I don't mean that. I mean about you not being blind.'

'You're a very perceptive woman,' I said, and winked at her.

I was smiling. I'd just remembered what I liked about weddings. It wasn't the sight of 'the happy couple'. It wasn't meandering speeches. Or alcohol. Or cake. It wasn't love. It was because there was always somebody who started dragging skeletons out of the cupboard. Clatter, clatter, clatter, right into the middle of the room. There was always somebody like Hedi.

It was the first social occasion of my new life and maybe that explains why I got drunk so fast. I kept bumping into people and having to apologise. At one point I was even seeing double (imagine Visser's face if I told him that!). Then Gregory appeared beside me. He had someone with him.

'This is Inge,' he said, breathing loudly through his mouth. 'Inge wants to dance with you.'

I looked at her. She was like one of those girls you see on the tram, her nose too long and not quite straight, her mouth too small, her eyes too mournful, one of those girls who sits down by the window and takes off her gloves, which are always pale-grey wool, and starts reading a textbook, mathematics, probably, or social science, one hand reaching up to fluff the hair above her forehead.

'I told you, Gregory,' I said. 'I don't dance.'

'But it's a special day. How can you say no?'

I sighed.

'You don't have to,' the girl said in a quiet voice.

And so we danced. A slow number, mawkish, just guitars and an accordion. The natural scent that rose off her skin made me think of fruit, somehow – of apple blossom. My hand felt too large against the small of her back, too hot. My right knee was trembling. Loots swung past my shoulder, his eyebrows halfway between his hairline and the bridge of his nose, the smile on his lips serene, professional.

I spoke into the air beside Inge's ear. 'Did someone put you up to this?'

She laughed.

'It was Gregory,' I said, 'wasn't it.'

'Nobody put me up to it. I wanted to.'

'Dance?' I said. 'With a blind man?'

She shook her head. 'The truth's more embarrassing than that.'

'Oh? And what is the truth?'

'Can't you guess?'

A feeling went through me, a feeling I'd forgotten. Like thick liquid being poured into a void. When the dance was over, I told her I needed a drink.

'Me too,' she said.

'I'll get you one.'

I made my way across the room to the trestle table in the corner, where I found Gregory easing the top off another bottle of beer.

'Was that so bad?' he said.

'Not so bad, no.'

'I think you're in with a chance there.' He gave my upper arm a squeeze.

I shook myself free.

'You're impossible, Blom.' He was slurring now: impossible and Blom were one word. 'You're bloody impossible.'

Dawn could not be far away. These days I could feel it coming; that first streak of red or purple in the east, I'd know it was there even before I looked. And then an electric milk-float passing. Birds in the trees. My vision was beginning to weaken. Very gradual, it was, that fade to grey. Gradual, but determined. Irreversible.

The party was almost over. Most people had gone home. Loots and I were still up, though. We were sitting in the kitchen with a bottle of Gregory's ex-wife's home-made plum brandy. A sticky, sweet drink that had a kick to it. A foot inside a velvet boot.

I'd last seen Gregory sprawled on the stairs.

'First I lose my wife,' he said, 'then I lose my daughter – '

'Yeah,' I said, 'that's true.'

'You're no help, Blom. You're no bloody help.'

I'd left him there, his bald head propped against the banisters, his fingers fastened round a glass.

I'd already told Loots I was thinking of going home and he'd said so, too, more than once, but neither of us had moved. Loots was dreaming at the end of the table, his sharp chin plunged into his hand. A fading image. In daylight it would take me hours to get back to the hotel. Somehow I no longer cared. This was the moment I'd been waiting for.

'You know you used to work in a circus?'

His face turned slowly on his palm. 'Who told you that?'

'Gregory.'

'He's such a blabbermouth.'

I sipped my brandy. 'I just wondered. What did you do exactly?'

'I'll give you a clue,' he said. And then he said, 'Listen.'

Ah yes, I thought. Here's somebody who understands. It wasn't just that he was using the kind of language someone blind could respond to. It was the timing of it. It felt as if he knew my vision had just failed and he was playing with it. Uncanny.

I heard him stand up and unzip his jacket. Then I heard a kind of singing sound as one . . . two . . . three . . . four . . . five . . . six metal things, I thought they must be knives, yes, knives, slid out of their individual sheaths into the air.

'You were a cook,' I said.

Loots began to laugh.

'A cook,' he said. 'I love it.'

He took me by the arm and led me out through the back door. It was cold suddenly. We crossed a yard, our feet catching in torn streamers, sending paper cups in giddy half-circles. My heart was beating fast. I felt like a child who'd got into a stranger's car. I asked him where we were going.

'It's another clue,' he said.

We were walking on grass. I heard the wings of geese carving through the damp air overhead. The house was quiet behind us. I wondered what Gregory would think if he happened to glance out of an upstairs window, glass in hand and yawning blearily.

Loots stopped. 'Ah,' he said. 'Perfect.'

We had to climb a fence. Loots made a step out of his hands for me. I put my foot on it and clambered over. Then dropped down, my feet sinking into spongy grass. Loots landed beside me, breathing through his mouth.

'All right?'

I nodded. 'Where are we?'

'The next-door neighbour's garden.'

We walked a few paces, then he pushed me up against a wall.

'Stand there.'

The wall was made of wood. Maybe it wasn't a wall. Another fence, then. No, I could feel where it ended. A shed of some kind. The side wall of a shed.

Six knives. The side wall of a shed.

'Hold on,' I said. 'I think I know.'

'Stand there,' Loots called out, 'and don't move.'

'*But I know* – '

Loots was chuckling, some distance off.

'It's perfect,' he said. 'You won't even see them comin – '

The g was cut off by the whistle of the first knife through the air and the thud a split-second later as it stuck into the wood next to my ear.

The other five followed, at two-second intervals. I dug my fingernails into the crack between two boards and held on, grateful that it was light and I couldn't see the blurred blades come hurtling towards me.

'*Hey!*'

'Who's that?' I said.

'It's an old guy,' Loots said. 'He looks angry.'

I grinned. 'It's probably the next-door neighbour.'

'That's right, it's the next-door neighbour,' the next-door neighbour said, 'and the next-door neighbour wants to know what the fuck six knives are doing stuck in the side wall of his garden shed.'

Loots tried to explain that he used to work in a circus and that he was just demonstrating the art of knife-throwing to a friend.

The next-door neighbour interrupted him. 'First I'm kept awake half the night, some wedding, now there's a fucking circus in my garden. Go demonstrate in your own garden, for Christ's sake.' He blew some air out of his mouth. 'Jesus.'

Loots retrieved his knives, then led me towards the fence.

'And don't fucking break my fence,' the next-door neighbour shouted after us, 'all right?'

We didn't start laughing until we dropped down on the other side. Then we couldn't stop. Every time Loots said, 'It's probably the next-door neighbour,' we started again. My stomach ached with it.

'Were you really a knife-thrower?' I asked him.

'Well, I trained as one,' he said, 'but they never actually let me loose on anyone.'

The two of us laughing, but more quietly now. Sitting on a damp lawn, with our backs against the fence. Dawn in the suburbs.

At last we walked back towards the house. There was something I was still curious about, though, and now seemed as good a time as any. I turned to Loots.

'Do you do any tricks with bicycles?'

'Bicycles?' He sounded baffled. 'How do you mean?'

'Oh, you know,' I said casually. 'Handstands, juggling – that kind of thing.'

'No, I don't know anything about that.'

I smiled to myself. Obviously he didn't want to talk about his bicycle trick. He was probably still perfecting it. I decided not to press him. Loots was a man of many talents, and some of them were hidden. If anyone understood the value of secrecy, it was me. The fact that he also had secrets didn't frustrate or discourage me at all; if anything, it lifted him higher in my estimation.

We travelled back into the city together. The tram was empty to begin with, then it filled. The people getting on hadn't been awake for long. They talked in murmurs, if they talked at all; they were still carrying their last night's sleep with them. I heard the stamp of tickets being punched in the machine. The wheels grinding on the rails. The whiplash of electric cables overhead. Loots fell asleep beside me, his cheekbone knocking against my shoulder. I opened the window and cool foggy air flowed in. November.

Just before my stop, I reached into my pocket to check that my key was there. My hand closed round a piece of paper. I lifted it to my nose. The scent of apple blossom still lingered.

Inge had suggested that I choose the place. Somewhere you're comfortable with, she said. Somewhere you know. While it was thoughtful of her, it wasn't easy. All the places I knew – or rather, used to know – I couldn't go to any more. I could only think of the Bar Sultan, which was in a small street on the east side of the railway station. Gregory had taken me there one night.

We'd agreed to meet at nine o'clock. I was there at three minutes past. I couldn't see her, though, so I took a stool at the bar and ordered a beer. It was a long, narrow place. Dark wood, framed photographs of local football teams (the owner used to keep goal for the city), and a juke-box and a pool table in the back. I wondered what would happen when she arrived. I didn't think we'd dance again; there was nobody to blackmail me into it this time and, besides, the music wasn't suitable. Maybe we'd talk. I didn't have much to say that anyone would believe, but I was curious about her. I knew so little. I drank my beer and when it was gone there was still no sign of her. I ordered another.

It's all right to be on your first drink when you're waiting for somebody, or on your second, that's all right, too. But if you're on your third, it starts to feel like something's wrong. I asked the bartender what the time was. Ten-thirty-five, he said. Inge was an hour and a half late. My neck ached from looking round whenever the door swung open. My head ached as well. I'd been looking forward to the moment when the crowd parted to reveal her, like something at the centre of a flower. I'd been looking forward to it, and now it wasn't going to happen.

By the time I ordered my fourth beer I was past caring. I drank it down in two savage gulps and ordered a fifth immediately.

Someone sat down on the stool I'd been saving for her. Well, she wasn't going to be using it. She wouldn't be coming now, and that was probably just as well. I couldn't even remember what she looked like. Somehow I couldn't bring myself to leave, though. It wasn't twelve o'clock yet, and, anyway, I didn't feel like going to Leon's. I went to Leon's every night. So there I was, five drinks inside me, sitting at the bar.

I couldn't have said exactly when I noticed the girl sitting on the stool beside me. Midnight, maybe. Maybe later. It seemed to me that she'd been sitting there for some time. Not saying anything. Just sitting there, like me. Her elbow touching mine. But I wasn't in the mood to talk to anyone. Not any more. I'd been stood up. Whatever dream I'd had, it was in pieces. The girl was still there, though, even after I'd registered all that.

'Have you got a light?' she said.

I found a lighter in my pocket. She cupped her hand round the back of mine and guided it towards her cigarette.

'Thank you.'

She inhaled, drank from her drink, then blew the smoke out. She was still sitting there. Dark-brown hair, with gold in it. Dark eyelashes.

'Can I kiss you?' she said.

I stared at her. I wasn't sure I'd heard her right.

She leaned closer. 'I'd like to kiss you.'

And before I could say anything, one of her hands reached up and rested on my shoulder, then her lips touched mine.

That girl from the wedding. Inge. Her small mouth. That tremor in her voice. *You don't have to*. She was actually, now I thought about it, pretty ugly. Repulsive even. Old, too. Thirty-five, at least. What had I ever seen in her? There was a kind of revenge in the way I kissed the girl who was sitting next to me, a vehemence that tasted sweet. And after that, another kiss. Longer this time. And suddenly all thoughts of revenge had lifted and there was only disbelief. That this girl, who was beautiful, had kissed me. That this was happening at all.

'There's something I should tell you,' I said.

She pulled back. 'You're married.'

I smiled at her. 'No, not that.'

'It's some disease then.'

'No.'

'I know,' she said. 'You don't like girls.'

'That's not true.'

'I can't think of anything else.'

'Well,' I said, 'I'm blind.'

She laughed. 'I knew that.'

I wondered how.

'That white stick of yours,' she said. 'Kind of gives you away, doesn't it.'

'You don't mind?' I said.

'No,' she said. 'I don't mind.'

The city was deserted. It must have been late.

Wide streets, silver tramlines bending off into the distance. A cold wind blowing.

Spiral staircases rose into the air, built out of newspaper, sweet-wrappers, empty bags of crisps. And sometimes there was a van parked on a street-corner with a flap open in the side of it. One fluorescent light. A man in a white jacket selling sausages, chips with mayonnaise, soft drinks.

Then just houses with dark windows, leaves on the pavement. The moon high up in the branches of a tree.

Nina, I whispered to myself. Nina.

That was her name.

I couldn't believe my luck. Hers was not a perfect beauty – she had a slight swelling on her upper lip, where she had run into an open window once, and there was a small right-angled scar on the bridge of her nose – but it was close; and that closeness made it better than perfect. Heads had turned when we left the bar.

'Are you tired?' she said.

'No, not at all.' I told her how I lived – going to bed at dawn, getting up in the afternoon.

'I do that, too.' She lit a cigarette, then talked with it in her mouth. 'I work in a club. It's south of here. The Elite.' Her chin lifted as she took the cigarette from between her lips and blew the smoke into the top corner of the car. I watched the street-lights edge her throat in orange. 'What were you doing in that place?'

'Waiting for someone.'

'Not me?'

I smiled. 'No, not you. Though it feels like that now.'

We were driving through the north-west suburbs of the city. Out there all the houses stand in gardens the size of parks, and the streets are silent, narrow, sinuous. Through the window I could see a field sloping upwards to a solid bank of trees. We were almost in the country. She was taking me to see a friend of hers whose parents were away on holiday.

'She'll be awake,' Nina said. 'She's always awake.'

But when we walked in and Nina called her name, there was no reply.

'The door was open. She must be here somewhere.'

Nina took my hand and led me through the house, a huge old place that smelled of the oil they used for heating it. There were double-doors between the rooms, and walls hung with tapestries, and stuffed animals with eyes that looked real (I stared at the otter in the hallway and it stared back, hostile, wary). There were mirrors two metres tall, with frames that seemed to have spent a century under the sea (I watched the two of us, shadows moving past the glass). There were fireplaces with gargoyle faces carved into the marble. At last we heard something. Nina said it was coming from the kitchen. A rhythmic creaking that was unmistakable. I thought I could hear Nina's friend too. The clicking sound she was making in the back of her throat was like the ticking of a bicycle wheel when the bicycle's been thrown down but the wheel's still turning.

'You're right,' I said. 'She's definitely awake.'

We decided not to go to bed, not yet. Maybe those two people in the kitchen had wrongfooted us. We crept back to the drawing-room instead and poured ourselves some drinks.

'Do you smoke?' she asked me.

'Sometimes.'

She rolled a joint and we smoked it on the sofa, her head against my shoulder. She told me what she thought when she first saw me. She said I was like ice, the way my eyes just kind of slid over the top of everything. Her included.

'I didn't notice you,' I said. 'I mean, not right away.'

'And then you did?'

'Your elbow. It was touching mine.'

'I had to do something.'

Can I kiss you?

I heard a siren in the distance. The sudden urgency seemed exaggerated, lonely, even pitiful, in the deep silence that surrounded it.

Later, as we climbed the stairs, she told me it excited her, knowing that I couldn't see. She said it was better.

'Better?' I didn't understand.

'Men can be so brutal,' she said. 'Looking at your tits or your ankles, telling you what's wrong with them.'

'They wouldn't say that to you,' I said, 'not the way you look.'

'I'm not good-looking. I never was.'

'You must be joking,' I said. And then, 'You are to me.'

She laughed softly.

'Martin,' she said.

It was dark in the bedroom. I watched her lift her blouse over her head. Her face was hidden temporarily; her stomach muscles hollowed, stretched. I undressed quickly. My clothes fell to the floor. Then she was pushing me gently back on to the bed. I watched her lower her body on to mine, her nipples touching me first – my thighs, my hips, my ribs. Her lips touching me next. We rolled over. I ran my tongue down the centre of her, through the sudden growth of hair, to where the skin delicately parted, to where it started tasting different. I saw the damp trail that I had left behind on her, and thought for a moment of my father. It was a strange time to be thinking of him.

'What is it?' she murmured.

'Nothing.'

She was looking at me over her breasts, her eyes half-closed. She had a triumphant expression on her face, almost greedy, as if we were playing a game and she was winning. Her breathing shortened and accelerated. 'I think I'm turning into a man,' she said.

I looked up at her again.

'My clitoris,' she said. 'I get erections.'

It wasn't an exaggeration. There was such wetness when she came, the sheet beneath that part of her was soaked.

All night I lay beside her while she slept. I watched her turn over, brush her face with the back of her hand. I saw how she gathered the corner of a blanket in one fist and brought it up below her chin. I listened to her murmur, lick her lips. Sometimes I thought I was imagining it all, and I had to reach out and touch some part of her, her shoulder or her hair.

When I heard the clock downstairs strike five I left the bed. She woke up, but quickly fell asleep again. After I'd dressed I wrote the name of my hotel and the number of my room on a piece of paper. I thought for a moment, then, underneath, I wrote, *Ice melts.* I put the note on the pillow next to her.

Outside, it was almost light. The air was so cold, I could feel the shape of my lungs when I breathed in. There was frost at the edge of the road and each blade of grass seemed brittle, as if a white rust had attacked it.

I was in the north of the city, out near the woods.

When I woke up the next day, the phone was ringing. I reached for it so fast, I almost knocked it over.

'Martin? You awake?'

My heart dipped. It wasn't her.

'Martin? Are you there?'

'Loots,' I said. 'How are you?'

He was ringing because tonight was his night off and he was just wondering if I'd like to come to supper. He thought we could eat late, maybe at around eleven. Nothing fancy – just fried chicken, some potato salad . . .

'That sounds wonderful,' I told him.

There was no tram to where he lived, he said, but he would be happy to pick me up. I felt ungrateful suddenly, ashamed that I'd been disappointed to hear his voice, especially in the face of all this generosity.

At eleven o'clock that night I was standing on the steps outside the hotel. I'd only been waiting a few minutes when a car pulled up.

'Martin?'

Loots was wearing a leather coat and heavy work-boots, but his shoulders still bounced as he walked towards me.

'Tell you one thing,' he said, as he walked me to the car, 'I'm not drinking any more of that plum brandy. I was sick as a dog.'

'Me too,' I said. Not because it was true, but because I liked him and I wanted us to have things in common.

Loots lived in the 9th district, an old working-class neighbourhood no more than a ten-minute drive from the hotel. On the way over, he asked me if I'd heard about Gregory. I said I hadn't. Apparently they'd found him the morning after the wedding party with his head in one room and his feet in another. He was lying face-down on the carpet like a dead man – Petra had suggested drawing a chalk line around him – and when they turned him over, he had the carpet's pattern printed on his cheek.

'First I lose my wife,' I said, 'then I lose my daughter – '

Loots laughed. 'Right.'

His apartment was at the top of a tall house. There was no lift, and the stairs were steep and narrow. He advised me to go carefully. People were always breaking their legs, he said, and that was people who could see. On the fifth-floor landing he edged past me and unlocked the door. Once inside, he showed me round. The rooms were small, with slanting ceilings, skylights in the bedroom and the lounge, and floors that sloped. A corridor ran the length of the apartment, front to back. This was where he threw his knives. The wall at the far end was covered with brown cork tiles, and on the tiles he'd drawn the figure of a woman. I admired his handiwork. I felt the smoothness of the tiles where the woman was, then I felt the knife-holes that surrounded her. Loots led me back to the kitchen and began to prepare the meal.

'So if they didn't actually allow you to throw knives at the circus,' I said, 'what were you doing there?' I was sitting at the kitchen table, drinking beer, while Loots fried some chicken breasts.

'It was just a labouring job,' he said.

He had to pitch tents, set up rows of seating, clean out cages. It was manual work, hard and tedious; if it hadn't been for The Great Miguel, he wouldn't have lasted.

'The Great Miguel?' I said.

The Great Miguel was the circus knife-thrower, Loots told me. For his performance he wore a red-and-white-striped blanket, a straw sombrero and a pair of knee-high boots with spurs. He whirled around the ring, flashing his eyes and shouting words like 'Caramba!'. Cleo, his assistant, appeared behind him, striking defiant poses against a painted backdrop of cows' skulls and cactuses. She wore a tasselled leather bikini, which was very popular with the crowds. She wore huge false eyelashes, too. And then came the moment when The Great Miguel closed in on her, eyes still flashing, and surrounded her with knives, machetes, even tomahawks. Cleo was The Great Miguel's second wife and it was testament to The Great Love she felt for him that she had asked to act as his assistant. He'd killed his previous wife, a knife severing the artery beneath her arm. The blood had drenched a party of children from the local school. She was dead in four minutes.

Loots had heard this story late one night as he sat in a roadside restaurant with The Great Miguel. They were drinking schnapps together, just the two of them. The Great Miguel talked a lot about superstition that night. He talked about the third knife, which was the one that had killed Agnes, his first wife. He would never throw a third knife again, he said. He didn't trust the number three any more. He would never take a room on the third floor of a hotel, for instance. If he was driving a car, he always went straight from second gear into fourth. The Holy Trinity was something he couldn't even begin to contemplate. At last Loots understood why The Great Miguel always threw his first two knives, but dropped the third, point down, into the sawdust at his feet, before continuing. He'd always assumed it was showmanship. Now he realised that there was tragedy in that dropped knife, and that it wasn't just fear either, but an act of remembrance, a kind of homage.

That same night The Great Miguel talked to Loots of passing on his craft. He drank too much, he said; his control was going. He held his right hand level in the air and showed Loots how the fingers trembled. 'No good,' he said. 'No damn good.' He drained the bottle that was in front of him and threw it past Loots' shoulder. Loots couldn't believe what he'd just seen. There was a huge plate-glass window behind him; he'd noticed it on the way in. He braced himself for the explosion, glass smashing glass. But, strangely, there was only silence. He turned round. The window was there, but someone had opened it. It was three or four seconds before he heard the bottle land, a faint sound on the road somewhere below.

Ordering another bottle, The Great Miguel went into a kind of rhapsody. He told Loots that he wanted to teach him the rhythm of the knife. The movement of a knife across the air was like a piece of music. That was what he said. You felt a bad knife the moment it left your hand. It had no rhythm to it. It didn't sing. You should almost be able to score the air the knife passed through. Loots listened, fascinated. His only worry was, The Great Miguel was drunk; by morning he would have forgotten all his promises. But he didn't. Loots was still paid to pitch tents and clean cages. Whenever he had free time, though, he watched The Great Miguel practising and studied his technique.

Loots paused for a moment, then he sighed. 'It was Cleo who spoiled it all.'

'Why?' I said. 'What happened?'

'I'd been with the circus about a year,' he said.

Then, early one morning, he was woken by a loud thud close to his head. Another thud. Then a gap. Then another. At first, still half-asleep, he thought somebody was knocking on his door. 'Who is it?' he called out. There was no reply, but the thuds kept coming. One after the other, at two-second intervals, against the side wall of his caravan. He remembered the gap after the second thud and thought: *The Great Miguel.* The Great Miguel was throwing knives at his caravan at six o'clock in the morning. But why? Several times he called out The Great Miguel's name – which, actually, was Erik – but still nobody answered.

At last he climbed out of bed and opened the door. He was just in time to see his mentor trudge away through the early morning mist, stoop-shouldered, still dressed in his striped blanket and his knee-high boots from the night before. Frowning, Loots walked round to the side of his caravan. There were thirty-six knives in all, not counting the one that stood upright in the ground, and between them they spelt a single word:

```
ooooo  o  o  o  oooo  oooo
  o    oooo  o  oo    oo
  o    o  o  o  oooo  o
```

It turned out that Cleo had become jealous of the attention The Great Miguel was lavishing on him. She'd told her husband that Loots had stolen money from their caravan. Some jewellery, too.

'So they fired you.'

'Yeah.' Loots nodded gloomily.

'But there wasn't any proof, was there?'

'There didn't need to be. I was just some kid they'd taken on to put up tents. He was The Great Miguel.'

'Erik,' I said, and gave Loots a wry smile.

Loots was silent for a moment. 'I'm not a thief, you know.'

'I know,' I said. 'I know that.'

Later, when we'd moved into the living-room and we were drinking coffee, I thought about The Great Miguel and how his story paralleled my own. There are some things that happen and then everything that happens afterwards is different. I wasn't thinking of forks in the road, small deviations. I was thinking of sudden change, extreme and violent. The third knife. A bullet fired from an unknown gun. I began to tell Loots about it, though it was difficult. I kept starting sentences I couldn't finish. I couldn't mention what kind of vision I had, and yet my story seemed empty without it, pointless and depressing; I didn't see how he could possibly be interested. I dredged up a few old anecdotes – Smulders talking in his sleep, Nurse Janssen's rubber balls – but even then I had to be careful. I wanted him to laugh, not feel pity for me.

Towards five in the morning I told him I ought to be going. He insisted on running me back to the hotel. I followed him down the narrow stairs and out on to the street. There was no sunrise, only a low sky and a drizzle falling; I pulled my jacket collar up and walked quickly to the car. Since the insertion of the plate, I no longer liked the idea of rain on my head. Maybe I was afraid I wouldn't feel it when it landed. Maybe I was afraid I'd rust.

'Are you all right to drive?' I asked Loots. I didn't want him losing his licence on my account.

'Why?' he said. 'You think it would be better if you drove?'

Laughing, he pulled out into the traffic. The first set of lights we reached, he turned to me. 'By the way,' he said. 'How did it go the other night?'

'How did what go?'

'With that girl. You know. The one from the wedding.'

'Oh yeah.' I smiled. 'She didn't turn up.'

'Really? I'm sorry.'

I didn't say anything. I was still smiling, though.

'You don't seem too upset,' Loots said.

'No, I'm not.'

Loots was staring at me. I could feel it, even without looking. Somebody behind us began to pound on their horn.

'Loots,' I said, 'I think the lights have changed.'

Four days had passed and still I hadn't heard from her. I sat on the edge of my bed with the phone on my knee. I was aware of my heart beating; it felt too close to the surface. When we were in the drawing-room of that mansion, stoned, she'd made me say her number over and over, until I had it memorised. She wouldn't have done that, would she, if she hadn't wanted me to call?

I dialled the number and then leaned back against the wall. It was a machine. Her voice, though. The usual phrases. *Sorry there's no one here. Please leave your name and number. I'll get back to you.* I left my name and the number of my room at the hotel, then hung up. I waited a few moments so the machine could re-set itself and called again. I just wanted to listen to her voice. This time I didn't leave a message.

She called twelve hours later, as I was preparing for bed. My window was open. Eight floors below the first tram of the day was pulling into Central Station – the sound of a knife being held against a grindstone. She said she couldn't talk for long. It was loud where she was. Music, voices. Glasses. I could only just hear her.

'Did you get my note?' I said.

'Yeah, I got it. I couldn't read it, though.'

'Really? How come?'

'I don't know. It looked like you wrote something and then you wrote something else on top of it.'

Strange. I could remember writing the name of the hotel and my room number on one line. Then, below it, on a second line, the message.

'What did it say?' she asked me.

I told her.

'That's nice. I like that.'

'Can I see you again, Nina?' The sound of her name on my tongue was unfamiliar, exotic – awkward, too, in a way. As if I'd been designed to say names, but not hers.

'Sure.'

'When?'

'We could meet tomorrow night,' she said. 'After I finish work.' She gave me the address of a bar. 'I get out earlier tomorrow. I should be there by two.'

There was a man at her table when I arrived. He was just leaving. I didn't get much of an impression of him: a baseball jacket, long blond hair parted in the middle – pretty nondescript. I sat down opposite her.

'You look good,' I said.

She leaned over the table and kissed me on the mouth. 'How would you know?'

I laughed. She was so easy with the idea of my blindness. She didn't adjust or patronise. She never said the things that other people said: *It must be difficult* or *I'm so sorry*. She just accepted it, as part of me. She even seemed to appreciate it, the way you might appreciate any physical attribute – the smell of someone's hair, the shape of their hands.

'There was somebody here,' I said.

She nodded. 'Robert Kolan. He comes from this old aristocratic family. He's one of my closest friends.'

They'd lived in the same house when they were students, she said. That was how they'd met. He always looked after her if she was tired or depressed or ill. He'd do anything for her.

'He'd kill someone for me if I asked him to.'

I didn't think she was boasting. It was just a simple statement of fact. If anything, she talked about this friend of hers, this Robert, with a kind of awe. As though she found it hard to believe that someone could devote themselves to her like that.

The waitress asked us what we were having. Nina ordered a cognac. I thought about it, then I ordered one as well.

'So,' Nina said, 'what do you want to do?'

She seemed different from the first night, more distracted, edgier.

'I've got something for you,' I said.

I took a package out of my pocket and handed it to her.

'It's soft,' she said. 'What is it?'

'Open it.'

The tissue paper quickly came apart in her hands.

'What is it?' she said. 'A scarf?'

'It's a blindfold.'

She didn't say anything.

'It's for when we're in bed,' I said. 'So we can be the same.' I realised I was deceiving her. Somehow it didn't feel wrong, though.

Our cognacs arrived. She picked hers up and drank some.

'Do you like it?' I asked.

'It's great.' She leaned over, kissed me again. 'Maybe we can try it out tonight.'

'Is your car here?' I asked.

'Yeah. It's outside.'

I drained my glass. 'Let's drive somewhere.'

We drove east, through the city. She talked about her car – what make it was, where she'd got it from, how many times she'd crashed in it. It was old and pretty beaten-up, but she loved it. The crack in the back window, for instance. That was one of the reasons she'd bought the car; she thought it looked just like some gangster's bullethole. She had a mascot, too – a plastic doll, which hung from the rear-view mirror. I reached up, touched the doll. I hadn't noticed it the first night. My eyes must have been too occupied with her.

'Her name's Doris,' Nina said. 'She's got the best tits in the city.'

'Second-best,' I said.

'You wouldn't say that if you could see her nipples. They've got red lights in them.' Nina was grinning.

Suddenly she turned off the road and stopped the car.

'Let's do it here.'

I looked round. 'Where are we?'

'Nowhere. Just a car-park.'

She moved closer to me and we kissed. Then she reached down. Her hand found my zip and opened it. Out of the corner of my eye I saw the dark curve of a wheel.

'What's wrong?' she said. 'Don't you want to?'

'It's not that.'

I told her about the shooting, how it had happened. Then I told her the rest: the months I'd spent in the clinic, the operations, the convalescence. I described the exact path of the bullet. I said the difference between life and death was one millimetre. She was nodding, her dark eyes moving between the empty car-park and my face. I could tell she liked this kind of talk. There was a danger, though. I wanted to tell her everything: the miracle in the gardens, Smulders naked, Nurse Janssen stripping – everything. I felt she might believe me, too. I had a thought that was treacherous and yet seductive: secrets become more powerful if you dilute them just a little.

'I've got an idea,' she said.

She started the car, turned on the radio. Then we were driving again. She lit a cigarette. The smoke from it flowered against the windscreen.

'Am I the first person you've slept with since it happened?' she asked me after a while.

I looked at her, but she was watching the road.

'Yes,' I said.

'I can't take responsibility for you. You know that, don't you.'

'Yes, I know that. I'm not asking you to.' I rested one hand on her shoulder. 'Don't worry.'

I turned and stared out of the window. The streets were still foreign to me. Unlit buildings. Wire-mesh fences and abandoned cars. It could have been anywhere.

'Where are we?' I said. 'Where are we going?'

'There's a motel about five kilometres from here.' She crushed her cigarette out in the ashtray and slid the ashtray back into its socket with the heel of her hand. 'It's called Motel Cherry.' She laughed. 'Do you like motels?'

Motel Cherry was a drab one-storey place, with rows of net-curtained rooms laid out along a strip of tarmac. On one side was a twenty-four-hour restaurant. Long-distance lorry-drivers hunched over cups of coffee. Cooks stood about in soiled white aprons, biting their nails. On the other side, there was a petrol station: ELF or DERV or ERG – the usual prehistoric brand-name. Between the tarmac and the road I could see a line of newly planted trees; they looked starved and grey, unreal.

We walked into reception. The man behind the desk reminded me of my father. The same sense of a life that could not be changed or redefined, a life that had to be endured. I thought of calling my father, but I knew it would only bring grief to the surface. It was like longing for a cigarette: the moment you had it lit, you wondered why you'd wanted it so much.

Almost the first thing Nina said when we were in the room was, 'I don't want you to get used to this.'

I looked at the orange bedspread and the yellow walls. 'You're right. Next time we should spend a bit more. Go somewhere nice.'

She came up behind me, put her arms around me. She'd taken off her shirt and I could feel her breasts flattening against my back. 'You know what I mean, Martin.'

I turned and kissed her. I could hear voices through the wall. A man and a woman talking. I thought I heard the word *divorce*. I began to undo Nina's jeans, but she pushed away from me.

'First I want to do something.' She took my arm and led me to a chair by the window. 'Sit there, would you?' She moved back towards the bed.

'I'd prefer it if the lights were out,' I said.

'Like people in the suburbs?'

I smiled. 'Is that how they do it?'

'Of course.' Nina walked to the door and switched the light off, then crossed the room again and climbed on to the bed. 'Is that better?'

I nodded. 'Much better.'

I could see her in great detail now; I could even see the tiny golden hairs glinting on her thighs as she eased her jeans down to her ankles. She kneeled among the blankets, facing away from me, her hair falling to the top edge of her shoulderblades. I noticed how her body tapered to her waist, two straight lines converging, then curved outwards suddenly below it. She leaned sideways, supporting herself on one hand while the other reached between her legs. She bent over, her face pressed into the pillow. With two fingers, she pushed her g-string to one side and parted the dark lips beneath it. Her breath caught, as if somebody had startled her.

She rolled, almost toppled, slowly on to her back. Her chin resting on her chest, she watched her left hand drift limp-wristed from one breast to the other, hovering above each nipple in turn, then dipping down to it, the way a humming-bird drinks from a flower.

'Do you know what I'm doing?'

It was hard for her to keep her voice level. Perhaps that was part of it.

I didn't answer.

'You don't know,' she said, 'do you.'

She seemed to favour her right breast, and the touching became rhythmical, repetitive, semi-circular. Her other hand was still hidden between her legs; the arm looked amputated at the wrist.

As she reached her first orgasm, there was a kind of fluttering on the surface of her skin, then her whole body shuddered, as though she was cold suddenly, and her back arched and lifted clear of the bed. Her head was turned towards me, her mouth half-open. She came twice more in that position, watching the man who was sitting on the chair by the window, a man who couldn't see what she was doing – or so she thought – and yet he was in the room with her, he was close to her, almost close enough to touch. Exhausted, she let her head tip backwards, over the edge of the bed. Her breasts falling softly in opposite directions, the neat pincushion of her pubic hair pushed high above her hip-bones. Her thighs, at a slight angle to each other. Her knees bent, her ankles still loosely bound by the g-string she'd only half-kicked off.

At last she called me to her. I stood up and walked over.

'You didn't mind, did you?' she said.

I didn't say anything.

'Now I'm going to do something for you.' Smiling, she handed me the blindfold I had given her. 'Tie this over my eyes, would you?'

Later, when she was in the bathroom, I lay on my stomach with my cheek resting on my arm. What had she said? Something about *not getting used to this*. I listened to the rush of cars on the motorway. You could almost believe you were in the country, with a river running just outside the window.

Towards the end of that week I invited Nina to the Hotel Metropole for dinner. It wasn't the food or the service that you went there for (they were both mediocre); it was the setting. You entered through a baroque archway laden with gilt from the previous century and draped in swathes of scarlet velvet. The room itself was painted cream and gold. Two storeys high, it had rows of windows looking down on it from other parts of the hotel. There was a stage on one side, with a dance-floor in front of it. The waitresses were always middle-aged, for some reason; they wore white, ruffled blouses and maroon skirts.

I was apprehensive walking in – I'd eaten there before, with friends – but no one recognised me, no one called my name. Once we were seated at our table, I relaxed. I looked around and nodded. It was all as I remembered it.

'That's odd,' Nina said.

I smiled. 'What?'

'Everyone's cigarette smoke's blowing in the same direction.'

I told her that the draughts were famous. Part of the experience, in fact. One Easter my parents took me to the Metropole for lunch. There was such a draught that day, my mother's hair lifted off her shoulders and flew horizontally in the air behind her; she looked as if she was riding in a speedboat or an open car. (I was exaggerating, but only slightly.) Another time a friend of mine sat too close to the door. He didn't notice anything at first. But, gradually, as the evening wore on, he lost all feeling in one side of his body. After the meal he had to be carried out of the hotel, like a footballer who's just pulled a hamstring.

Nina was laughing. I took a small box out of my pocket and slid it across the tablecloth towards her.

'What's this?' she said.

'It's a present.'

'You're always giving me things.'

'It's nothing,' I said. 'Just something small.'

It was a silver-plated cigarette-lighter that used to belong to my father. I'd had it engraved: FROM M TO N – LOVE IS BLIND (a bit obvious, perhaps, but anyway). She looked down at it and shook her head. Light caught the gold in her dark-brown hair.

'It's lovely,' she said. And then, a few moments later, 'You shouldn't give me things.'

A band played while we ate. The saxophonist was slope-shouldered, shifty-eyed. His gaze kept sliding sideways and lingering on Nina. And no wonder. She was more beautiful than ever – her hair loosely pinned, a long black dress clinging to her body, a smile lurking at the corners of her mouth as if she'd just thought of something illicit.

The main course arrived. My roast pork with plums smelled like a piece of old carpet. Tasted like it, too. The keyboard-player sneezed eight times during one song. Nobody danced. Another vintage night at the Metropole.

'I don't think I've ever been so cold,' Nina said. 'Well, maybe once.'

'When was that?' I asked her.

She told me that when she was seventeen she'd had an affair with a married man. They had flown to a city in the south together. He was on a business trip, and they'd stayed in a luxury hotel. But something she said had upset the man. He'd thrown her out. She had no money and no coat. It was February.

She found herself standing next to a park. Snow had fallen early that morning and the streets were still soft with it. Cars came creeping up behind her. You could hardly hear them. If you wanted to make the sound, she said, you had to take a piece of cardboard – an empty cereal packet or the back of a letter-writing pad – and you had to hold it close to your ear and tear it very slowly. That was cars on snow. There was a fairground in the park, she remembered, but it was shut for the winter. There was a Big Wheel. Freezing fog hid the top of it. She stood on the road, clutching her ribs in both hands. She had no idea what to do.

A car went by, more stealthy than the rest. Its wheels fat, its white exhaust fumes flapping. Some foreign make. It slowed down, pulled up just beyond her. She ran towards it. The window on the passenger side slid down. She stooped, that position you see whores in – a figure seven; she could feel the tendons taut in the back of her thighs. The man looked warm, though – that was all she could think of. She stood there looking in at him, his round glasses and his overcoat, the sound system playing opera, the seats of pale leather, and she thought how warm he looked. He was foreign, like the car, but he spoke to her in her own language.

'How much?'

She said the first amount that came to mind. He didn't understand her. She had to draw the number on the outside of his windscreen, in mirror-writing. She didn't know whether it was a little or a lot; she didn't have any idea of the prices. He looked at the number and smiled faintly. Reaching across, he unlocked the door and pushed it open.

'Your coffee.' A waitress had appeared at our table. Late forties, with a moustache. As she set the coffee down in front of me, it slopped over, spilled into the saucer. She shrugged her shoulders, walked away.

I turned back to Nina. 'Then what?'

'We drove,' she said.

Through the city and out into the country. Women were sitting under umbrellas along the roadside, selling apples out of wooden boxes. The land was black and white, the sky a heavy, even grey. She saw three deer cross a rising, snow-covered field.

They arrived at a small house on the edge of a village. It had mustard-yellow shutters and a dark, thatched roof. When they were standing inside, he held her gently by the shoulders and said something which she took to mean, *Stay here*. Then he drove away. She made herself a cup of hot chocolate. Through the kitchen window she watched two children skating on a pond. In the afternoon she went to bed and slept.

That evening he returned. He cooked supper for her, then they spent the night together. In the morning he drove her back to the city. When he let her out of the car, he handed her an envelope. She didn't open it until he'd gone. There was money inside, almost twice the amount she'd asked for. She bought a coat with it, and two pairs of woollen tights, and she still had enough to catch a train home.

I watched her light a cigarette and sit back in her chair.

At first I thought she might have made the whole thing up. But then it seemed so like her – drawing an amount of money on a stranger's windscreen, drinking hot chocolate in a stranger's house – that I decided it had to be true. I still wasn't sure what it meant to her, though. Was she proud of her resourcefulness, her spontaneity, the fact that she could make her own luck? Or was it some kind of talisman in itself, proof that the world could treat her well?

'So,' she said eventually, tapping her cigarette against the edge of the ashtray, 'that's the coldest I've ever been.' She paused and looked round, then she said, 'Though I have to admit, this comes pretty close.'

Smiling, I asked our waitress for the bill.

Afterwards Nina took me to a bar she knew. We both drank whisky, to warm up.

'I hear you're seeing someone,' Gregory said.

I looked across at him. 'No smoke without a fire, Smoke.'

Loots chuckled.

We were in Leon's, the three of us. It was early December, and the walls were covered with shiny paper decorations, red and green and gold, many of them already curling in the humid atmosphere. Bunches of balloons clustered in the top corners of the room. Above the counter, suspended from the ceiling, was a sign: SEASON'S GREETINGS TO ALL OUR CUSTOMERS.

'So it's true,' Gregory said.

I nodded.

'So who is she?' He was like an old dog who was trying to gnaw on a bone, but couldn't seem to get it into the right position between his paws.

'Her name's Nina.'

'Because you know Inge liked you . . .'

'What is it about you?' Loots said. 'What's the secret?'

'I'm a cripple,' I said. 'They feel sorry for me.'

'They feel – ' Gregory almost choked. 'Did you hear that, Loots? They feel sorry for him.'

'I don't feel sorry for him,' Loots said, 'do you?'

'Well,' Gregory said, sounding thoughtful, 'it can't be easy.'

He missed the point completely. As usual.

'She takes me to motels,' I said. 'We always go to motels. The

Cherry, the Nero, the Astra – I know them all now. Or we sleep in other people's houses, friends of hers.'

'Where does she live?' Loots asked.

'That's just it. I've no idea.' I stirred some sugar into my coffee. 'I think she likes being anonymous,' I said. 'This whole thing with me, it's not because she's sorry for me, but it *is* because I'm blind. Because I can't see her. That's what she likes – being invisible. It makes her feel less pressured. More free. It's kind of a fantasy for her.'

'Did I tell you about Anton?' Loots said.

'Anton?' I shook my head.

It was a week ago, Loots said. There had been a knock on the door of his apartment and when he opened it his old friend Anton was standing there. Anton was a clown. He belonged to a circus that toured the provinces, playing to small towns and villages. They talked about the old days for a while, but Anton became increasingly restless and distracted. In the end Loots had to ask him if there was something wrong.

'This is going to sound strange.' The clown coughed nervously into his fist. 'It's The Invisible Man. He's disappeared.'

Loots stared at his friend.

'He just vanished,' Anton said, 'into thin air.'

'The Invisible Man?' Loots said.

'Yes.'

'He's disappeared?'

'I told you it would sound strange,' Anton said.

He told Loots that The Invisible Man was the best act in the circus, the act people came to see. It always began in the same way. The Invisible Man walked into the ring and started telling a funny story. He looked funny, too: short, with bright-red hair and a scar on his chin. Soon everyone was laughing. They forgot he was supposed to be, you know, Invisible. Then, suddenly, halfway through the story, he vanished. Just by turning round.

'It's like he hasn't got a back,' Anton explained. 'It's like there's only one side to him.'

Without him, Anton continued, they would probably be ruined. They'd have to look for other work. And how could they do that? The circus was all they knew. The circus was their life. Anton's voice was cracking and his eyes had filled with tears.

'And you think he might be here,' Loots said, 'in the city?'

Anton nodded. 'Someone heard him talking about it. I've been sent up here, to find him.'

He needed help, though – Loots' help; there was nobody else he could ask.

I sipped my coffee, imagining a clown in Loots' apartment. His voice would probably be thin and quaint, like the high notes on a mouth organ. I saw tears dropping on to the toes of an enormous pair of shoes.

'So,' I said, 'you're helping him?'

'I'm trying to,' Loots said.

He'd tracked down a woman who used to work with The Invisible Man. Her name was Madame Fugazi. She lived in a basement somewhere in the 7th district. But she hadn't seen The Invisible Man for fifteen years. 'Yeah, it must've been fifteen years, at least,' she told Loots. 'He weren't much good in them days.' Madame Fugazi had dyed black hair that was flat at the back where she had slept on it. 'He used to bow and wave his arms about and do all that stuff they do,' she said, 'and then he'd kind of spin round fast and he was supposed to be, you know, *gone*, and I'd have to yell out, "I can still see you." He really hated it when I did that.'

Loots asked her if she had any idea where he might be now.

'I told you, love. It was fifteen years ago.'

But as he turned to leave she spoke again: 'You'd have found him easy in them days. He couldn't have disappeared, even if he'd wanted to.' She licked her finger and rubbed at a stain on her leopardskin print dress. 'Now I'm not so sure. People say he got better at it.'

'Three steak,' Leon shouted from behind the counter.

Loots stood up. 'I'll get it.'

I waited until he was sitting down again. 'One thing occurs to me.'

'What's that?' Loots said.

'Suppose he doesn't want to be found?'

'Well, maybe he doesn't, but we don't know that, do we?' Loots poked at his pickled cabbage with a fork. 'For all we know, he could be in some kind of trouble . . .'

Gregory leaned back in his chair.

'About this Nina,' he said. 'What do you mean, it's a fantasy for her?'

The Relax Motel, early December.

One of Nina's favourites, the Relax. It had a green neon sign with the name of the motel on it. The first two letters didn't work: all you could see from the motorway was the word LAX flashing on and off. A few years back, in the forecourt, they had built a swimming-pool. On the black metal fence that surrounded it was a sign that said, GUESTS ONLY. The pool was empty. According to Nina it was always empty, even in the summer; she said the only time it had water in it was when it rained. The place was run by an old woman who had rheumatism. Some days she couldn't use her hands at all. She couldn't hold a pen. You had to write out your own bill.

Our room had cheap wood-panelling and cone-shaped orange lampshades, and if you put a coin in the box on the wall, the whole bed started shaking. Nina was lying on her side, one hand under her head, the other in between her thighs. The knot on the blindfold had come loose; it had fallen from her eyes. The curtains drawn behind her. The lights in the room switched off. *Like people in the suburbs.*

I heard a car pull up down below. A door opened, then another. Two voices arguing. Nina reached for a cigarette and lit it. It began to rain.

I followed the faint light that filtered from the car-park into our room. I noticed how it chose parts of her body, made different arcs out of her shoulder, her hip, her calf, her heel. She looked as though she'd been drawn in mercury.

'I miss you.'

She turned to look at me. 'What?'

'When you're not there. I miss you.'

'You're with me now,' she said, 'right next to me . . .'

'Am I?' I rolled on to my back. 'Am I really?'

'I told you before. That's not what we're about.'

'What *are* we about? Tell me again.'

'This,' she said, and took my hand and brought it to her breast. I knew it so well already, that curve up to her nipple, and the nipple itself, no bigger than a medal, and pale, but not too pale, the skin there soft and glossy. I watched the side of my thumb as it moved in the gentle, semi-circular patterns I had learned from her.

'I've been lying to you,' I said.

Her nipple stiffened as I spoke.

'It's not lying, exactly. It's just something I haven't told you.'

My thumb still moving.

'I'm not blind.' I paused, wanting to be clear. 'Well, I am in the daytime, but not at night. At night I can see.'

She sat up, backed away and leaned against the headboard, staring at me. 'Why are you telling me this?' she said.

'It's true. The white stick, the dark glasses – I don't really need them at night. I just carry them around in case I'm out late and it gets light.'

She laughed, but the laugh cut out suddenly, as if someone had turned the volume on her down to zero.

'You're the only person I've told,' I said. 'Since I left the clinic, I mean. You mustn't tell anyone else either. Nobody knows – '

'Stop it, Martin.'

'What's wrong? Don't you believe me?'

She didn't say anything.

'It's just between the two of us,' I said. 'It'll be like talking a language no one understands. It'll be our secret – '

Suddenly she was pushing both her hands along my thighs.

I looked at her. 'What are you doing?'

'I want you to fuck me.'

'What?'

'Fuck me.'

What I'd said, had it excited her? Had she understood me after all? I reached out for her. I kissed her neck, her chin. Her mouth. It took a long time because we'd already done it twice. There was a place she had to get to, though; she wouldn't let me rest till she was there. It was cold in the room and yet the sweat was running down my face. My hand slid across her rib-cage like an ice-cube on a mirror. When we'd finished, the sheets were damp and there was someone banging on the wall. Nina just banged back.

'Probably those people who were arguing,' I said.

'Pricks,' she said.

She walked into the bathroom and shut the door. I heard the toilet flush. The bed softened suddenly, drew me deep into itself. I closed my eyes.

Outside, the wind took a handful of rain and flung it against the window.

Nina had told me she'd be at the Kosminsky by one, but I knew she wouldn't turn up before two at the earliest. After she finished work she often had a drink with Candy, who was a dancer at the bar. At two-thirty she still hadn't arrived. She hadn't called either. I wondered if she'd got tired and gone straight home. I rang her house. Eight seconds of machine-gun fire, then a beep. She'd been getting some weird phone-calls recently, she'd told me. Men just breathing.

I opened my window and looked out. It was zero degrees, the middle of December. Orange light was bouncing off the low cloud-cover; it hung over the grey buildings in an eerie, artificial dome. I watched the late-night traffic moving past the station, the whisper of car tyres in the slush. The people who sold cheap fur coats and sheepskin gloves had left a long time ago. The fast-food stand on the corner was still open, though: pizza, hot dogs, soft drinks, cigarettes. On an impulse I picked up the phone and asked Victor to call me a taxi. Then I put on a hat and coat and left the room.

The car was outside when I reached the street.

I got in. 'The Elite. It's a club.'

The driver said he knew it.

I sat hunched over in the back, chewing my bottom lip. It was strange she hadn't called. Though I hadn't seen her for almost a week, I'd spoken to her several times. I'd told her about Sprankel and the black paint, and she'd seemed intrigued. We'd arranged for her to come and see my room. She laughed when I said she'd better bring some matches or a torch.

'So what's happening at the Elite tonight?'

The last time Victor called me a taxi, the driver didn't open his mouth once. I'd been hoping for the same man.

'My girlfriend works there,' I said.

'What's that?'

'My girlfriend. She works there.'

The driver nodded. 'I was up for a job there once. Didn't get it, though.'

My head ached. I wasn't in the mood for this. If he said something else, I'd lodge a complaint. For talking? Sure. Why not?

But he didn't. Not for five minutes, anyway.

Then he said, 'There's some nice girls working at that place. Real nice.'

I leaned forwards. 'What's your name?'

'Maximilian. People call me Millie.'

'I don't mean to be rude, Millie,' I said, 'but would you just shut the fuck up and drive?'

Millie giggled. 'Anything you say, chief.'

I pressed the backs of my fingers against the cool pane of the window. Nina not showing, it seemed like part of the pattern. That night in the Relax Motel, when I was half-asleep, I'd had an idea. It was a missing persons poster. At the top it said, HAVE YOU SEEN THIS MAN? Underneath there was a big blank space. In fact, most of the poster was blank. There was one line along the bottom: THE INVISIBLE MAN IS MISSING. WHEN HE'S NOT INVISIBLE, HE'S ONE METRE SIXTY-TWO WITH RED HAIR AND A SCAR ON HIS CHIN. I told Loots about it when I saw him next. He thought it was brilliant. He had some posters and leaflets printed, and we spent two nights distributing them in police-stations, at tram-stops, outside shops. Then someone from the radio had picked up on our campaign and broadcasted a series of appeals.

But it hadn't worked – or, rather, it had worked too well. It had created a kind of atmospheric disturbance. Hundreds of people had contacted the police, claiming to have 'seen' The Invisible Man. If a door slammed for no reason. If a picture changed its position on a wall. If leaves moved on a tree, but there wasn't any wind. Even if things just somehow felt different, in a way you couldn't quite put your finger on. For instance: a couple in the western suburbs were convinced that The Invisible Man had gatecrashed one of their dinner parties – that was why the mood that night had been so awkward. And then there was the woman who insisted she'd been sleeping with The Invisible Man for the past four years. 'It's only weekends,' she told a journalist. 'Friday nights, I hear the key turn in the door. I don't even have to switch the light on. I know it's him.' There were hoaxes, too. One man rang the radio station, saying that he was The Invisible Man and that he was calling from a phone-box on the street outside. 'Which phone-box?' the DJ asked. The caller laughed. 'Which one do you think? The empty one, of course.' The unexplainable was out there, part of everybody's lives. All they needed was a hook to hang it on.

The taxi clattered over potholes. South central streets: a non-stop fun-fair ride. We were getting close now. Through the steamed-up window I saw a derelict factory, a junk yard, part of a canal.

At last we pulled up outside the club. It didn't look like much. A one-storey building, the word ELITE in pink neon script above the entrance. Nothing too surprising there.

'Careful when you get out,' Millie said. 'The kerb's a high one.'

I thanked him, then opened the door. Maybe I'd been too hard on him before. I asked him if he could wait. He said he would.

A helicopter chattered in the sky. As it faded, I heard bass and drums. My stick was in my hand now. Scanning the ground in front of me. Making sweeps. There were times when I used my stick like worry-beads: it was just something to do.

'What's up, pal?'

That belligerence, that phoney cool. It snagged on something in me; I felt heat rise, collect in my titanium plate. They get to feel so fucking big, these bouncer types, just because they're stuck outside some club in a tuxedo.

'You deaf or something?'

I showed him my white stick. 'Not deaf, no. Guess again.'

'You threatening me?' The bouncer laughed. It was four high-pitched sounds. Like a hinge.

'I'm not deaf and I'm not threatening you. All right?'

'So let's hear it.'

'I'm looking for Nina. Nina Salenko. She was working here tonight.'

'Ain't here now.'

'Do you know where she went?'

'Nope.'

'Is Candy here?'

'Now what would you be wanting Candy for? You got a sweet tooth or something?' That laugh again. Bad joke, too.

I could have broken his nose with my stick. I could have got Nina to get her friend Robert Kolan to kill him. I could have reported him to the Chronically Sick and Disabled Persons' Association. But I didn't do any of that.

A breeze moved across my teeth. I must have been smiling.

Back in the car Millie turned to look at me. 'Trouble?'

I shook my head. 'Just drive me home, will you?'

What did I think I was doing, going to look for her like that? She'd be in the lobby of the Kosminsky, smoking a cigarette with Arnold (Nina was the one person who might get someone like Arnold to loosen up and talk). Or else she'd have gone home to her mysterious apartment and there'd be one small light flashing on her machine – my message. What had I been thinking of? I sank lower in my seat, moulding my shoulderblades into the upholstery.

I'd known her for three weeks. Three weeks since she appeared in that bar. Sat next to me, her elbow touching mine. Three weeks since that first kiss. Then we were in her car, we were driving . . .

An old mansion in the suburbs. We lay on a sofa talking, smoking joints, while someone I'd never met fucked someone else in the kitchen (we heard a saucepan crash). The club she worked in, she was a waitress. Some nights there were shows – exotic dancing, talent contests, cabaret. She lived near the flower market. She was twenty-two.

I remembered how I heard a clock chime five somewhere, how I got up and began to dress. I remembered that my jacket smelled of her perfume.

She shifted in the bed behind me. 'What time is it?'

I told her.

'Are you leaving?'

'It's easier now,' I said, 'while it's still dark.' She couldn't have understood what I was saying, of course, but at least it had a kind of ambiguity. 'Can I see you again?' I asked her.

'Something I should tell you,' she murmured.

'You're married.'

She didn't laugh. 'I'm seeing someone else – '

There are people who unload their disappointments early. I stood in that bedroom, someone else's bedroom. I stood quite still for a moment and told myself it didn't make any difference. But there was an ache in my throat, as if I'd been crying.

'Martin?'

'Yes?'

'I've been seeing him for a while.'

'Can't I see you as well?'

'Maybe . . .' She was asleep again before I'd finished dressing.

But it was those four words of hers that I was thinking of as Millie drove me home: *I'm seeing someone else.*

I looked out of the window at the cold glare of the lights. The streets iced over, treacherous. It was strange. Though she kept saying that everything was temporary, unstable, she never seemed to want to bring things to an end. I had the feeling that maybe I could change her mind. There was room for hope. And this uncertainty produced a genuine erotic charge, a desperation, a kind of fever: each time we slept together could be the last. Sometimes I wondered if it was deliberate, simply her way of sustaining interest. Whose, though, hers or mine? (I didn't think mine needed much sustaining.) I felt I was caught in a storm. I was clinging to a tree and waiting for the wind to drop. I had to cling so hard, my arms were numb. But I didn't dare let go.

The man outside the club, the bouncer. He had shoulders like the slopes of a volcano and diamond studs in both his ears.

Or they could've been gold.

It was warm in the back of the car. I dozed off. Straight into the dream and running. I feel my fingers loosen at the knuckles. I start to come apart.

Then the driver's shaking me. 'Mr Blom? Mr Blom?'

'OK,' I mutter. 'I'm awake.'

I lean forwards. And, just for a moment, as I reach for the door, I've got no hands.

It snowed that week. The powerlines were thick with it, the rooftops smooth and white. A hush to the traffic, people's feet. I knew Nina had been home because there was a new message on her machine. No voice. Just a church bell tolling, then a beep. Was this the death of our relationship? Twice I put the phone down, trembling. The third time I left my name and number. I waited in my room till dawn. I didn't eat. Outside, the snow kept coming down. You wouldn't think the sky could hold so much of it. She never did call back.

The hotel was different, too. Quieter. Even on the second floor. I hadn't forgotten Arnold's lecture, but I found myself ignoring it. Night after night I walked the corridors. I sat on the black vinyl sofa by the lift. I was waiting for something to happen. Anything. Once I saw a man in a silk dressing-gown putting his shoes outside his room. I wished him a good evening. He looked at me sideways, as if I might be dangerous, then withdrew without a word. Otherwise it was silent, deserted. Unrecognisable. I could only think that the police had exposed the operation, closed it down.

I walked the streets in sub-zero temperatures. I felt I was part of something that was decaying. During the day there was the illusion of purpose – activity, movement, noise – but it was just the obscene bustle of maggots on a corpse. At night the truth revealed itself. The wind could be heard on the avenues and in the squares. The buildings with their blank façades. People sleeping in tram shelters, cardboard boxes, alleyways. People drunk and bleeding. I stood in front of a travel agent's window. The posters looked surreal at four o'clock in the morning: sunshine, laughter, turquoise water – some lunatic's hallucinations. But everybody fell for it.

Towards the end of that week I returned from Leon's to find Victor taping a notice on to the lift.

'It's out of order,' he said.

'What? Again?'

'They're going to fix it tomorrow. Arnold said.'

'They're always fixing it. But it's always broken.'

'I know, I know. But what can I say? This isn't the Metropole.'

I began to climb the stairs. When I reached the second floor I instinctively glanced in both directions. And there, in her crisp white uniform and her starched white hat, was Nurse Maria Janssen.

I stared at her in disbelief.

She began to walk towards me, smiling. Her eyes were looking into mine. Her hands reached out to me. I could almost hear her voice. *Outside your window there are three beautiful trees . . .*

But then, as she came nearer, I realised it wasn't Maria Janssen at all. This woman was older. She must have been standing under the light. That was the only possible explanation. The light in the corridor had deceived me.

'I saw you,' the woman said. 'The other night.'

Now she was closer she reminded me a little of Gregory's ex-wife, Hedi: the peroxide hair, the drinker's skin. Certainly she looked nothing like Maria.

'You were lost,' she was saying, 'don't you remember? I should have helped you, but I didn't. I don't know why . . .'

I could smell vermouth, I thought. Stale tobacco, too, and soiled underclothes. My stomach heaved. Why was the woman talking to me? Was she mad?

'What's wrong, dear?'

'I'm sorry,' I muttered. 'I thought you were someone else.'

I turned away from her and suddenly I was falling. I saw the banister rotating past me like a stick flung to a dog. I ended up at the bottom of a flight of stairs. I wasn't sure exactly how it had happened. I must've turned too quickly, lost my footing. I'd have to be more careful in future. Look where I was going.

'Are you hurt?'

Oh God. The woman was still there, somewhere above me. She was wearing slippers that were like my mother's – brown leather with a pattern of embossed gold flowers, and black fur trimming round the ankles.

'I'm fine.' My elbow hurt. My left leg as well. But it was only bruising.

'Are you sure?' She was peering down at me in that way I hated. 'If you come to my room,' she said, 'I'll bandage it for you.'

What? Bandage what? I wished I could bandage her. I'd start with her mouth. 'Look,' I said. 'All I want is to be left alone. All right?'

'Oh.' She straightened up. 'I was only trying – '

'I said, leave me alone.'

'But – '

Some people never get the message, do they?

'Will you just PISS OFF!'

At last she shook her head of brittle hair and climbed back up the stairs. I watched her fat hips glumly oscillate. A few moments later I heard the click of a door closing further down the hall. I stood up shakily and leaned against the wall. That backside of hers, when she turned in the confined space of the stairs! It reminded me of a cat in a litter tray. What was she doing on the second floor? Some old whore, I supposed. Must have been pensioned off by the Kosminsky brothers. Given a cheap room in recognition of her years of faithful service.

Maybe I'd been wrong to shout at her. I couldn't help it, though. I was angry with myself for having been so careless. For having panicked like that.

For having lost control.

Later that night, after bathing my injuries, I sat in front of the TV. At about three in the morning, the phone rang. There was only one person it could be. I picked up the receiver.

'Martin?' She sounded breathless, as though she'd been running.

'Nina,' I said. 'Where are you?'

'I'm at work. I can't talk.' She wanted to meet me, but it had to be on neutral ground, somewhere public. Before I could ask her why, she said, 'I was thinking of the city library. Tomorrow. Two in the afternoon.'

'I never go out in the day. You know that.'

'Just this once. For me.'

I wouldn't be able to see her. And I'd have that blankness to contend with, blankness I usually slept through. But the last few days had been hard on me. Empty, too. If this was all she was prepared to offer me, I had no choice. It was a measure of my desperation.

'Where in the library?' I said.

She had it all worked out. 'There's a reading room on the first floor. Rare Books and Manuscripts. In there.'

The next day the streets were icy, and my left knee was stiff and swollen. I allowed an hour and a half for what would normally have been a twenty-minute walk. I was still late. I tapped my way up the library steps at two-fifteen and in through the revolving doors. Once there, I had to ask someone to guide me to the information desk.

'Is it Braille you're looking for?' the information officer said.

'No,' I said. 'Rare Books.'

He escorted me across the foyer to the lift, then travelled with me to the first floor. He had trouble with his sinuses. All kinds of snorts and snuffles. We turned left out of the lift and walked thirty paces. He held a door open for me and I passed through it.

'Rare Books,' he said.

I thanked him.

I knew he was watching me, waiting to see what I was going to do. I didn't *do* anything. I just stood there, both hands resting on my cane, as if savouring the air, or just thinking. In my experience blind people are often viewed as mentally deficient, and it amused me to play on this misapprehension. I listened to his footsteps as he walked away, hesitant at first, because he was looking back at me over his shoulder, but becoming more rapid, more definite, as he decided to leave me to my own devices.

I used my white cane to explore. There were twenty-eight rows of metal shelves, with narrow aisles between them. The rows of shelves were bisected by a wide central aisle. I could smell dust and old paper, and the two smells seemed related, part of the same family. At the far end of the room was a reading area, with tables, chairs and lamps. I found an empty place and sat down. Not wishing to attract attention, I took off my dark glasses and opened a newspaper. Trust Nina to be even later than I was.

The minutes passed. I turned to the next page of my paper. A man coughed. The doors at the far end of the room swung open – but it was only someone with a trolley. The trolley had hard rubber wheels. For a moment I was back in the clinic.

Then something touched me on the shoulder.

'Come with me,' Nina whispered.

I followed her into one of the narrow aisles. There was a small table at the end of it, by the wall. She sat me on a chair. For a moment I thought the sun had come out; I could feel it against my back, the warmth of it. Then I realised it was just a radiator. It was the heat coming off a radiator that I could feel.

'This is difficult,' I said.

Something creaked. The table. It was Nina, leaning against it. I had no way of telling what kind of mood she was in.

'Have you been here long?' I asked her.

'About half an hour.' She paused. 'You sat right next to me. It was uncanny.'

'You were already here, you mean?'

'Yes. I was early.'

'Why didn't you say anything?'

'I was watching you pretending to read the paper. You even got it the right way up.'

I could smell her perfume. It didn't belong there. Perfume, ancient paper, dust: it felt wrong as a combination.

'I didn't make it to your place,' she said. 'I'm sorry.'

'I noticed.'

She didn't say anything.

'That was five days ago,' I said. 'You didn't call.' I hesitated. 'I was worried about you.'

She still didn't say anything.

'I went to the club – '

'I know,' she said. 'They told me.'

I ran my hand along the edge of the table. It was rounded, worn. I stared at where my hand was, but I couldn't see anything. I shouldn't be here, I thought. I should be in bed. Away from all this. As far away as possible.

'Did you hear the message?' she said. 'On my machine?'

'Yes, I did.'

'It was for you.'

'It sounded like a funeral.'

'You told me about your name once, how it was like a bell. Don't you remember?'

I was looking up into the corner of the room. Where the corner of the room would be if I could see it.

She sighed. 'Why are you being like this?'

'Like what?'

'This isn't going anywhere,' she said.

I almost said, What isn't?

'This conversation,' she said, 'is not going anywhere.'

'I love you, Nina.' I just blurted it out.

She eased down off the table. I heard something metal touch the radiator. A belt? A ring? I didn't even know what she was wearing.

'I love you,' I said.

Then it was silent.

'There's a man down there,' she said. 'He's got a tattoo on his neck. A spider's web.' She paused. 'Only you can't see it.' She paused again. 'Because it's daytime.'

'Nina – '

'Reach out,' she said. 'Your left hand.'

I reached out slowly through air that seemed to thicken, to resist the passage of my fingers. Slowly through the air, so any contact would be gentle, soft as the contact between capsules when they link or separate in space.

I felt the heat of her skin before the skin itself. She took a quick breath, then she seemed to hold it. My hand didn't know where it had landed. Her bare skin – but where? It moved one way, then the other. Identified a curve. Moved further over. At last the tiny hairs explained it. Her thigh.

She was wearing almost nothing. Had she arrived like that? If not, I couldn't imagine how she'd taken off her clothes without me hearing.

My hand moved softly inwards, upwards. I felt her body arch and stiffen against the point where I was touching her.

'I don't think you should leave me,' I said.

'Oh?' she said. 'Why's that?'

'It's too exciting.'

'Really? Who for?' She could hardly talk.

'You.'

'And not for you?'

She was leaning back against the radiator. I imagined the ridges on the metal printing a row of vertical lines across her buttocks and her upper thighs. As if that part of her was in jail.

'I mean, who else could you do this with?' I said.

She moved against my hand. She didn't answer.

'Is there anyone else you could do this with?'

'What are you telling me?' she murmured. 'You're the only blind man in the city?'

'How many do you know?'

Her breath rushed fast and soft across her bottom lip.

'How many?' I said.

Her inner thigh began to tremble. That shallow trough, that channel in the muscle. Trembling.

'I bet you don't know any others.'

Her whole body shuddered. I pulled her towards me.

'Not even one.'

Loots called me late that afternoon. As soon as I picked up the phone he started talking. He'd had some news. There was a man on the eastern border who claimed to have seen someone disappear right in front of his eyes.

'Another hoax?' I said.

'I don't know,' Loots said, 'but I'm going out there anyway. Do you want to come?'

An hour and a half later we were on the motorway, heading east. For the first sixty kilometres you drive through thick pine forest. There are silver birches in the foreground, a tinge of red to their dead foliage, but it's the pines you notice, massing behind the metallic speckled trunks, deep and darkest-green – impenetrable. The road feels blinkered. Most of the traffic was coming towards us, bound for the city. Loots leaned over the steering-wheel, his eyes narrowed against the dazzle of their headlights.

There was a dusting of snow along the hard shoulder and in the grass verges, but on the road itself the snow had melted, and the surface was glassy and wet. Each time a car passed, it reminded me of the library. Each car that passed was someone asking us to be quiet.

'Did I tell you about the house?' Loots said.

I looked at him. 'What house?'

Someone had offered him a house for Christmas. It was more of a cabin, really – a log-cabin. It stood on the shore of a small lake, all on its own. He was taking his girlfriend down there. Maybe I could come along as well, he said, with Nina.

'Then I'll get to meet her at last.'

In his voice there was a trace of something rueful, a kind of fatalism, as though what he was hoping for was unlikely, if not impossible. Nina, I thought. That was Nina. I watched the telegraph poles flash past. Black trees unreeled on both sides of the car. I felt like a thirsty man who'd drunk something with too much sugar in it. I felt unquenched.

'I didn't know you had a girlfriend,' I said.

'Her name's Helga. She works at the factory. I told you I was in Sponge Cakes?'

I nodded.

'Well, she's next door. In Chocolate Éclairs.'

I asked him what she was like.

'Gorgeous,' he said. 'Half the men in Jam are after her.'

In two hours we had reached the place. It was a run-down farmhouse, three kilometres from the nearest town. We sat in the kitchen – a bleak and cheerless room, its whitewash stained floral yellow by the damp. There were tools leaning against the walls, and the wood stove in the corner had burned down far too low. I could smell dogs, mildew, washing. The man offered us a schnapps, which we both accepted. Cold from the drive, I drank mine down in one.

'I never saw nothing like it before.' The man's hands fumbled the top back on to the bottle. He had the kind of hands that look as if they don't feel anything, that look numb.

Loots asked him what it was exactly that he saw.

'I were inside the shop and he were outside of it, just, you know, peering in the window, see if something took his fancy. He were an ordinary-looking bloke – or so I thought until he disappeared.' The man wiped his nose on the side of his forefinger, which was rough as pumice-stone, and reached for the schnapps. He poured us both another glass. 'I don't mean he disappeared into a crowd or nothing. There weren't no crowd around him. Weren't nobody near him at all. He just disappeared.' The man wiped his nose again. 'Short bloke, he was. Ginger hair.'

We drove into the town. The shopping precinct was deserted except for a couple of youths sharing a cigarette by the fountain. A weekday night in the provinces, rain tumbling through the dull orange light of the street-lamps. We stood outside the shop where it had happened. In the window there were power-tools, lawn-mowers, rolls of wire-mesh fencing. We trawled the damp air for the missing man. But there was only the scrape of waste-paper on concrete and the crackle of archaic neon. The next time I looked round, we were alone in the place. Even the two youths had gone home.

We ate in a cheap restaurant on the main road. It, too, was deserted, apart from four drunk men in hunting-caps who were sitting in the corner singing songs. I didn't have much appetite; I could only eat half the chicken dish I'd ordered. I wasn't sure what I was doing there.

Loots thought we should stay the night, though. 'It was only two days ago that he was seen. I've got the feeling he's still here somewhere.'

I agreed, but without much enthusiasm.

As we left the restaurant, turning our collars up against the rain, something unexpected happened. Two men approached out of the darkness and introduced themselves. A reporter and a cameraman from a local TV station, they wanted to do a report on The Invisible Man for a regional news programme. They'd already talked to the farmer who'd actually seen The Invisible Man. Now they wanted to talk to me.

'You'd be better off with Mr Loots,' I said. 'He's the one who organised it all.'

'No, no,' they said. 'You don't understand. It's you we want.'

They explained that a blind man was a more potent image, a more poignant symbol of the quest. It would be good television, too. I'd just have to take their word for it.

Loots pulled me aside. 'It's OK, Martin. You do it. But listen. Talk to him directly. It'll work better than answering questions. And use his real name. I think that's the mistake we've been making – not using it.'

I thought Loots had a point. One thing worried me, though. If I was on TV, people would see me. Maybe even the people I'd left behind would see me. Claudia. My parents. Dr Visser. Then I remembered that we'd be broadcasting from an obscure town near the eastern border, at least two hours' drive from the capital. A programme like that might actually work in my favour, as disinformation: it would throw everybody off the scent. I suddenly became amused by the idea: someone who didn't want to be found looking for someone who didn't want to be found. It was like a lift with mirror walls: if you stand in the right position you can replicate yourself, there are hundreds of you, nobody can tell which one of you is real. I patted Loots on the back and walked over to the reporter.

'All right,' I said. 'I'm ready.'

Towards eleven that night we checked into a small family hotel on the road that led out of the town. We took a room with two single beds. While Loots showered, I watched an old black-and-white movie on TV. Aliens were taking over the planet. I thought of Nina, who loved science fiction. I sat on a chair by the window with the phone on my lap. The receiver smelled of cleaning fluid. Lemon flavour.

Loots emerged from the bathroom, wrapped in a towel.

'Did I do OK tonight?' I asked him.

'You were great,' he said. 'Specially that bit you said – what was it? "We're not trying to put any pressure on you. We just want to be sure that you're all right."'

'You think that was good?'

'Great. And at the end, when they pulled back and showed you standing all alone on that empty street. Even I felt sorry for you.'

I smiled.

'I'm going to get some sleep,' Loots said. 'I'm really tired.'

'Does the TV bother you?'

He said it didn't. Springs winced as he climbed into bed and drew the blankets over him. He was asleep in minutes.

I sat on my chair by the window. The aliens were going to lose. They always lost. There was always something on earth which they just happened to be allergic to, something ridiculous like toothpaste or concrete. I dialled Nina's number, expecting her machine. I didn't mind if I got the machine; at least I'd hear her voice before I went to sleep – or maybe there'd be another sound-effect intended specifically for me. But she answered and, for a moment, I couldn't think of anything to say. Then I remembered how she liked to start conversations in the middle.

'Do you think he saw us?' I whispered.

'Who?'

'The man with the tattoo on his neck.'

'I don't know,' she said. 'Maybe.'

'Do you think he liked it?'

She laughed softly, but didn't answer.

'I liked it,' I whispered. 'All of it.'

'Why are you whispering?'

'Loots is asleep.'

I told her where we were. She didn't ask what we were doing. She didn't even sound surprised. Sometimes it bewildered me, this utter lack of curiosity. It made me feel irrelevant, disposable. I didn't think it was intentional. She had her own world, that was all. But still. I changed the subject. I talked about the house that Loots had mentioned earlier, the house by the lake. I said she was invited, too.

'You should see the clouds tonight,' she said. 'Orange and grey, and swirling round and round, like someone's stirring them . . .'

'It's raining here.'

'Do you remember clouds? From before you were blind?'

'I've got memories,' I said. 'You go blind, you don't lose everything.'

There was a moment's silence.

'I was with Greersen,' she said.

I didn't follow.

'The night I didn't show up. I was at Greersen's place.'

'Oh.'

Greersen ran the Elite. That was all I knew about him.

'I was there all night,' she said.

I walked to the window. The phone was in my hand. For a few seconds it had the feeling of a weapon.

'Quick,' said someone on TV. 'Get down.'

'Sorry,' she said, 'but I never promised – '

'I know.'

'Does it matter?'

I parted the brown curtains. The rain was still falling. In the building opposite, there was a man sitting on a chair. The room was pale-green. He was alone.

'Martin?'

'Yes.'

'It doesn't mean – '

'It doesn't mean what?'

There was another silence, then she sighed.

'I think I'd better go,' I said.

I waited.

As I took the receiver from my ear, she said something. I only caught a fraction of it, her tone of voice rather than the words themselves; I thought she sounded anxious. I tried to call her back, but the line was busy. I stood by the window with the phone in my hand, watching the rain fall on a town I didn't know.

•

By late afternoon I was in a multi-storey car-park, waiting for Loots. It had been a wasted day. We'd got nowhere. That farmer in his kitchen, the empty shopping precinct, Nina's confession on the phone. I felt tired and desolate. I didn't like standing in car-parks either, no matter how many storeys there were. I started imagining men with T-shirts on. I started imagining tomatoes.

At last I heard footsteps approaching. I didn't hear any keys, though. Loots had this habit of bouncing keys on his hand as he walked towards his car. A lot of people do it. It's slightly irritating, actually. It's like people who shake the ice-cubes in a drink just before they finish it. I listened to the sounds surrounding the footsteps. I listened hard. No keys.

'Loots?' I called out. 'Is that you?'

The footsteps stopped. A voice said, 'Mr Blom?'

'Yes?'

'You were on TV last night.'

'That's right,' I said.

'It seems you've been looking for me.'

I turned to face the voice. 'The Invisible Man!'

'Used to be.'

It was still daylight and I had no vision, so I did the only thing I could think of: I held out my hand.

'Pleased to meet you,' I said.

And I shook hands with The Invisible Man. It was the most curious feeling. The hand was there – but, at the same time, it was not. It was recognisable as a hand and yet it was absent, somehow. Recognisable by its absence. Maybe that was the best way of describing it. Absence of hand – or, maybe, hand-shaped air. In any case, an unforgettable sensation.

'By the way,' he said, 'I liked the poster.'

One light laugh, and the hand withdrew. He was gone.

Then I heard Loots' footsteps. He was whistling. The car keys tingled on his palm.

'Did you see him, Loots?' I called out.

'Who?'

'The Invisible Man.'

'You're joking. He was here?'

I talked all the way back to the capital. I'd formed a theory; it was based on that one phrase: *used to be*. The Invisible Man was tired of being different, special. Tired of living up to expectations. He wasn't interested in being THE INVISIBLE MAN! He wanted to be ordinary, with no exclamation mark after his name – invisible in the way that normal people are. So that was what he'd done. Become invisible, with a small i. Or, more appropriately, visible. With an ordinary v. You could be sitting next to him on a bus or a train, in a restaurant or bar, at home on the sofa, you could be sitting next to him right now and there'd be nothing invisible about him, nothing invisible at all. That was what had happened, I was sure of it. And that, I told Loots, was what he should say to Anton when he saw him again.

The city seemed to welcome us as we drove in – green lights all the way and rockets exploding in the bright, snow-heavy sky above the Metropole. We'd done the impossible. We'd found The Invisible Man. I wanted to tell everyone I met. I suddenly wished I had more friends. Well, at least there was Gregory. I dropped in at Leon's and there he was in his donkey jacket, white hair rising off his head like steam, his shiny hands wrapped round a cup of coffee.

'I haven't seen you for ages,' he said. 'Where've you been?' His head was lowered, bull-like, and he was glowering at me through a kind of undergrowth: his eyebrows.

'Smoke,' I said, 'you won't believe what happened.'

I told him the story of the last twenty-four hours. As I reached the end I saw that he'd forgiven me. I bought him a dessert, just to make sure: Leon's famous blackcurrant jelly, with a dome of whipped cream the size of the Kremlin.

When I unlocked the door of my room just after two o'clock, the phone was ringing. I snatched it up.

'Blom.'

Never had my name sounded less gloomy. The m hummed happily, like bees in summer.

'It's me.'

Nina!

'I have to see you, Martin. Right away.'

What she was saying seemed to prove the theory I had about her, that there was always room for hope. I'd already decided Greersen didn't mean anything to her. It had been a whim, an aberration (she probably regretted it now). There was no reason why I couldn't go on seeing her. Who knows, maybe we could even get married. It would have to be a night wedding, of course. I'd invite Gregory, Victor, Leon. I'd invite The Invisible Man, too. Loots could dance with Nina in that quaint, old-fashioned style of his.

'Will you meet me somewhere?' she was saying.

'Of course,' I said. 'Where?'

She told me she'd drive over. There was an all-night café-bar inside the train station. She'd see me there in twenty minutes.

I put the phone down. Half an hour later I walked into the café. Nina had taken a booth at the back, near the toilets and the cigarette machine.

'Sorry I'm late,' I said. 'Have you been here long?'

'No,' she said, 'not long.'

She was wearing a fake-fur jacket and a beret, and no lipstick. All I could think about was kissing her. The waitress came and stood beside our table. I ordered coffee and a pastry.

Nina waited until the waitress had gone. 'You don't like pastry.'

'I'm celebrating,' I said.

'What are you celebrating?'

'We found The Invisible Man. Me and Loots.'

'Oh. Right.'

'I talked to him, Nina. I actually shook his hand.'

'That's great.' But she put nothing of herself into the words. They were hollow, empty. Insincere. I felt my good mood being gradually dismantled.

'What did you want to see me about?' I asked her.

She touched her beer mat, just the corner of it, with one finger.

'It must have been important,' I said, 'for you to drive all the way over here at this time of night.'

'It is important.'

My coffee arrived.

'I don't love you,' she said.

'Who do you love? Greersen?' I stared at her in disbelief.

She didn't answer. She lit a cigarette, then started turning her beer mat on the surface of the table.

'Maybe I loved you in the beginning,' she said, after a while, 'but I don't any more.'

'Maybe you'd like to say it again,' I said. 'Maybe I didn't hear it the first time.'

She sighed. 'I'm sorry.'

I stared at my pastry, its flaky crust baked to a perfect gold, its dusting of spotless white sugar. I wished I was blind. We should have met in the daytime, like before. Or some bright place. Somewhere with fierce lights, preferably fluorescent. Then I wouldn't have been able to see her. Then I wouldn't have known what I was missing. Then I wouldn't have been staring at a fucking pastry.

'Guess what?' I said. 'I was on TV.'

'Were you?' She was somewhere else, though. She'd hardly heard me.

'It doesn't matter,' I said.

'No, tell me.'

I stood up. 'I'll pay on the way out.'

'I've got to go to the bathroom,' she said. 'Will you wait for me?'

I sat down again. This hurt more than almost anything else. *Will you wait for me?* So trivial, so everyday – and yet it meant there was something between us. We were connected, together.

I didn't watch her walk away. Instead, I looked at the place where she'd been sitting. There was a shallow indentation in the plastic. I reached over, touched the indentation. It was still warm. Then I noticed her bag on the seat. She'd left it behind. Without thinking, I slipped my hand inside it. The usual jumble of lipstick, make-up, money. A notebook, too. Scalloped edges to the pages. Her addresses. I picked up the book and tucked it into my pocket. I wasn't sure why I'd done it. And by the time I thought about putting it back, it was too late. I heard the door to the toilets open. She was walking towards me.

'What?' she said.

'Nothing.' I pointed at the seat. 'You left your bag.'

She was staring down at me. No warmth in the look, no suggestion of any intimacy at all. It was more sort of dissatisfied. Disillusioned even. I obviously wasn't handling this the way she'd hoped I would.

'Is there anything you want to ask me?' she said.

I sat there for a moment longer, trying hard to concentrate. I kept thinking of her address book in my pocket. I still didn't know why I'd taken it. I shook my head. 'No.'

She walked ahead of me, up to the cash-register. She reached into her bag.

'I already told you,' I said. 'This is on me.'

She took her hand out of the bag again. She hadn't noticed that her address book was missing. I paid for two coffees and a pastry.

'Didn't you like the pastry?' the waitress said. She seemed to be taking it personally, the fact that I hadn't touched it.

'I lost my appetite,' I said. 'I'm sorry.'

When I walked out of the café, Nina was waiting in the station concourse. There was that whispering again, the sound I'd heard when I first returned to the city. Voices lifted into a great emptiness. Voices appealing to something they didn't even know was there. She took hold of my arm. 'There's a man staring at me.'

'There's always men staring at you,' I said, irritated suddenly. 'The saxophone-player the other night. He stared at you, too.'

'How do you know that?'

'I told you. I can see at night.'

She didn't say anything for a moment. Then she said, 'This is different. I've seen him before.'

I looked around. I couldn't see anyone. 'Who is he?'

'I've no idea. I've seen him before, though.'

I looked up at the roof, moving my feet inside my shoes to warm them up. She was still clinging to my arm.

'Will you walk me to my car?' she said.

I said I would.

'You don't mind, do you?'

'No.'

We left the station by the main exit and turned right, into a side street. Our breath speech-bubbled up into the air. It was very cold.

'So you're not coming away for Christmas?' I said.

'Coming away? Where to?'

I reminded her about the house by the lake.

'I don't think that's a very good idea,' she said, 'do you?'

I didn't answer.

'There's too much going on. I need some time.'

'Sure,' I said. 'I understand.'

The wind rose. Snow blew sideways across the street, vicious as ground glass. I thought I could hear footsteps on the pavement behind me, but when I glanced over my shoulder there was no one there. I nodded to myself, remembering the clinic corridors at night.

'He's still there,' Nina said. 'He's following us.'

'Where's your car?' I said.

We had to cross the street. I tucked my chin into my collar. My feet felt as if they were made of something different to the rest of me.

'Is that where you live?' she said. 'The Kosminsky?'

I nodded.

'That's the place you wanted to show me?'

'Yes.'

'Will you show me now?'

'I don't think that's a very good idea,' I said, 'do you?'

She'd parked right outside the hotel. I left her by her car. Just walked away, towards the steps.

'Martin?' she called out.

For a moment I couldn't move. Her voice had that power over me, the power a dream has, to lock muscles, making it impossible to run. I didn't look round. Instead, I hunted through my pockets for my room-key. It was a charade. I didn't have the key on me. I'd left it in a pigeon-hole behind reception.

'Martin?' she called again, more urgently this time.

But I had reached the doors, and they were beginning to revolve.

I was inside the building when I heard the car door slam. The engine spluttering, the crunch of gears. And then a sound that was like a seagull's cry: Nina's tyres spinning as she took the corner. It wasn't her fault. It was the new road surface they'd put down. It happened to everyone.

Friday came. I was in my room, watching a carol concert on TV, when the phone rang. It was Loots calling from downstairs, in the lobby. I closed my suitcase, put on my coat and left the room. Loots was standing outside the lift when the doors slid open.

'Where's Nina?' he said.

'I forgot to tell you. She can't come.'

There was a sudden switch in the expression on his face: eagerness to disappointment. 'What's wrong? Is she sick?'

'No, she's not sick.' We passed reception. 'Well, Happy Christmas, Arnold.'

'It's Victor, actually. But thanks, anyway.'

I shook my head. I could've sworn it was Arnold I was looking at. Maybe it was just that Victor had taken up smoking.

'If she's not sick,' Loots said, 'what is it?'

'I'll tell you later.'

I followed him out of the hotel and down the steps, and climbed into the back of the car. He introduced me to his girlfriend, Helga. We shook hands. Loots pulled out into the evening traffic.

As we turned right at a set of lights, I thought I saw Dr Visser on the pavement. If it wasn't Visser, it was a man of the same height and build, with a similar moustache. I sank down in my seat, below the level of the window. Probably he was just doing last-minute Christmas shopping. In fact, I was sure I'd seen some packages under his arm. Or maybe it wasn't even him. A narrow escape if it was, though. Very narrow.

'Martin?' Loots said. 'Are you all right?'

'Yes. Yes, I'm fine.' I sat up straight again. 'I just dropped something, that's all.'

I settled back. It felt good to be getting out of the city for a few days. I'd been thinking of staying behind, in the hope that Nina might call, but then I'd decided against it. I'd done the right thing. If she called now, I wouldn't be there. She wouldn't know where I was either, and she'd have no way of finding out. I drew some comfort from this small, imagined revenge. More to the point, if she didn't call, I wouldn't be sitting there, depressed.

Besides, it was Christmas. Most people left the city. I thought back to a holiday weekend one summer when I was twenty-two or -three. I had stayed in my apartment, thinking that I would learn the city's secrets, thinking that, if it was empty, it would be more likely to reveal something of itself to me. I could still remember the streets – sunlit, yet grey, somehow, and utterly deserted. And that dusty colour, that emptiness, had crept into my blood. I could remember lying on a single bed under an open window. Sometimes a car drove by. There were smells of rotten fruit and chip-fat; there was the smell of the canal. The phone didn't ring at all. One night I slept for more than thirteen hours. And then, at last, the people returned. They were tanned and easy in themselves, full of entertaining stories. I found that I had nothing to say. I couldn't even seem to make my loneliness sound funny; every time I cracked a joke about it, I felt as if I was about to cry. An eternity had passed. What had I done?

'Are you warm enough?' Loots called out.

I told him I was fine. Just fine.

I listened to Loots and Helga discussing junctions, exits, distances – which route would be the best to take. Though much of what they said was practical, desultory even, I couldn't help but feel envious. Their voices were like the gentlest kind of acid: all thoughts of revenge on Nina quietly dissolved in it. I just wished that she was sitting next to me, her head against my shoulder, as we travelled towards the cabin by the lake. Her face as the motorway lights washed over it. Her voice dreamily describing clouds, the sky . . .

'Martin?'

'Yes.'

'The police are here. They'd like to speak to you.'

The police? Heat rushed to my titanium plate and coalesced. I had to sit down on the edge of my bed. I could feel cold air reaching through a gap in the window, but I was sweating.

They're on to me.

'Martin? Are you there?'

I asked Victor what it was about. He couldn't tell me. They wanted to come up to my room, though. They wanted to speak to me. That wasn't convenient at all, I said. I'd been sleeping; I'd have to put some clothes on.

'How long will you be?' Victor asked.

'Ten minutes. No, wait. Fifteen.'

As soon as I put the phone down, I cursed myself. Fifteen minutes? It wasn't enough. I had to think. They were on to me. Had my parents reported me missing – or was it Visser, acting out of some notion of responsibility? That TV appearance, I really regretted it now. I'd reminded people of my existence when all I wanted was to be overlooked, ignored, forgotten. I'd reminded people that they were worried about me.

There was no time to pack a case. I took the plastic bin-liner out of the waste-paper basket and emptied it on to the floor. I tipped a drawerful of socks and underwear into the bag, together with my suit, my medical supplies and my tactile clock, then I put on my dark glasses and picked up my white cane. I opened the door and peered out. No one in the corridor. I locked my room. I was hurrying towards the fire stairs when somebody called my name. Too slow, too slow. My father's snail blood. If only I had one side to me, like The Invisible Man. If only I could've vanished, just by turning round. The voice was a policeman's voice. There were two of them. I could hear them walking down the corridor towards me.

'Well, well. This *is* a coincidence.'

I wasn't sure what the policeman meant by that. His voice did sound familiar, though. It was a soft voice. A softness that was comfortable, almost soporific.

'It's Detective Munck. I came to see you at the clinic.'

'Of course,' I said, turning round. 'The pears.' I shook hands with him and we exchanged a smile.

'You remember my partner, Slatnick?'

'Yes, I do.'

This was the first time I'd set eyes on Slatnick. He was chewing gum again (he had knots of muscle in his cheeks, he'd chewed so much of it). His forehead sloped backwards, the same angle as a snow plough. He seemed older than Munck, and less intelligent.

He stepped forwards. 'You were going the wrong way.' His nostrils were unusually wide and round, and they were aimed at me, like a shot-gun. 'The wrong way,' he said, 'for the lift.'

'Was I?'

'You were heading for the fire exit.'

'I'm always getting lost in here,' I said. 'It's a big hotel. Confusing.'

'What's in the bag?'

'The bag? Nothing. Laundry.'

'You weren't trying to make a run for it, then?'

'A blind man? Making a run for it?'

Munck seemed to enjoy my last remark, though he faced away from Slatnick, sending his smile back down the corridor.

'And anyway,' I went on, 'what would I be running from?'

Munck took me gently by the upper arm. 'Is there somewhere we can talk?'

I suggested the cocktail bar on the first floor.

As we descended in the lift Munck asked after my health. My responses were polite, but distracted. I still didn't know what they wanted. And Slatnick was standing right behind me; I could feel the air being fired from the twin barrels of his nose into the back of my neck, into my hair.

The bar was empty, as usual. A dark, cramped room with mustard-yellow curtains, it smelled of stale cigarette smoke and the liquid soap they use for washing glasses. Munck showed the bartender his police ID and asked him not to disturb us. We sat in a corner booth. Munck put a folder on the table, opened it and leaned forwards, one hand placed on top of the other.

'You know, I've got this theory,' he said.

I waited.

'It's to do with free-floating anxiety,' he said. 'Nervous breakdowns, too. Paranoia. It's why they happen.'

'Not the aliens again,' Slatnick grumbled.

Munck silenced his colleague with a look. 'It's my belief,' he said, 'that there are intelligent life-forms living on the moon.'

I stared at him.

'Do you think I'm mad?' he said.

I didn't know what to say.

'Slatnick thinks I'm mad.'

'Life-forms,' I said. 'On the moon.'

'They're very advanced,' he said. 'They're beyond anything we can imagine. And they're watching us right now, the same way we watch ants – '

'How come the astronauts didn't notice them?'

'What? A couple of bouncing men in big white suits?'

Slatnick sniggered.

'All they did was pick up stones,' Munck said, 'like children. And that's what we are, by comparison. Children.'

'I see what you mean,' I said.

'They're sophisticated. They're where we'll be in a millennium – if we last that long.'

'So they're watching us?'

'Yes.'

'Which explains why we feel paranoid sometimes?'

'Exactly.' Munck paused. 'You, though. You've got a reason of your own.'

There was a long silence, which I didn't understand.

'You mean, because I was shot?' I said eventually.

The two policemen stared at me.

'Is that what this is about?' I said.

'No.' Slatnick popped his chewing-gum. 'It's nothing to do with that.'

'It's just a routine enquiry.' Munck consulted one of his sheets of paper. 'It concerns a Miss Salenko. Miss Nina Salenko.'

'What about her?' My heart had lurched at the mention of her name. Or was it simply that I'd been expecting something else?

'She's disappeared,' Slatnick said.

I almost laughed. 'What? Again?'

Another silence.

'I'm sorry,' Munck said. 'I don't know what you mean.'

Now that it seemed I wasn't the subject of the investigation, I became quite talkative. I told the two policemen that she was always disappearing. I mentioned the evening that she was supposed to meet me downstairs in the lobby. How she never arrived. And how she didn't call either, not for five days.

'Were you a friend of hers?' Munck asked.

'Yes, I suppose I was.'

'A close friend, would you say?'

'It depends what you mean by close.'

'Did you know her,' and he cleared his throat, 'intimately?'

Slatnick stopped chewing for a moment and looked at me sideways, across his right shoulder.

'Yes,' I said. 'We slept together a few times. I wouldn't say I knew her very well. We only met two months ago.'

'When did you last see her?'

'It was a Tuesday night. About ten days before Christmas.'

'Did she seem upset?'

'No, not especially.' I wanted to tell him that I was the one who was upset, but I checked myself. Now was not the time – as Munck himself might have said.

'She didn't say she was going anywhere?'

I shook my head.

'And you can't think of a reason why she might have wanted to leave the city?'

'No.'

I remembered standing at the bottom of the hotel steps and hunting through my pockets for an imaginary key. Her calling out. *Martin?* The sudden shriek of tyres as she pulled away. That was the last time. I'd tried to phone her since New Year, but she was never there.

'What about her car?' I said.

'She had a car?'

I nodded.

'I don't think we knew that.' Munck glanced through the papers in his folder. 'No, there's no mention of a car.'

I described the car for him as best I could: the make, the colour – the naked woman dangling from the rear-view mirror.

'A naked woman?' Slatnick's mouth had fallen open.

'A doll. One of those little plastic ones.' I smiled. 'She called it Doris.'

Munck took up the questioning again. 'Did she like driving?'

I remembered that Munck was fond of habits, but I didn't want to mention the motels so I generalised. I told him that she loved driving.

She was always driving places, often in the middle of the night. She was impulsive, some might say reckless.

'In which case,' Munck said cautiously, as if he was trying the flavour of a new idea on his tongue, 'this might all be a fuss about nothing.' He paused. He didn't seem to like the way the idea tasted. 'It was her mother who reported her missing. Do you know Mrs Salenko?'

'No.'

'You've never met her?'

I shook my head. 'Never.'

'Attractive woman,' Munck said. 'Still young. She's a croupier.' He paused again. 'Well,' he said, 'I think that'll be all. For the time being, at least.' He straightened the papers in his folder. 'Oh, one last thing. You registered under a false name . . .'

I had to admire his technique. That quizzical smile of his told me the positioning of the question was deliberate, thought-out: he'd waited until the interview was over and I was off my guard.

I returned his smile. I tried to explain how the shooting had affected me. I told him that the life I used to live was dead. I was living a new life now, as a blind person. I'd adopted the false name because I thought it might help me to adjust. If I had a different name, I'd feel different. That was the logic. It was a symbol of my determination to leave the past behind, to begin again.

Though pleased with my improvisation, I was aware that what I was saying sounded suspicious, guilty even, and I wasn't sure how the two policemen took it. Munck, at least, seemed satisfied. He shuffled his papers once more and then stood up.

'May I ask you something?' I said.

'Certainly.'

'How did you find me?'

'You were on Miss Salenko's answering-machine,' he said. 'Well, you left the name of the hotel and the number of your room.'

'You didn't know it was me, though?'

'I had no idea.'

'It must've been quite a surprise.'

'Yes.' Munck smiled. 'Yes, it was.'

We passed through the door of the bar and out into the corridor. The two policemen thanked me for my assistance. I wished them luck.

'If you hear anything,' I said, 'will you let me know?'

'Of course,' Munck said.

I took the stairs back to my room. I was thinking about Nina's address book. Without it, Munck's investigations might be hampered, but I couldn't bring myself to hand it over. Not yet, anyway. Was I obstructing justice, I wondered, by holding on to it?

When I reached the fifth floor I put my bag of clothes down and leaned on the windowsill. I didn't know what I felt, exactly. On the one hand, there was relief: nobody was after me. On the other, Munck knew where I lived. And Slatnick.

And then there was Nina, missing . . .

I was looking out over the side street where she'd parked her car that night. It was dimly lit, deserted – two transit vans, a stack of oil-drums, some wooden pallets. Then I saw him, in silhouette against the sky. He was on his bicycle, as usual, only this time he was riding through the air, and uphill, too, from the curved, wrought-iron roof of the railway station to the clock tower of a nearby church. He was at least twenty metres above the ground, and yet he seemed nonchalant, one hand on the handlebars, the other in his pocket. There had to be a line strung between the two buildings, but I couldn't make it out. I thought of calling to him, then decided against it. He probably wouldn't hear me anyway; he'd be concentrating, in a kind of trance. As I resumed my climb I could've sworn I heard him whistling. Loots, I thought to myself. The Great Loots. And I too began to whistle.

I hadn't been back in my room for long when the phone began to ring. I thought about ignoring it. But after it had rung perhaps ten times I reached over and picked up the receiver. It was Victor. He wanted to know what kind of trouble I was in. He promised not to tell Arnold.

'Sorry to disappoint you, Victor,' I went on, 'but it's not me who's in trouble, it's a friend of mine. The police are looking for her. I'm helping them with their enquiries.'

Putting the phone down, I shook my head. Victor.

I turned the TV on: ballet on one channel, ice-skating on another. I turned it off again. I sat by the window on my plastic chair and smoked. Outside, it was snowing. In the distance I could hear the bells of the cathedral, those three descending notes, always descending. A kind of panic spread throughout my body, pushed against the inside of my skin. I remembered the story Nina had told me, the night I took her to the Metropole. I kept thinking of her standing on that road with the Big Wheel behind her, its brightly coloured cars lost in the mist.

At ten o'clock I took the lift down to the lobby and walked out through the revolving doors. The taxi I'd ordered was waiting at the kerb.

'Mr Blom!'

I got into the car. 'How are you, Millie?'

'I'm fine,' he said. 'You know, I saw you on TV.'

'Seems like everybody saw it.'

'I thought you were great. Really great.'

I thanked him.

'I thought maybe you should make a career out of it,' he said. 'You know. Presenter.'

I smiled at the idea.

He pulled out into the traffic. 'It's the Elite again, right?'

'Right.'

'TV,' he said, a few minutes later. 'One day I'll be on it.' The way he said it, he made it sound like a desert island.

When we reached the club, I asked him to call back in half an hour, then I set out across the pavement. There were no helicopters flying this time. The weather was too bad.

'It's fifteen to get in.'

A different man was on the door. If it had been the same man, he would've recognised me. That was something to be grateful for.

'I want to see Greersen,' I said. 'Tell him it's a friend of Nina's.'

Five minutes went by. Then another five.

The wind sliced through the telegraph wires above my head. My ears were almost numb.

At last the door opened. A man said, 'I'll take you to Greersen.'

Inside, the music was loud and slack, and someone had been smoking grass. It was dark: just a couple of red table-lamps and a strip of ultra-violet where the bar was. A blonde girl in a spangled g-string was dancing up on stage. Her hair swung across one shoulder. A tattoo covered both her breasts. A bird, it looked like. An eagle. Wings beating as she moved. I wondered if she was Candy. But then I remembered Nina telling me that Candy was black. I tapped through the place with my stick. I'd decided to act blind. It might give me an edge. I knocked against somebody's knee and almost fell. Then I apologised. You have to make it real.

I followed the man through a velvet curtain and down a corridor. We climbed a flight of stairs. The music was muffled now, as though it had been gagged. Greersen's office was on the first floor, at the back of the building. The room was brightly lit. I could smell dust burning on the naked bulbs.

'I'm Greersen.'

He had flat black hair and a thin moustache. His voice was thin as well. Two people were in the room with him, but I wasn't interested in them.

'My name's Blom.'

'So?'

'Is Nina here? Nina Salenko?'

'No.'

'She been here tonight?'

'She hasn't been here for weeks.'

There was always a perfect moment for a silence, and this was it. It was a technique I'd picked up from Visser. You could use it like a polygraph, to test the veracity of what had just been said. Greersen's words hung on in the hot air of the room. He didn't sound guilty at all, more curious – or mocking.

I broke the silence first. 'She said you were sleeping with her.'

A woman was sitting on the sofa to my right. I saw the corners of her mouth turn down. Then she lit a cigarette.

'What's it to you?' Greersen said.

'I'm sleeping with her, too.'

'Got nice tits, hasn't she?'

'The rest of her's not so great,' the woman said.

'Who's looking at the rest of her?' a man behind me said.

The woman didn't say anything. Her paste ear-rings flashed as she reached for the ashtray.

'She's gone missing,' I said.

Greersen put his feet up on the desk. 'You came all the way down here to tell me that?'

'I happened to be passing.'

'What's wrong with the phone?'

'I wanted to meet you. Face to face.'

'It's not exactly face to face, is it,' and Greersen laughed, as if he'd just said something clever.

'It's good enough for me.' I took a step towards him, my hand tightening on my cane. There was a sudden movement on my left. Someone's arm, probably. Someone else's arm restraining it.

I took my dark glasses off and peered down at Greersen. I was doing it deliberately. I knew that it was hard to take. Those blank eyes peering, close up.

'I wanted to get a good look at you,' I said.

There was a smell coming off him. You know that spinach you can buy, pre-washed, in sealed bags? Well, leave it for a week, then open it. That was Greersen. Except he was trying to hide the smell with a cologne. It wasn't working. The smell squatted underneath the perfume like a toad.

'Find out what kind of creep I was dealing with,' I said.

Someone was right behind me now. The man who'd brought me up the stairs, presumably. I broke out into a sweat that was slick and cold. He might have a gun, I was thinking. He might use it. The woman on the sofa was turning her cigarette in the ashtray. Turning it and turning it, sharpening the lit end to a point.

'Get him out of here,' Greersen said.

Two men threw me out of the back door. My shoulder ached from where it had hit something on the way downstairs. I could see the shapes of cars in the darkness, cars drawn up in rows. The glimmer of radiator grilles, the curve of tyres. They couldn't have done it better if they'd tried.

I found my cane and brushed myself down. When I reached the front of the building again, Millie called my name. I crossed the pavement, opened the car door and toppled in.

'What is it, Mr Blom?' he said. 'What happened?'

I couldn't say anything just yet. The scorched smell of the office was in my nostrils. My head felt like a bag of broken glass.

'They roughed you up a little, didn't they.'

I nodded, let him examine me.

'I'm taking you to my house,' he said. 'Get you cleaned up.'

'That's not necessary.'

'But you've cut yourself – '

'I've got a headache, that's all.'

I wanted to go straight back to the Kosminsky, but Millie insisted on driving me to a twenty-four-hour chemist first. He said the best pain-killer was codeine and he could get some for me. We wouldn't need a prescription because a friend of his worked there. He didn't charge me for the detour. He wouldn't let me pay for the pills either.

Just before I got out of the cab I touched him on the shoulder. 'You know that TV show I'm going to have?'

'What about it?' he said.

'I want you to be my first guest.'

Sitting on the steps of the hotel, I dabbed at the cut with a tissue. Greersen. Maybe I shouldn't have upset him. I couldn't resist it, though. Sometimes if a pond looks too still you throw a stone in it.

It had stopped snowing and the moon showed in the gap between two banks of orange cloud. I felt I could see through the moon's thin skin to the organs underneath. Its life seemed as fragile as my own.

Someone was walking up the hill towards me. I didn't think anything of it until he came and stood in front of me. I thought he was going to ask me for the time, or some directions, but all he did was say my name. I didn't recognise him. Was this the moment I'd been dreading, the appearance of a person from my past? Or was it just another member of the public who'd seen me on TV?

'I'm sorry,' I said. 'I don't know you.'

'My name's Robert Kolan. We met once, in the station café.' He hesitated. 'Well, we didn't meet exactly. I was just leaving.'

The blond hair parted in the middle and tucked back behind his ears. The creaking leather jacket. Robert Kolan.

He wanted to talk about Nina.

'Let's talk inside,' I said. 'It's warmer.'

'Yeah,' he said. 'Right.'

We sat in black vinyl armchairs, in the corner of the lobby.

'Nina's disappeared,' he said.

'I know. The police told me.' I told Kolan what I'd told Munck and Slatnick, how Nina was always disappearing.

Kolan interrupted halfway through. 'This is different.'

'What's different about it?'

'It was her father's birthday on the twenty-ninth of December. She never misses her father's birthday.'

I realised that I'd never heard her mention her father (or her mother, for that matter). I had a sudden sense of how thoroughly she'd excluded me, not just from her apartment but from her life.

'Well,' I said, 'it's really not my problem now.'

'You don't care what happens to her?'

'I used to. She left me, though.' I remembered what she'd said about Kolan. *My closest friend*. 'I thought you would've known that.'

'I did know.'

'Well,' I said, and opened my hands.

'So she leaves you and suddenly you don't care about her any more?' He scraped his hair back behind his ears. He was leaning forwards, his eyes jumping between my face and the floor. 'Just like that?'

Suddenly he irritated me. All this talk about caring and friendship. This sanctimoniousness of his. He'd probably been dying to fuck her for years. I wanted to shock him.

'Maybe I wish she was dead,' I said. 'Has that occurred to you?'

I stared at the sofa opposite. I thought of Nina's seat in the station café, which had kept her imprint after she was gone.

'People who've been left by someone,' I went on, 'they often wish the other person was dead. That,' I said, 'is not uncommon at all.'

'She meant that much to you?'

I didn't want to look at him. I looked at the carpet instead – meaningless swirls of orange, brown and black. I heard him light a cigarette. The sharp intake of breath as he inhaled sounded exactly like surprise.

'Do you know Greersen?' I asked.

Kolan was silent.

'I went to see him tonight.' I paused. 'I just wondered. Was Nina sleeping with him?'

Kolan's silence lasted.

'Greersen,' I said. 'The owner of that club.'

'I know who you mean. She couldn't stand the guy.'

'So she wasn't sleeping with him?'

'No.'

I believed him. Greersen had lied about it to get at me. That made sense. Why had Nina lied about it, though? And, if she was lying, who was the someone else that she was seeing?

'You know what Greersen said?' I went on. 'He said he hadn't seen her for weeks.'

'Nobody's seen her for weeks.'

'Do you know who saw her last?'

Kolan hesitated. 'I thought it was you.'

'Me?'

'Yeah. That's why I'm here. I thought you might know something.' He leaned forwards and crushed out his cigarette.

He told me he was over at Nina's place on the Monday night. Nina had called me up. It was late, maybe three in the morning. She drove to the 14th district to meet me, dropping him off outside the station. Nobody had seen her since.

'I didn't realise,' I said.

'You can't tell me anything?'

I shook my head.

He got up out of his chair. He parted his hair again with two hands, training it behind his ears. 'I should be going.'

'Have you talked to the police yet?'

'Not yet.'

'What will you tell them?'

'What I told you.' He paused. 'Why? You've got nothing to hide, have you?'

I watched him leave through the revolving doors, then I rose to my feet and crossed the lobby. Arnold was watching TV. A lit cigarette lay on a groove in the ashtray; the smoke made a series of spaced loops or coils, the way a spring might if you stretched it. He glanced round at me.

'The lift's out of order,' he said.

'You know why, don't you.'

Arnold shook his head. 'Why?'

'Sex,' I said.

It didn't surprise me when he appeared not to understand. He understood all too well – but he would never admit it.

I took the stairs.

First floor, then the second. And, sure enough, there was the lift. Just standing there, with its doors jammed open. There was nobody inside it. But if you dusted the edges of the doors, at a point not too far above the carpet, you'd almost certainly find delicate deposits of human skin, the faint print of a woman's hips.

I glanced down the corridor. One couple fucking silently against the wall.

A quiet night.

The following afternoon, as I was shaving, the phone rang. I saw myself in the mirror, hesitating. I couldn't hear the phone without thinking of Nina, without hoping that it might be her. It wasn't her, though. It was Munck.

'We found the car.'

He wanted me to identify it for him. I'd mentioned certain features, he said. The so-called bullethole. The doll.

Half an hour later he picked me up outside the hotel. He opened the door for me and I got in. There was one last pale streak of daylight to the south-west, but otherwise the sky was dark.

It was cold in Munck's car. He told me the heating was broken. He apologised.

'A policeman's salary,' he said.

Outside, the streets were wet, but the temperature was dropping; they would freeze during the night. There was a tension in the car, which I took to be anticipation.

As we passed beneath the ring road, Munck told me where we were going. A suburb on the outskirts. Right on the edge of the city. I knew the area. Railway arches, scrapyards. High-rise slums. Children tortured cats in concrete corridors. Babies fell out of windows. It was always drizzling.

I peered through the windscreen. We turned down a wide, deserted avenue. A park appeared on the left. The grass was littered with empty bottles, newspaper, women's shoes.

In ten minutes we were there. Munck jerked the handbrake upwards, then he faced me. I saw his teeth at close range. Not just the texture of celery, but the colour, too: palest yellow-green, a kind of chlorophyll.

'Have you been here before, Martin?'

I shook my head. 'Never.'

It wasn't until he got out of the car that I realised it had probably been a trick question. Was I really here for purposes of identification? Or was I here to incriminate myself?

Munck opened my door. 'The car's to your right.'

He walked me towards it.

It was just a piece of waste-ground, near a flyover. The seashell roar of traffic. Blocks of apartments loomed like prison ships. I glanced over my shoulder. Two motorways reared up and tangled with each other in the sky.

'There's tyre tracks stretching ten or fifteen metres,' Munck said. 'The car braked suddenly, for no apparent reason. Both doors are open, as if the occupants left in a hurry.'

I moved slowly round the car, my white cane tapping on hard ground. I found the crack in the back window – a crazed area, something like a spider's web, with a neat hole at the centre. Then I knew it was Nina's car. I went on checking, anyway. I thought I recognised the dent in the bumper: Nina had reversed into a bollard one night, in the car-park of the Motel Astra. When I reached the door on the driver's side I bent down and looked in. No Doris. But I remembered how she'd dangled from a piece of ribbon, and there was a bit of it still knotted round the rear-view mirror. I straightened up.

'It's her car,' I said.

Munck nodded. 'Why would she come here?'

'I've no idea.'

'Did she have any friends in the area?'

'Not so far as I know.' I paused. 'But like I said, I didn't know her very well.'

I took a deep breath, turned away. And then, as I stared out across the waste-ground, I noticed him. He was standing some distance off, with his left shoulder propped against one of the concrete pillars that supported the flyover. He was wearing a herring-bone overcoat and a pair of black shoes; and he was holding both his gloves in his right hand. There was frost in his moustache.

I must have looked strange because Munck took me by the arm.

'Martin?' he said. 'Are you all right?'

I couldn't answer.

Visser was looking right at me, with a smile on his face. It wasn't a malicious smile; it wasn't gloating or unkind. If anything, he seemed to be taking a kind of patriarchal pleasure in the sight of me. It was almost welcoming. But, at the same time, there was an edge to it that disturbed me: it was as if he'd seen a joke that I had yet to see.

'You've gone as white as a sheet,' Munck said.

'I don't feel very well.'

'It must be a shock for you. Perhaps I shouldn't have asked you to come.'

'No, no,' I said. 'I wanted to.'

Visser watched me climb gingerly into Munck's car. As we pulled away, he didn't make any attempt to follow us. He didn't even move. And the smile lingered – indulgent, strangely relaxed.

On the way back to the city centre I started to explain what I thought had happened to me. In a sense, I was just elaborating on certain things I'd talked about in the hotel bar two days before. Ironically enough, it was Visser's predictions that I was trying to remember and repeat, what Visser had told me I'd experience. I ran through the phases: numbness and shock; depression, self-pity, suicidal tendencies; the gradual emergence of a new personality (I made it sound natural but squeamish, a snake shedding its skin – as if, somewhere in the city, in a hotel room, perhaps, there was a transparent version of me, a twin, identical but lifeless).

'A new personality?' Even Munck found it hard to believe.

I laughed. 'I don't think I'm quite there yet.'

I introduced a few variations on the theme, lurid variations of my own. I told him about migraines, rushes, panic. I blamed it on the titanium plate. Maybe sub-zero temperatures affected it. Nobody really knew. I was a unique case, I said. An extraordinary phenomenon. I was like those people with shrapnel in their legs who always know when it's about to rain.

Munck was nodding now. I thought he was beginning to understand. And, gradually, I brought the subject round to Visser, which had been my intention all along.

'Did you ever meet him?' I asked Munck innocently.

Munck looked as if he was trying to remember.

I prompted him. 'He was my doctor. At the clinic.'

'I think it was Dr Visser who gave us permission to see you,' Munck said. 'Yes, I think I must've met him.'

'You don't know him, though?'

'Oh no. I only saw him that one time. The second time, it was a nurse. Why do you ask?'

'Just curious.'

I asked Munck to drop me outside Leon's. I didn't want Visser knowing where I lived – though it occurred to me that, in order to be standing on that piece of waste-ground, he must have been following Munck, and if he was following Munck he must have seen me walk out of the hotel that evening. Possibly he already knew all there was to know. Still, I wasn't going to hand it to him on a plate.

I looked up and down the street. There was no sign of that salt-and-pepper overcoat, no sign of any shiny shoes. I watched Munck drive away, then I turned and walked through the glass-and-metal door, through the heavy vinyl curtain, into Leon's. Loots was sitting in the corner. He called me over.

'Was that a police car?'

I hadn't seen Loots for a day or two and he knew nothing of Nina's disappearance. I repeated most of what I'd learned from Munck. Then I told him where I'd been that evening.

'That's a bad area,' he said.

'I know.'

He bought me a coffee and a brandy, and brought them over to the table.

'Thanks, Loots.'

'I never did meet her, did I?'

'She was hard to meet,' I said, 'even for me.'

Not all the news was gloomy, though. On New Year's Day Loots had seen Anton. The circus hadn't folded after all. They'd found a contortionist known as The Rubber Man who could pass himself through a piece of garden hosepipe. The crowds were back.

By the time we left the restaurant, it was one in the morning and the city was deserted. Street-lamps spread a thin metallic light. At the bottom of the hill, one last tram curved past the station, its yellow windows almost empty. I doubted Visser would be following me tonight. It was too cold to stand in the shadows or sit in a parked car. It was just too cold. Outside the hotel Loots wrapped his arms around me.

'Don't worry. She'll turn up.'

I said good-night, then turned and walked to the entrance. The doors were spinning slowly when I reached them. I waited a moment, then stepped forwards, moving in time with them, as if we were a couple dancing.

The coast, out of season – there's a smell to it. Briny, damp. It's everywhere: in hotel rooms, in taxis, in cafés. I'd never liked the coast much; I always seemed to slow right down, as though my ankles were caught in seaweed.

I'd eaten in a small place by the train station. The man who ran it was a foreigner. He wore a pale-blue suit and white patent-leather shoes with gold buckles, and he had that clammy seaside skin. I ordered chicken salad and a beer. He stood in front of me, staring down with slightly bloodshot eyes, a sack of gelatinous flesh beneath his chin. When he spoke, his words blurred on his tongue.

'Your first time here?'

I shook my head. 'No.'

'You like?'

'No.'

'Me also,' the man said. 'I don't like.'

He dropped his shoulders, moved away. At the bar he picked up a hand-mirror and studied himself for a long time with no change of expression. Then he began to pluck his eyebrows, a faint pop each time a hair came loose. I imagined the root of every hair he plucked; I saw the tiny pellet of skin they were embedded in. I drank my beer, but left most of the food.

Karin Salenko lived in a modest stucco building on the seafront. I leaned against the balcony outside, the plaster flaking away beneath my hands. I could hear breakers behind me, like something being dynamited. Why had I come here? Was it to get away from Visser? (Could he have followed me?) Was it because I was curious about Nina's life, a life I'd been excluded from? Or did I think I was some kind of detective, trying to unearth the truth about her disappearance? I brushed the dust off my hands and turned to face the apartment. Maybe I just wanted to hear somebody talk about her. Maybe all I wanted was to hear her name. I knocked on the door. When it opened, the security chain was still in place.

'Karin Salenko?'

'Yes.'

'My name's Martin Blom. I called you yesterday.'

'Oh yes.' Karin Salenko unhooked the chain. 'Come in.'

Once I was settled on a sofa in the lounge, she asked me if I'd like a drink. Something cold, I told her. Anything, really (I wanted to wash the taste of that restaurant out of my mouth). She brought me a beer from the fridge. Then she sat down opposite me, with the light behind her. I thought she must be working later, at the casino, because she was wearing a glittery, skin-tight turquoise dress that was split to the thigh. Eye-shadow, too. Mascara. And then there was her blonde hair, back-combed and lacquered at the front, and falling in a sheen of gold past her right shoulder. She had a tall glass in her hand.

'You wanted to know about Nina.'

I nodded.

'There's not much to tell,' she said, 'not recently. I haven't seen her for a while. We talk sometimes, you know, but, well . . .'

She had a lazy voice, but there were edges to it. She knew how it sounded, the lazy part. Maybe she even pushed it a little. It wasn't hard to see how it might work with men. The edges, she couldn't do anything about. The edges were memories. Things that hadn't gone right, things that had taken too long. Things that had never happened at all. I don't know. Maybe I was reading too much into it.

'When did you see her last?'

'August. I was in the city, for a convention.' She looked at me. 'I'm a croupier.'

'I know,' I said. 'Where did you meet? Her apartment?'

'No, we had lunch together. A Chinese restaurant she knew. We argued about Christmas.' She smiled faintly. 'We always argued about Christmas. And Easter.'

'What was it about, the argument?'

'She didn't want to come and see me. She wanted to go to her father's place. I said she was always going to her father's place. She was there in the summer, for instance. "That's right," she said. "I was."' Karin Salenko lowered her eyes.

'So you argued about it?'

The ice-cubes rattled in her tall glass as she drank. 'You have to understand. She adores her father. When I left him, she blamed me for everything.'

'And you haven't seen her since then?' I said. 'Since August?'

'That was the last time.' Suddenly she began to cry.

At first I didn't realise she was crying because she cried in a way I'd never seen before. She kept her head very still, level, too, and stared out across the room. She didn't try to hide the tears. I asked her if she was all right. If I could get her anything. She didn't answer.

'You see, I have a bad feeling,' she said eventually.

She pushed the knuckles of her left hand into her eye.

I saw the car standing on that piece of waste-ground, both doors open, like an insect on the point of flying. But it didn't move.

'How did you find out that she'd disappeared?' I said.

'My ex-husband rang me up. She hadn't sent him a birthday card, that was the reason. He'd called her three nights in a row, but she was never there. He wondered if I knew anything.'

'You didn't, though.'

'No.' Karin Salenko reached behind her neck with both hands and, lifting her hair off her shoulders, twisted it a couple of times and then released it. I'd seen Nina do the same thing. 'I was almost happy when he told me. I was glad. But then I started thinking, she'd never do that, not Nina. She'd never forget his birthday.'

I took the address book out of my pocket and handed it to her. 'Your ex-husband,' I said. 'Could you tell me if his address is in this book?'

She stared at the book for a moment before she opened it.

'Yes, it's here,' she said. 'Jan Salenko.'

I held my hand out for the book. She hesitated, then gave it back.

'Other people walking around with her things,' she said. 'It's like she's dead or something.'

'I was a friend of hers,' I said, 'before all this.' I paused. 'I loved her.'

There was a silence.

'I'm sorry,' she said. 'I didn't know.'

I wanted to change the subject. I was looking down at the book I'd stolen, a dark shape on my palm. 'You kept his name.'

'Sorry?'

'You still call yourself Salenko, even though – '

'Oh, I see. Yes. Well, I never liked my name before.'

She left her chair and walked to the window. Her feet were silent on the carpet. All I could hear were the ice-cubes in her glass. The sound of her moving behind me was the sound of a chandelier in the wind.

'We're not a close family,' she went on. 'Sometimes it seems like we tried to get as far away from each other as we could.'

'You too?'

She was staring out into the darkness. 'Especially me.'

When she talked about her family, the words seemed to curdle in her mouth and, just for a moment, she reminded me of myself. She'd had some kind of bullet fired at her. The way she was behaving now revealed it. The path of the bullet, the rhythm of the knife.

Thunder rolled on the horizon. It was so continuous, so unbroken, it could have been a plane circling in the sky, waiting for clearance.

At the window, Karin Salenko shivered. 'I think it's going to storm.'

I thought I should leave. I rose to my feet, but didn't move towards the door. I just stood in the middle of the room. The carpet was deep-pile, ice-blue. I drew a pattern on it with my stick.

'I had her when I was sixteen. It was too young.' The edges in her voice, they'd taken over. 'In that part of the world,' she said, 'you know, people . . .' She tailed off again, in that way she had.

'Sure,' I said. 'I know.'

I didn't, though. I didn't even know what part of the world we were talking about. She went to the fridge and brought me another beer. I hadn't asked for one. It was because she wanted a drink herself. I watched her drop new cubes into her glass.

'You don't have to drink it,' she said.

'It's all right,' I said. 'I'll drink it.' I sat down again.

She stood over by the window, as before.

'It's ironic, really,' she said. 'He isn't even her real father.'

'Who isn't?'

'Jan. Jan Salenko.' The ice-cubes jangled as she drank. 'I already had her when I married him.'

'So who's her real father?'

She turned to me, her dress flashing in a hundred places as it caught the light. 'You don't understand. I was raped.' She was laughing. 'I don't know why I'm telling you all this.'

Because I was blind? Because she was drunk? I didn't know either. I was still drawing patterns in the carpet with my stick.

'Did Nina know?' I asked her.

'I always kept it from her. But maybe she found out. Maybe that's why she disappeared – '

'Found out?'

'The truth.'

I hesitated. 'Which is what?'

She didn't answer. She'd lowered her head and she was shaking it from side to side.

'You can't talk about that?' I said.

'No,' she said. 'I can't talk about that.'

'Can anyone?'

She lit a cigarette. It was a long cigarette, with a white filter. When she spoke again, her voice was bitter, almost vitriolic. 'My mother. Edith Hekmann. She'd probably tell you.' She took the smoke into her lungs, then blew it out as if she hated having it inside her. 'Up there in the mountains. It's like a different century up there.'

'Where?'

She mentioned the name of a village. I'd never heard of it.

She stared into the corner of the room. The tears came again. I waited for a moment, and then I muttered something about my train. I heard her follow me across the room.

'No, that's the kitchen,' she said.

'I've never had much of a sense of direction,' I told her with a smile. 'Ever since I was young.'

'Is that when you went blind? When you were young?'

'No, no. It happened last year.'

At the front door she touched me on the arm. 'You came all this way. And I behaved so – I just cried the whole time.' She fumbled in her bag and handed me a card. 'It's a special discount voucher for the casino,' she said. 'You get a pile of free chips to start you off.'

I looked down into her face, which was eager suddenly, her eyes bright behind the smeared mascara. 'Do people ever say that you and Nina look alike?'

'They used to,' she said. 'When Nina was thirteen, fourteen. They used to think we were sisters. But it was probably just because we were so close in age.' She studied the end of her cigarette for a moment. 'Inside, we're not alike at all.'

'I'm sorry,' I said. 'About what happened.'

She nodded quickly, sniffed. 'That's all right,' she said. 'It was a long time ago.'

Outside, the wind was stronger. Clouds sliding past the rooftops like the world was under ice and moving fast.

She'd told me there were always taxis on the seafront. I flagged one down. All the way to the train station there was that smell. The smell of things wedged under rocks. Things in shells.

I left the voucher on the seat. There'd be someone who'd appreciate it. Who knows, maybe they'd even get lucky.

I'm on my way to Nina's apartment. It's not far from the flower market. When I reach the street, it's dawn and people are unloading vans. The stalls are open, colourful. The cool morning air has seams of fragrance running through it.

I walk into a courtyard, pass beneath an archway. I climb a narrow winding staircase. It's on the third floor. A dark wooden door on an even darker landing. Part of me's excited. *So this is where she lives.* Her house-keys are warm, almost illicit in my hand. And yet I feel as if I know the place, as if I've climbed these stairs before, with her, after a dinner out somewhere, or a party, our arms around each other, drunk.

Then I'm in her bed. The pillow smells just like her skin. I lift my head. She's standing by the window.

She's wearing a long, dark-blue dress; her arms are bare. There's an expression on her face I can't decipher. It's not surprise at seeing me in her apartment, or anger. It's not even curiosity.

'Nina?' I say.

She's standing by the window, looking down into the street. The wall behind her is plaster: grey and cream and pale-pink. A slab of bright, white sunlight falls across it.

'Nina?'

'I used to be,' she says.

I'm crying out as I wake up. There were two people in the compartment with me before I fell asleep. I begin to apologise.

'I'm sorry,' I say, 'a nightmare – '

Then I look around and realise I'm talking to myself. The compartment's empty.

By the time I reached the Kosminsky it was almost two in the morning. Three messages were waiting for me at hotel reception, all of them from Munck. Upstairs in my room I dialled his number at police headquarters. It didn't surprise me when the switchboard put me through. I'd already identified Munck as a man who worked late into the night. Either he'd never been married or he'd been married too long. He'd forgotten how to go home.

'Munck,' I said.

'Ah, Blom,' he said. 'Feeling better?'

'Much better, thank you.'

Two youths had been arrested, he told me. They were to be charged with the theft of Nina Salenko's car. He described them for me. They were both fourteen years old. One wore a denim jacket with the arms cut off. His hair was light-brown, shoulder-length. The other one was thin, with cropped hair and a speech impediment, a kind of lisp.

They didn't sound like anyone I knew.

Munck described part of the interrogation. Both youths were shown a photograph of Nina. The one in the denim jacket took a long, close look.

'Wouldn't mind a bit of that,' he said.

Munck asked him if he'd seen her before.

The youth grinned. 'Didn't know we was here to talk about girls.'

Slatnick came up behind the youth and clouted him on the head with the back of his hand.

'You should've seen Slatnick,' Munck said. 'Like the shadow of a cloud, he was, the way he came up behind that boy.' He chuckled. 'The boy never knew what hit him.'

'I can imagine,' I said.

Munck described how the youth bellowed, as much in shock as pain, and clamped one hand over his ear.

'You've never seen her before?' Munck asked the youth again.

'I told you. No.'

He turned to the friend, the thin one with the lisp. 'You?'

'No.'

The story that emerged was simple. The two youths had been in the city centre, drinking. It was a Wednesday night and they were bored. When they saw a car with the keys left in the ignition, they couldn't believe it. It was like an invitation, a gift. How could they say no?

I interrupted. 'The keys were in it?'

'Yes.'

'Did they see anybody on the street?'

'Nobody. It was late. Two-thirty in the morning.'

'You believe them, don't you.'

'Yes, I do.' Munck sounded gloomy.

It was a breakthrough, but it took him backwards. Nina had disappeared – but not in the car. That was all he knew. Or anybody knew. There were fewer facts than ever.

'Would you mind coming in tomorrow?' he said. 'I need to talk to you.'

I went to bed early. It had been a long night and I was tired. As I lay on my side, waiting for sleep, I thought of Karin Salenko – her lacquered hair, that lazy voice of hers, the tall drinks. I would never have guessed that she was Nina's mother. I remembered what she'd said about looking like her daughter. She'd said something else, too, something unusual. *Inside, we're not alike at all.* I could only think one thing: it must have been the inside that I was looking at.

The next evening, just after sunset, I left the hotel. The police headquarters was located in the 2nd district, on the west bank of the river. I took the most direct route, over one of the city's famous bridges. There were old-fashioned street-lamps, which gave the stonework a deceptive warmth, and on the balustrades there were statues of nineteenth-century statesmen and generals. I was thinking of Visser as I walked along. He hadn't shown his face since that evening with Munck in the suburbs. He was following me, though. I knew that much. What else would he have been doing on that lonely piece of waste-ground at six o'clock on a Tuesday evening? Halfway across the bridge I stopped and leaned on the parapet. I looked down. Currents twisted like muscle in the slow green body of water. Weeds floated by in clumps. Broken branches, plastic bags. Was Visser watching me now? And, if so, what would be going through his mind? Did he think I was suffering? Did he think I might jump? I glanced over my shoulder. Stranger after stranger walking past.

When I arrived at the police headquarters I was told to wait. It was a grim eight-storey block, with metal grilles fixed like cages over the ground-floor windows. The radiator next to the front entrance had been covered with a piece of carpet. I thought it was probably because the police didn't want to hurt offenders accidentally on their way into the building. They'd rather hurt them deliberately, in a room with no windows, somewhere higher up. From where I was sitting I could see an officer in dark-green fatigues, with his back against the wall and his legs on a bench. He was reading a comic-book that Victor sometimes read. A man walked in off the street and sat down opposite me.

'All right?' he said.

I nodded. 'How are you?'

He wore a soiled check jacket and trainers, and he had a deep cut on his forehead.

I waited almost half an hour. At last a metal door scraped open and Munck emerged. It could only have been Munck. Each step he took, his foot flicked at the air, then slapped down on the floor. The way he walked, it always sounded as if the floor was wet. But there was someone with him, someone I didn't recognise.

Munck shook my hand. 'I'm sorry to have kept you, Martin.' He turned to include the other man. 'This is Jan Salenko. Nina's father.'

Salenko took my hand awkwardly and shook it for too long. 'I just arrived in the city this morning,' he said, 'by bus.'

He was one of those people who say too much, either out of nervousness or a desire to please.

'I thought we'd go round the corner for a drink,' Munck said. 'Mr Salenko?'

'Yes. A quick one, maybe. Thank you.'

I asked Munck if Slatnick was coming.

'No,' Munck said. 'He's off sick.'

Psychological problems, I imagined. That stone-age buckle of bone above his eyes, that shot-gun nose. It couldn't be easy.

Munck took us to a place called Smoltczyk. He liked it, he said, because it was entirely without character. There was nothing to look at. No pictures, no hunting-horns, no china donkeys. It was just a bar, with drinks in it. I nodded. Salenko nodded, too. We ordered three brandies.

'That should keep the chill out,' Munck said.

As soon the drinks came, Salenko leaned forwards, both hands round his glass. 'I understand from the detective here that you were the last person to see . . .' He hesitated. 'To see my daughter.' He couldn't bring himself to say her name.

'So they tell me.' I stared at him, but I couldn't establish any physical resemblance. Then I remembered what Karin had said. Of course. Why would Salenko resemble Nina?

'That's what I'm told,' I said.

'How was she? Did she seem,' and his hands opened, showing me his glass, 'upset?'

'Not really,' I said. 'Actually, it was me who was upset.'

My answer seemed to take Salenko by surprise. It took me by surprise as well. But I'd been asked the same question so many times. There was what I'd felt, and I was tired of walking round it.

'I'd been going out with her for about six weeks,' I went on. 'That was the night she told me it was over.'

I wasn't looking at Munck, but I knew his eyebrows were halfway to his hairline. This was the first he'd heard of my rejection.

'I'm sorry,' Salenko said.

'Yeah,' I said. 'I was sorry, too.' I sipped at my brandy, felt the warmth spread through me. 'Strictly speaking,' I said, 'you're not her father, are you?'

'Not strictly speaking, no.'

'You know who is?'

'No. I never asked.'

I watched Salenko carefully. The silence seemed to embarrass him.

'I just treated her like my own,' he went on, 'and she grew up believing it. She was only a few months old when we were married, her mother and me. Not even talking yet.' He paused, thinking back. 'First word she ever learned was Dad.' He smiled sadly, looked down into his drink.

Then he roused himself. 'Karin, she never told me anything. She didn't like to talk about the past. If it ever came up, she'd throw things. Or she'd drink. Or leave the house.' He tilted his glass on the table and watched the brandy climb the side. 'I didn't want to lose her, I suppose.'

'But you did,' I said.

'Did what?'

'Lose her.'

'In the end I did,' he said, 'but that was later.'

He took a deep breath. When he breathed out, I could hear his heartbeat in it.

'Something you've got to understand,' he said. 'I didn't deserve her. That's what I felt when I first set eyes on her, and I never stopped feeling it the whole time we were married.'

There was a river outside the village where he lived and one day he was standing on the bridge. A truck was parked at the far end, facing away from him. He saw a girl climb into the back of it, over the tailboard. Her dress looked handed-down – too big for her, anyway; it swirled around her skinny legs, made climbing difficult. She was about eight years old. Then a man walked out of the field and up the grass bank, and the truck lurched with his weight as he got in. The girl was standing in the back, both hands on the metal rail that ran along behind the cab. The man shouted something from the window, probably, *Hold on*, then the engine caught and the truck set off down the road, heading west, and that was all there was to remember, think of, dream about: that girl clinging to the rail as distance claimed the truck, her brown hair loose and streaming against the shoulders of her ill-fitting, pale-blue dress. Afterwards he was still standing on the bridge, only the road was empty now, and the wires that linked one telegraph pole to the next, the sun was shining through them, and the way their shadows fell across the tar, it looked as though a car had braked hard, as though there'd been some kind of accident.

By the time she was fifteen – the age he'd been that morning on the bridge – she was the prettiest girl in the county. She didn't seem to know it either; it was as if she'd never looked in a mirror, or even in a window, or a pond. He was nothing special, though. He won a memory contest once by reciting an entire page of the local telephone directory, not one name out of order either, but where would that get him with a girl who could turn his stomach over like a ploughed field just by looking at him? And besides, his memory was something people mocked him with. There was a rhyme that everybody in the village knew:

Jan Jan
The Memory Man
Remember remember
As much as you can

Remember you're ugly
Remember you're weak
Remember that rubbish
Comes out when you speak

With his memory, of course, it was impossible for him to forget the rhyme – and verses existed that were far less innocent.

Jan Salenko smiled ruefully into his drink. He didn't think Karin had ever called him 'Memory', as the others did, nor had she ever chanted those rhymes at him. When she saw him in the village she'd say, 'Hello, Jan Salenko,' as if the sound of his name said all at once amused her. She was always friendly, but somehow that was worse than if she hadn't noticed him at all.

Then something happened. Nobody knew for sure what it was, only that Karin wasn't seen around any more. The autumn he was twenty-three and the whole of the winter that came after. She just disappeared. And when she appeared again, in the spring, she had a baby. But there was no mention of a husband. And nobody could say who the father was. There were jokes, of course – immaculate conception, virgin birth; there was even some sarcastic talk about the second coming (the trouble was, the baby was a girl). The year before, Karin had been courted by half the boys in the county. Now they stayed away, every single one of them.

He gathered his courage. One morning towards the end of April he walked out to old man Hekmann's place. It was a fine day, clouds running in the sky, trees with their new leaves. He found Karin crouching in the shadows on the back porch. She had her baby with her. No one else was about.

'Oh,' she said, 'it's you.'

She stepped out into the sunlight. Her eyes were dull and her face looked thin. Her brown ringlets were tied back with a piece of chicken wire.

He stood in front of her and began to remember her out loud. He remembered every time he'd ever seen her in his life, starting at the bridge eight years before. He described where and when each meeting had taken place, how the weather had been on each occasion and what she'd looked like, not just the clothes she was wearing, but the smallest details – how long her hair was or whether she had a graze on her knee. If she'd spoken to him – or to anyone else, for that matter – he recalled the words for her. If she hadn't spoken, he told her whether she'd smiled or not, and what kind of smile it was. At last he reached the most recent encounter, which was still happening, of course, and he told her what he'd remembered so far – the April sun, the wind, her faded dress, the wariness he saw in her, the split in her lip (had someone hit her?), the baby sleeping in her arms, her first three words.

Afterwards, she was silent for a moment, then she looked at him in an entirely new way and said, 'That's the best present anyone ever gave me.' Then she looked off into the trees for a long time.

They didn't talk much after that, but he wasn't uncomfortable sitting on the porch with her. He didn't think she wanted him to go. He felt he fitted cleanly into the air beside her. They could've been two staves in a fence.

The next time he sat on her porch, three days later, she turned to him with the baby in her arms and said, 'Sometimes I think I'm going to drown the both of us.'

Her eyes moved to the trees and the shallow pond that lay beyond the clearing, just an area of grey light on the ground. 'Better to be done with it,' she murmured. 'No one will have me now, not with a child.'

He had to wait until his heart slowed down. He remembered the exact look of the trees and the temperature of the air.

'I would,' he said. 'I'd have you.'

She stared at him, and then she laughed. He didn't know what she meant by the laughter. For a moment he feared that the rhyme might follow it. *Jan Jan The Memory Man* . . . But the laughter stopped and she was still staring at him.

'Why don't you marry me then,' she said, 'and take us away from here?'

Leaves whispered at the edge of the clearing and the sun went in.

'Marry me, Jan Salenko.'

Salenko cleared his throat, then looked across at Munck. 'I'm sorry. I ran on a bit.'

Lifting his glass, he finished his brandy. I finished mine, too. I knew something Jan Salenko didn't. His ex-wife, Karin, had told me how the child had happened. We were the same, I was thinking, Nina and I. We'd both come close. With me it was a bullet. With her, that shallow pond beyond the trees.

'Another drink, Mr Salenko?' Munck said.

'Thank you, no. I should be going. My bus . . .' He rose out of his chair.

When he'd gone, I looked at Munck.

'I'll have one,' I said.

'This case,' Munck said.

He had something on his mind. I waited. The brandies arrived.

'You knew her pretty well,' he said, 'didn't you.'

'I don't know about well.' I swirled my new drink in its glass. 'I told you. I only met her in November.'

'She took drugs.'

'Probably.'

'Probably?'

'I never saw her take any.'

'No, of course not.' Munck drank. When the brandy went down, it made a sound that doves make when they're nesting – a kind of muffled squawk. 'She was a stripper, wasn't she?'

'As far as I know, she worked behind the bar.'

'In a strip club.'

'In a club that has dancers,' I said, 'sometimes.'

He let that go. Cradling his drink, he peered down into it. 'She slept around.'

'She slept with me,' I said. 'That's all I can be sure of.' I leaned forwards. 'What are you getting at, Munck?'

'I'm just telling you what they're saying at the precinct.'

It was another example of Detective Munck's technique. He could say anything he liked in that soporific voice of his, the worst thing he could think of, and then he could step back with his hands raised and disown it all. It allowed him to provoke you and remain your friend.

'They're saying, girls like her, they disappear.'

I drank some of my brandy. It was very smooth. I thought it must be imported.

'Down at the precinct they're saying she's probably gone off somewhere. Be a hooker, something like that. Make some money.' He mentioned a port in a neighbouring country that was famous for its red-light district. 'They're saying, girls like her, that's what they do.'

I swallowed some more brandy. Definitely imported.

'They're saying, girls like her, forget it. They've got it coming, they're asking for it, they get what they deserve.' He paused for breath. 'Are they right?'

'Munck,' I said.

'That's what they're saying.' He shrugged, then he emptied his glass. 'You want another?'

'No. I think I'll go now.'

He ordered one for himself.

'What else are they saying?' I asked him.

'They're saying she could've been killed. That wouldn't surprise them, a girl like her. That wouldn't surprise them at all.'

I lifted my glass to my lips, but there was nothing in it.

'Sure you don't want another?' Munck said.

'I'm sure.'

'You loved her, didn't you.'

I nodded.

'She told you it was over.'

'Yes.'

He paused long enough for me to hear the whole line of a song that was playing on a radio somewhere.

'You want to know what they're saying, Martin? I'll tell you what they're saying. They're saying you could've done it.'

That night, at one o'clock, I unlocked the door to Loots' car and climbed into the driver's seat. I turned the steering-wheel from side to side, just to get the feel, the weight of it. I tested the pedals with my feet. Down to the floor they went, resisting; up they sprang again. I moved through the gears once or twice. The transition from second to third was awkward; you could end up in fifth, if you weren't careful. Then I was ready to fit the key into the ignition. When was the last time I'd driven? A Thursday evening, almost a year ago.

I'd called round on Loots after my drink with Munck. Loots didn't know I was coming, and his enthusiastic welcome startled me. I was still labouring up the stairs when he leaned over the banisters and shouted, 'Blom, there's someone here I want you to meet.'

On the landing he took my arm and led me into the apartment and down the corridor. He stopped me in front of his cork-tiled wall.

'I want to introduce you to Juliet,' he said. 'She's going to be my assistant.'

Juliet was a sex dummy, one of those plastic inflatable models with a mouth shaped like an O. She stood against the cork tiles with a look of shock on her face. I knew exactly how she felt. I'd been there myself.

'What do you think?' Loots said.

'Does she have any experience?'

Loots laughed.

'Why Juliet?' I asked.

'She's beautiful – and young . . .'

I reached out and touched her. Her breasts were small and sharp, like ice-cream cones. 'Loots,' I said, 'you're going to have to buy her a bikini.'

He thought that was funny, too.

I explained why I'd dropped in. I wanted to know if I could borrow his car. 'Don't worry,' I said. 'I'm not going to do the driving.'

Loots chuckled at the idea.

'I've got someone to drive me,' I said, leaving a silence that seemed suspicious, loaded with unanswered questions.

'And who's that?' he asked, as he was supposed to.

I acted a little shy about it. 'You remember that woman at the wedding – '

'The one who stood you up?'

'That's her.'

'And now she's seen the error of her ways?' Loots was shaking his head. 'How do you do it, Blom?'

'It's only for tonight,' I said. 'I'll bring it back first thing in the morning. Anyway, you won't be needing it. You'll be quite happy here – with Juliet.'

I was grinning as I turned the key in the ignition.

The first part was more difficult than I'd expected. It was the lights of other cars, their headlights as they came towards me: they literally blinded me for a moment. I had some problems with spacial relationships as well, though perhaps I was simply adjusting to a car that wasn't mine. I turned out of Loots' street, making for the Ring. I passed the blue neon sign of the Saskia Hotel, the Royal Gardens and the floodlit Doric columns of the National Philharmonic. I crossed the river west of the city centre. From the elevated road I could look down on the community housing of the 15th district: tower blocks and parked cars and meaningless areas of grass. Sometimes I thought I was driving too slowly. At other times I felt as though I was going to hit something or get pulled over. But nothing like that happened. In twenty minutes I was easing into the slow lane on the motorway and heading north.

The bright lights were all behind me now. I stepped on the accelerator. If a car got too close, I tilted the rear-view mirror so it couldn't dazzle me. The motorway climbed into the hills and darkened. People always claimed this stretch of road was dangerous – but what was dangerous for everybody else was safe for me. I relaxed my neck and shoulders, leaning back against the headrest, straightening my arms. My white cane and dark glasses were lying on the floor behind my seat. If I was stopped, I'd give the police a false name and address (though not the same as the ones I'd given Arnold). If they tracked me down, I'd deny all knowledge of the incident. I'd look shocked, incredulous. 'I'm blind,' I'd say. 'How on earth could I be driving?' I'd be staring past the policeman's shoulder and I'd be smiling at nothing. My head would probably be wobbling, too. 'I can't drive,' I'd say. 'There must be some mistake.'

The road was still climbing and I had to shift into third. There were patches of fog now. I felt as if someone was hurling rags at me; it made me want to duck. I took the next exit, a two-lane road that twisted eastwards through the hills. There wouldn't be much traffic on it; I'd have it to myself. And it was then, as I saw the empty road ahead, the unbroken darkness on either side, that I had an inspiration. Obvious, really. I couldn't believe I hadn't thought of it before. *Turn the headlights off.* If only Visser could've seen me! With his earnest face and his Stalinesque moustache. My laughter filled the inside of the car.

For a while I just drove, not thinking at all. What a relief it was to be out of the city – away from the wide, grey streets, away from the grime and the decay. I was in a trance, half-dreaming, when I saw a car swing round the bend, its lights full-beam. It was in the middle of the road and heading straight towards me. At the last minute it swerved, tyres shrieking. I watched its tail-lights yo-yo in the rear-view mirror. Shake a soft-drinks can and pull the ring. That's some indication of how my heart felt then. I could only suppose the driver hadn't seen me. Still, nothing had come of it.

Not long afterwards a huge, veined leaf slapped on to the windscreen. I jumped, then grinned. I was wondering how they'd write that sound in Victor's comic-books. SHLOK! maybe. Or WHAP! I stared at the leaf: a deformed hand, with five attempts at fingers. My dream was happening to leaves. There was a fizzing in my chest again. That narrow miss, and then the leaf. WHAP! I turned my wipers on and sent it skimming back into the night.

Slowly my thoughts spread sideways.

So. I was a suspect now. I could see how Munck (or Munck's colleagues) might have arrived at that conclusion. I'd been the last person to see Nina alive. Add to that, I'd tried to make a run for it in the hotel (after registering under a false name). And I'd behaved suspiciously when called upon to identify her car. I even had a motive. It was an old motive, one of the oldest there was, but it was good enough. She'd told me she was leaving me. She'd said it was over. Jealousy, resentment, wounded pride – that was all it took. The circumstantial evidence was overwhelming. Once, when I was working in the bookshop, I'd picked up something on aircraft technology. I'd only read a few pages, but one passage had always stuck in my mind – a description of the computer targeting system in certain fighter planes. The target appeared on a screen, with four white lines round it. The white lines formed a square known as 'the kill box'. Whatever lay inside the square could be destroyed by the aircraft's missiles. That I was thinking of it now was no coincidence. It didn't necessarily have to do with being annihilated. It was simply the idea that you could be targeted by forces that were beyond your control. Nina had disappeared and I was thought to be responsible.

I was up in the hills. Up in the hills and heading east. I'd opened the window and cold air was rushing through the car. In the rear-view mirror I saw papers rise up off the back seat like a flock of ghostly birds. They whirled about, they jostled one another. A big brown envelope dipped past my shoulder and flew out into the night. I watched it shrink in the darkness behind the car; I hoped it wasn't anything important. I took a deep breath and breathed out slowly. The air was so fresh. It had an aromatic edge to it. I wasn't sure if it was fir trees releasing resin or some herb that happened to be growing wild.

Nina had disappeared.

I pulled the car off the road. I shifted into neutral, put the handbrake on, switched off the engine. Behind me I heard the papers settle. Buttoning my coat, I opened the door and got out.

There was the city, far below. A loose collection of lights, milky and blurred, as if seen through frosted glass. Over to my right, the motorway – one long illuminated line, bright as the past that I'd forgotten. My new life was the gloom on either side of it, the darkness between roads. I could sense a headache forming, the amorphous shape of it – a pressure. I emptied two pills on to my hand and swallowed them.

Nina.

I was the one she'd left. I should've been the only one who was missing her. But suddenly there were dozens of us, all missing her in different ways: Karin Salenko, Jan Salenko, Greersen, Detectives Munck and Slatnick, Robert Kolan . . .

Christmas had been difficult for me. I stayed up late most nights and went for walks around the frozen lake, thinking of Nina. Once, on New Year's Eve, I ventured out across the ice, my footsteps echoing as if in some great hall. A fine, powdery snow blew towards me, thin snaking lines of it, reminding me of electricity, or the way light moves on the surface of a swimming-pool. I would never see her again, yet images of her rose constantly before my eyes. In motel rooms, in cafés, in her car. Our dinner at the Metropole. Or the first night, in that mansion near the woods . . . I had to put her behind me, I knew that. My life would go on without her. Still, I thought it might be easier if I pretended she no longer existed.

To some extent, I must have succeeded. Because, when Munck came to me in January and told me that she'd disappeared, I wanted to say, *I know. I made it happen. Like a magician.* Of course, he was talking about disappearance at another level. A level that was, to me at least, irrelevant. As far as I was concerned, she couldn't disappear any more than she already had. It's the same as someone telling you that someone you used to know has died. Since you were no longer actively aware of their existence, from your point of view they might as well have been dead all along; you might even see their death as a form of overkill. Earlier in the evening Munck had said, *They're saying you could've done it*. I was being blamed for something that had happened in another dimension. He might as well have told me that I'd killed a ghost. It was abstract, esoteric. Tautological.

I was floating now, the codeine dreaming in my blood. Slowly I turned away from the view. I noticed a car parked on the other side of the road. Its lights were dimmed.

Curious, I walked towards it. I thought I could see someone inside, a shape behind the wheel. But as I walked towards the car, it started to reverse.

'Who are you?' I called out.

It was moving backwards, silently, its lights still dimmed. I was already too far away from it to make out who the driver was.

I began to shout. 'Visser? Is that you?'

I was running now, but I couldn't keep up.

'Visser?' I was shouting. 'What do you want?'

I watched the car withdraw into the darkness further down the hill. I stood on the road, uncertain what to do. A crack opened in my skull. White light poured in, bounced from one curved piece of bone to another. Gasping, I bent down. I clutched my head between my hands. My cane dropped away without a sound.

I tried to count the seconds – one . . . two . . . three . . . four . . .

Then I could see again. That codeine, it was dying on me. Or maybe I'd taken too much of it.

Walking back to Loots' car, I didn't look behind me once. I didn't even listen for tyres on the road below, an engine firing in the distance.

But there was a fear.

The fear that, any moment now, I'd feel a gentle nudging at my legs and that, when I glanced over my shoulder, the car would be behind me, right behind me, its front bumper touching the back of my knees and no one at the wheel.

I parked Loots' car outside his apartment and dropped his keys through the letterbox in an envelope. When he rang me later that day I still hadn't been to bed.

'You sound upset,' he said.

I told him I was fine, just tired. There was a deadened area inside my head, like the shape a hare leaves in the grass where it's been sleeping.

'How did it go last night?'

I didn't say anything.

'She didn't show up, did she?'

'Well – '

'I thought so.'

I asked him what he meant by that.

'My car,' he said. 'It doesn't look as if it's moved.'

I stood outside the building where Robert Kolan lived and looked both ways. Rain dripped from the trees on to the paving-stones below. The street was empty. As I paid the taxi-driver, I thought I saw a man in a herring-bone overcoat standing on the corner, but it must have been an illusion, the moon shining through bare branches, a chance pattern of light and shadow.

I'd called Kolan earlier to arrange a meeting. I had to talk to somebody about what Munck had said, and Loots and Gregory were no use to me; they'd just sympathise. I wanted somebody who knew Nina, and Kolan seemed the obvious, almost the only, choice. But when I called him, his first question was: 'How did you get my number?'

I tried Munck's theory on him. 'There are intelligent life-forms out in space,' I said, 'and they're watching you right now.'

'Don't give me that shit. I asked you a question.'

I grinned into the phone. 'What are you so nervous about?'

'I'm hanging up – '

'Wait a minute, wait a minute.' Kolan's paranoia didn't bother me;

I'd already prepared an answer. 'Nina gave it to me once,' I said. 'She made me memorise it, in case of an emergency. She told me I had to call you first.'

He seemed satisfied with that. (I'd known he would be; it addressed his vanity.) And once that awkwardness was dispensed with, he agreed to see me.

It was an old house, with tall trees in front of it which resembled the trees outside the clinic. Pieces of plaster and roof-tile had fallen into the garden and a sun-dial lay under a bush, its markings cloaked in moss. Kolan had told me there was a flight of stone steps on the right-hand side of the house. His apartment was at the top. Though it was three in the morning, I could hear music. He was still awake.

I found a door at the top of the steps and knocked on it. I had to knock four times before it opened. Kolan stood there, holding a cigarette. 'I thought you were the police again.'

'They've been here then?'

He looked past me, into the darkness. 'You'd better come in.'

The lighting was low in his apartment and there was a stick of incense burning. I watched Kolan as he sat on the threadbare carpet and began to roll a joint.

'Was it Munck?' I asked him.

'They didn't tell me their names.'

'They always tell you their names.'

'In that case, I forgot.'

He trickled grass into a cigarette paper that was already filled with a thin roll of tobacco.

'The police,' I said. 'Did one of them chew gum?'

'Christ, you're as bad as they are.'

I sat down on a chair by the window. His music reminded me of the music they play when something unpleasant's about to happen. You hear it in airports and mental homes. You hear it at the dentist as well. Sometimes you hear it as you lift out of an anaesthetic.

'They told you about the car,' I said.

'Yeah.'

'They're saying she might've been killed.' I paused. 'They think I might've done it.'

He licked the narrow strip of glue on the cigarette paper and stuck it down, then he ran his finger and thumb along the length of it several times, making sure it was sealed. There was a kind of fussy expertise about the way he built his joints. He should've been exhibiting at country fairs, along with the basket-weavers and the ceramicists.

'I've even got a motive,' I said.

'What's that?'

'She was leaving me. I didn't want her to.'

'Do you smoke?'

'No.' I reached into my pocket for my bottle of pain-killers. I tipped two pills on to my hand and knocked them back.

'What's that you're taking?'

'Codeine. For my head.'

'Yeah, right.' His joint crackled as he drew on it. He must've missed some of the seeds. 'Her frame of mind,' he said. 'I've been doing some thinking about it.'

Something had been worrying her. He had the feeling that was why she'd asked him over on Tuesday night. And she'd made a date to see him on the Wednesday, too. He often sat in her apartment while she talked. He never said much. What happened was, she'd launch into a kind of monologue. But he had to be there, otherwise she couldn't do it. Sometimes there were drugs as well, to help the process. He'd score for her. There was someone in the 15th district, out near the cemetery. He could get them anything they wanted.

'She won't do it herself. Thinks it's squalid.' Kolan's voice pinched as he held the smoke inside his lungs. 'If I'd seen her Wednesday night, that's what would've happened.'

'You've no idea what it was?'

He studied the roach. Then he brought it to his lips, inhaled three times quickly, dropped it on to a saucer. 'I was thinking about her being worried,' he said, 'and it reminded me of something else.'

She'd called him a couple of weeks back. She'd had a strange experience. A man had walked up to her on the street and he'd shown her a picture of herself. She didn't know the man. She'd never seen him before. He was a complete stranger. But it was definitely a picture of her. It unsettled her. Maybe she'd been living the wrong way, she said. She couldn't explain it. It was just a feeling. But things had to change. A different job, a different apartment. Maybe even a different country.

'She told me I could come too.'

Kolan smiled absent-mindedly. Then he started to roll another joint. He had to keep scraping his hair back behind his ears, otherwise it fell over his face and he couldn't see what he was doing.

'Maybe that's what she did,' he said. 'Maybe she just left and decided not to take me after all. Or she just forgot.' The smile was still there – absent-minded, self-deprecating. 'Keys in a car, it's like clothes on a beach, you know what I mean? It's a smokescreen. It's the kind of thing she'd do.'

I thought about it for a while. I remembered what she'd said on the street that night, just before I turned away from her. *There's too much going on. I need some time.* Then I remembered what had happened just before that.

'What is it?' Kolan said.

'It's something she said that night. I forgot all about it.' A chill spread across my shoulderblades. It was in my hair as well, at the back. 'She said there was someone staring at her. Following her. She said she'd seen him before.' I looked at Kolan. 'You think it was the same man?'

'Don't know. Could be.'

'This man she told you about,' I said. 'She didn't know him, but he had a picture of her.'

'Right.'

'What kind of picture was it?'

'It was a photograph.'

'How did he get hold of it?'

'Who knows?' Kolan stood up and walked over to the stereo. 'She wasn't really interested in the guy with the picture. Not in itself, anyway. It was what they meant, that's what interested her. She saw it as a sign, an omen.' Once he'd changed the music, he sat down again. He was holding his new joint between his fingers and looking at it. 'Or maybe she saw it as a warning.'

'Did she tell you what he looked like?'

'You're not listening, man. She wasn't interested.' He lit the joint and took his first hit off it, then he lay back on a pile of cushions. 'She said there was something weird about him. The way he looked at her or something.'

When I got back to the hotel I called Munck. He didn't answer. Well, perhaps that wasn't so surprising, at five-thirty in the morning. I tried again just after sunrise. This time he was there, yawning into the phone. I told him what had happened at the railway station.

'She seemed afraid suddenly,' I said. 'She asked me to walk her to her car.' I paused. 'I thought it might be important.'

'This man,' Munck said. 'Did she say anything about him?'

'She'd said she'd seen him before.'

'She didn't describe him to you, though?'

'No.'

'Why didn't you tell me this before?'

'I don't know. I forgot all about it.'

Munck didn't say anything.

'You don't think she was just imagining it, do you?' I said. 'I mean, that's what I thought at the time.'

'Excuse me, Martin.' Munck spoke to someone who was in the room with him, then came back on the line. 'We'll check with Central Station, see if they can tell us anything.'

After he'd hung up, I lay on my bed thinking about what Kolan had told me. What I realised was this: for all her unpredictability, Nina was a still point. She was attractive, in the literal sense: people were drawn to her. She was the box of matches for their stack of firewood. This could be good or bad. There was loyalty and then there was obsession. They shared the same root. *He'd kill someone if I asked him to.*

My eyes were closing. I could have slept, but I resisted it. I had the feeling I was getting somewhere.

So. Things collected around her. Things accrued. I imagined she was often surprised when she found out. No, more than surprised. Astonished.

Even, sometimes, frightened.

That was one way her disappearance could've come about. The man with the photograph was a blueprint for it. Leave that magnetic quality in place, but change the situation, change the details. Funny. I'd always thought of her as somebody who made things happen. I'd thought that was her brand of magic, her particular gift. I'd thought that was her. Now I wasn't so sure.

What if you turned the whole thing round?

Suddenly I saw her as the centre of an area of ignorance. She was ignorant of how she was being affected, and ignorant, in turn, of her effect. You could map it like an earthquake. Where she was, the ignorance was at its most intense. It wasn't stupidity exactly; more a simple lack of knowledge or awareness, which wasn't the same thing at all.

Just before I fell asleep, a question floated to the surface. I'd been thinking about Nina, yes – but hadn't I also, in some indirect way, been thinking about myself?

The next night I sat in the Elite drinking beer. Beside me, there was a stool with no one on it. The stool unsettled me. I didn't know who was going to sit there first, Nina or Bruno Visser. I tried to distract myself by looking round. A girl was dancing on the low stage to my left. She had the fixed smile of an air hostess as she drew a pale feather boa between her legs. There were the usual men, middle-aged and nondescript, their faces absorbed but, at the same time, curiously bland and empty of expression.

I saw the dark car back away from me, its tyres like treacle on the tarmac. Towards the end of my last conversation with Munck I'd asked him if I was under surveillance. 'Not so far as I know,' he'd replied. But if it wasn't the police, then surely it had to be Visser, didn't it? I saw him propped against that concrete pillar in his expensive winter coat. Of course he could always claim that he was merely concerned for my welfare. What had he said on the phone once? *It's important that we don't lose touch.* But following me in a car with the lights switched off? Wasn't he taking things a bit far?

I sifted my memory for something he might've let slip, a casual moment, a careless phrase. *You're an extraordinary case. We've never had anyone like you. You're unique.* He was good, though. He was very good. Everything he said could be taken two ways – innocent or implicated; if he stood accused of one, he could always take refuge in the other. He'd mastered ambiguity. I thought of all the time I'd spent, either tranquillised or under anaesthetic, time that had been explained away by words like neuro-surgery, post-traumatic amnesia, and depression. Technical jargon. Generalisations. Vagueness. I'd have given anything for a detailed account of my stay in the clinic. Maybe Nina was a centre of ignorance. But, in that case, so was I.

'*And now, the gorgeous . . . the talented . . . Miss Can-dy!*'

I turned towards the stage. I could only remember one thing Nina had said about Candy. Nina was sitting on a motel bed at the time, sheets tangled around her waist and legs. She was holding a breast in each hand and looking from one to the other. 'They're not bad,' she was saying. 'They're not as good as Candy's, though. You should see Candy's. She's got great tits.'

It was true. She did.

Candy was wearing leopardskin chaps and a stetson, and that was about it. She had a bullwhip in her fist. There was a half-naked man kneeling in front of her. It was some kind of dominatrix routine. She stalked round the man, cracking the whip, light skidding off the high gloss of her skin.

'What the fuck are you doing here?'

I didn't even have to look round. I recognised the smell. 'What's it look like?' I said. 'I'm drinking a beer and watching the girls.'

'You're fucking blind. How can you watch girls?'

I turned, looked Greersen up and down. His tie was too wide and his shoes were grey. 'Who says I'm fucking blind?'

My nostrils filled with the stench of rotten spinach. I thought Greersen must be like a skunk: he released foul odours when he was furious or scared. He seized me by the collar of my jacket and pulled me off my stool.

'This guy's a friend of mine, Greersen,' a girl's voice said. 'I invited him.'

Greersen swung round. 'I thought you were dancing.'

'It's my break. Listen, he's a friend of mine. Let me take care of it, OK?' She took me by the arm and led me through a curtain and down a corridor. 'You're Martin, aren't you,' she said. 'Nina told me about you. I'm Candy.'

She showed me into her dressing-room behind the stage. It was a bare room, with mirrors along one wall. I could smell hot light bulbs and hair-spray. 'You all right?' she said.

'I'm fine. Thanks for rescuing me.'

'Don't mention it.' She sat in front of the mirror and began to wipe the make-up off her face. 'I don't have long,' she said. 'I have to go on again in fifteen minutes.'

'You won't get in trouble, will you?'

'Trouble?' She chuckled. 'Not me.'

'I don't think Greersen likes me very much,' I said.

'I hate the little shit. He's always throwing his weight around, what there is of it.'

I grinned.

'You heard anything about Nina?' she said.

'No, not really. What about you?'

'Not a thing.' Candy dropped a ball of cotton-wool into the waste-paper basket. 'How long's it been now? Three weeks?'

I nodded.

'You know, it's probably none of my business,' she said, 'but I think you made a mistake with her.'

'What do you mean?'

'You scared her.'

'Scared her?' I said. 'Oh, you mean because I'm blind?'

'No, she liked you being blind.' Candy laughed. 'No disrespect, but she always did go for the strangest men. No, what scared her was when you told her you could see.'

'I don't remember her being scared.'

'Yeah, well. She probably, you know, disguised it. You get pretty good at that, working in a dump like this.' She lit a cigarette. She was one of those people who put the filter to their lips and seem to drink from it. 'One night, in some hotel, you stared at yourself for an hour, apparently. That really freaked her out. A blind man staring at himself in the mirror.'

I thought I remembered it. I'd just told Nina my secret. Then we had sex. She insisted on it; she seemed desperate, violent, almost possessed. It exhausted me and I fell into a deep sleep. Towards morning I woke up suddenly. I'd had one of my dreams. I left the bed and sat on a chair in front of the mirror. It was what I did sometimes, to calm myself. But Nina was asleep the whole time. I looked at her every now and then, and her head was under the covers, only her dark hair showing on the pillow and the fingers of one hand. What Candy was saying made no sense to me.

'I didn't realise,' I said.

'I don't know anything about it, really.' Candy stood up, touched her hair. 'We got on pretty good, Nina and me, but I can't say I ever understood her.' She put her cigarette out, half-smoked. 'I'm black,' she said. 'Did you know that?'

'Yes. Nina told me.'

'Once, in the club, there was this guy. I don't remember where he was from. Anyway, he saw me and Nina sitting at a table together. You know what he called us?'

I shook my head.

'Night and Day.' She laughed, and this time it was soft, like water from sprinklers falling on a lawn.

There was a pay-phone at the end of the corridor, outside the toilets. It was depressing down there. The walls were bare brick and the ceiling leaked. On the floor there was a puddle with cigarette butts floating in it. The phone smelled of other people's breath. I fed two coins into the slot and dialled Munck's number.

'About the man in the station,' he said.

I asked him what he'd come up with.

'Not much. Somebody saw a man behaving oddly.'

'How do you mean, oddly?'

'Staring through the café window.' I heard Munck shuffling his papers. 'Tall man, apparently. Pale hair.'

'I don't know anyone who looks like that.'

'Well,' Munck said, 'we haven't been able to trace him, anyway.' He sounded weary. I could hear the melancholy slap of his feet as he paced the office.

'Is there any other news?' I asked.

He'd spoken to Karin Salenko again. This time she'd come clean. She'd seen her daughter at the beginning of December. On that occasion it appeared that she had told Nina that Jan Salenko wasn't her real father.

I leaned my head against the cold brick wall. So Karin had lied to me. All those sentences that tailed off, that was Karin running out of the truth. But Munck was still talking.

'The feeling here is, it's some kind of family crisis.'

I stood in the draughty corridor and thought it through. Nina had learned the truth about her father – or part of it, at least. It had been a shock to her and she'd gone away to try and come to terms with it (it had upset her enough to make her forgetful: she'd left the keys in her car). The theory fitted the facts, such as they were.

'And anyway,' Munck went on, 'she's over twenty-one. If she wants to go off somewhere without telling anyone, that's well within her rights.'

'So you don't still think I did it?'

'Did what?'

'Did away with her,' I said. 'Because I was jealous.'

Munck was silent for a moment. 'I don't think anyone did it,' he said, 'not until there's a body.'

I felt a sudden rush of affection for this tired, disillusioned policeman. 'Maybe we should have another drink sometime,' I said. 'We could go to Smoltczyk again.'

He seemed surprised by the idea, but not unreceptive.

After I'd hung up, I tried Karin Salenko's number. I wanted to tell her that I knew she'd lied to me. But the phone rang fourteen times and nobody answered.

I waited at a tram-stop not far from the club. By now it was late, and when the tram came it was almost empty. Just a couple of drunks and a teenage girl wearing a pair of clunky workman's boots and a nose-ring. Through the window I saw a circus poster on the corrugated-iron wall outside a building site. CIRCUS ROKO, it said. In the picture there was a clown and an elephant and a woman with a snake. There was also a man emerging from a hosepipe. Across the poster, in bright-blue letters on a yellow background, was a flash: INTRODUCING THE INCREDIBLE BALDINI! MASTER OF CONTORTION!

In the Kosminsky Arnold was flicking through a magazine, a cigarette burning in the ashtray beside him. The smoke spiralled past his shoulder, thick and rope-like, something he could almost have climbed. Arnold slid my key across the desk. The lift was working for once; I didn't have to think of any jokes.

I punched 8 and waited. Up I went. When the doors opened, I stepped out. Then stopped, rooted to the floor in shock. There, standing in front of me, was Visser. He was wearing a brown tweed suit and black shoes. I saw him first, and he was smiling. But when he saw me, his smile stiffened, and he started to back away, down the corridor.

'What are you doing here?' I said.

He didn't answer me. He just kept backing away, almost on tiptoe, his eyes fastened on mine, and I knew then that it must've been him behind the wheel of that mysterious car. I thought I knew what he was doing, too. He was pretending he wasn't there. He was trying to hypnotise me into thinking I was imagining it all.

I walked towards him. 'What are you doing here, Visser? What do you want?'

Suddenly he turned away, began to run. I ran after him.

'Visser?' I shouted. 'Visser?'

Keeping up with him was hard. Like pistons, those black heels of his. It surprised me that he was fit, that he could run so fast.

There was one moment when I almost grasped one of the flapping tails of his jacket, but I overbalanced in the attempt and lost valuable ground. I didn't know where he was making for. The fire exit, maybe. Or the service lift.

I was shouting at him, telling him to stop. Doors were opening up and down the corridor. People stood around in their pyjamas, complaining. I ignored them.

Then I was on my back on the carpet. I could see explosions to my left. And there was something sliding down my face. I tasted it. It was blood. I must've tripped and hit my head.

I looked round. The corridor was deserted. Visser had got away.

Lights pulsed in front of my left eye.

'Are you all right?'

It was Gregory's voice. His sweat a subtle distillation of cod, his hair floating above his head like mist.

'Did you see him?' I said.

'Who?'

Sometimes I couldn't believe Gregory. I just could not believe him. The man was fucking blind. He had to be. He couldn't even see things when they were going on right under his nose.

'No wonder Harold got off with your wife,' I said.

'What do you mean?'

'Nothing.' I took a tissue out of my pocket, held it against the left side of my face. 'Smoke, listen,' I said. 'There was a man – '

'I didn't see anyone.'

No, of course not. *Jesus Christ.*

'You shouldn't be running like that,' Gregory was saying. 'Not someone in your condition. You could really hurt yourself.'

I left him standing in the corridor and took the lift back down to the lobby. Arnold was still flicking through the same magazine, as if nothing had happened. There was a cigarette in the ashtray, and it was resting at the same angle, but it was longer than before. A different cigarette, then. He'd kill himself at this rate.

I asked him if anyone had left the hotel in the last five minutes. Not that he'd noticed, he replied. I leaned on reception, thinking. Visser was wily. He must have used the back door.

I tried another approach. 'Did you notice anyone come in?'

'Lots of people've come in.'

'I mean, someone you haven't seen before . . .'

Arnold fell silent.

'Someone with a brown moustache . . .'

'Nobody like that.'

'You're sure?'

'Quite sure.' Arnold seemed to hesitate. 'You're bleeding.'

'I know. It was an accident.'

I took the lift back to the eighth floor. Gregory was nowhere to be seen. I double-locked my door and lay down on the bed. The lights were still pulsing. They reminded me of Leon's Christmas decorations. Then the room began to spin.

I thought I might be sick, but I wasn't. I made my way to the bathroom and took two codeine with a glass of water. When I returned to my bed, it was painted white. A glossy, creamy white.

I lay down again.

All the hookers on the second floor were blind. Visser patrolled the corridors in his black shoes.

If I looked out of my window I knew what I would see.

Three beautiful trees.

I must have slept, because suddenly it was afternoon. I couldn't open my left eye at all. I touched it gently with the fingers of one hand. There was a flaky substance that I couldn't explain. Then I remembered my fall in the corridor and how I'd hit my head. It had to be blood.

I hauled myself from my bed. As I stood in the bathroom, gripping the edge of the basin, my stomach convulsed. I leaned over, retching. All that came up was bile. It was the colour of pearl light bulbs and thick as old-fashioned paper-glue. I spat and spat, but couldn't seem to rid my mouth of it.

I'd seen myself in the mirror. My left eye had closed completely; the skin above and below it was tight and fat. My nose and left cheek were swollen, too. Blood had spread across the left side of my face, then it had dried into a brittle crust and cracked, like glaze.

I sank down on to the ice-cold tiles next to the toilet and put my head between my knees. I heard a clock somewhere strike five. It would be dark by now.

Eventually the nausea passed.

I saw Visser on that piece of waste-ground, an image I'd returned to in perplexity a hundred times. I saw him closer, on the eighth floor of my hotel. The knowing way he'd looked at me both times. His interest in my case – obsessive, almost pathological: he'd actually been following me. My secret power, I thought. What if it wasn't a secret at all? Or rather, what if it was a secret everybody knew about *except me*? What if it was actually a secret I'd been *excluded from*? And what if it was being monitored? What if it had been monitored all along? The questions broke over me, one after another, remorselessly, like waves; I felt I was being flattened on some barren shore.

At last it came to me, as I sat on the cold tiles, weak, and wet with sweat, and shivering. It came to me. *He knows I can see.* He'd known all along. That was why he'd been following me, with that smile on his face. *He knows.*

The thought was chillingly magnetic. It attracted instant evidence. The endless consultations. That visit to my parents (two hundred kilometres from the clinic!). The file marked HIGHLY CONFIDENTIAL. Those things he'd said. *Extraordinary case. Unique.* Well, of course. I would be, wouldn't I?

I leaned over the toilet-bowl again, my whole body arching, straining to yield something, my hair spiked with sweat – but there was nothing there. The convulsions were so violent, it felt as if I was about to tear a muscle in my stomach. When the nausea subsided, I sat back against the wall and moaned out loud in sheer relief.

I tried to think as clearly as I could. The titanium plate. It had to be an implanted device. Some kind of receiver or decoder that was capable of interpreting the signals being sent back by my eyes. All my theories about a chance connection, some freak hook-up, my own fragile miracle, they all crumbled in the face of something so logical, so scientific.

Obviously it was a prototype, though. That night in the gardens, objects had appeared through a kind of green gloom. There'd been little or no sense of colour at that point, just shape and movement – a night-camera effect. Then, slowly, almost imperceptibly, it began to change. The scarlet of those capital letters slanting across the cover of my file. The pale-yellow of the tiles in Leon's restaurant. The glittering blue of Loots' circus pullover. And yet it was far from being infallible. Which explained my lapses of judgement, my miscalculations. They weren't clumsiness, as I'd sometimes thought, or panic. They weren't my fault at all, in fact. They were simple malfunctions. A temporary loss of picture. Do not adjust your set. No wonder Visser spent night after night working late in his office. No wonder there were cranial X-rays everywhere, and confidential files. The system was still in development. He was still perfecting it.

I kneeled by the basin, put my mouth to the cold tap. First I rinsed the water round my teeth and spat. Then I drank some, felt it cool my aching throat.

At last I could see through him. That docile voice (about as docile as a snake sleeping on a rock!). His infinite patience, his solicitude (genuine and false, both at the same time). How close I'd come with that question about research, and how expertly he'd fielded it! It wasn't the way I'd thought it would be – glimpses of the truth, gradual revelations. No, it was more dramatic than that, and more fundamental. The whole ingenious façade had dropped away, like plaster from a wall with damp in it.

It seemed to me that we'd both been playing games of subterfuge, bluff and counter-bluff. I wondered if, by appearing to discourage me, by insisting that I should face what he called 'reality', he hadn't actually been provoking me a little. Providing me with a regime I could rebel against. Indirectly pointing out the course he hoped I'd follow. How clever of him to allow me to think of him as stupid! He'd wanted me to believe that I was in possession of a secret power. He'd been curious about my reactions, curious to see how far I'd go. I'd been part of an experiment. His experiment.

I still was.

Later that evening I called Directory Enquiries and asked for the number of the eye clinic. There was no reason to hide, not now that I'd seen Visser less than twenty metres from my room. I would probably meet my parents next, weeping tears of joy as they came whirling through the revolving doors. Or Claudia, in one of those ghastly négligés that are supposed to put the excitement back into your sex life. Or, even worse, I'd step out of the lift and find my entire past gathered in the hotel lobby, like some nightmare episode of that famous TV programme. There'd be girls I'd betrayed. Relations I'd never written to. Friends I'd abandoned. There'd be people whose faces I couldn't even remember – but they'd remember me. Oh yes, they'd remember! They'd be standing there, with glasses of cheap champagne and toothy smiles. Grimacing, I dialled the clinic. When the receptionist answered, I asked for Visser. In my mind I was walking those endless corridors again, and my heart had speeded up, as if I could hear footsteps behind me. The phone rang internally – once, twice, three times. I was almost hoping there was no one there. But on the fourth ring, someone picked it up.

'Visser.'

I hesitated. The idea that I shouldn't have any contact with the man had become so deeply ingrained that, for a moment, I couldn't speak at all. Then I heard myself: 'Surprise, surprise!'

'Who's speaking, please?'

I swallowed. 'It's me. Martin Blom.'

'Martin!'

Oh, he was good. That lift in his voice. The inflection was perfect. Concern, astonishment, delight – even a little relief. They were all there, and in exactly the right proportions. That voice of his, synonymous with deceit, with exploitation. Suddenly I found my tone.

'You must be tired, Doctor.'

'Tired?'

'Up half the night,' I said, 'in strange hotels.'

He tried to speak, but I talked over him.

'A man of your distinction,' I said, 'in a hotel like that. And running, too!'

'Where are you, Martin?'

'You know where I am.'

'I've been worried – '

I interrupted him again. 'I'm fed up with games, Doctor. I want the truth.'

'What about?'

'The plate you put in my head. The titanium plate.'

'Are you feeling some discomfort?'

I had to laugh. 'Discomfort? That's good.'

He waited for me to continue. He gave me time, as always.

'No, I wouldn't call it discomfort exactly,' I said. 'More like malfunction.'

'I'm sorry. I don't follow you – '

'All right. I'll be as straightforward as I can. I think you're experimenting on me. No, wait. I don't think. I know.'

'Martin, that's absurd.'

'That's one word for it. There's another word. Obscene. Or here's one that might get through to you. Unethical.'

'Martin, listen to me – '

'That's the whole problem right there. I listened to you. All along I listened to you. I should never have done that.'

'Martin, listen. I warned you about this the last time I saw you. I told you that you might experience phases of denial, or even recurrences of your hallucinations. You've been pushing yourself too hard. You've taken on too much. I think it would be best if you came in to see me. Then I could – '

'I'm surprised you're still bothering with that old story. Especially after last night.'

'I think you should come and see me at the clinic. I really do. Or I could come to you, if you'd just tell me where you are . . .'

I was laughing again. He was like an actor who goes on playing his part, even after the curtain's gone down.

'So you're not going to admit it, Doctor? You're not going to come clean?'

'Admit what?'

I couldn't listen any more. The calmness, the compassion. That slight anxiety. All totally dishonest. Bogus. Fake.

'Fuck you, Visser.'

I slammed the phone down. Then I picked it up again. He was still there.

'Hey, Visser. Fuck you. All right? FUCK YOU.'

I sat on the edge of the bed, trembling. What would he do now? Would he send a private ambulance? Would he come for me, with muscular attendants? Would he pump me full of tranquillisers?

Would he operate again?

Just after six-thirty in the morning I heard a bicycle bell, and I knew from the sound of it that it was Loots returning from the factory. I turned to look and there he was, upside-down as usual, only this time he was juggling a pint of milk, some eggs and two or three bread rolls. His breakfast, presumably. Even though my situation was desperate I found that I was grinning.

By the time he stopped outside the building he was the right way up again, with his provisions safely stowed in a brown-paper bag. Whistling to himself, he locked his bicycle to a lamppost. I was sitting in the shadows, on the stoop, and he didn't notice me until he started towards the front door, brown-paper bag in one hand, keys bouncing in the other.

'Martin?' he said. 'What are you doing here?'

I stood up. My bones ached from the long wait in the cold.

Loots was eyeing my suitcase. 'What's happened?' He came closer and peered at me. 'What happened to your face?' His voice had lifted an octave, in shock.

'I tripped and fell. It's nothing.'

'It doesn't look like nothing. Have you seen a doctor?'

'Loots,' I said, 'could I possibly stay with you for a few days?'

'Of course. Stay as long as you like.'

'It seems like I'm always asking you for favours – '

'Nonsense. Juliet will be delighted. She's taken quite a shine to you.' He put an arm around my shoulders. 'Are you hungry?'

We ate breakfast at his kitchen table – fresh rolls with butter and honey, slices of cheese, a pot of coffee (I wondered what had happened to the eggs). The radio was on, low-volume. Some news programme.

'Are you going to tell me what this is all about?' he said.

'I'm sorry, Loots. I can't just yet.' I paused. 'And, if I did, you wouldn't believe it.' I yawned. 'God, I'm tired.'

But Loots wouldn't let me sleep until he'd seen to my injuries. There was a deep gash where my left eyebrow joined the bridge of my nose. He cleaned it with iodine and stuck a plaster over it. Then he gave me a bag of ice to hold against my swollen cheek while he made up a bed for me on the sofa in the living-room.

'One last thing,' I said. 'I don't want anybody to know I'm here. Nobody, Loots. Do you understand?'

'OK.' He spoke hesitantly, still puzzled by my behaviour.

'I appreciate this,' was all I could say. 'I really do.'

When we woke up in the afternoon, he told me that he didn't have another night off until the weekend. He hoped I'd be all right on my own. He'd get some keys cut before he went to work.

'There's no need,' I told him. 'I won't be going out.'

'What? Not at all?'

I shook my head.

He laughed. 'I wouldn't either,' he said, 'not if I looked like you.'

This hadn't occurred to me as an excuse, not until Loots mentioned it, but I seized on it with gratitude. 'I may be blind,' I told him rather pompously, 'but I still have my pride.'

Though I'd moved away from the Kosminsky, I didn't feel as if I was out of danger (after all, I could easily have been followed to Loots' apartment). I took a number of precautions. I decided not to leave the house, for instance, not under any circumstances. Not even at night. I devised an escape-route, too. As soon as Loots left for work in the evening, I double-locked the door and jammed a kitchen chair under the handle. I took another chair and stood it directly beneath the skylight in the living-room. I climbed on to the chair, opened the skylight and pushed my white cane out on to the roof. On the floor beside the chair I placed a travelling bag that was already packed with a few necessities – money, codeine, a change of clothing. I practised my emergency exit several times that week. It began in one of two ways: a ring on the bell downstairs or – more urgent this, more threatening – a knock on the door of the apartment itself. The procedure was the same, though. I would slip the strap of the bag over my shoulder and climb on to the chair. Then I'd reach above my head and, gripping the frame of the window in both hands, I'd haul myself up into the night. I knew I could be out of the room and across the rooftops in less than the time it would take to force the door. My only worry was the chair. Its position under the skylight might betray me. After a great deal of thought, I decided to leave it facing the TV, with the newspaper on the floor in front of it. The newspaper would be opened on the page that listed the programmes for that day, and certain of the programmes would be circled. That would explain the chair's position in the room. Even if it didn't work, it ought to buy me a few precious minutes. It was cold in the apartment with the skylight open; I had to wear a coat and gloves. I would close the skylight when I heard Loots' footsteps on the stairs, but he often remarked on the temperature when he walked in. I'd put a grin on my face and breathe in deeply. 'Ah,' I'd say, 'fresh air.' Each night, after he'd gone, I'd be back on the chair with the skylight open again and my eyes fixed on the door. Before too long, I knew it intimately. Every nick and dent and scratch. Every pattern in the grain. Say it went missing and the police wanted a description. They couldn't have done better than to question me.

When the knock came, on my fourth night in the apartment, I was ready. Like a spirit departing from a body, I rose out of the chair and stood beside it, in a kind of half-crouch, scarcely breathing. The knocking came again, more insistent now. The wood seemed to bulge each time the stranger's fist pounded on it. Curved lines appeared in the air, the way they do in comic-books, to show the power of the blows.

'Blom? Are you there?'

It was Gregory. Surely they couldn't have recruited Gregory? They must have been more desperate than I thought. I was still standing beside the chair, motionless, hunched over.

'I know you're in there, Blom. Open up, will you?'

But I wasn't opening the door for anyone. I had a curious sensation suddenly. The door wasn't made of wood at all, I felt, but glass, and Gregory could see me through it. He was staring at me through the door, and I was crouching there, next to the chair, pretending that I didn't exist. It was absurd. But it was unnerving, too, somehow.

'Come on, Blom. Open up.'

The blows on the door were harder still, and there were more of them. They came in groups of five instead of two. I reached down, hooked the strap over my shoulder, then I placed one foot on the seat of the chair. My heart had a heavy, sluggish beat to it, as if the blood it had to pump round my body weighed too much.

'Blom? Come on, Blom.'

I must have stood on that chair for fifteen minutes. Eventually I realised that Gregory wasn't about to break the door down. At first I was angry to have been disturbed in this way, for no good reason. Then I thought that perhaps it had been good practice – a useful false alarm. In the end, though, I just felt sorry for him. I almost stepped down off the chair and unlocked the door. But how could I have explained the delay? His blows grew weaker, less impassioned. I heard him murmuring outside, like something dying. I was astonished he'd kept it up for so long. Is persistence a sign of wisdom or stupidity? Normally I would have said, Well, it depends. But we were dealing with Gregory. Wisdom wasn't even part of the equation.

Sometime later I watched him from the window as he walked off up the street, his shoulders hunched inside his donkey jacket, his scalp showing through the usual thinning mist of hair. Yes, I felt sorry for him – but what could I do?

During that same week I noticed a dramatic alteration in my vision. I was watching the door one night when a kind of whiteness flashed in front of me. I didn't think of TV interference, not right away, but later I realised that that was exactly what it had been like. There'd been a buzzing, too, loud at first, then fading to nothing. And suddenly a woman was standing in front of me. She was holding a packet of soap powder. And she was smiling, as though she knew me.

My first instinct was to climb on to the chair. But even as I did so, I realised it was too late. *The woman was already inside the apartment.* I looked down at the woman. Her smile didn't seem to be affected by the sight of me standing on the chair. She didn't seem to find it peculiar, or even funny (she didn't make any jokes about mice, for instance). I was about to ask her who she was and what she was doing in Loots' living-room and, more to the point, *how she'd got in, for Christ's sake*, when I noticed that it wasn't his living-room that she was standing in. It wasn't a living-room at all, in fact. It was a kitchen. And not his kitchen either. Slowly I lowered myself back down to the floor.

The woman showed me a soiled T-shirt. She seemed downcast, dismayed. I'd no idea why she was showing it to me. It wasn't mine. And it didn't look as if it belonged to anyone I knew either. I could hear her talking about stains. I heard the words *grass* and *blood*. I watched her put the T-shirt into a washing-machine and add some powder from the packet she'd been holding. When she took the T-shirt out again, only seconds later, it was clean and white. She held it up for me to see. Her plump cheeks shone with happiness. It occurred to me that I was watching TV, even though the TV wasn't on. I was watching TV *inside my head*.

I tried to stay calm, establish what was happening. It was a commercial channel, but not one I recognised. When the commercials were over, I was returned to a film which had something to do with police corruption. It had all the usual car chases and shoot-outs and, every twenty minutes, there were more commercials: cars, beer, holidays – and soap powder, of course. I saw the woman with the T-shirt so many times that night that I knew almost every second of the thirty seconds it took her to find happiness.

When Loots came home, he found me pacing up and down in a state of disturbed excitability. The skylight was still open, and the chair was facing the door. The woman was about to take the clean white T-shirt out of the washing-machine again.

'What is it, Martin?' Loots said. 'What's going on?'

But I couldn't find an answer for him. I just stood at the window, staring out.

'Is it dark, Loots?'

'Yes,' he said. 'It's still dark.'

I stared out of the window, but I couldn't see the chimney-pots in their uneven clusters, or the slanting, tiled rooftops greasy with rain, or the pale, dome-shaped glow of the city sky beyond. I couldn't see them, even though I knew they were there. All I could see was a beach of pure white sand and a girl in a blue bikini.

So it was true. Some kind of transposition had taken place. It wasn't vision that I was getting, not any more. It was television.

What I was beginning to believe was that the eye clinic was affiliated to some government agency – one of those secret research establishments, rows of long, low buildings protected by attack dogs and electric fences. Visser worked both for the clinic and for the agency, though in what precise capacity I couldn't be sure. There was something a bit too smooth about him, a bit too seamless – I'd always thought so. This new theory of mine explained the misgivings I'd had about him, misgivings I'd never been able to justify in rational terms.

Visser had lost contact with me in the physical sense, but his mental hold on me was as strong as ever; if anything, he'd tightened it. It appeared that they'd found a way of feeding TV channels directly into my brain. They were broadcasting on my own internal screen. I'd become a hybrid – part human being, part television. And someone else had the remote.

One night I watched the same channel for hours. The next night it was twitch-time: a different channel every five seconds. As to why this might be happening, I had no idea. I was sure of only one thing. I had no control over it. None.

I talked to Visser again. I decided beforehand that I would keep it short and to the point; after all, I didn't want the call to be traced.

'Visser here.'

'It's working, Visser. I just thought I'd let you know.'

'Is that you, Martin?'

'That's right. It's me.'

'Good,' he said. 'Because the last call ended, how shall I put it, somewhat abruptly.'

'There's been a new development,' I said, 'as I'm sure you're aware.' I was using his phrases deliberately. I wanted him to taste his own medicine.

'A new development?'

'You've really surpassed yourself this time.'

There was a silence.

'I'm getting pictures,' I said. 'Images.'

The silence lasted. It was an uncomfortable silence on his part. Guilty, I would've said. He knew I was on to him.

'I'm getting signals,' I said.

'And what's your interpretation?' he said at last, struggling to sound objective, to remain uninvolved, aloof.

'I think it's television. I think I'm receiving electromagnetic waves and internally reconverting them into visual images.' I paused. 'Strange thing is, I don't recognise any of the channels. I think I must be getting cable.'

'Extraordinary,' he muttered.

'That's what I thought. You must be pretty proud of yourself.'

'Martin, I'm worried about you. I've spoken to your parents. They're worried, too.'

I walked to the window. Though I could feel the cold glass beneath my fingers, all I could see was a game of football. I'd been getting a sports channel for some days now. There was a team in a red strip playing a team in white. I couldn't identify any of the players; it was probably some foreign league. In any case, the score was 0–0 and the red team was in possession, on the halfway line.

'The trail's gone cold on you, hasn't it?' I said. 'You don't know where I am.'

'I think you should tell me, Martin. I could help you.'

Smiling, I turned back into the room. I'd lost him. That was all I needed to know. Perhaps I could allow myself a little more freedom now. Perhaps I could even venture out at night. As for the rest of it, Visser was no different from Arnold. He wasn't going to admit what he was up to. There was too much at stake. Maybe he'd even signed some kind of official secrets act, forbidding him to talk about his work.

'I'm going now.' I grinned to myself. 'I just wanted to make sure you were all right – '

'Martin, wait – '

Against the run of play, a white forward beat two defenders and drove the ball into the top left-hand corner of the net. A brilliantly taken goal. Mouth wide open, arms outstretched, he raced towards the touchline. The red team stood around with their hands on their hips, looking at the ground.

'One–nil,' I said. Then I hung up.

That night I watched thirteen hours of TV – thirteen hours without a break; the titanium plate was hot, it had been on so long. I liked the game show best, though I forget what it was called. The host was a middle-aged man with a sun-bed tan and a toupee. He flounced. He twirled. He was constantly opening his eyes too wide, or flapping his hands, or rounding his lips into an O. He got on with everyone – but that was because everyone had been told to be nice to him. He was like an invalid, I thought, or a dictator. My favourite moment came when he revealed the prizes, when the contestants learned that they'd won a holiday for two in a resort nobody had ever heard of. Or a set of crystal glasses and a travel rug. Or luggage. How I longed for somebody to bellow, *What? Is that all?* But no. They whooped, they punched the air; they shook both fists at the same time. One woman even cried. Appearing on TV was clearly a powerful homogenising force.

My mind jumped sideways. If this was an experiment, then what kind of experiment was it exactly? What was the rationale behind it? What were its aims and goals? It was difficult to concentrate with a game show going on in my head, but that, in itself, set me thinking. The way I saw it, there were two possibilities (or maybe they were different applications of the same basic principle). Firstly, it was an attempt at social engineering. Ideally, everybody would be fitted with a small titanium plate. It was a simple operation. The scalp healed in no time, the hair grew back. By feeding people with TV – intravenously, as it were – you could keep them distracted, pacified. It was lobotomy on a grand scale. There would be no crime, no violence. You'd have a nation that was incapable of rebellion or dissent.

The second possibility was no less sinister. Obviously, this new generation of television (drip TV, as I had started calling it) could be used as a form of persecution. It's hard to think when there's a TV on inside your head. It's hard to have much of a sense of yourself. People could be driven mad that way. And perhaps that was what was being explored. The use of visual images in psychological warfare. Torture by satellite. TV as a weapon. No wonder Visser didn't want to talk to me: either I was part of some hush-hush weapons research programme, or else I was the first in a long line of passive citizens (or PCs, as they would doubtless come to be known).

Visser didn't want to talk to me. It was only to be expected. Strangely, this realisation didn't depress me. In fact, there was a sense in which it cleared the air. If I wanted to get at the truth, there was only one way to do it.

The doorbell jangled as I walked into Sprankel's shop. I'd waited for a break in transmission before leaving Loots' apartment, so I was able to see that Sprankel had changed his layout in the past two months. Instead of plastic waste-bins there were TV aerials. Hundreds of TV aerials. They were dangling upside-down on lengths of string, twisting slowly in the dark air near the ceiling.

'Sprankel?' I called out. 'Where are you, Sprankel?'

'I'm right here.' His head appeared above the cash-register, which, reassuringly, was still lined with Astroturf.

'There's no need to hide from me, Sprankel. I'm not going to hurt you.'

'I wasn't hiding, sir.'

Poor old Sprankel. It was embarrassing, really.

'I need two pairs of gardening gloves,' I said, 'a torch, and something to cut glass with.'

Sprankel's eyes began to twitch and hop behind his glasses. I knew he was curious – a glasscutter? gloves? a torch? – but probably he remembered how stern I'd been with him the last time.

'Before you start guessing, Sprankel,' I said, 'I'll tell you. I've got a job.' I tapped the side of my nose. 'A job. Know what I mean?'

'No, sir. I – '

I threw my head back and laughed. The tips of a thousand TV aerials reached towards me, glittering and complicated.

'I'm going to be doing a spot of burglary, Sprankel. Yes,' I said, 'there's something very important that I've got to steal.'

Sprankel was chuckling almost before I'd finished the sentence and he went on chuckling much longer than I expected him to, much longer, in fact, than I considered necessary. Surprised at his sense of humour, a little puzzled, too, I stared at him. I'd never realised how small his teeth were.

'If you don't give me a good price,' I said, 'I might have to make you an accessory.'

He was still chuckling.

'And will you be needing any black paint today?' he asked me.

'Oh no,' I said. 'Those days are over.'

'Those days are over,' he repeated, half to himself.

He wrapped my purchases and I paid for them and put them in my bag. On the way to the door I paused, turned back.

'By the way, Sprankel, I like your display,' I said, pointing at the ceiling. 'Very imaginative.'

The following afternoon I was woken by what I thought was someone knocking on the door. I lay quite still, my body heating with anxiety. Sweat collected on my chest, behind my knees. Surely it couldn't be Gregory again? But after listening carefully, I realised the knocking sounds were coming from inside the apartment. Also they were grouped in sixes. It wasn't someone at the door at all. It was Loots, throwing knives at Juliet.

I wrapped myself in a blanket and moved towards the corridor.

'I'm sorry,' Loots said. 'Did I wake you?'

'No, no. I was just dozing.' I watched his knives fit snugly to the curves of Juliet's hips and thighs. 'Gregory called round the other night.'

'Yeah? How was he?'

'I don't know. I didn't let him in.'

Loots lowered the knife that was in his hand and stared at me, his eyebrows high on his forehead, like they were when he was dancing.

'I asked you not to tell anyone where I was,' I said.

'But Gregory's a friend – '

I stepped closer to Loots. 'I trust you, Loots. That's why I'm here. But there isn't anyone else I trust. I certainly don't trust Gregory.'

Loots didn't speak for a while. Then, finally, he said, 'You'd better tell me what all this is about.'

'I'm hiding from someone.' I saw his eyebrows lift again. 'Don't worry. It's not the police.' I turned back into the living-room. 'If you get me a drink, I'll tell you everything.'

I had no intention of telling him everything. That was the mistake I'd made with Nina. I was in possession of secret knowledge, but unlike most secrets, mine had a foolproof quality. Each time I tried to tell it to someone, it became unbelievable, untrue; it was like a command built into the substance of the secret itself, that it could not be shared. I would tell him as much as I could make him believe, and no more. I sat down on the sofa. He handed me a small glass of his uncle's peach brandy. I thanked him and swallowed it in one. I felt its quiet fire rise through me. I wondered how to begin. I thought I'd use words that had worked with him before – the words of Anton the clown.

'This is going to sound strange,' I said.

I started with the missing bone, the part of my skull that had been shattered by the bullet. I described the operation to replace it with a specially measured piece of titanium. I saw Loots wince and look away. I waited a moment, then asked if he'd ever heard of people who had so many fillings they could pick up radio stations on their teeth. Yes, he thought he'd heard of that. I told him that was what was happening to me, only it was more sophisticated. The titanium plate, I said. They were using it to experiment on me. It was a device that allowed them to transmit images directly into my brain. I looked at Loots. His eyes had filled with water. I had frightened him.

'Images?' he said.

I spoke more softly now. 'Pictures,' I said. 'Like on TV.'

The man responsible for the experiment, I went on, the man in charge, was my neuro-surgeon, a certain Dr Visser. I described Visser's unhealthy interest in my case. He had a file on me, for instance, which was marked HIGHLY CONFIDENTIAL. He'd been following me, too.

'He even appeared at the Kosminsky.' I shook my head; I still couldn't believe it. 'That's why I had to leave so suddenly. That's why I was sitting on your doorstep the other morning.'

Loots poured us both another drink.

'I never heard of anything like this before,' he said.

We both drank.

He asked me what I was going to do. I reached down into my travelling bag. I took out two pairs of gardening gloves, a torch, and a tool for cutting glass, and I laid them on the table in front of him.

'You're not a thief, Loots. You told me that.'

'That's right,' he said. 'I'm not.'

I left another silence, then I spoke: 'How do you feel about breaking and entering?'

As Loots drove through the city, I felt a pleasant tension, a kind of burning, in the pit of my stomach. I pictured Visser in his swivel chair. He looked tired, dispirited. I thought I detected a trace of grey in his moustache. I'd spent weeks trying to fathom his motives and his strategy, weeks attempting to evade him, out-manoeuvre him. Now I could sense the tables turning. Now, for the first time, I was taking the initiative. And it was the perfect night for it. There was no moon. The sky was cloudy, almost brown. When we stopped at traffic-lights, I felt the car rock on its suspension. It was the wind, gusting out of the east. That would help us, too. Any sound we made, the wind would cover it.

I talked for most of the journey. Partly it was to reassure Loots, to drive away any remaining doubts he might have. Partly it was my own adrenalin. Visser had a secret file on me. I wanted it. That was all. We had to break into the clinic in order to steal the file, but we would do as little damage as possible. It wasn't revenge I was interested in, but proof. Proof of the way I'd been exploited. Proof of the crimes that had been committed against me. We weren't the criminals. They were.

'Do you see, Loots?' I said. 'Do you understand?'

'Yes,' he said. 'Yes, Martin. I do.'

We drove north, through the wide, grey streets. The puddles on the pavements had iced over. It was almost three o'clock in the morning.

The clinic was on a main road. We parked in a quiet, residential street directly opposite. I could just make out the building, with its towers and chimneys, black against the dull brown of the sky. We walked towards it through the shadows. I turned to Loots, saw the tightness in his shoulders and in the muscles near his mouth.

'We're not the criminals,' I told him again. 'Remember that.'

We found a section of the clinic wall that wasn't overlooked, then we pulled on our gardening gloves. Loots made a step out of his hands and I clambered over. He clambered after me. On the other side, we crouched in the bushes. Listened. The only sound was the trees dreaming above our heads.

We crossed a wide expanse of grass. The wind dropped and I thought I could hear crows in the distance like old doors opening on rusty hinges, doors in horror films. Then only the keys in Loots' pocket and our breathing. A sudden whiteness sizzled through the air in front of me. I had to stop and hold my head.

'What is it?'

'I can't see.'

Loots didn't say anything.

'It's almost like he knows I'm coming,' I muttered. 'Like he's making it difficult for me.'

I'd been expecting a TV programme to follow that flash of white, but it didn't happen. Instead, I could see the grey lawn reaching down towards the lake.

'Do you remember where his office was?' Loots said.

'Not really.' I tried to think. 'There was a walkway outside. A metal walkway . . .'

Trees surrounded us. I glanced up into their branches, bare of leaves. I would like to have explained their significance to Loots, but there wasn't time. A clock somewhere was chiming the half-hour. Loots tightened his grip on my arm. We were passing the main entrance.

He chose a window in the west wing of the clinic. It was more isolated, he said. No lights. He cut a small hole in the glass and knocked it through into the room. After waiting a moment, he cut round the edge of the pane, next to the window-frame. He put one hand into the hole and gripped the glass, then tapped on it sharply with the other. The pane came loose. He reached in, turned the handle.

'You first,' he said.

We stood in a room that smelled faintly of methylated spirits.

Loots crossed to the door and opened it. I asked him what was out there.

'Nothing,' he said. 'Just a corridor.'

I warned him about the corridors – their labyrinthine qualities, their disturbing acoustics. If he thought he heard somebody behind him, he was not to worry; it was probably just his own footsteps, echoing. I spoke of the scale of the building, too and, while I was on the subject, I mentioned Kukowski's memory techniques. Not that they'd ever helped me much, I said, but maybe he'd do better. It was important to remember which way we went in case we had to leave in a hurry. Loots listened with a slightly lowered face. He seemed to be absorbing everything I told him.

We left the room and began to walk. We were in a part of the building I didn't know; I didn't recognise the corridors at all. Every now and then a sizzle of white moved across my field of vision. That sudden, blinding wash of magnesium light: it was as if I'd put my face inside a photocopying machine. I didn't want game shows, not now. I didn't want the nervousness, the hysteria.

Once, we heard footsteps. It was a good example of what I'd been talking about, and I was just going to point it out to Loots when he opened a door and pushed me through it. I began to protest, but he put a hand over my mouth. I heard the footsteps grow louder, move past us, fade into the distance.

'It was a nurse,' he whispered.

A nurse? It could have been Maria Janssen on the early morning shift. What would she have said if she'd discovered us? Was she aware of what they'd done? I saw her walking among the pear trees with Visser. It was possible. When she was first assigned to me, they might have thought it best to let her in on it. Perhaps that explained her initial awkwardness with me. There'd been times when she seemed to be floundering, out of her depth . . . It might also make sense of the night when she took off all her clothes. That strip-tease could even have been part of the experiment.

Our luck held. We found ourselves passing a series of doors, and on the wall beside each one there was a plaque with a doctor's name on it. Loots read them out to me. Metz . . . Czarnowksi . . . Feleus . . .

'. . . Visser!' he exclaimed.

The door wasn't locked. When we were both inside the office, he switched his torch on and began the search. There were no files lying around, he said. No X-rays either. The room was neat and orderly, with every surface cleared of paperwork. He checked the drawers of Visser's desk, but all they contained was stationery, a few memoranda, some business correspondence. The only place left was the filing cabinet, which was locked. I took this to be a good sign.

'We're going to have to force it,' I said.

I handed Loots the screwdriver I'd brought with me and watched him work it between the drawer's edge and the framework of the cabinet itself. The lock snapped open. The drawer slid forwards on its rails.

I paced the room impatiently as he searched the contents of the cabinet. 'Have you found it?' I asked him, every fifteen seconds. I couldn't help it. So much depended on it.

At last Loots sat back on his heels and sighed. 'It's not here.'

'It must be.'

'They're not files,' he said. 'They're articles. Some of them Visser wrote himself, but most of them are by other people. There aren't any files in here at all.'

I thought we should go through the desk again.

'There aren't any files in the desk either,' Loots said. 'I've already looked.'

'Maybe he's got a safe . . .'

Loots stood up. 'There's no safe.'

'We'll have to look somewhere else then.' I went to the door and peered out. The corridor had a familiar shine to it, a mocking emptiness, like a mirror with nobody looking into it.

'It's almost six,' Loots said. 'It'll be light in an hour.'

'I don't care.'

A sizzle of white and this time pictures followed it. I saw rows and rows of beds, with wounded men in them. Men with their heads wrapped in bandages, men with limbs missing. They could have been refugees from my dreams. Through the hospital window pillars of black smoke were visible. Grass lay flat as a helicopter came down. A man in a uniform was searching the hospital. There were stretchers everywhere. One had a girl on it. Her face floated beneath his distracted gaze for a moment, her dark hair pushed back from her forehead, her skin pale, drained of blood, her eyelids closed.

'Nina?' I couldn't believe it. 'Nina? Is that you?'

Loots seized me by the arm. 'Quiet, Martin.'

'I thought I saw Nina.'

'She's not here.' Loots was shaking me. 'There's nobody here.'

'OK, OK,' I muttered. 'It's just a film.'

But the girl on the stretcher had looked so like her.

We were half-walking, half-running now. Loots was afraid that someone might have heard me shouting. Fighter planes swooped through the smoke. Their guns sounded like people typing. Somehow Loots found his way back to the same room. We climbed through the open window, dropped to the ground below. He took my hand. 'There's only lawn in front of us. Just run.'

I ran. But it was difficult. Shells were landing all around me. Flashes of white light and then fans opening in the air, fans made out of earth. I wanted to throw myself down on the grass. I might get killed otherwise. But Loots still had me by the hand and he wouldn't let go.

Once, he stopped and stood there, panting. 'I thought I heard something.'

'I can't hear anything,' I said.

How could I? The hospital had just been hit. A fireball engulfed it, orange edged in black. A cauliflower of flame.

We ran on, plunging through some bushes. At last we reached the wall. Loots gave me a leg-up, as before. I waited for him on the other side, but he didn't appear.

'Loots?' I whispered.

There was no reply. Only a startled, anguished cry and then Loots came scrambling over the wall. He rushed me across the road. It took him three attempts to open the car door. I heard another cry.

'What *is* that?' I said.

But Loots wouldn't speak. He didn't say a word until we'd driven fast for several minutes. 'I dropped my keys,' he said. 'It happened when I was helping you over the wall. I looked around a bit. Found them. The next thing I knew, there was a man . . .'

The man asked him what he was doing. He must have been the nightwatchman or the gatekeeper. He was standing up against a tree. Loots quickly drew one of his knives and told him not to move. He thought he'd pin the man to the tree by the arm of his coat. Slow him down. Discourage him from taking any further action.

'Good thinking, Loots,' I said.

'He moved,' Loots said.

'What?'

'He moved. Only a fraction, but it was enough.'

'He shouldn't have done that,' I said. 'He shouldn't have moved.'

'I know. I feel strange about it, though. It's against the principles of knife-throwing. Knife-throwing,' and Loots paused, 'the whole point is, you're supposed to miss.'

I turned and looked at him. There were helicopters flying through the place where Loots should have been.

'Where did you get him, Loots?'

'I wish he hadn't moved. It would've been all right if he hadn't moved.'

'Where did you get him?'

'In the ear.'

'What?'

'I pinned his right ear to the tree. Didn't you hear him yell?' Loots began to laugh. High, thin spirals of laughter. Then he stopped.

'It wasn't your fault.' I thought for a moment. 'How come you had your knives on you?'

'I always carry them. For luck.' Loots laughed again. Only once this time. Bitterly.

'Can they be traced to you?' I asked him.

'No,' he said.

'What about the man? Did he see you? Clearly, I mean?'

'I don't think so.'

I settled back in my seat. 'I'm sorry about all this.'

'I'm sorry, too. We didn't even get your file.'

I was staring at a battlefield – shelled farm buildings, burned-out army vehicles. Smoke rose from a blackened tree-trunk into the thin grey air. One soldier was helping another across the devastated landscape. They both looked close to collapse. The words THE END appeared.

I couldn't believe that was the end. I just couldn't believe it. Couldn't there have been an exchange of weary smiles between the two soldiers? Or a symbolic close-up of a green shoot in the mud?

What about the future?

What about hope?

'Ah, Martin,' Visser said. 'Still getting cable?'

I smiled, then sat down. A waitress appeared at my elbow. I ordered tea, with lemon.

To arrange the meeting had taken some courage on my part. In the time that had elapsed since our last encounter – more than two months – Visser had assumed a different persona (rather as I was supposed to have done). He'd become more unpredictable, more threatening. More veiled, too. I no longer had the slightest idea what it was that he intended. In our conversation on the phone I'd offered to meet him, but only under certain conditions. It had to take place after dark. He was to come alone. And the venue should be a neutral one. To all of this he agreed. I'd chosen the café with great care. It was located in the old quarter of the city, the 7th district, which was famous for its maze of narrow, winding streets and its clandestine squares. And I had Loots standing by, with his car. As soon as I stepped out of the café, he would draw up alongside me, I'd jump in, slam the door, and we'd be gone. Visser would be left on the pavement, too stunned even to have noted down the number-plate. It had been like planning a bank robbery; in fact, I'd been inspired by a film I'd watched at the weekend.

When I saw Visser, over by the window, I had the feeling that he was going to come clean at last. I'd been doing some thinking about it. Yes, he could feed anything he liked into my brain. But what good was it if he couldn't monitor the process? He needed my co-operation in order to continue the experiment, so it was time for him to sit down at the negotiating table. I could read imminent capitulation in his face as I walked towards him. That was the reason why I could smile at his little joke. Obviously, there had to be some play-acting first. A bit of light-hearted banter, repartee. He had to ease himself into a position where he could admit that I'd got the better of him.

'Cable?' I said. 'Yes, I'm getting cable. I'm getting channels most people have never even heard of.'

I sipped my tea. Visser was looking well. He'd trimmed his moustache (though it still looked as dictatorial as ever) and he was slightly tanned. He must have been away – some kind of conference or symposium, no doubt.

'It's a nice café.' He smiled and, turning in his chair, looked round. He seemed to be taking it all in: the marble tables, the waiters in their starched white aprons, the wall-lamps with their red shades. 'You know, I used to come here when I was a student,' he said. 'That was years ago, of course. I used to think I was really living it up.' He smiled again, this time at the folly of youth.

Living it up? That was an unusual phrase for him to use. Almost slangy. He was probably just trying to create the right mood. Relaxed, informal.

'It's my first time,' I said, and I, too, looked round. 'But it is nice, yes.' My eyes found their way back to him. 'How have you been, Doctor?'

'Very well.' He paused. 'You know, we had a break-in over the weekend.'

'At the clinic?'

'Yes. Nothing was taken, though. It's a bit of a mystery, actually.'

'So all your secrets are still safe?' I said.

He laughed heartily – rather too heartily, I thought.

We both reached for our cups of tea and drank.

'So tell me, Martin,' he said, 'why is it that we have to be so furtive? Why the cloak-and-dagger atmosphere?'

'I'm giving you another chance,' I said. 'In fact, it's your last chance. I'd like you to tell me the truth.'

'The truth,' he said.

'Yes.' I leaned back, crossed my legs. 'I'm not going to kick up a fuss about the fact that you're experimenting on me. I mean, you saved my life and I'm grateful for that. It's just that I don't want to be alone any more. Alone in what I know. I need you to admit that you know, too. That you've known all along. Right from the beginning.'

'Known what, Martin?'

'Known that I can see.' It occurred to me suddenly that if it was a state secret we were discussing, then he might not want anyone to overhear. And there was a man behaving suspiciously behind him. The man was pretending to be an intellectual. He had all the props: a left-wing newspaper, round glasses with wire frames, cigarette ash on his lapels. But the glasses didn't sit quite right on him. And he kept glancing at me sideways, past the edge of the page. I leaned forwards. 'Nurse Janssen knew,' I said, in a low voice. 'That's why she took off all her clothes. You know, too. You wouldn't have been following me otherwise. You wouldn't have turned up at the hotel.'

Visser didn't say anything, so I went on.

'First you gave me nocturnal vision, a kind of night-camera effect. I expect you called it something fancy, didn't you? Noctovision or something. Not much sense of colour, though, was there? Everything at the end of the spectrum looked black, for instance. White showed as pale-green. Yellow was slightly darker. Hard to tell the difference between a lime and a lemon. Could make gin-and-tonics difficult.' I gave him a wry smile. 'Then you began to feed the colour in. Just magical. But you know, it happened so gradually, I never even noticed. I just kind of took it for granted. And now, of course, I'm getting TV. And, I have to say, apart from the odd film, the occasional game show, I think I prefer the old night vision. Actually, I was thinking of asking you to reinstate it.'

I looked down at my hands for a moment. 'About the pornography,' I said quietly. 'It's a bit much. I mean, twice a week, fine. But not every night. Take Sunday, for instance. Sunday! I got nine hours of it. Nine hours of people taking their clothes off every time a door closes. Nine hours of women going, *Oh God, that's so great*, and men with that stupid look on their faces going, *Yes, Yes, Yes*. Incidentally, why do the men always look much more stupid than the women? Or is it me? Anyway. All night there were people fucking in my head. And then, just to round it off nicely, that home movie someone kindly sent in with the two thalidomide sisters and the Alsatian. I mean, Visser. What's going on? You think you're doing me some kind of favour? Favours like that I can do without. So, please. Let's have the old night vision back. In fact, that's really why I'm here. I want to come to some arrangement with you. I'm willing to co-operate.'

I leaned back in my chair. There was a long silence while Visser stirred his tea. The way he studied the spoon's elliptical motion in the cup, it could have been revealing something of the utmost importance.

'Let me get this quite clear,' he said at last. 'You think that I'm responsible for these various forms of vision which you claim to have?'

'I do.'

'You think that I'm controlling your vision? You think that I can switch it on or off at will?'

'Precisely.'

'And how am I able to achieve this?'

'I told you on the phone. You're using the titanium plate as some kind of substitute for the visual cortex. It's able to interpret the information that's being gathered by my eyes. You've even found a way of overriding it. You can feed signals into it from outside. It's remarkable, really. Very impressive. I should be congratulating you, Doctor.'

But Visser didn't beam with pride, as I'd expected him to. Instead, he let out a sigh. 'You know what I'm going to say, Martin, don't you?'

I swallowed nervously, looked down into my empty cup. The tea-leaves on the bottom said that I would shortly be receiving some bad news about a personal matter.

'You leave me no choice,' he said.

'What about?'

'Let me ask you something. Do you have any vision at the moment?'

'Yes.'

'What kind of vision is it?'

'It's night vision,' I said. 'You know that.'

'All right. Suppose you describe something for me. Something in this room. Anything you like.' His voice had lightened, as if we were playing a game.

'What about you?'

'Perfect.'

I sat back and looked at him. Where should I begin? Not the moustache. Too obvious.

'Well, let's see,' I said. 'There's your shoes. They've got metal on them.'

'You can hear that.'

'Just testing.' I smiled. 'Testing your alertness. Your shoes are black – '

'They're not black.'

'They're such a dark brown, I thought they were black.'

'What else?'

'Your hair,' I said. 'It's brown.'

'You knew that already. I told you, in the clinic.'

'All right.' I stayed calm. 'Your face, then. Let's start with your moustache – '

'I don't have a moustache.'

I stared at Visser in disbelief. 'But I'm looking right at it.'

'You're imagining it,' he said. 'The moustache is an illusion. It's part of the imaginary picture you've built up.'

He was trying to undermine me, establish control. He had that smile on his face, not so much indulgent now as patronising. We were back to square one. Square minus one.

'You must've shaved it off,' I said.

'Martin,' he said, still smiling, 'I've never had a moustache.'

'You're lying to me. Why are you lying to me?'

'No, Martin. You're the one who's lying. To yourself.'

I stormed out of the café. I was so furious, I knocked a table over on my way to the door and I didn't even stop to apologise.

Loots brought the car to the kerb as planned and I jumped in. He took the first corner fast, the steering-wheel spinning. I saw a woman leap backwards, her arms and legs outstretched, like a starfish, her mouth the same shape as Juliet's. I thought of Visser stirring his tea. Stirring it so fucking carefully, it could have been nitroglycerine. *You know what I'm going to say now, don't you.* I smashed my hand against the dashboard. Then I smashed it again.

Loots slowed down. 'It didn't go too well, I take it.'

I took off my dark glasses and rubbed my eyes with the hand that wasn't hurting. No, it didn't, I thought. It didn't *go too well.*

Would it ever?

It was something Karin Salenko had said to me while she was standing at the apartment window in that glittery turquoise dress. *Up there in the mountains, it's like a different century*. I asked Loots to look the village up for me. It wasn't in the atlas, but he found it on a touring map of the north-east. The area used to be known for its hot springs, he said. His uncle had told him about it once. His uncle lived in a small town on the same latitude, some distance to the west.

'Do you like your uncle?' I asked him.

Loots looked at me oddly, his head seeming to rise into the air above his collar. 'Yes, I like him.'

'How long since you saw him? Two years? Three?'

'About eighteen months.'

'Don't you think it's time you saw him again? I mean, after all,' and I paused heavily, significantly, 'he isn't getting any younger.'

Loots' head was still suspended in the air – puzzled, curious, and slightly blank, like a balloon. He suspected me of something, but he didn't know what it was. I was not unfamiliar with the look.

'I was just thinking,' I said. 'We could get away for a few days.'

'It's a long drive.'

'I know. But you could use a break. You look terrible.'

Loots laughed, but he knew I was right. Not long after he'd driven the getaway car for me, he'd punctured Juliet. He'd thrown a knife too close to her and it had grazed her rib-cage. She didn't explode or burst. She just withered, aged – which, if anything, was worse. He mended her, using a bicycle-repair kit, and blew her up again, and she stayed blown up, but his confidence was damaged. He'd stopped throwing knives in the afternoons before he left for work. He'd started dreaming about The Great Miguel. I knew why, too. It was that gatekeeper's ear. He'd read an article about it the next day in the paper. A small headline on page nine. MAN HAS EAR PINNED TO TREE. There was no comfort for Loots in the fact that he hadn't been identified. He'd hit somebody with a knife for the first time, and it had shaken him.

'So what's in it for you?' he said.

While he was visiting his uncle, I told him, I'd stay in the village, which was in a valley surrounded entirely by mountains. In the mountains, I said, people often had problems with their TVs. With reception . . .

Loots interrupted. 'You'll stop getting those programmes!'

I went to seize him by the shoulders, but in my enthusiasm I missed completely, embraced the air instead and overbalanced.

What was in it for me? What *wasn't* in it for me? The signals that Visser was transmitting would lose their way. The further north I went, the weaker they'd become. Until they faded altogether. I'd regain my night vision by a process of elimination, as it were, and Visser would have no say in the matter. The mountains would defend me. In the mountains I'd be free.

'It'll be like old times,' I said. 'You know, when we were looking for The Invisible Man.'

There was no breaking and entering involved, I told him. No dangerous driving. In fact, for one of my ideas, it was astonishingly mild. Harmless, even. We could travel up and back together, in his car.

'Just like old times,' I said again.

We left at six in the morning, while it was still dark, but daylight came and, with it, nothingness. The hours passed slowly; I'd forgotten how dull it was, how utterly interminable.

I'd spoken to Karin Salenko the day before. I wanted to learn a little more about the village. But when she answered, I didn't know how to begin. It was awkward, since our only common ground was Nina. I said the first thing that occurred to me: 'I met your husband.'

'Jan Salenko?'

'Yes,' I said. 'He was telling me about when you were eight, climbing into your father's truck – '

'He doesn't forget a thing, does he.'

'He said you were the most beautiful girl in the village.'

'That wasn't difficult.'

I smiled.

'You didn't ring up to talk about me, though,' Karin said.

'No.' I told her about the trip I was planning. I couldn't go into the real reasons behind it, so I presented it as a pilgrimage, a journey to the birthplace of someone I still loved, a kind of homage.

Karin was quiet for a few seconds, and when she spoke again, her voice was uneven, as if she'd been crying. 'I've only been back once,' she said, 'and that was years ago.'

'What was it like?'

'A mistake. I've had nightmares about it ever since.' I heard her tall glass clink against the phone. 'You mentioned my father,' she went on. 'It was to do with him.'

When she was fifteen, he had a stroke. He couldn't talk much after that. The next year, in the spring, she ran away, and it was impossible to keep in touch with him. Sometimes she called the hotel where her mother worked. She used to think she could hear him listening on the other end. She wrote letters, too. But it wasn't enough. Still, it was three or four years before she returned. Her mother was standing on the porch that day, wearing a pair of spectacles that made her eyes look twice the size of other people's. There was no sign of her father. Karin asked where he was. Upstairs, her mother said. In the back.

She found him sitting by the window, strapped into a bath chair with leather belts. The room smelled of his incontinence. He didn't know her at first. He leaned forwards, peering at her through his eyebrows. One of his hands moved constantly, the way plants do underwater. She took the hand and held it. Then he said her name.

'Yes,' she said, 'it's me.'

He didn't answer any of her questions, though, and he didn't ask her any either. There was only one thing he would talk about and that was his wife, her mother: Edith Hekmann. Karin wasn't prepared for the flood of bitterness and rage that he unleashed. After sitting with him for an hour, she realised that he didn't know her at all. It was a coincidence, him mentioning her name when she walked in. Her name was just a reflex. Something he repeated over and over, like a prayer, to anyone who happened to appear in the room. It had no meaning. She remembered staring at the steam rising from the sulphur pond and the fir trees, ghostly, beyond. Beside her, a man whispering her name. *Karin, Karin.* Piss grew in a dark pool on the floor. When she kissed him goodbye, he gripped her wrist with his good hand and she could feel the useless fury trembling in it.

'In a way, I was lucky,' Karin said. 'Three weeks later he was gone.'

I couldn't think of anything to say.

'And now you're going there . . .' She drank from her glass again.

'Your mother,' I said. 'Does she still work at the hotel?'

'She owns it now.' Karin lit a cigarette. 'It's not hard to find. It's the only hotel in the village.'

'Should I give her any message?'

She let a few moments pass. It was so quiet, I thought the line had gone dead.

'Mrs Salenko?'

'No,' she said. 'No message. In fact, don't mention me at all.'

After I'd put the phone down, I sat in the apartment for a long time, listening – the fridge, a car starting, rain on the skylight . . .

I turned to Loots. 'Where are we?'

He told me the name of the town we'd just passed through. I'd never heard of it. I opened the window, but it was drizzling, so I had to close it again.

I reached for the radio and switched it on. The news was just beginning. A feeling went through me, quick as an eel.

It was exactly one year to the day since I'd been shot.

Towards midday we blew a tyre. There was a flat bang and the car began to swerve, first one way, then the other, as if we were dodging missiles. We ended up on the wrong side of the road, two wheels in a shallow ditch. I could tell that Loots had been startled by the incident: a smell was rising off him, sharp and bitter, like the milky fluid in the stalks of plants.

We pushed the car back on to level ground. The air was damp; I could feel it sticking to the walls of my lungs. The south-bound traffic hurtled past us. Up here they judged you by your number-plate, and we were city people. No one was going to stop for us.

I asked Loots what the scenery was like. He said it was nothing special.

'You have to describe it for me,' I said. 'I want to see it.'

He sighed. 'It's flat. Just fields, really. Some hills off to the right. That's about it.'

'And the sky?'

'Grey.'

I thanked him.

He muttered something under his breath, then I heard him unlock the boot and lift out his tools. While Loots changed the wheel, I stood at the edge of the road with my hands in my pockets. I was looking eastwards, imagining the fields, the hills.

We drove on. I knew he was in a better mood half an hour later when he suddenly announced that the landscape had changed. The hills had moved closer, he told me, and more rock was showing through. It had holes in it, he said, like cheese.

'Really?' I said. 'Like cheese?' I chuckled.

At four in the afternoon we stopped at a roadside restaurant. I could smell coffee as soon as we walked in – a sour, boiled-down smell that meant it had been brewing for hours. They were playing music which managed to sound the same all the time without ever quite repeating itself. Robert Kolan came to mind. I took a table by the window and Loots sat oppositie. Our waitress seemed nervous. I thought it was probably me. Blind men are bad luck for some people, like the wrong number of magpies or a hat left on a bed. I wanted to explain that I was only blind during the day and that it wouldn't be long before I could see her waiting on me, any moment now, in fact – but then she'd think I was deranged as well.

Our meat and dumplings arrived. We hadn't eaten since dawn and the food smelled good. During the meal Loots talked with the long-distance lorry-drivers at the next table. He asked them about the road conditions further north. They told him rain was forecast. It might be a bit greasy in places. Watch the bends.

'We already blew a tyre,' Loots said.

'Where are you headed?' one of them asked.

Loots told him the name of the village.

'Don't know it,' the man said.

'I do,' said another. 'There's nothing there. Nothing but a bad smell, anyway.'

A couple of the men murmured in agreement.

'That'll be the sulphur springs,' Loots said. 'My friend here, he's got a condition. Kidney stones. We heard about the springs, that they were good for that.'

I could feel the lorry-drivers' eyes move over me. I knew what they were thinking. *Kidney stones as well? Poor bastard.* I was impressed by Loots' performance. That story about my condition, I could use that later on.

While we were eating our dessert, the lorry-drivers filed past us. They told us to take it easy. We said we would. The door to the restaurant creaked and then they were outside. I could hear them talking in the car-park, short sentences, no more than phrases, really, lobbed from one man to the other, like a game played with an invisible ball.

'Are you ready?' Loots said.

I nodded.

Outside, the wind was blowing hard. The car-park was the first thing I saw that evening. It was almost empty, the men already gone. I looked back towards the restaurant, a white timber building with a row of coloured lights along the roof. Loots buttoned his coat and tucked his chin into his collar. Beyond him there were clouds, high up, all moving at the same speed. A thin moon haunted the corner of the sky.

As soon as we were driving, a man's face appeared in front of me: it was the President, addressing the nation from his private office in the capital. He'd been criticised in the press for his economic policy, and there'd been rumours of an affair as well. Now he was on TV, to reassure us. He sat at his bureau desk in a a sober dark-blue suit. His grey hair swept neatly over the tops of his ears, and his hands were folded on a rectangle of green leather. Everything about him was scripted, composed – except for his left thumb, that is, which was twitching.

I opened the window. Loots took a deep breath, shifted in his seat. I couldn't see him, but I could imagine him: he always hunched over the wheel, his shoulders up around his ears.

'I'm sorry about the tyre, Loots.'

'That's all right. Anything on TV?'

'Only the President.'

We drove northwards, with the leader of our country still on air. He was doing something that politicians often do: he was smiling every fifteen seconds, and his smile never had anything to do with what he was saying. It reminded me of the smile some adults use with children. It means they've been confronted by something they're not familiar with, and might even be frightened of. I found him bearable if I concentrated on his thumb; it was the only part of him that seemed natural, the only part I trusted.

And, suddenly, as I watched, his whole face wobbled, buckled, then slid sideways, like a wax figure melting in a fire.

My turn to smile. The mountains. We were almost in the mountains.

Loots saw the signpost first. Then I saw it: white, and sharpened at one end. Fourteen kilometres to the village. It pointed left, a thin road that wound up from the valley floor.

'We're almost out of petrol.' Loots looked anxious.

'Don't worry,' I said. 'There's bound to be some in the village.'

For a few minutes we drove along the bottom of a gradually ascending gully. Fir trees rose above us on both sides. The smell of woodsmoke found its way into the car. There was a mountain ahead of us and the road swung westwards, around it, clinging to the lower slopes. I could see the snow now, glowing, high above. We were still among the fir trees, though, a forest that turned black when you looked into it. Loots hit a pothole, muttered something. The surface of the road was disintegrating. Probably it was hardly ever used.

Then, without any warning, the trees stepped back, and there was land on either side of us, rough pasture by the look of it, with slabs of rock showing, smooth and rounded in some places, jutting like the fins of fish in others.

We rounded a sharp right-angled bend and suddenly I could smell it. A hot, damp smell. Sulphur. We crept on to a bridge of narrow wooden slats that spanned a stream. I could see the shallow water breaking over beds of stones.

'We'll only just make it,' Loots said.

I was peering through the windscreen. 'Can you see the hotel?'

'Yes. There's someone standing on the porch. A woman.'

'It must be her,' I said.

Edith Hekmann was watching us approach. And there was a word in her head, too. I could hear it across the sloping patch of grass that separated us, as clearly as if she'd shouted it: *Strangers*. The word always meant the same thing to somebody like her. Just one thing. *People who are in the wrong place*.

Loots parked in front of the hotel. As he shifted into neutral, the engine spluttered and cut out. He turned the key in the ignition. The engine fired, then died again.

'We've run out of petrol.' Loots was talking through his window to the woman on the porch. He sounded apologetic.

She just watched us. She had grey curls and thick, stockinged ankles, and she wore a shapeless dress with a cardigan over it. One of Loots' hands rose from the steering-wheel and touched the growth of bristle on his chin.

'You passing through?' the woman said.

'No,' Loots said. 'We're looking for a place to stay.'

'The petrol station's down the road,' the woman said, 'about a kilometre.'

Loots thanked her.

'But it'll be closed now,' the woman said.

I opened my door and got out. I stretched, then moved round to the back of the car. I was wearing my dark glasses and tapping at the unpaved road with my white stick. I started drawing in the dust with it. I drew a woman's face. Eyes, nose, mouth – all in the right place. Then, remembering what Karin had said, I added a pair of spectacles. The woman crossed the patch of grass. She stopped beside me and stood with her head at an angle, examining the picture. In the meantime I filled the background in. Behind the face was the hotel. A porch with a chair on it. Steps. Two windows. A stone chimney at the side. I even drew the pump on the front lawn. Though I got the handle wrong, deliberately.

'Not bad for a blind man,' the woman said.

I studied her through my dark glasses, as though she was something I might be interested in buying. If the price was right. 'You must be Mrs Hekmann.'

She grunted.

'You run the hotel,' I said, 'don't you.'

The cigarette in her fingers had burned down to the filter. One flick of her wrist and it was past me, into the road.

'The waters are famous,' I said. 'I heard about it.'

'It's sulphur water. It's not going to do much for you.'

My head dropped. I moved my white cane on the ground – one way, then the other. 'Well,' I said, 'I heard about it, anyway.'

She was still staring at me. It didn't bother her that she might have offended me, not even remotely. She was simply coming to some decision of her own.

'We don't usually get people at this time of year.' She paused. 'We don't usually get people at all.'

'If you know of somewhere else . . .' Blindly, I looked away from her, into the great dark night. Trees breaking like waves on the far side of the road.

'It's fifteen each,' she said, 'and that includes the pool.'

'The pool?'

'The waters. What you came here for.'

What I came here for.

'What's the reception like up here?' I said.

'The reception?'

'You know, the reception. On TV.'

'You mean the picture?'

I nodded.

'You don't get much of a picture, not up here,' she said.

'Loots?' I said. 'Let's get the cases out.'

I woke in a kind of panic, an orange sky above me and, closer than the sky, the dark arc of a car's tyre, and I could hear the sirens circling. I lay still, my body hot and damp. I waited until I knew I was in bed. Until I knew which bed it was. The drive north: I remembered it slowly, and in detail – the puncture, the lorry-drivers in the restaurant, some fin-shaped rocks, my sketch of Edith Hekmann. I remembered myself all the way back to where I was, shivering a little as I felt the sweat begin to dry.

I swung my legs on to the floor and waited again. Then I stood up. I crossed the room to the small basin in the corner. I ran the cold tap. Cupping my hands under it, I brought the water to my face. Once, twice, three times. I couldn't find the towel, though. I had to use the curtain instead; it smelled unpleasantly of mildew and tobacco. As I stood there, drying my hands and face, I heard a light tapping on the door.

'Who is it?'

'It's me. Loots.'

I opened the door. Loots' narrow face floated up out of the darkness on the first-floor landing. He was wearing an overcoat. And socks. He moved past me, into the room.

'Are you all right?' he said.

I closed the door. 'Yes. I'm fine.'

'I heard shouting.'

'I had a dream.' I went and sat on the bed. 'I'm sorry. Did I wake you?'

'No.' He shook his head. 'I was already awake. It was something else.' He stood at the window and parted the curtain with one hand. 'Did you hear anything?'

'Like what?'

'Footsteps. Outside.' He turned back into the room. He was picking at the skin around a nail; it was as if only one of his hands was alive, and it was preying on the other. Something had woken him, he was saying. When he looked out of the window he saw a man crossing the car-park. The man was tall and thin, with pale hair, and he carried his arms at some distance from his body, the way you might if your clothes were wet. At the top of the steps that led down to the pool the man stopped, glanced round, his head on one side, listening, then he turned and disappeared into the steam.

'There was something about it,' Loots said. 'I don't know what.' He was shivering. I could hear his teeth.

'It was probably a guest,' I said.

'There aren't any guests apart from us. I looked.'

'Maybe you were dreaming.'

'No,' he said. 'I don't think so.'

After Loots had left the room, I went to the window. Leaned against it. I'd just remembered something. *Tall and thin, with pale hair*. They were more or less the same words Munck had used about the man in the railway station. The man who had stared at Nina. Followed her.

What was this, a coincidence?

I looked out of the window. The car-park was empty. Dead leaves blew over the gravel, moving in loose formations, like birds, or dancers.

I closed the curtains.

It had been a disconcerting evening. We checked into our rooms, which were next to each other, on the first floor. While I was unpacking, Loots called through my door, saying that he'd meet me in the dining-room downstairs; though we'd arrived too late for supper, Edith Hekmann had agreed to put something out for us. Nine o'clock was striking as I locked my door. Looking left, there was a window with a view of the car-park. In front of the window stood a small upholstered chair and a table which had a telephone on it. The main body of the landing stretched away to my right. I walked until I reached the top of the stairs, then, on impulse, I walked further, discovering two more rooms, numbers 6 and 7. At the far end of the landing there was a door with no number on it. I tried the handle; it was locked. Was this where Karin's father had been kept? I bent down and put my nose to the keyhole, but all I could smell was dust and varnish.

'Is there something I can help you with?'

It was Edith Hekmann's voice. I straightened up, turned round. She was watching me from the top of the stairs.

'I was lost,' I said.

'I thought I heard somebody fall.'

'I didn't hear anything.'

'It's always dark up here,' she said. 'We try and keep the lights turned off. It saves on electricity.' She paused. 'I don't suppose it makes much difference to you.'

'No difference at all.' I smiled.

'Were you looking for something?'

'No, not really. Well, the stairs, I suppose.'

'That door you were listening at,' she said, 'there's a notice on it.'

'Is there?' I reached out with blind man's hands. 'What's it say?'

'It says Private.'

I started to apologise, but she was already walking back down the stairs, smoke trailing from her cigarette.

I saw her again in the dining-room, a large draughty space at the back of the building, with windows on two sides. The floor was made of creaking boards that gave under your feet. On the walls were several dismal paintings of farmyards, cottages and cattle. I joined Loots at a round table near the door. One low-voltage light bulb hung above the white-lace tablecloth. Shielded by a wide, pale-pink china shade with a scalloped edge, it gave me the feeling that I was looking up a woman's skirt, at something that was glowing.

Loots spoke in a whisper. 'It's more like an old people's home than a hotel – '

But he couldn't elaborate because Edith Hekmann was walking across the room towards us. She served a plate of cold meat, some warmed-up cabbage and a few slices of stale bread, with tinned fruit to follow. Tap-water to drink. Though she'd already eaten, she sat with us throughout the meal. Between courses, she smoked a cigarette. Every once in a while, as I leaned close to her, I thought I could smell alcohol on her breath. She asked where we'd come from. Loots told her. She'd only been to the city once in her life, she said, making no attempt to hide her obvious distaste. She'd seen enough.

'It must've changed a lot since you were there,' Loots said.

'It was six weeks ago.' She left the room. I heard her talking to the girl who was washing dishes in the kitchen.

'I was only trying to be polite,' Loots whispered.

I imitated him. 'It must've changed a lot since – '

He kicked me under the table.

Everything I'd eaten or drunk that night carried the flavour of slightly rotten eggs. I didn't mention it. Instead, I complimented her on the meal. Her mouth widened and she touched the palm of one hand to her hair, feeling the shape of her hair rather than the hair itself. It was a gesture I recognised. My mother always used to do it. On her it seemed pretentious, neurotic. When Edith Hekmann did it, however, it betrayed a strangely haunting vanity. The vanity of a woman who had lived her life in isolation and had never been admired. She could believe that she was beautiful because she had nobody to contradict her. I realised that I was looking forward to being alone with her. Alone, I could indulge her, draw her out. Alone, we would get on; I was sure of it.

I leaned towards her, smelled the alcohol again. 'You said not many people come here now. What about before?'

That was all the encouragement she needed. She launched into a history of the inn. It began when a man came from the city to study the water. Inside his suitcase were hundreds of tiny bottles no bigger than rifle cartridges. He collected samples, did tests, wrote reports. At the end of his stay he told the people of the village that the water had all kinds of beneficial powers and properties. He even listed the chemicals it contained, and in what proportions. Largely on the strength of what he said, a family called the Bohlins built the inn. It was a modest place, but each room had a balcony with its own hanging basket of geraniums, and there was a natural hot sulphur pool among the rocks at the back. To begin with, the inn was often full. Statesmen, actors, dukes – they all drove up from the city to take the waters; it was the fashionable thing to do (in Mrs Hekmann's mouth, the word had a disdainful twist to it). During the day they lounged in the pool with their newspapers and their cigars, or played croquet on the lawn (there'd been a lawn back then). They spent the evenings on their balconies, sipping the foul-tasting water and telling each other how much better they felt. The inn had kept her father in work. A carpenter by trade, he'd built most of the furniture. He used to carry out repairs on the property as well. All this was before her time, of course. Though even when her older brother Karl took over, the place had been popular. By then it catered more to people who had read about it in books, or people who had genuine ailments, but somehow they weren't made to feel welcome by Karl and his wife, and they seldom came back. Soon even the locals stayed away, and during the last few years it had become a lodging-house where old people from the village lived, people who had no family left, people who could afford to pay for bed and board.

'Now, if someone comes,' she said, 'we wonder why.'

She left the table again. This time I heard a cupboard open and close. I thought I heard a cork spring from a bottle, too. There was no mistaking the smell clouding the air around her when she sat down. Something sweet, it was. Sherry, perhaps. Or a liqueur.

'All those sick people we got,' she said.

I smiled to myself, but she didn't even notice.

People with skin disease, gallstones, rheumatism, they all came to the springs thinking they could cure themselves; sometimes they even left thinking they were cured, which was good for business, of course. In her opinion, they were fooling no one but themselves. All the water did was make your skin soft when you bathed in it, soft in a way that didn't seem quite natural. In the end your mind went soft as well. She'd never spent much time in it. In fact, in her family, they'd never even learned to swim.

'My husband swam in it,' she said, 'but it didn't do anything for him.' She paused. 'He's dead, in case you're wondering.'

'Oh,' I said. 'I'm sorry.'

'I can't say I am.' She laughed. 'Towards the end, it was – ' She paused to light another cigarette and left the sentence dangling. 'We never got on very well,' she went on. 'We never did see eye to eye about much.'

'Do you live here alone then?'

She hesitated, as if the question had several answers and she had to choose between them. 'No,' she said at last. 'I have a son.'

'I haven't seen him,' Loots said.

'He's away.' She tapped her cigarette against the edge of a saucer. We were drinking coffee by then, so weak you could taste the water in it. 'I had a daughter, but she left. That was twenty years ago.'

Karin, I thought.

'Yes,' she said, 'there's just the two of us now. Everybody else is either dead or gone.'

What stayed in my mind, what was still there as I lay in bed, seeing nothing but the window and the rain on it, was the satisfaction in her voice. They were the last words she'd spoken before she left us, and they ran together, they were slightly slurred, but there was none of the self-pity or regret you might have expected. If anything, she seemed to be taking a kind of pleasure in what had happened. She was almost gloating.

After dinner I'd walked down to the pool with Loots. The night was cold and clear. In the moonlight his cheekbones looked more rounded than ever, and polished, too, like bedknobs. He stood on the terrace with his hands in his pockets and his shoulders hoisted. He talked about the steam rising off the water, how odd it looked, almost artificial. I thought of Gregory's bald head.

'You didn't mention Nina,' he said suddenly. 'You didn't say you knew her.'

'No, I know. I'm not sure why. And now it feels too late, somehow.' I walked across the terrace to the wooden rail that bounded it. 'Maybe it'll just come up naturally,' I said, 'in conversation.' I leaned my forearms on the rail. Beyond it, the ground plunged into darkness. In the distance, on the far side of the valley, I saw trees outlined against the sky. The sky was lighter than the trees, the division between the two uneven, serrated, as if a piece of torn black paper had been placed on a piece of paper that was grey. 'They're not a very close family,' I went on, after a while. 'It wouldn't surprise me if she didn't even know that Nina's missing.'

Loots joined me at the rail. 'She's strange.'

'You think so?'

'It's the way she looks at us.'

'I didn't notice anything.'

In the silence that followed I could hear the sulphur water rushing along its narrow channel in the rock and tumbling down into the pool. I thought Loots was being dramatic. Her prickly manner had to do with where she lived; it was as natural as a dialect. You couldn't judge her for it.

'She's a country person,' I told him. 'You know what country people are like. They're suspicious. They don't like strangers.'

'She runs a hotel.'

'Yes, but nobody's stayed here for ages.'

Loots didn't say anything.

'There's just a couple of fucked-up old people to look after,' I went on. 'You'd be strange.'

'Maybe.' He didn't sound convinced.

He stepped back from the rail and began to take off his clothes. I asked him what he was doing.

'I'm going to take the waters,' he said.

He stripped down to his underpants, which were baggy and misshapen. He was very thin: shoulderblades like triangles (I thought of the signs you see on the back of trucks sometimes, or outside nuclear facilities, the signs that mean CAUTION: RADIOACTIVE MATERIAL). I watched him spring into the air, turn over twice and slide into the water, exactly the kind of acrobatic dive that I would have predicted. There was no need to comment on it. Instead, I asked him what the water was like.

'Warm,' he said. 'Kind of silky, too.'

'Silky?'

'Yes. Like there's oil in it. Are you coming in?'

'I don't think so.'

I found a bench and sat down. Loots floated somewhere below me. I'd never liked swimming. Even before I was shot, I didn't like it. And afterwards, it just got worse. I went swimming at the clinic once. Therapy, they called it. I panicked. It was the four sides of the pool – I didn't believe they were there. When I stretched a hand out, there'd be no tiles, no ropes – nothing to hold on to. It was like being someone who thought the world was flat: the pool was something I could reach the end of and, when I did, I'd fall over the edge.

'You're sure you don't mind me going tomorrow?' Loots said.

'I don't mind at all. How long will you stay at your uncle's?'

'Till Wednesday.'

'And you'll come for me on your way back?'

A note of uncertainty must have crept into my voice, because he laughed.

'Of course,' he said. 'I wouldn't just leave you here, would I.'

I lay awake on the first floor of the hotel, rain still landing on the window, making the glass look torn. It was Saturday night. Wednesday wasn't far away. And I had no sense of what might happen after that. I wasn't sure that returning to the city was such a good idea, and yet I could hardly stay where I was. It was as if I'd found myself in the pool after all. I couldn't keep swimming indefinitely, but how could I get out if I didn't trust the edges?

In the morning I walked to the local garage with Loots to buy petrol. A kilometre, Mrs Hekmann had told us, but it was more like three. Loots claimed she'd misled us deliberately, out of some perversity or spite. I disagreed. It was simply that the road was so familiar to her; she thought of it as shorter than it actually was. In the end, it didn't matter. We enjoyed our walk. Loots described the countryside as we passed through it. There were pine forests, stands of silver birches. There were houses made of wood and painted the same colours as the land, green or brown or yellow, many with carved balconies and eaves. There were farmyards inhabited by geese with orange beaks, and barns weathered to an even grey, the skins of scavengers and rodents nailed to their walls. Loots was more observant than the day before, more specific, his descriptive powers honed, no doubt, by the knowledge that he would soon be gone. Once, though, his voice lifted in genuine excitement as he noticed a cow standing on a frozen stream and drinking from a hole in the ice.

Later, I stood outside the hotel and listened to him drive away. At the last minute he'd asked if I wanted to come with him. It wasn't too late, he said. I smiled. The truth was, I was eager for him to leave; there was a great impatience in me that I couldn't have explained.

The sound of the car was a shape in the air that slowly sharpened to a point, then sharpened still further, into nothing. It was only then, in the silence, that I felt uncertain. I went up to my room and slept.

When I woke up, it was dark but I thought I had time to stretch my legs before dinner so I put on my overcoat and a pair of gloves, and went downstairs. The hallway was deserted. I opened the front door and stood on the porch. Smoke blew past my face from a chimney somewhere not too far away. The wood they burned in the village had a sweet edge to it and, for a moment, I had the feeling that I'd travelled back in time, that I'd been returned to some much earlier part of my life.

I crossed the road and ducked between the rails of a fence, then climbed down a steep grass bank into a field. Edith Hekmann had told me there was a river at the end of it. I took a few steps, stopped and listened. I thought I could hear the water, though it could have been the wind in the trees. And besides, if that stream the cow was drinking from had frozen over, then maybe the river was frozen, too.

As I wandered through the long grass, the city came to me, the city as it had been when I moved back to it – those first few weeks of freedom. Night after night I'd walked down empty shopping streets, through parks, over bridges: a process of reacquaintance, a new life laid over the old one. In the red-light district the whores would hiss and whistle as I passed their ultraviolet doors. Some of them even learned my name, I walked that way so often. To them I wasn't blind or strange; I was just a man, like any other. Who else knew me? Gregory, brooding over a schnapps in Leon's. Loots on his bicycle, juggling unlikely objects with his feet. And then there was Nina, whose appearance was no less magical. *Can I kiss you?* What kind of opening line was that? In some ways, I felt like Jan Salenko: I could remember every time I'd ever seen her – from the first moment, in the Bar Sultan, to the last, outside the Kosminsky. I could remember every motel and every drink. I could remember every drive. She was the only person I'd ever told my secret to in its entirety. I didn't think I'd frightened her, whatever Candy said. I thought Munck had it right. It was a family crisis. She'd had to sever all connections, I understood that now. I understood. The city would look after me.

But Visser had ruined it. He found me and everything began to fall apart. I had to leave my hotel room, my home. I had to hide like some kind of criminal or refugee. I had to start again, from scratch. I couldn't forgive him for that. A thought went through my head, as random as a bird across the sky. *Suppose I killed him.* Not for revenge, but for relief. I'd be acting in self-defence. You couldn't call it murder. Not after the way he'd persecuted me. Manslaughter, maybe. But not murder. So. Say Visser was dead. What would happen then? Would there be somebody waiting to step into his shoes, some Visser-worshipper, some eager protégé? Or would the entire project be shelved, its secret files stored in dusty vaults under the clinic, ignored, forgotten and even, in the end, destroyed? There was no way of knowing. It was an idea, though. To do away with him. To liberate myself.

The ground sloped downwards suddenly. I had to be careful; it would've been easy to turn an ankle. Still, I thought, I was free of Visser for the time being. The far north-east of the country, a place most people had never even heard of. Of course it was tempting fate to think that way. Visser was master of the surprise appearance: like a tragedy or a natural disaster, he always struck when you were least expecting it. I stopped and looked around. Looked for his face floating in the darkness of the field. Looked for that earnest, condescending face. But there was nothing. Only grass sloping downwards, combed by the wind. Only trees huddled in a grove and a hard cold sky above.

At last I reached the river. It wasn't frozen; it slid below me, almost motionless. There wasn't much to look at. A narrow footpath wound its way along the bank. Up ahead, a bend to the right, the river's elbow silver where the moonlight landed on it. In the distance I could see a bridge of wooden trestles. Was that the bridge Jan Salenko had spoken of? The place where he first saw his future wife, then only eight years old?

To liberate myself.

I sat down on the river bank. I took out a pen and a blank page which I'd torn out of the back of the hotel bible. I wrote, *Kill Visser*. The words looked good together, sounded good. They had some kind of natural affinity. I would move back into my old room at the Kosminsky. Arnold would be his usual miserable self (maybe he would even remind me not to loiter on the second floor!). Would the lift be working? I doubted it. The first priority was to get hold of a gun. Loots would know someone who knew someone. Or Gregory. Someone would know. Then I'd simply wait for Visser to appear . . .

One night, I hear him walking up the corridor in his highly polished shoes. I know it's him: I recognise his footsteps from the clinic. I'm not sure how many shots I'm going to fire. That stranger in the supermarket car-park only fired once and look at me. I'm not dead. So two, then. Maybe even three. Do I want him to confess before I kill him? Does that really matter any more? The door opens cautiously. Some light spills in around him, but it's not enough to make any difference.

'Stop right there,' I say.

He stops. 'Martin?' He always uses my Christian name. It's a technique. It's supposed to make me treat him as a friend, and trust him. Or treat him as a parent, and obey him. I'm not sure which. 'Is that a gun?'

'I wouldn't try anything,' I say.

'I wouldn't dare,' he says. 'A blind man with a gun?' It's his own joke, but he laughs at it anyway. Well, someone's got to.

I quieten my voice right down and give it metal edges. 'That's right, I'm blind,' I say, 'but I can hear the outlines of your body. I can hear where your body ends and the air begins . . .'

He hesitates. I tell him that it's true what people say about enhancement of the senses. Your eyes go, and the efficiency of your nose and ears and all the rest instantly increases by hundreds of per cent.

'For instance,' I say, 'I can hear your heart beating. It's a bit faster than usual, and no wonder. It's a tense situation.' I pause. 'I can hear your liver purifying what you drank last night. I can hear your bowels. There's turbulence down there . . .'

He takes a step backwards, into the corridor. He's about to make a run for it. I fire. He cries out, crumples in the doorway.

'Oh, don't go,' I say.

He's on the floor. 'You shot me.'

'Is it serious?'

'It's my leg.'

'Well,' I say, 'I did warn you.' I shift in my chair. The moulded plastic one. 'I could shoot you again,' I say. 'I might get you in the balls this time. It wouldn't be deliberate. I mean, how could it be? I'm blind.' I raise the gun.

'No. No, it's all right. I'll tell you everything.'

I stand over him. I'm smiling.

'You're lucky,' I say.

'Am I?' he whispers. He's not so sure.

'Yes. No one's ever seen my room before.' I bend over him. 'So,' I say, 'how do you like it?'

The wind plucked at my piece of paper. I smoothed it down. Slowly I drew a line through what I'd written. I couldn't even kill Visser in my head. What chance would I have in real life?

I stood up and walked on, along the river bank. Wednesday. There was no avoiding it. But surely there was something I could do. Here, in the mountains, I was free of Visser's signals. No housewives, no game-show hosts, no pornography – nothing. Wasn't there some man-made way of reproducing that effect? There had to be. I thought of a friend of mine, who worked in broadcasting. We'd never been particularly close, but I knew him well enough to call him. His name was Klaus – Klaus Wilbrand. He'd be able to advise me. It was crossing the line drawn by the bullet, it was stepping back into the past, but I could see no alternative.

I looked up. The bridge didn't seem to be any nearer. Suddenly I wearied and a chill went through me. I didn't think I could make it to the bridge. Maybe some other night. I should go back. I left the footpath, climbing a slope into what I took to be the field I'd crossed not long before. But I walked for several minutes and still I couldn't see the lights of the hotel. An owl startled me, swooping through the air just overhead. I saw its flattened face, the smudges around its eyes. I heard the beat of its wings, stirring the heavy air, the same speed as my breathing. I stood there in the middle of the field. I couldn't see any lights at all. I couldn't see where the road might be either. Was I lost?

I felt I should go back the way I'd come, but the thought exhausted me. Instead, I cut diagonally across the field. At the end of it, there was no grass bank, no road, only a barbed-wire fence and another field beyond. I stood still. I could hear a dog barking in the distance. Away to my right I could see lights, small yellow squares in the great mass of darkness that surrounded me. They looked like windows. A farm, perhaps. They appeared, disappeared. Appeared again. As if someone was signalling. I thought it had to be the trees between us, shifting in the wind. I didn't believe they were the lights of the hotel, but I decided to make my way towards them.

I crossed the field, climbed through another fence, and found myself in a kind of pasture. The ground was rougher here, more uneven. Though I tried to watch where I was putting my feet, I stumbled several times.

After a while I looked up and noticed that the lights were gone. I waited for them to appear again, but they didn't. The darkness was absolute and unrelenting. I could only think of one explanation: the people must have gone to bed. I was tired now, and my trousers were cold and slippery with mud. I was in country I didn't know. No landmarks, and nobody to ask for guidance. It had been foolish of me to think I could just go out for a walk. I wasn't in the city.

I wondered how much time had passed. An hour at least, maybe two. People would be going to sleep soon, if they weren't asleep already. There was nothing for it but to try and get some sleep myself. When dawn came, I could begin again. With luck I'd find somebody who could tell me where I was.

I was standing at the entrance to a wood. I followed one edge of it, hoping to find a hut, a lean-to, some kind of shelter. I quickly gave that up. Instead, I walked in among the tall trunks and the undergrowth. Here, at least, I might be able to escape the wind. I found a tree that I thought would give me some protection. Its roots were raised above the level of the forest floor; they reached out like fingers from the base. I gathered sprays of bracken and a few dead branches, then I stacked leaves in one of the gaps between the roots. I arranged some bracken over me and weighed it down with the branches I'd collected. I lay there with my eyes shut and my knees drawn up against my chest. Sleep wouldn't come, though. The cold had already found its way into my bones, and there were sounds all around me – the sound of the woodland shifting, straining, groaning; I could have been lying on the deck of some huge old-fashioned sailing ship. I opened my eyes, looked up into the intricate bare branches of the tree. If only Visser knew what lengths I'd gone to, just to avoid his TV programmes! I smiled, but it was a smile that stayed inside me. I pulled the collar of my coat up around my ears and closed my eyes again.

I must have slept, if only in snatches, because I remember having a conversation with my sister, Gabriela. We were standing in the garden at home. We were both excited, talking as though we knew each other, as though we were friends. I had no memory of what we said. I only remember watching her run down the garden to where my mother and my father were. Their three faces turned towards me, small and round and blank, like plates. I stayed where I was – the house in the distance, the warm summer air, the almost golden grass.

I sat up. There were leaves in my mouth, my hair. My body was stiff with cold. It surprised me that I'd slept at all. I slowly pushed the bracken and dead branches away from me and stood up. One of my knees had stiffened during the night, but I thought I could walk on it. It would be best to try and return the way I'd come, though in daylight, of course, that wouldn't be easy. I was a blind man in a strange country. I might just get lost in a different kind of way.

I'd been walking for half an hour or so, a light drizzle falling, when I heard a noise I hadn't heard before. I stood still, listened. Grating, clinking, grinding. The sound of wheels. No engine, though. It had to be a horse and cart. I started shouting and waving. There was no reply, but I noticed that all the noise had stopped; a new silence had descended. I hurried towards it. Suddenly the ground disappeared in front of me and I fell forwards. A hand reached down and hauled me to my feet.

'Thank you,' I said. 'Thanks very much.'

I must have been an odd sight, with my dark glasses and my white stick, and standing in a field with mud all over me, at dawn.

'I'm lost,' I said.

'I thought so.' It was a man's voice, and there wasn't a trace of irony in it.

I told him the name of the village where I was staying, the name of the hotel.

'You're a long way from there,' he said.

'Am I?'

His thoughts came one at a time, and they were scarce, like cars on a motorway at night. There was a gap between everything he said, a time-delay, which made it feel as if nothing was happening. But I was already grateful to him, grateful just for the sound of his voice.

'Which way do I go?' I asked him.

'You're in luck. Just so happens, I'm going there myself.'

He helped me up on to the cart and told me to sit on the side of it, as he was, with my legs dangling over the edge, then he clacked his tongue against the roof of his mouth and shook the reins and we moved off. The drizzle had slackened; the air was still damp and I could hear the trees and bushes dripping. The man had a strong smell to him, a smell that was like old butter, but peppery as well.

'That's Mrs Hekmann's place,' he said, after a few minutes.

'That's right. You know her?'

'I thought of marrying her once.'

I looked in his direction. 'Really? What happened?'

'Nothing.' He paused. 'I never asked.'

Though I was curious, I didn't speak just yet; I brushed at the mud on my coat instead. It seemed natural to slow down, talk at his pace.

'How come you never asked her?' I said eventually.

'I just never did.' He shook the reins again and muttered something at the horse. 'The most I ever asked her was to dance. She wouldn't.' There was a long silence. Then he cleared his throat and spat. 'Most people, they steer clear of her now.'

'She seems friendly enough,' I said.

He didn't talk much after that.

At last I heard the boards of a bridge rattle as we passed over it, and I thought it had to be the same bridge that Loots and I had crossed on Saturday evening. On the far side, the man climbed down on to the road and began to walk. All of a sudden, he let out a cry. Haunting, it was – more animal than human; I almost jumped out of my skin. A few moments later he cried out again, only this time I realised what it was: he was a rag-and-bone man. The cry was repeated every few paces, and it had no effect whatsoever on our surroundings. He didn't seem unduly troubled. Probably he was used to the indifference; it was part of his trade.

When we stopped outside the hotel, I thanked him again.

'I was coming through here anyway,' he said.

'Still,' I said, 'I appreciate it.'

I crossed the patch of grass and climbed the steps to the hotel. Behind me, his cry grew fainter as he moved on down the street. I felt for the front door.

'Siding with the enemy now, are we?'

I turned round. 'Mrs Hekmann?' She must have been standing on the porch the whole time, watching me.

'That man you got a lift with,' she said, 'you know who he was?'

'He didn't tell me his name.'

'That was Jonas Poppel. One of the Poppel family.'

I didn't know what she was talking about. 'If it hadn't been for him,' I said irritably, 'I'd still be wandering the fields.'

'You missed dinner.'

'I know. I went for a walk. I got lost.'

'Have you been out all night?'

I nodded. 'Yes.'

'Did you sleep at all?'

'I tried to. Under a tree.'

'We used to sleep outside,' she said, almost dreamily, 'my brother and I. But we were young then and it was in the summer.' She was sitting in her rocking-chair. I could hear the creak of it now, like breathing. 'You should see yourself.'

I smiled faintly.

'You know what would do you good?' she said. 'One of our special baths.' There was a pump-room in the basement, she explained. Nobody had used it in a while, but she was sure that Mr Kanter could get it working. Mr Kanter was a part-time masseur. He'd learned some interesting techniques when he was abroad. It was just what I needed, in her opinion.

'Maybe later,' I said. 'When I've slept a little.'

Upstairs in my room I drew the curtains. I took off my trousers and left them soaking in the basin, then climbed into bed. I was too tired to call Klaus; it would have to wait a few hours. The sheets were cold and the mattress sagged, but I could feel myself falling, sinking down – that long, parabolic drop into unconsciousness. Somewhere far away I heard the sound of spoons in cups and knives and forks on plates, as delicate and mysterious as an oriental language. The old people would be eating breakfast in the dining-room below.

Since there was no phone in my room, I used the one in the corridor. I called Directory Enquiries and they gave me a number. I sat there, with the receiver in my hand. It was Monday, a few minutes after six. Klaus Wilbrand always worked late. It was a good time to try him.

When I dialled the broadcasting company, a woman answered. I asked for Klaus and she put me through.

'Hello?'

'Klaus, is that you?'

'Who's this?'

'It's Martin Blom.'

There was a shocked sound on the other end. It must've been at least two years since we'd spoken to each other.

'Martin. Jesus. How are you?'

'I'm fine. Listen, I want to – '

'You were shot, weren't you?' His voice had incredulity in it, regret as well, and a kind of awe. It's a special voice. People use it when they're speaking to someone something bad has happened to.

'That's right. I was.'

'Someone said you – '

'Yes, yes. But listen, Klaus. I want to ask you something. It's about television.'

'OK . . .' He sounded doubtful. Or perhaps it was just that I'd interrupted him. Well, I didn't have all day, and this was important.

'Say I was in a room,' I said, 'and I wanted to stop TV signals from coming in. How would I do it?'

'Well, you'd have to insulate the room somehow.'

This was better. He was alert suddenly. Excited. It was his work we were talking about. I thought he was probably relieved, too, not to have to discuss the shooting, all that awkwardness.

'How would I insulate it?' I said.

He told me there were several ways. I would have to use a conductive material. Wire-mesh would do – though not just any wire-mesh, since the holes had to relate to the frequency of the signals.

'And I attach it to the walls or what?'

'That's right,' he said. 'The ceiling and the floor as well.'

There was also something called metallic foil plaster-board, he went on. You could buy it at any do-it-yourself shop. Or I could even use plain old aluminium foil. If I covered the room in foil and then earthed it, that would work just fine.

'How do you mean, earth it?'

He explained that all the panels of silver foil would have to be taped together, so they overlapped. Then I'd have to fix a screw into each panel and run a wire from the screws down to a plug in the wall. Or, better still, into a metal pipe embedded in the ground. I could use a meter to check that the flow of electrical current was continuous.

'It wouldn't be very sightly, of course,' he said. 'That's why I suggested a metal cage of some kind. But the silver-foil method would be cheaper.'

'And that would block the signals?'

'Nothing would get through. Nothing at all.'

'Klaus,' I said, 'you're brilliant.'

He laughed. 'When am I going to see you?'

'Well, I'm up north at the moment . . .' I promised to call when I got back, though I didn't think I would. I thanked him for the information (that, at least, was perfectly sincere) and said goodbye.

I put the phone down and then I held my cane in both hands, parallel to the ground, and did a little dance in the corridor, just like they used to in the old musicals. I hummed a tune to go along with it. I could already imagine the scene in Walter Sprankel's shop – the jangle of the bell, his eyes fidgeting above the till . . .

I would build myself a room out of aluminium foil and bits of wire and screws. It would be a silver room, and I'd live in it, insulated and at peace, spared all forms of interference. I'd see what I wanted to see. My thoughts would be my own.

I was still dancing when someone coughed behind me.

'Mr Blom?'

'Yes?'

'Your sulphur bath is ready. Down in the pump-room. If you'd like to follow me . . .'

I glanced round. At the top of the stairs I saw a short, wooden-looking man with ginger hair and a mole in the middle of his cheek. Mr Kanter, presumably. The masseur.

I beamed at him. 'I'd be delighted to.'

That night I sat at the same round table, under the same pale-pink china lampshade. Nothing would ever be different in that room, no matter how long I stayed. I couldn't imagine another guest, for instance. I couldn't imagine it in summer.

The old people had eaten earlier, and I was alone with Mrs Hekmann. I thought she'd forgiven me for siding with the enemy, as she called it; in fact, she seemed to have forgotten all about it. I could feel her suspicion lifting with each minute that went by. Her hand moved forwards, into the light; her index-finger tapped her cigarette against the edge of the ashtray. She smelled of alcohol already; she must've started earlier than usual. I could see the kitchen doorway over her shoulder, a rectangle of yellow that was interrupted, every now and then, as the silhouette of Martha, her hired girl, passed through it.

'And how was it,' she said, 'with Mr Kanter?'

I had to smile. 'I've never come across anything quite like it.'

'There's nothing like it in that city of yours, I'm sure.'

'Not that I know of.' Like most people who live in the country, she wanted to be told that there was nowhere better, and I was quite happy to oblige.

'I didn't think so,' she said.

It had been an unusual experience, to say the least. I'd followed Kanter down a flight of stairs, into the basement. Though he hardly spoke, there was an air of ritual about the whole procedure. In the pump-room two enamel baths stood side by side on a floor of wooden slats. He'd already filled one for me. The water was hot, he said, naturally hot, and sprang from almost directly underneath the building. It was beneficial for the joints, the muscles and, most of all, the skin. You could drink it, too, though the taste was, how should he put it, acquired. The water also fed the pool. People said it was red, but actually it was more of a brown colour.

'It's quite a smell,' I said.

He chuckled and tugged absent-mindedly at one of his ears. 'I've lived here so long, I don't notice it.'

He left me alone while I took off my clothes and lowered myself into the bath. I was surprised at how quickly I became accustomed to the smell. I was surprised at the texture as well, until I remembered what Loots had said on our first night.

When I'd soaked for about fifteen minutes, Kanter told me it was time to take a shower. After the shower he dried my shoulders and my back, then asked me to lie down in a small, wood-panelled room, under a sheet. I was supposed to relax, he said. He was an awkward man, not talkative at all, not tactile either, and yet his work demanded a certain intimacy with strangers. You'd think he would have become less awkward as the years went by, but he hadn't; instead, he'd grown so used to his awkwardness that, like the smell of sulphur, it was something he was no longer aware of.

I 'relaxed'. In fifteen minutes Kanter was back again. He led me into another room. I lay face-down on a bed that was narrow, high and padded, like the bed in a doctor's surgery. Kanter opened a bottle and worked some perfumed oil into his hands. Then he began.

Towards the end of the massage I felt him place one forearm lengthways across the small of my back. Leaning all his weight on it, he drove it repeatedly up my spine towards my neck. He grunted a little with the effort. I had the feeling I was being crushed.

At last he stood back, panting. I sat up. He handed me my shirt.

'Was that one of your special techniques?' I asked him.

'That's right,' he said. 'I bet you feel good now, don't you?'

I could hardly deny it.

I smiled at Edith Hekmann. 'What's for supper?'

'It's stew.' She lifted the lid on a cast-iron pot. 'You walking all night like that,' she said, 'it's just like something my son would do.'

'Really?'

'There's something about you reminds me of him.' She looked at me carefully. 'I think it's your eyes. You've got the same eyes.'

I watched her ladle a generous helping of stew on to my plate. I put my face above it and breathed in.

'Smells good,' I said, wanting to seal myself in her favour.

I began to eat.

She rose from her chair and crossed the crooked floorboards to the kitchen. I heard her talking to Martha. The collision of cutlery and dishes, the murmur of voices underneath. I remembered something that had happened when I woke that evening. For a few moments I was aware of TV signals. I didn't get any pictures, though. Just a million white fast-moving molecules on a black backdrop – a blizzard, violent and quiet. It was Visser, trying to get through. How apt the image was! How perfectly it captured his frustration and his impotence! And just think. Soon I'd have my silver room. Then I'd be free of him for ever, out of reach, immune.

Mrs Hekmann returned. She brought the smell of alcohol with her, stronger than before. I ate; she smoked a cigarette. There was the sense that things could not be otherwise.

I could hear the wind in the yard outside. I felt a storm was on its way: leaves shifting like chicken feathers, something metal falling over – it was as if the air itself was changing shape. When Edith Hekmann began to speak, her words were so much a part of it that I knew she'd felt it, too.

'It was a day like this my brother died.' She paused, the wind rising to fill the silence. 'North of here, it was. Down by the lake.'

CARVING BABIES

Some sulphur water got into the lake that year. There are springs everywhere under the earth and one of them must have burst sideways, found a new path to the surface. I remember that was the first thing I did when I saw the truck. I bent down at the water's edge and put my hand in it. I touched my fingers to my tongue. The taste was faint, but it was there. Like gas.

I stood up.

There was a creaking in the woods around me, the sound of doors opening. I wasn't scared, though. I wasn't scared. I saw a bird go catapulting through the trees, a red line high up in the green. There was a wind up there, too, the leaves and branches all tumultuous, but that was far away. Where I was, everything was still.

My eyes came down.

The crashed truck on the lakeshore with its headlamps staring stupidly into the water. And two bodies, neither of them moving. One with its arms and legs spread crooked on the roots of a tree. The other sitting behind the wheel, chin on chest, no sign of any hands.

The forest creaking and that smell lifting off the lake. Smell of the devil, smell of health – people were always saying one thing or another. To me it wasn't anything like that. To me it was the smell of something that was unexpected, out of place. I couldn't argue with it, though. In fact, it made a kind of sense to me.

My mother left us when I was too young to remember. The story was, she'd died of a fever, but there was no stone in the cemetery, at least none that I could find. When I was older I asked my father about it.

'Where's the stone?' I said.

He sat at the kitchen table for longer than it takes to boil a kettle. He was tall, Arno Hekmann, even when he was seated. A stiff-jointed, thick-skinned man, with sharp bones to his elbows. Words came slowly to him at the best of times, though he could explode with anger, if provoked. I remember looking at his hand, which was driven deep into his hair, and thinking of a spade left in the ground when the day's work is over – but this was work that had scarcely begun.

I said it again. 'Where's her stone?'

He didn't have an answer. He didn't even have a decent lie. He could have said we were too poor to buy a stone. He could have said it wasn't a stone at all, it was wood, and he'd carved the name on it himself – but it had rotted, or it had been washed away by floods, or undergrowth had buried it. Or it was marble, the best that money could buy, and somebody had stolen it. He could've said any number of things to lay my curiosity to rest. But he didn't.

And that was the most I ever got from him – a silence stubborn as an animal's. Eventually he would push me away with the flat of his hand, shout at me to do a chore that didn't need doing, but when I looked at him upside-down, through a crack in the kitchen door, his face was the shape of the stone I was asking about, the shape of stones I'd seen on other people's graves, and I knew then that he was keeping things from me. Uncle Felix knew something, he was fidgety with knowledge, but he was too cowardly to part with it. If he so much as mentioned her name, he said, my father would cut him into pieces with his chisels and his saw and drop him down between the walls of whatever house he happened to be building. (In our family, Uncle Felix was the one with the stories.) Karl, my older brother, was just as silent on the subject. If I asked him where the stone was, he stared at me until I felt his eyes had passed right through my head and stuck in the wall behind me. Once, he tried denying she had ever lived, his eyebrows gathering into one dark line across his forehead.

'We must've come from something,' I said.

'Think what you like,' was his reply.

Axel, the youngest, was the only one who wasn't hiding anything. He didn't have anything to hide: there could hardly have been time for him to be born before she left.

Years later someone told me that she'd run off with another man. You'd never have guessed it, though, not from looking at my father. He didn't seem to miss her at all, nor did I ever hear him curse her memory. Instead, his pride solidified. Stood thick and still in him, like dripping or cold grease; there were days when you could almost touch the thick white shape of it. He believed in himself the more because his wife had not. When lightning blew a hole in the roof of our house, he paid no heed. Maybe he thought it was a test of his fortitude, his patience. Maybe he thought he answered the lightning by building the roof back on. I don't know. I always felt he should have listened, should have moved us on. West, to where the water in the ground was clear and had no smell. Or south, into the pastureland. Maybe that would have been the end of it then, instead of just the beginning.

My Uncle Felix bore no resemblance to my father, not in his build nor in his nature. He was altogether more excitable, more harmless, too – a frothy man with a left eye that winked without him meaning it to and a smell to his skin like sour milk. He never married, though he considered himself a ladies' man. I loved to watch him getting ready for a dance. He would stand in front of the tin mirror in the kitchen, legs apart and slightly bent, flattening his wild hair with lard. Then he'd step back, turn one cheek to the mirror, then the other, and he'd shoot air through the gaps in his teeth, a kind of whistle that was like a rocket going off. He always wore his Sunday trousers, which were wide at the thigh, but much wider by the time they reached his ankles.

The turn-ups were so roomy, we used to hide things in there – dead frogs, cigar stubs, empty sardine tins – knowing he'd discover them later, in the middle of a waltz, perhaps, or even, though I couldn't quite imagine it, an embrace. The next morning he'd come after us with a belt, the buckle coiled around his fist, the rest of it licking at the air. A threat was all it was. We didn't have to run too fast to stay out of his way; his right leg had been withered by polio when he was a boy. That was also the reason that he never worked much, relying on my father and Karl to bring in the money while he stayed at home and split wood, or swept the floors, or boiled bones for soup.

Once, when it was autumn and my brothers were gone for the day, helping my father with a job, Uncle Felix took me walking through the forest to a spring he knew. It was historical, the water. Centuries old. You could tell by looking at the rock, which was stained a strange red colour, as if tea had been drunk from it. Some famous theatre actresses had bathed there naked once. Or were they ballerinas? He couldn't remember now. It was difficult for him to climb down the steep steps with his bad leg, but he seemed determined. There was a place that was his favourite, out of sight of the footpath and screened by trees. He told me I should bathe there. If I bathed, I'd grow into a woman. I'd be beautiful.

I wasn't sure.

'It smells bad,' I said, wrinkling my nose.

He grinned. 'So does medicine,' he said, 'but it makes you better, doesn't it.'

I looked at him, sitting on a shoulder of rock, with his knees drawn up tight against his chest and his walking-stick beside him.

'Don't you want to bathe?' I said.

He stuck his lips out and shook his head. 'It's too late for me.'

'Didn't you do it when you were young?'

He smiled, but didn't answer. He told me to hurry or else the sun would drop behind the hill and I'd catch cold. I took off all my clothes and handed them to him. He placed them next to his walking-stick in a neat pile. I walked over the rock, part of it red, as he'd promised it would be, part still white and crystalline. I stepped down into the pool, which was only knee-deep, and stood under the rush of sulphur water. It crashed on to my shoulders, exploded, sprayed out sideways. And all the time Uncle Felix was sitting above me, where it was dry, just watching me and smiling.

It didn't seem unnatural to me at the time, but later, when I thought about it, it gave me a strange feeling. Whenever I was naked, I'd look round, expecting him to be there, staring at me. I'd be alone and yet I'd feel as if I wasn't. Even years afterwards, when he was dead.

I could never tell anyone about it – not even Axel, during the time when I was closest to him. It wasn't because it was a secret (Uncle Felix didn't ever use the word). It was because it was too delicate a thing to find words for. If I told it to someone else, they'd turn it into something far more obvious; they'd turn it into something that it wasn't.

He never actually touched me, you see. He just watched.

There's love and everybody talks about it, but not all of us come close to it – or, if we do, it's not in the expected way.

What Uncle Felix said about becoming a woman, becoming beautiful, it didn't mean much to me. In our house we were all treated the same. I was still being passed off as a boy, even when I was twelve or thirteen. It was easier for everyone to pretend that I was just like them rather than to start thinking about what I was really like. I understood that, somehow. I understood that it might also make life easier for me. I kept my hair cut short. I swore, and spat, and kicked at stones and car tyres and empty cans. I shared my brothers' clothes – Axel's usually, or Karl's when he grew out of them. My body seemed to play along. My blood, for instance: it came late, as if worried it might upset things. I didn't learn grace or guile or any of the tricks girls played with make-up; there wasn't anyone to learn it from. Not that they were coarse men particularly; they behaved the way they'd behave in a bar or any other place where there were men together and no women. If I'd been pretty, with a soft, red mouth and honey curls, maybe it would've been different. Maybe they would've put me up high like something holy, trod silently around me with faces raised in fear and awe. But the most that anyone ever said of me was, *She's got something*, and that was Uncle Felix. I didn't know what he meant by that either. If I look at the only photograph of me that still exists – I'm at a country fair, aged nine – I can see that my spine had a certain straightness to it and there was something steady in my eyes. Maybe that's what he meant. Or maybe it was just that he'd seen me naked one September, under that hot, rust-coloured water.

The first time I put on a dress, nobody knew where to look. They all seemed to lose something, all at the same time. Their eyes searched the rafters, the fireplace, the gloom beneath the kitchen table. Or ran along the mantelpiece, the skirting-board. Or just rested on their boots. Uncle Felix had bought it for me off a van that came through the village every Tuesday, creaking under the weight of household goods and new clothes wrapped in cellophane. It was harvest festival, a dance at the church hall, and I sat with my back against the wall all night. I couldn't even down a few glasses, the way I might have done at home – I was a girl, and girls couldn't be seen to drink, at least not in public. My green-and-purple dress was too new; it wouldn't lie against my skin, but stuck out as stiffly as washing when it freezes on the line in winter. I watched my uncle crawl past me like a crab, some toothless woman nailed to him by the hands and feet. From a distance there seemed to be a monstrous creature loose in the room. My head ached with the music, a bow pitching on the strings of a violin like a ship's deck in a storm. I began to feel sick. Nobody paid me any heed. I saw Karl with a brown bottle upside-down in his mouth, his Adam's apple jumping as he drained it dry. I sat there so long, my legs grew into the floor. If anyone had come to me then, it would've been too late. I'd have shaken my head, my brushed-out hair catching on the foolish lace collar of my dress, my body made of the same wood as the walls, the chairs, the door.

They were all drunk on the way home, boasting about how they'd danced with this one, then with that one, and the moon rolled among the bare branches of the trees like the woman I'd seen outside the hall, falling from one man's arms into another's. The truck lurched and swayed on the dirt track, and my uncle hit his head on the window, and when he touched his fingers to the place, they came away black, as if they'd been dipped in ink.

'I'm hurt,' he cried, 'I'm hurt,' but he was laughing.

It was Karl driving, his eyes splayed on his face, his hands bouncing on the wheel, he couldn't seem to get a grip on it, and all the others shouting, their voices loud against the hard curve of the roof, lifted by the alcohol.

Then we saw the house.

A hole blown clean through the roof, scorched walls and, when we moved closer, lines burned all the way across the floor, as though some great cat had stretched out, leaning on its claws, and done its scratching there.

'Jesus,' Karl said. 'Jesus Christ.'

I could only whisper, 'Who did it?'

My father stood in the blackened house with one hand wrapped over the back of his neck. People in the village often said Arno Hekmann was a good man in a crisis because he didn't rise too fast. Just one word came out of him that night and we waited minutes for it.

'Lightning,' he said at last.

Though he looked at me in my stiff dress, as if it wasn't lightning he was thinking of, but women. His laughter was one hollow sound and then nothing.

I looked down at my hands, with their hard palms and their broken nails, a boy's hands on a girl's dress, and I remembered the pretty little thing that Karl had brought home the year before and how one kiss on the porch had left her drained, like a flower needing water, her head drooping, her eyes half-closed.

We slept under the firs and pines that night. The air still felt astonished; I could smell the hole the lightning had made, not just in the timbers of the house, but in the sky. I curled around a tree-trunk and when I woke, the cold had poured into all my joints and set. My brother Axel was the only one who'd slept in a straight line on the ground. The rest were huddled, crooked, folded-up. Opening slowly as they came round. Old pen-knives, almost rusted solid.

October, that was. After a night of watching people dance.

It was a small village, even in those days, population three hundred and fifty or so, but out in the hollow, which was where our house was, it was population five – my two brothers, my father, my uncle and me.

By the following spring, that was no longer true.

It was a bitter winter. The first snows fell at the beginning of November, before the roof was mended, and lasted till the middle of January. At dawn I'd have to shovel snow off the kitchen floor while the others worked above me (some of it I used for making tea). We had no money coming in. Two of our goats died. We lived on potato soup and boiled white beans. The only luxury was that hot spring Uncle Felix had taken me to. For three days I tunnelled through the drifts with Axel. At last we reached the place and, shivering, stripped off our clothes. We stood for what seemed like hours under that stream of strange, rusty-looking water, and we were so warm suddenly, we couldn't stop laughing. During the summer Uncle Felix had often asked me to go down to the spring with him, but I always said no. If he'd come with us that day, I wouldn't have minded. But he was in bed, with a chill.

Over the New Year storms descended on us. The new roof held. Then, towards the end of January, the wind suddenly sank out of the world like the last of the water running from a bath and there was a night of perfect silence. You couldn't even hear a dog bark or a car cross the bridge, and the air was clear all the way from the cold crust of the earth to the surface of the moon. That was the night we listened to Uncle Felix breathe. It was the breathing-in we heard, a thin, urgent sound, almost plaintive, like someone straining repeatedly to lift a weight, and failing.

Karl murmured, 'Maybe we should get a doctor.'

'In the morning,' I heard my father say.

But Uncle Felix kept us awake for much of the night and we slept later than usual. When we woke up he was dead, his mouth open, as if he'd thought about saying something and then decided against it.

'I told you.' Karl was leaning against the window, staring out. 'I told you we should've got a doctor.'

My father shook his head. 'It would've been too late. There was nothing we could have done.'

I thought he was probably right. Felix had gone to bed in his Sunday jacket and his wide trousers that grew wider as they reached the floor. His hair was greased flat and there was a dried rose in his lapel. He had prepared himself as thoroughly as he would have done for any dance.

My father drew the blanket over his brother's face.

Later that morning, before the undertakers arrived, I hid a few objects in the cuffs of Uncle Felix's trousers, and it seemed odd to think he wouldn't be coming after us this time. In the left cuff, a small bottle of water from his favourite spring; I had to seal it tight, or it would smell. In the right, the comb he always used when he stood in front of the tin mirror, and a picture postcard of a beautiful woman, which I'd found in the top drawer of his desk. She was standing on a tigerskin rug in a long tight dress, with her face in profile and her head thrown back, a cigarette pointing like a thin white pistol at the ceiling. I wondered whether she was one of the famous theatre actresses he'd talked about. I tried to imagine her naked on the stained red rocks, with her head thrown back, her cigarette alight and pointing at the sky.

We buried Uncle Felix in February, which meant it took pickaxes to dig the hole, and even then it wasn't nearly deep enough. I wore the dress he'd bought for me the year before – it was still the only dress I owned, though it was softened now by many washes. My father had built the box himself, with cuts of wood left over from the roof. On the lid he carved FELIX HEKMANN and, underneath the name, he carved a pair of dancing shoes. As they lowered Felix into the hole, I glanced at Axel. His face was pale and serious, and someone had parted his hair; I smiled across at him, to comfort him. He held my look and then, still serious, he winked at me with his left eye. Then winked again, three times in succession, very quickly. It was an uncanny imitation. I had to put a hand over my face. My shoulders shook and tears poured from my eyes. Everybody thought I was crying, and they were very gentle with me when the funeral was over.

That night, or one soon after, I saw Felix in a dream. He was standing under the hot spring in his best clothes and he was laughing the way he'd laughed the night we drove home in our truck, knowing nothing of the lightning or the ruined house.

The spring I turned sixteen, Axel took me to the willow tree. I'd always known it was there – I paddled close to its trailing yellow branches every summer – but it was just a tree to me, a tree like all the others.

It was warm for the time of year, and we'd both woken before dawn. Axel whispered in my ear, something about going for a walk, something about the stream, and I nodded in agreement. We eased out of the bed. Karl, who'd slept like a stone ever since I could remember, slept heavily on, one of his arms reaching to the floor, his fingers just touching it, making him seem delicate. My father was also asleep, lying on his back, with his hands folded on the outside of the blanket.

We went out through the back, past the shed where the goats were penned. Their shoe-shaped faces turned; their yellow, devil eyes slit upright at us. We told them to be quiet. Then down into the field below. The sun was still behind the ridge, though the trees up on the crown were coloured with it, as if the bark had been stripped away, as if they were down to naked wood.

The grass licked at my bare legs.

Axel wasn't wearing any shoes. I watched his heels rise, with something of the mill-wheel in their rhythm. The left one, the right one, the left one – one after the other, they kept rising. I watched his heels, shiny with dew, as I followed him across the field.

A grey bird curved through the air like a flung stone.

We stopped above the stream. There were trees there – poplars, willows, oak and fir. That time of year, the stream was swollen, snow melting further north and running down to us. My brother sat on the bank where it lifted clear of the fast-flowing water. It was a flat place, just mud and tufts of grass.

'If we wait here,' he said, 'the sun'll come to us.'

I sat beside him. Stared at the water where it swirled around a root. The root arched out of the water and curved back down again in a kind of bow. If you looked at the root and its reflection both at once, as if they were joined, as if they were one completed thing, they made a shape that was exactly like a mouth.

The sun was above the ridge now, to our left, but it hadn't touched us yet. We were still sitting in the shade.

'You never kissed anyone, did you?'

I turned to look at him. His head was bent and he was scratching at the mud with a piece of stick he'd sharpened. 'How do you know?'

'I just know.'

He was still scratching at the mud. It wasn't drawings he was doing, just lines that didn't look like anything.

'Maybe I did,' I said.

'Who with then?' He looked sideways at me, his lip curling. Then he said the name of a boy who lived in the village.

I laughed in his face. I was like that sun bursting over the curve of the hill and landing on everything in the world at once and turning it a colour suddenly.

His head dipped again.

'You didn't do it yet,' he muttered. 'I know you didn't.'

I was strong now. I could say anything I liked. Even the truth.

'So what if I didn't.'

His body went still. All of it. The hand with the whittled stick in it stopped moving. Even his head, which wasn't moving anyway, seemed strangely motionless. It was as if he was listening to himself think.

'So what,' I said.

He lay back with his head against the willow's trunk. He didn't look at me. He looked up into the tree instead, its pale-yellow waterfall of leaves and branches.

'Would you like to?' he said, without moving.

There's a way of holding on to a moment, of making it last almost indefinitely, but anything you do, you have to do it slowly, and in absolute silence, and you have to separate your mind from it, it's not you who's doing it, it's someone else.

I placed my lips where his were and I pressed. I remember thinking of the school teacher, and the way she held that spongy pale-pink paper against a piece of writing to make it dry.

Then I leaned on one elbow, looking down at him.

He just lay there and smiled. I almost hated him in that moment. His light-brown hair falling forwards, his lazy mouth. A scattering of freckles across his nose.

'Try it again,' he said.

There was a bird awake somewhere near by. Its call was like a see-saw. Backwards and forwards, the call went. Backwards and forwards. It was then that I thought of Uncle Felix. I felt he was watching, even though I knew he was dead. If I looked round, he would be there, on the other side of the stream, with his knees drawn up against his chest and his walking-stick beside him. He'd be smiling.

'What is it?'

But I didn't look round. I looked into my brother's eyes instead and saw the black parts widen suddenly. I seemed to be rushing down towards him.

I thought I'd startled him and so I said, 'It's nothing.'

Before I could move, he sat up. One of his hands was on my shoulder. Then he covered my mouth with his. I was inside him then. His face so close, it was blurred. I could taste his breath.

'It's your mouth that should be open,' he said, 'not your eyes.'

I did as he said.

We stayed kissing until the sun reached us. When I opened my eyes again, everything in the world was blue and we had shadows.

That was the morning Axel told me about the trees. He said we'd been born in a house that was made of the wrong wood. Unlucky wood, it was. The kind of wood that if you make railway sleepers out of it, the train crashes. Or if you turn it into matches, girls set fire to their dresses. Some trees were haunted at the core and if you used them to make a house, the haunting spread from the wood into the people, like a disease. Those trees were only good for burning, and even then you had to have your wits about you; a fire built out of that kind of wood might stubbornly refuse to burn, or else it might burn too well and greedily consume whole forests. Our father was a carpenter. He should have known. Which trees helped, which hindered.

'And this one?' I remember asking.

Axel looked up into the weeping willow. 'You might think from its name that it's sad. It isn't, though.'

'What is it then?'

'It's a pleasure tree. You don't find them hardly ever. I've looked and looked and this one's the only one I've found.'

'A pleasure tree?' I said. 'What's that mean?'

He looked across at me. 'What do you think it means?'

We began to go further. The tree showed our hands new places. Always at dawn, with goats' eyes watching as we left the house, and then that walk through wet grass to the stream. At dawn, with everybody still asleep.

Summer came. Our shadows followed us, grew longer.

One morning he undid his trousers and pulled down his pants and there was his thing, smooth as stripped wood, blond, too, like a kind of pine, and it grew in the sunlight, faster than any tree, faster than a plant, and it jumped, almost as if it was counting.

I took it in my fingers and it still felt smooth, softer than I'd imagined, it was strange, the softness of the skin and the hardness just beneath, and moving one against the other, and then I put it in my mouth and closed my eyes, and my eyelids burned as the sun lifted over the ridge, reached through the trees, another day.

'Who else have you been learning from?' I heard him say.

But because there was admiration in his voice, I didn't need to answer.

There was a moment just before the juice from him was in my mouth, when I had already the taste of it: I could see his head on the ground, turned sideways, and his left eye narrowed, almost closed, the tip of an arrow drawn in charcoal, and his back arching away from the earth, just shoulderblades and buttocks touching, and as his body twisted, a hollow appeared between the raised muscles of his stomach and the bay where his hip-bone was, and his ribs pushed upwards through his soft, tea-coloured skin.

There never was someone more beautiful than that.

With his light-brown hair slipping down into his eyes, and his body, whippet-lean, and the stories he could tell, such stories, Axel Hekmann could have had any girl he wanted. I saw the way they looked at him – sideways, along their cheeks, or upwards, through their eyelashes, or even over their shoulders as they walked away from him. And yet he chose his sister. His plain sister. There had to be some kind of perversity in him. Maybe it was the sense of doing wrong – or else he somehow knew I'd go along with it. It was a question I never asked. I didn't dare. There was the fear that I'd be opening his eyes to something he hadn't seen, and that everything would then, quite suddenly, be over. And I couldn't imagine that, it being over; I felt raw on the inside if I thought about it, as if I'd been scraped out with a spoon. But I couldn't imagine the future either. Each time he reached out at night and touched me on my breasts or between my legs, we had my father and my brother lying in the same room with us, and my uncle watching, too, his hair smoothed down with lard and a postcard of an actress in his hand. Certain kinds of secrets, they're quiet and dead; they can be kept. There are others, though, that are alive and growing, and have a tendency to reveal themselves.

Sometimes he was so rash, so obvious, I thought that what he really wanted was to be found out. There was the time he took my hand and put it inside his pants while we were riding in the back of the truck, with Karl and my father right in front of us, in the cab. If they'd turned round, looked through the narrow pane of glass, they would have seen. But he did it on my hand anyway and then laughed when I tried to work out what to do with it. I let the wind take it in the end and then I spat on my hand and wiped it on a piece of sacking, though I couldn't get rid of that pale-green smell it had, sweet and salty at the same time, nothing like a girl's. Another time we were in the grocery store and I was wandering between the shelves of outdoor things. I liked the smells – the green rubber waders, the orange leather work-gloves. He came up behind me and his breath was in my ear. I could feel his thing against my hip.

'Minkels is deaf. He'll never know.'

'What if somebody comes in,' I hissed, 'to buy something?'

He grinned. 'We'd have to be unlucky. It's only once or twice a week that happens.'

I let him do it, not inside me, but between my thighs, among the hurricane lamps, the leaning towers of hunting-caps (which toppled just before his stuff came out), the knives with dainty deer's feet for handles, and he was right: Minkels never knew.

I dreaded being caught, though. As the older of the two, I'd be blamed for it. And besides, I was the girl and girls always led boys on; girls were always guilty. Axel didn't seem to worry. It just never entered his head. Sometimes I think that quality of his rubbed off on me and that, unknowingly, he prepared me for much of what came after. Or maybe it was in our blood and he was simply showing it to me. I often wondered how deep it went, and at what point it would turn into treachery. If we'd been caught, would he have pretended it had nothing to do with him? I could see it, somehow. I could see him smiling at me from some blameless place while I stood there in the sun with fingers pointing at me. He'd be smiling the way he'd smiled that first morning by the stream. Under the yellow leaves. Sometimes it seems to me that what I did was in revenge for this imaginary betrayal. Though there was an actual betrayal, of course. There was that, too, eventually.

When I was seventeen, Karl married the Bohlin girl. I didn't know much about her, except that she wasn't the one I'd seen standing in his arms on the back porch like something in need of water. Her name was Eva. She was the only daughter of the people who owned the inn on the edge of the village. They were old for parents, almost the age of grandparents, and they were eager for her to take a husband so they could hand the business over. They already knew Karl on account of the work he and my father had done for them, and they were delighted to have him as a son-in-law. My father was pleased as well, partly because it sealed the bond between the two families and partly because he thought that Karl was bettering himself, marrying not into money, it was true, but into property, which was the next best thing. And, with a hotel, there was always the possibility of wealth.

'You can make a go of it,' he told Karl at the wedding party. 'The place needs work, that's all.'

He was right. Baskets still hung above the balconies, though they'd been bleached by the weather and most of the geraniums had died. The rooms were bare and gloomy, plagued by mosquitoes in the summer, and by draughts and damp in winter. The natural sulphur pond had filled with fungus and algae. But Karl only nodded and, turning away from his father's long, excited face, said, 'Maybe.'

There was dancing in the Bohlins' garden that evening. Though it had rained earlier in the day, the clouds had blown away and the sky was almost clear by the time dusk fell. There were paper lanterns dangling from the trees and strings of pearly light bulbs and red tin ashtrays in the shape of hearts. I thought of Felix flat on his back in his cheap box, already dressed for the occasion. He would probably have danced with Mrs Bohlin's widowed sister, a small woman with a fierce gaze and pointed teeth. I could imagine them waltzing together on the damp grass, the bare bulbs silvering his greased black hair, his left eye winking.

'Uncle Felix should be here,' I said.

I was dancing with Axel. We were pretending to be brother and sister, keeping a respectable distance between us, even exaggerating it, but every now and then, as we passed through a dark corner of the garden, he drew me close to him and I could feel his thing pressing against my belly.

'Felix,' Axel said. 'Do you remember the time we put yoghurt in his trousers and it spilled all over that woman's shoes when they were dancing and she thought – '

I was laughing even before he'd finished.

We whirled past our father, who was drinking schnapps with the bride's uncle. I could tell from the way his jaw swung that he was already drunk.

Axel nudged me. 'Look, there's Edwin.'

'What about it?' I said.

'He's got his eye on you.'

I gave Axel a look. Edwin Bock was the ugliest boy in the village.

Axel grinned. 'He has. Look.'

I glanced sideways. Bock was sitting on a chair under a tree with his hands wedged between his thighs. When he saw me looking, his eyes slid sideways and he blushed.

'Bock's a nobody,' I said.

'Why don't you dance with him?'

'I don't want to.' We'd come to a halt, but I could still feel Axel's warm hand on the small of my back.

'Think how embarrassed he'd be.'

'He's already embarrassed – '

'Oh, go on. Dance with him.' Axel was grinning again. 'You'd really make his evening.' The wind gusted suddenly and blew his hair into his eyes.

'Since when did you care about making Edwin Bock's evening?'

I let go of Axel's hand and, turning away, ducked under a string of light bulbs and crossed the grass to the table where the food had been laid out. I saw Eva Bohlin through the crowd. She was a full-breasted, slow-boned girl with dull black hair. She had the curious habit of looking at Karl, no matter who she was talking to. I supposed it must be love that made her behave like that. When Axel came over and stood beside me, I handed him a piece of pumpernickel bread with pickle and smoked cheese on it. I asked him what he thought of Eva.

'Not my type.' He bit into the bread and cheese.

'What *is* your type?'

He didn't answer.

'It'll be strange for Karl,' I said, 'with all Dad's furniture around. It'll almost be like still being at home.'

'It'll be better than that.' As Axel glanced up at the inn, his face took on a darkness, a kind of discontent, I hadn't seen before.

'Will it?' I said, staring at him. I didn't think so, and nor, I thought, should he. We were each other's reason why.

'Well,' he said after a while, 'at least there'll be one less in the bedroom,' and he looked at me and then he began to smile.

I would lie next to Axel with my head on his chest, the stream trickling over stones below us. His body had altered, grown. I couldn't remember Karl without hair on his face and legs. That summer Axel had it as well, though it wasn't coarse and black like his brother's. It was finer, softer – almost coppery. Sometimes he was restless now. His face would shadow over and he would shift suddenly, shake me off like sand. I would sit up with my arms around my knees and watch the shallow water run. But I was happiest with my eyes closed and my cheek against his skin and the smell of it as sunlight touched him, the smell of wood-shavings, sea salt, apricot.

It was almost time to climb back through the field to the house, but as usual I didn't want to go. I didn't feel like mopping floors or drawing water from the well or boiling sausage. I couldn't bear to see my father's teeth lunging at his fork, or his mouth, glassy with grease. I wished there was somewhere else we could go. Then Axel spoke, and what he said was so close to what I'd been thinking that all of me went still:

'I've heard about a place.'

'What place?'

He began to describe it for me. The valleys were smooth as dust, and pale-pink or, sometimes, silver-grey. There were no walls or fences, and almost no trees. Everything was open. The people's faces were yellow and wrinkled, like leaves in autumn. Their eyes were narrow. They wore skirts – not just the women, the men, too – and they rode small horses with thick, black manes. The country was high up, but the mountains were even higher – unimaginably high and jagged and dazzling with snow. Up there the sky was always blue, and the air was so pure and clear it hurt your lungs the first few times you breathed it. The castles in those mountains looked like the castles in fairy-tales. They were real, though. Holy people lived in them. From the battlements you could see halfway round the world. You could see so far, in fact, that in the distance the surface of the land began to bend. It was the curve of the earth itself that you were looking at.

'If only we could go there,' I murmured.

His face didn't alter; he didn't seem remotely affected by what I'd said. I thought it was probably because he'd taken himself there so many times already, with his knowledge of the place, with his own descriptions. He'd already been.

After that, I was always asking him to describe the place to me so I could be there with him. He never tired of it. Sometimes what he told me could have come from an encyclopaedia – how to avoid altitude sickness, what the local music sounded like, why certain flowers could grow high up. Other times he gave me impressions that were arbitrary and vague, like memories. I asked him how he knew about it. He'd seen some pictures once, he said. They were in a magazine that somebody had left at the inn. When he looked for the magazine again, though, it was gone. It didn't matter, really; he could still remember it. He found some other magazines from the same series, but there was nothing in them that interested him much.

One morning I asked him what the name of the country was. It was strange I hadn't thought of asking him before. He said he didn't know. I watched him as he stared up into the branches of the willow tree.

'The highest mountain in the world,' he said, 'what's it called?'

'Mount Everest.'

He nodded. 'It was somewhere near there.'

It was hot, July or August, with a white sky that hurt to look at, and I came up out of the garden with vegetables for that evening's meal.

From the barn I heard my father sawing and I thought of Uncle Felix and the night he died, but the breathing of the saw was out, not in – out as it cut down into the wood, in as it drew back, out as it cut down again. I stopped in the doorway. As my eyes adjusted to the gloom, I saw my father bent over the sawhorse, his right arm moving like one of those rods that drive the wheels on a train. I noticed a square frame behind him, low on the floor, and a wide half-moon of blond wood propped up against the wall.

'Is that a bed you're making?'

'Yes, it's a bed.' He didn't pause in his work; his sweat dropped on to the pine and darkened it.

'It's for the inn, I suppose.' My father had been hired to build some furniture – wardrobes for the bedrooms, chairs and tables for a restaurant. Karl and Eva had taken his advice. They were trying to make something of the place.

'Didn't you hear yet?'

'Hear what?'

'We're losing Axel.'

I didn't have the slightest idea what he was talking about.

My father stopped sawing, straightened up. 'He's fixing to get married. This bed's for the wedding night.' He ran one hand carefully over the headboard, and his long teeth showed.

'Married?' I said. 'Who to?'

'The Poppel girl. I thought you knew.'

The white sky beat against my neck. Standing on the line between the darkness of the barn and the brilliance outside, I felt caught between two worlds, adrift suddenly, abandoned. I knew Axel had been seeing Eileen Poppel and, though I sometimes wondered why, I certainly never thought it would come to anything. The Poppel family – scrap-dealers from across the valley. And Eileen, their only daughter. Not exactly what you'd call a catch, though, with her mouth too small and her wrists that you could snap in your hands like kindling, if you'd a mind, and that pale-blue vein wriggling through the thin skin at the edge of her left eye. She looked like, if you shouted at her, she'd just lie down and die. I could feel the white sky burning, burning. Married? Certainly I never suspected it would come to that.

'At least there'll be some help for you around the place.' My father spoke to me from the world he belonged to, a dark world, steeped in wood-chips, sweat, and resin.

'You mean they're going to live here?' I stared at him.

'Only till they get a place of their own.'

I walked back into the glare below the house. Five shrivelled heads of beetroot nodded in my hand. I wanted to start running, but I didn't know which way to go. I wanted to burst into flame. Instead, I stood at the kitchen sink with a knife against my thumb and the cold tap dripping, and I skinned the beetroots and sliced their wet, violet flesh on to a plate.

The next morning Axel woke me at the usual time. I followed him out of the house, across the clearing. It wasn't light yet; the goats shuffled in their pen. Past the shed, along the footpath, down into the field.

Then, halfway across, I stopped. I just stopped and watched him walk away from me. His feet rising, falling, rising. He thought I was still behind him. He didn't realise. The stupidity of those feet of his.

'I'm not coming,' I called out.

He looked over his shoulder. 'What's wrong?'

'Is it true you're getting married?'

He nodded slowly. 'Yes, it's true.'

'Why?'

'She's going to have a baby.'

'So what?'

'It's my baby.' He began to walk towards me, not looking at me. Looking at the grass.

'No,' I said. 'Stay there.'

He kept walking until I could see the freckles on his face.

'One last time,' he said.

'No.'

'Edie.' He grasped my wrist and tried to pull me towards him. My arm was horizontal in the air, but my feet hadn't moved. 'One last time.'

'Didn't you hear me?' I shouted. 'I said no.'

He held on to my wrist with both hands. Then, at last, he let it go. My arm returned to me, like a boat cast loose on dark water.

'Three days ago,' I said. 'That was the last time.'

His face brightened suddenly. 'You're jealous.'

In one flowing, almost circular movement I picked up a fallen branch and swung it at his head. He caught the blow on his forearm. It still hurt, though.

'You're dead,' I said.

'What?' Holding his forearm, he stared at me. 'What did you say?'

'You heard me.'

I threw the branch down in the grass and walked away from him. After a while I looked round. I was surprised how small he was. There was half a field between us and a wind getting up, clouds blowing southwards. If I spoke now, he would hear me.

'It was your choice,' I said.

One night I hacked the marriage bed to pieces with my father's axe. I woke up and lay quite still – shocked, fearful, regretting what I'd done. I put a coat over my nightshirt and crept out to the barn. How was I going to explain it? My father would be furious. All that work.

But when I saw the bed standing on its four legs in the moonlight, not finished yet, but whole, somehow, and beautiful, I changed my mind. I wished I'd done it after all. I stood there, undecided. The axe I'd used in the dream was hanging on the wall; its newly polished steel seemed to beckon me. The axe began to speak. *Edith. Take me down. Do it.* I turned and ran out of the barn. Ran straight into my father who had heard a noise and come out with his gun.

'What are you doing up?'

'The bed – I wanted to make sure it was all right.'

He gave me a look of bewilderment as I moved past him, back into the house.

For most of that week I didn't talk and no one talked to me. I was out in the vegetable garden every day, planting for the spring. Carrots, I put in. Potatoes, too, and radishes. The wind brought squalls with it. I laboured on as the rain came down, soaked to the skin and shivering. In the barn behind me, the bed took shape, its headboard carved with the names of the bride and groom, and round the names there was fruit – apples and wild figs and grapes – and over them, a canopy of leaves. Axel was hardly there, except to sleep. Either he was working with my father, repairing storm damage, or he was over at the Poppels' place, a muddle of shacks on a side road, half an hour's walk from where we lived. I still couldn't understand it. The Poppel men were a bunch of good-for-nothings, drunks. They passed you in their cart sometimes, horse teeth in their heads and startled, bloodshot eyes, and nothing on the back except some bedsprings, maybe, and a punctured tyre. But that was where he went, to drink with them and play cards and lie down on something with that pale girl.

The wedding was still weeks away and suddenly I could stand it no longer. I asked Karl and Eva if I could move into the hotel. In return, I'd be a chambermaid, a gardener – anything. Karl listened to me as if I was talking to him from somewhere very far away and when I'd finished he just nodded. He didn't query my decision or my motives. All he said was, 'We could use another pair of hands round here.'

They gave me a small, north-facing room on the first floor. It had a single bed; the headboard was plain, varnished wood – no fruit on it, no names. I had a wash-basin, too, and a tall wardrobe that leaned forwards, away from the wall, like a waiter taking orders. Standing at the window I could see the pool below me. There were fir trees at one end, to shelter bathers from the wind. A flight of steps led down to the water. The steps had been cut out of the rock and then reinforced with cement. Beyond the pool was a wooden terrace; this was where the famous people must have strolled in the past, with their silk dressing-gowns and their cigars.

I had more contact with Eva than with Karl and, though she could be remote at times, she couldn't match his almost total lack of interest. Five years older than I was, she would sit me down at the kitchen table and question me. For instance, she wanted to know whether I'd fallen out with my family. I said I hadn't. I told her that my brother Axel and his wife would be living in our house and I thought that, as newly-weds, they ought to have some privacy.

'Then what's that on your arm?' Eva was pointing at the dark-red, wedge-shaped scar that ran in a straight line from the edge of my right hand towards the inside of my elbow.

'I did it on the stove,' I said. 'I tripped and fell against it.'

'It must've hurt.' Drawing greedily on a cigarette with her pale, plump lips, she seemed to *want* it to have hurt.

I nodded.

It had happened the day I told my father I was leaving. Breakfast was finished and I was clearing the plates away. Axel had already left the room.

'You're walking out on us?' My father's eyes were pewter-coloured in the gloom of the kitchen and his hands lay on the table, red and swollen at the knuckle.

'I'm going to live at Karl's. He needs help with the hotel.'

'There's plenty of work around here.'

I shrugged. 'That Poppel girl can do it.'

'You're walking out,' he said, 'just like your mother.'

'I thought she died.'

His head turned slightly to one side, as if he wasn't sure he'd heard me right. He was looking at me all the time, though, his anger rising, slowly rising. It was like watching milk come to the boil.

But I couldn't stop myself. 'She wasn't my mother, anyway,' I said. 'I never even knew the woman.'

Through the window I watched Axel cross the clearing, carrying a struggling guinea fowl by its feet.

I said it again. 'She wasn't my mother. Your wife, maybe. But not my – '

I didn't see the hand coming. I thought for a moment that I must have rushed forwards suddenly and hit my face on something. The room spun round and I fell against the stove. My right arm touched it first. I felt the flesh melt. I couldn't tell if I'd screamed or not. There was a kind of echo of a scream, in the walls of the kitchen, somehow, up near the rafters. And the sweet, rotten smell of my own skin burning. Axel came running in. My father was standing over me. I could see the air between his trouser pocket and his hand.

He pushed Axel across the room. 'Get some butter.'

'We haven't got any.'

'Fat then.'

Axel came towards me with a scoop of white lard in a spoon. He sat on his haunches in front of me and let a whistle through his lips. 'Nasty wound.'

Which wound? I almost said. The one you did, or the one done by the stove? But I kept silent. I took the spoon from him and melted the fat on to the burn myself.

'What happened to your mouth?' he asked.

'Must've hit it when I slipped.'

My father hadn't spoken at all. From where I was sitting, on the floor, I saw his right boot shift sideways, scrape at a mark made by the lightning years before.

'Leaving,' he muttered. 'Usually it hurts the ones that stay behind.'

If there was any feeling of triumph in moving out, I don't remember it. My life at the inn – the Hotel Spa, as it was now called – was lonely. Karl was eight years older than I was. He worked all through the day; in the evening he sat in the parlour with a beer. He rarely spoke to me and when he did, his voice had a kind of distance in it, as if I wasn't family, but a stranger he felt he had to be civil to. Nights were the hardest, thinking Axel's hand might reach across, wanting it so much, on my shoulder, in my hair, anywhere – and then remembering. I was eighteen and no one touched me any more. I'd get up before dawn and stand by the window, facing north; I'd watch the steam lift from the pool. Most mornings I was sick in the basin. It occurred to me that I might also be carrying Axel's child. Then he'd have to marry me as well. I imagined two brides walking up the aisle in the village church. *Do you take this man to be your lawful wedded husband? I do. I do.* I saw my smile in the wardrobe mirror, and it was not a pleasant one. But my blood came halfway through the month, as usual. And anyway, I was losing weight, not gaining it. It got to the point where it didn't matter whether Karl spoke to me or not. But I only had to think of Axel's face in the field that morning, his face just before I hit him with the branch, and the anger rose in me until my hands shook so hard that I couldn't dress. My anger wasn't unlike my father's – slow-burning, rarely visible, but almost impossible to put out.

The day before the wedding I left the hotel early, walking along the road that led west out of the village. The leaves were red, and the high, baked grass of summer was beginning to soften with the frost. I passed Miss Poppel's house. She was the only one of them I had any time for. She lived alone, with three stray cats and a car that had been painted an unusual shade of brown. When she drove down the street, all you could see was its huge, disappointed face and then, dimly, through the windscreen's milky glass, her spectacles tilted upwards as she peered over the wheel and a headscarf which was actually a pair of old silk stockings. The front of her place was heaped with empty bottles and rusting engine parts the way all the Poppel family's places were. With her, though, it was character, not squalor. She had chimes made out of door-hinges, each one the size of a man's hand. She'd strung them together on a piece of wire and hung them from a withered crab-apple tree. They were so heavy, the wind didn't move them much. But they did clang if a storm got up. I could sometimes hear them through the open window of my room at the hotel.

I crossed the bridge, looking down between the wooden slats at the coating of pale-green scum on the water below. Beyond the bridge, the road ran uphill to the horizon, three kilometres away. I took the first turning on the left, a narrow track of mud and leaf-mould. I passed the plough that had been there for years, half-grown over now.

There was a keen edge to the air that quickened my muscles as I walked, and I forgot for a moment that it was anger I was carrying.

I saw the clearing ahead of me, the dun-coloured walls and black windows I knew so well. Instead of entering the house, I circled it, taking a path that struck off through the bracken-skirted trees just to the east. I parted brambles, then scrambled down a steep bank to the stream. There was the willow. And there, beneath it, was the flat place where we used to lie. I reached inside my coat and pulled out the folded manila envelope I'd taken from the hotel office. I began to strip one of the branches of its yellow leaves. When the envelope was full, I sealed it shut. I sat down on the bank and took out a pencil and wrote AXEL & EILEEN HEKMANN on the front, then I put the pencil away and laid the envelope beside me on the ground. I stared at the water for a long time. It ran as it had always run in the autumn, loud and purposeful, tumbling over the stones. You could sit there pretending that nothing had ever changed.

The next day, after the ceremony, the Poppels held a party at their farm. While I was there, one of the men came up to me. He stuck his thumbs in his belt and gave me a slanting look.

'How come you're against the marriage?'

It cost me a great effort to be polite, but it was someone's wedding day and besides, I weighed it up and I decided that, in the end, politeness would be more insulting.

'I'm not against it.' I smiled. 'Who said I was against it?'

'I heard something.'

'Rumours,' I said.

'What about the yellow leaves?' He altered the angle of his head. 'What was all that about?'

'In our family they mean something special.'

'That so?'

'Didn't he tell you?'

'No,' the Poppel man said, 'he didn't tell us.' One of his brothers or cousins had joined him, wearing a brown suit and chewing on a blade of grass.

'Well, ask him,' I said.

'So you're not against the marriage?'

I sighed. 'No.'

'You fancy a dance?' said the man in the suit.

'No,' I said. 'Excuse me.'

I walked across the yard to where a boy was pouring home-made beer and I asked him for a glass of it. I could feel their eyes on me, like snails. I was glad I'd sent the leaves – especially as they were yellow, and yellow meant what it did . . .

I looked across at the two men. I nodded, raised my glass.

Then I drank.

It was a Friday afternoon and I'd been working at the inn for almost exactly a year. I was sitting on the front porch, taking a short break before I started to prepare the evening meal. The warm weather had lasted longer than usual, and the trees were only now beginning to lose their foliage. My father wiped the sweat off his forehead as he walked up the road towards me, his trousers fluttering and flapping round his ankles. He looked like a man who was standing still in a high wind. I rose slowly to my feet. I'd been wondering when he would come.

He stood at the bottom of the steps. 'Axel took the truck at half-past seven this morning and I haven't seen him since.'

'Where was he going? The market?' There was a market every Friday morning in a town a few kilometres to the north.

'Yes. But it's three o'clock now.'

'Maybe he's driving around. You know how that wife of his likes to drive around.'

My father shook his head. 'I told him to be back at midday. There was something he had to help me with.'

I felt my heart begin to churn. 'You think he broke down?'

My father turned and stared into the trees on the other side of the road, one hand twitching against his leg as if his brain was in that hand and it was thinking.

'Get Karl,' he said.

Karl had the use of an old four-seater that belonged to Eva's parents. The two men climbed in the front, with Karl behind the wheel. I sat in the back. First we drove out to the Poppels' place. The mother was in the yard, feeding her chickens. She stood below us, one arm circling a bowl of corn meal, the veins and tendons showing through her transparent skin.

'I ain't seen nobody all day.'

Karl spun the car round, ran it fast across the ruts and potholes, back on to the road, the springs complaining loudly all the way.

'I told you we should've fixed the truck,' he muttered.

My father just stared out through the windscreen. I noticed how his shoulders curved under his jacket.

I thought of the time I'd met Axel in the village. I was buying candles for the restaurant. Eva said candles would create atmosphere. That's what people want, she told me. Atmosphere. It must have been early spring because I could remember what my first words were.

'I hear the baby's born.'

'Yeah.' He scuffed his boots on the floor. 'It's a boy.'

'I heard that, too.' I paid Minkels for the candles and moved towards the door. 'What are you naming it?'

'Michael. I call him Mazey.' He grinned quickly.

'Mazey?'

'I don't know why. That's what I call him, though. It just feels right.'

I nodded. 'You got a place of your own yet?'

'We're getting one.' He told me there was a small homestead out towards the lake. It didn't have any water, but he knew where they could dig a well. There was some land that came with it. He might try farming. Sheep, most likely.

I was staring at him, thinking of how I used to lay my head against his shoulder, thinking of the sweet, split-wood smell of him as morning sunlight spilled over the ridge, when suddenly I realised that I was still angry. It was like some huge sea-creature surfacing. It startled me. I'd forgotten it was there.

'It couldn't have gone on, you know,' he said.

'What?'

'You and me.' He had dropped his voice down low. 'We couldn't have gone on like that.'

'You don't have to whisper,' I said. 'Minkels is deaf, remember? He won't hear a thing.'

'Edie – '

'I hope the property works out.' I laughed my father's laugh, one hollow sound and then nothing, because I already knew what I was going to do. I didn't know how yet, but I knew what.

I walked out of the shop. I heard the bell jangle above the door as he came after me. I turned to face him. His hair seemed to have darkened at the roots. He stood there.

'Don't you remember what I told you in the field?' I said.

He shook his head, but not because he didn't remember. He looked out into the street. It was a still, grey day. There was nothing to look at. He shook his head again. Then, with his face lowered, and a smile on it, he turned and walked away. Just for a moment the street was not dust and a stray dog and two parked cars, but grass, the coarse grass of the field, and a path was visible, but only to us, and the stream was at the end of it, over a stile and through a copse, and I was following him down . . .

'Which way would he have gone?' Karl said.

I glanced out of the window. We were at a fork in the road. The town where the market was held lay directly ahead of us, but so did the lake. If we turned left, we had to double back along a road that circled the shore. If we turned right, the road climbed up on to the hills that bordered the lake on its south-east side. My father was looking one way then the other, trying to gauge which was the more likely.

'We'd better try them both,' he said eventually.

Karl had been staring at him, waiting for an answer. Now he faced the windscreen again and muttered something that I didn't hear.

'Left's quicker,' I said, 'if he was in a hurry.'

It was a road with no markings, scarcely wide enough for two cars. On the right and way below, the lake. You could only see bits of it between the trees, smooth as something planed, though I'd seen it in a gale once, with slabs of water lifting clear and flying through the air like houses in a tornado. Some days it was blue, others it was black. That afternoon it was green – the deep, dark green of marrow skin. To the left the ground climbed steeply through beeches that had been there for two hundred years. We drove slowly, heads turning from one side to the other, but we didn't see the truck. We rounded the south-western corner of the lake, and the trees thinned and the ground levelled out. We stopped at a crossroads.

'So much for that,' Karl said. 'Now what?'

My father said we should drive on into the town.

By the time we reached the market square, it was almost deserted. Traders were packing the last of their goods into the backs of vans. Nobody knew anything. We tried the bars. There was one man who remembered a young couple with a baby. It was because of the baby, he said; his first was due in a month's time. He thought he'd seen them leave in a dark-red truck.

'When was that?' Karl said.

'Eleven. Maybe twelve.'

Karl looked at my father, but he didn't say anything.

We headed north, out of the town. The road took us through farm country, then it veered east and began to climb up to a ridge. This was the second route. To the left you could see the bare brow of the hill, all outcrops of rock and windswept grass. On the right, there was a long drop to the lake below – a steep scree-slope which plunged into the water at an angle of seventy-five degrees and kept on going.

There was no sign of the truck.

When we arrived at the fork again, Karl stopped the car in the banked-up leaves at the side of the road and left the engine idling. He sat there, staring through the windscreen.

It was after six o'clock and the sun had almost gone; what was left of it was pink and raw, like part of a skinned animal. We'd been looking for almost three hours. It seemed hopeless. But, without meaning to, I spoke: 'I think we should try the first route again.'

The two men didn't say anything, but I could hear their reluctance, their exasperation. 'I'll walk it if I have to,' I added.

Karl was motionless for a moment longer, then he shifted into gear and pulled back on to the road.

We'd only been driving along the lake for a few minutes when I saw it. I shouted at Karl to stop the car, then I opened the door and jumped out. We were on a bend. The road swung left, away from the lake, though it was still just visible about thirty metres below. I ran back to the tree, crouched down. There. A piece of bark had been torn away at bumper-height and the blond wood under it was smeared with plum-coloured paint. I'd only missed it the first time because I'd been looking for the wrong thing. I began to make my way down the slope towards the lake. The ground was so steep, it was hard not to lose control and fall headlong.

I followed the trail of damaged trees, some creaking, as if they were still recovering from what had happened, some scratched or gouged, some split wide open. I saw Eileen Poppel first. She must have been hurled through the windscreen, hurled clean through. You wouldn't have thought a little thing like that would have weighed enough to break the glass. She lay at the foot of a tree, her arms spread over the roots, her face in profile, like someone worshipping the earth. Her cheek and her forehead were ribboned, crazed with blood. At last they seemed appropriate, those eyes of hers, which had always looked as though someone's thumbs were pressing at them from the inside. I ran on down the slope.

I found the truck with its radiator grille dipped in the lake, like a cow drinking, its headlamps staring gloomily into the silent, dark-green water. I could see my brother in the cab, his chin resting on his chest. I called his name softly, but he didn't move. It was then that I noticed the smell of sulphur. I dropped to my knees, put my fingers in the water, tasted it.

I stood up. It didn't feel as if my feet were quite in contact with the ground. I walked to the door of the truck. My brother seemed thinner. I knew what it was. The steering-wheel had pushed his ribs up against his spine, and the organs had been forced sideways. His face was unmarked, though, and there was no blood on him at all. I wondered when his skin would turn yellow, when his eyes would narrow. I knew he wouldn't want to look like a foreigner in the land that he was going to. I could imagine him on the battlements already, watching me from halfway across the world, watching me as I stood beside him.

I was aware of everything around me, trees and sky and ground, and I was at the centre of it, and I knew then that it was right, what I had done. I took a deep breath and let it out, and then I heard the two men come trampling through the leaves towards me, and I heard something else, too, not a cry exactly, but a voice, a small voice, and I looked down into the cab and saw the child, not more than six months old, my brother's child. The wooden drawer he always travelled in was on the floor next to the gear lever and he was lying on his back in it, staring upwards through the shattered windscreen at the trees. He was holding his arms away from his body, moving the inside of his wrists against the air.

' – I *told* you it needed work.'

'I only looked at it a few days ago. I didn't notice anything – '

'You didn't notice anything. When was the last time you *noticed* anything?'

I rocked the baby in the crook of my elbow. He made no sound. He just stared up into my face the same way he'd stared up into the trees.

'There, Mazey,' I whispered. 'There.'

Five days later I stood beside the grave.

The weather had changed. A cold October wind pulled at the blanket I'd wrapped Mazey in. I folded it more tightly around him. I'd lost a brother and inherited a son. I was nineteen years old.

All I could think of was what I'd said after we found the bodies. In the car, on the way back to the village, I was the only one who'd spoken.

'That stupid son of a bitch,' I said. 'He never could drive.' Then I burst into tears.

I cried for hours. Most of it was sheer frustration. If only he'd listened to me, none of this would've happened. If only he'd thought for once. It was nobody's fault but his. He'd chosen it.

So there I stood, on that cold October day.

My father had built the box, as he'd built Felix's seven years before. It took him longer than usual. One evening, shortly after the accident, I walked out to the house. I found him on the back porch, staring into the darkness. I asked him how it was coming, but he didn't answer. I went and looked in the barn and saw the box lying on trestles, less than half-built. I wondered if he was using the right wood. Axel had said there were different kinds, but he'd never taught me how to tell them apart. Returning to the porch, I took the chair next to my father's. From where he was sitting he could see the truck, parked next to the goat shed on the far side of the clearing. There were people in the village who thought he should've sold it for scrap, but he insisted on keeping it. For parts, he said. It wasn't morbid, it was practical, and he wouldn't be persuaded otherwise. I had no idea what he was staring at. Maybe it was the truck. Or maybe it was the small pond glimmering beyond it, among the trees. Or maybe it was nothing. I didn't know what he was thinking – I'd never known – and he wasn't about to tell me either. I sat beside him for an hour and we were silent the whole time. When he finally spoke to me, I was almost asleep.

'You remember your uncle's box, with the dancing shoes on it?'

I sat up. 'Yes.'

'What about Axel?'

That wasn't difficult.

'A mountain and a castle,' I said, 'and snow, too, because it's high up where the castle is.'

He turned and looked at me.

'It's a place he always dreamed of going,' I explained.

He was still looking at me, and it was a while before he spoke. 'I'm not sure I can do snow.'

The two boxes were lowered into the same hole, first Eileen's, then Axel's. My father had surpassed himself. He'd carved a range of mountains that stretched the entire width of the lid. He'd also carved the castle, perched high up in a lonely pass. He'd even carved a snowline. I noticed several members of the Poppel family peering suspiciously at Axel's box, and I thought they were right to be suspicious. That lid, it was a hint. Axel wasn't with Eileen in the ground at all. Axel had gone to a completely different place.

I glanced down at the child in my arms. He was wide awake and staring up into the sky, a sky filled with racing clouds and frantic autumn leaves. His eyes moved to my face. His mouth opened and his hands moved this way and that in the air, palms upwards, as if he was trying to balance it. He didn't make a sound, though. Not a sound.

Most people had caught a glimpse of the truck when it was towed back through the village. Others had visited the site of the accident. Some had even seen the bodies of the deceased. No one could believe the child had survived. It was a miracle, they said. Equally miraculous was my eagerness to adopt him – especially to the Poppels. They'd always doubted me and, even now, suspected that I might be up to something. They set their narrow minds to work on the problem, but they got nowhere with it. There wasn't anywhere to get. I could have told them that.

It was with a querying air that Mrs Poppel came up to me after the service. She offered her condolences. I offered mine.

'Well,' she said, 'at least they're together.'

I nodded. *That's what you think.*

She gave me a look that lasted seconds, then she stooped over the baby and tickled him under his chin. I stared down at her – the reddened eyelids, the dirt under her fingernails.

At last she straightened up. She stepped back, gathering her black shawl around her shoulders. 'He's good, isn't he?'

'Yes,' I said. 'He is.'

Not long after the funeral I was preparing supper for my father one evening when I heard the jingling sound of reins outside. Through the window I watched a horse and cart lurch to a standstill in the clearing behind the house, two lanterns swinging from the tail-board. Several people clambered down on to the ground. I saw a woman first and recognised the high, pinched nose on her.

'It's the Poppels,' I told my father.

Five of them had come. Mrs Poppel, her sister, her sister's daughter (or granddaughter – you never could tell, with the Poppels) and two sons, including the one who'd asked me for a dance at the wedding. They sat against the kitchen wall on straight-backed chairs drinking cherry brandy, which was all we had in the house. The two men took out tobacco pouches and rolled cigarettes that were as thin as matches. They smoked quickly, furtively, their eyes high up in the corners of the room.

Not until Mrs Poppel had drained her glass did she begin to speak. It was about the child. She was grateful to me for having taken him. She thought it was fitting. I was family, after all; I was blood. What's more, I was the right age – just two years older than her poor Eileen. A tear fattened on her lower eyelid. I watched it burst and spill across her cheek.

'And it's one less mouth for you to feed,' I said.

They bred like rabbits, the Poppels. Like rabbits.

'Well, yes,' she said, 'there is that, of course . . . ' She looked at my father, who had hardly said a word. 'And if you should ever think the child might need a father,' and she glanced at her son, the one sitting across the room, the one who liked dancing, 'well . . . '

Her son was staring at the wall. The hand holding the cigarette rested on his thigh, the cigarette pointing inwards, at his wrist. His eyes sprang towards me and then away again, as if the look was attached to a length of elastic.

'A baby's one thing,' I said. 'A husband's quite a different matter.'

My father cleared his throat and spat into the fire. The phlegm sizzled. 'Contributions,' he said, 'would always be welcome.'

I wasn't sure he meant it. I thought he was probably just telling the Poppels that their visit was over. He wasn't a great one for socialising, Arno Hekmann.

I waited until the cart had disappeared up the track and then I turned to him. 'Contributions?' I said.

My father lit his pipe. 'I don't see why not.'

As he leaned back in his chair and lifted his eyes to the smoke-blackened ceiling, I thought I saw a smile cross his face.

Later that night, though, he told me he was worried about money. There was less work than there used to be. He wasn't sure we could afford to keep the child. I reminded him that I was working now. And I would go on working. They didn't pay me much at the hotel, but it was better than nothing.

'If all else fails,' I said, 'I'll get married.'

My father contemplated me through coils of blue pipe-smoke.

'But not to some Poppel,' I added.

Now that Axel and Eileen were gone and my father was alone, I spent half of every week at the house. In the mornings I would walk into the village with Mazey bound tightly into a blanket on my back. When I reached the hotel I would lay him in a drawer, the same drawer that I'd found him in (it wouldn't be long before he grew out of it). If I was cleaning, I carried the drawer from room to room with me. If I was sweeping the terrace or scooping leaves out of the pool, I took the drawer outside. If I was cooking, the drawer stood on the kitchen table, among the fruit and vegetables. He was never any trouble. It was only his hands opening and closing in the air above the drawer that told you he was there. Eva didn't mind my bringing Mazey to work with me. She had two children of her own now, Thomas and Anna, yet she seemed more interested in mine. She thought there was something different about him. She was almost envious.

'He's so quiet,' she said, 'so,' and she bit her pale bottom lip, trying to think of the word, 'so *peaceful*.'

He had always been quiet. I could only remember him making one sound, and that was when he called out to me from the floor of the truck, to tell me he was there. He'd been quiet ever since. To me, that was normal. Also, it was an absence of something; it would have been hard for me to notice it, this being my first child. He didn't cry at night; in fact, he seldom cried at all, not even when he cut his teeth. Eva told me this was unheard of. She'd never come across a child who didn't cry when it was teething.

'You must be giving him something,' she said.

'I'm not.'

Her eyes narrowed. 'You're not giving him alcohol?'

'No.'

'Some kind of herb, then?'

I shook my head.

It was Eva who told me about the rumours that were spreading through the village. People thought Mazey might be a prophet or a saint. That was the reason he'd survived that terrible plunge through the woods. That was the reason he'd been spared the fate of his unfortunate parents. You might almost say that they'd been sacrificed on his behalf. They had died that he might live.

'That's absurd,' I said.

Eva lifted a finger to silence me. 'I didn't tell you about the miracle.'

The week before, she'd taken Mazey shopping in the village. It was late afternoon, already dark. Several people were in the grocer's when she walked in. While she was waiting to be served, her arms grew tired and she sat Mazey on the counter. Suddenly there was a violet flash in the square outside and then a loud crack overhead, like a dry stick being snapped in two, and all the lights went out.

'He was sitting on the counter,' she said, 'and somehow there was this glow around him, I don't know if it was a reflection or what it was, but anyway, everybody noticed it. And because everybody in the shop was looking at him, they all saw him lift his arms up and at the same moment that he lifted his arms, the lights came on again – *but only in the shop*. The rest of the village was still in darkness.' Eva stared at me with eyes that were wide and glistening, mesmerised by her own re-telling of the story.

It sounded like a coincidence to me.

'I know,' Eva said, 'but people are talking.'

The next time I cut Mazey's hair, she asked me for a lock of it. I gave it to her without thinking. A week later, while I was cleaning the lobby, I found the lock of hair. It had been laid on a square of brown velvet, then sealed into a small gilt box with a glass lid on it. The box had been fixed to the wall above the entrance to the hotel. When I asked her what it was doing there, kinks appeared in both her eyebrows; they could have been about to tie themselves in knots.

'It's so there's calmness in the house,' she said, as if it was perfectly obvious, '*his* calmness,' and she sent a glance to the corner of the kitchen, where Mazey lay sleeping. She took me by the arm and led me into the shadows by the cellar door. 'Tell me, is he talking yet?'

I shook my head.

'Not even one word? Not even,' and she lifted her shoulders towards her ears, and smiled a smile that was as small and plump as a ripe plum, 'not even – Mama?'

'No. Nothing.'

She frowned for a moment, then her dark eyes widened. 'Perhaps he's about to make an utterance. Who knows, perhaps he'll speak in tongues!' She moved closer. 'Don't mention it to Karl,' she said. 'The lock of hair, I mean. If you don't say anything, he probably won't notice. Men generally don't.'

If it had only been Eva who was acting in this manner I would have put it down to one sulphur bath too many and thought little more about it. But one afternoon in February a young couple, recently married, approached me as I was walking home. They wanted me to bring Mazey to their house, so he could bless it. It wasn't far, they said. Just round the corner.

Was it their eagerness that I succumbed to? Was I reminded of myself and Axel, the way we used to be – the way we could have been? Or was I just too tired after my day's work to think of an excuse? I don't know. In any case, I followed them and stood on the threshold of the house with Mazey and he was silent, as usual, and he stared, as usual, then we left. That was the blessing.

Winter moved northwards, leaving the landscape brown and sodden. We visited a rich man who'd been afflicted with a painful and incurable disease. I stood at his bedside, Mazey in my arms. We had only been there for half an hour when the man opened his eyes and said, 'He just sits there, doesn't he,' and then he smiled and died. There was the feeling among the family that the child had lifted the rich man's suffering and eased his difficult transition from this world to the next. There was the belief that the child had done good. I believed it, too. I was his mother, after all, and I was proud of him.

After that, we were often summoned to the beds of the dying to give them succour. We were summoned to the fields as well so the harvest would be plentiful. We were even summoned by the childless, in the hope that they might conceive. Each time Mazey appeared somewhere, the tales of his mysterious powers were enhanced and multiplied. More miracles were reported. Mazey passed an orchard and all the apples ripened. Mazey touched a sack of flour and when it was opened there was a gold coin in it. Just about the only thing he didn't do was bring somebody back from the dead – but he was probably saving that for his adolescence. Presents were showered on him: slaughtered animals, fruit and vegetables, alcohol, cigars – even money. Far from not being able to afford to keep him, my father and I found that he was more than paying for himself. I was worried, though. The Poppels were becoming interested again. I knew how their minds worked. I could see them driving through the village and the surrounding countryside with Mazey sitting on a piece of velvet in the back of their cart. There would be giant banners, painted in red and gold: SEE THE HOLY CHILD! TOUCH HIS BLESSED GARMENTS AND BE HEALED! and also, naturally, CONTRIBUTIONS WELCOME! They would grant audiences with him. They would sell locks of his hair. They would guarantee fertility, good fortune, peace of mind. He would make them rich.

The Poppels were stupid people and it would take them time to realise all this, but when they did, it would be hard to convince them of my innocence. They'd remember how swiftly I'd adopted him and suddenly they'd see everything that had happened in a new light: the child was gifted, even sacred, and somehow I'd known it all along. This was the truth they'd been trying to get at during the week of the funeral. This was the knowledge I'd cunningly concealed from them. The Poppels were only a threat if they felt they might have been wronged in some way. Well, they would feel wronged. And, like most stupid people, once they'd got that idea into their heads, it would be almost impossible to dislodge it. Mazey had already become, to some extent, the property of the village: the track to our house was being worn out by the feet of supplicants. How long before the Poppels tried to claim him as their own? He was all I had, but I would lose him if something wasn't done.

We celebrated Mazey Hekmann's second birthday. That morning my father had told me that certain people in the village wanted to build a shrine to him. It was to be erected on the shore of the lake, in the place where we had found the truck; people were saying it was the site of his spiritual rebirth. My father was sitting in his chair by the stove, his pipe unlit in his hand.

'They'll probably ask me to build it for them.' He laughed his hollow laugh. 'Strange thing is, I could use the work.'

I looked up from the cake I was icing and for once I could see we were both thinking the same thought: Where will it end?

Curiously enough, it was the church that saved us.

One night there was a knock on the door. I opened it and peered out into the darkness. The village doctor was standing there.

'You've got the wrong house,' I told him. 'There's no one sick in here.'

'That's what I'm here to find out.' He stepped forwards into the light and removed his hat. 'I've come to see the child. The pastor sent me.'

The doctor was a small bald man with a fragile manner. He always looked to me as if he'd just broken something valuable and was expecting punishment. His name was Holbek, and it was said of him that he wrote poetry at night.

He spent a long time examining Mazey with all kinds of tools and instruments which he produced from his black leather bag. At one point he asked me if Mazey could talk. I shook my head. Not yet, I said. Does he ever smile? the doctor asked. I looked at my father. I don't know, I said. I can't remember.

At last the doctor turned to face us, one of his hands clasped in the other.

'It's as I thought,' he said.

I stood beside my father, waiting for the doctor to continue.

'Well,' he said, 'the child may be a saint, for all I know, but he is also,' and he lowered his eyes for a moment and then lifted them again, 'he is also retarded.'

'I knew there was something about him,' I exclaimed.

Holbek gave me a watchful look. The child's mind was a seed that would never grow, he said, quoting from a poem he had not yet written. He couldn't be sure whether the condition was inherited or whether it was the result of the terrible accident that had robbed him of his parents. He simply couldn't say. However, it would be a great strain on all of us. He hoped we understood.

I tried to conceal my relief. No one would take him from us now.

'Please assure the pastor that I intended none of this,' I said. 'Quite the opposite, in fact. I don't know how it started, but I'm glad it's over.' I moved closer to the doctor, who was looking at me strangely. 'Please let it be known throughout the village that my child is not a holy child, but a simple one.'

The doctor nodded.

'His mother was a Poppel,' I said. 'That probably explains it.'

I thanked the doctor for coming, then showed him to the door. I stood in the yard and watched him walk away, his short dark figure merging quickly with the night.

During the next few weeks the village turned against us. Doors closed as we walked along the street. Faces looked away. They'd been deceived, not by the child or by me, but by themselves – though that wasn't how they saw it, of course. They'd put their faith in Mazey, and he'd made fools of them. Their reverence was replaced by wariness at first, and then by fear. His eyes weren't calm; they were blank. His silence wasn't serenity, but emptiness. So it is that people are betrayed by their desperate craving for gods. But we lived on, as we had always done, in our house out in the woods – my father, my son, and me.

There came a time when the hotel's fortunes began to change for the better. Eva was convinced it was because she'd taken the gilt box down from above the door and ceremonially burned the contents, but the fact was, our national economy was booming and the new prosperity could be felt, even in the more remote corners of the country. We had guests most nights. They weren't the actors and statesmen of half a century before. They were ordinary people who wanted to escape for a weekend: pensioners, businessmen, romantic couples. Over the years, as Karl had started drinking heavily, first at home, then in the nearby town, Eva had come to rely on me. By the time I was twenty-four, I was practically running the place. I worked hard, with only a part-time cook and a chambermaid to help me. I saw less of my father, less of Mazey. It was a condition of my employment, in any case, that Mazey be left at home. As a baby he'd been no trouble, but things were different now that he was five. 'It's those eyes of his,' Eva would say, shivering dramatically. 'They put people off.'

It was true. Mazey was tall for his age, with pale-blond hair that fell across his forehead, just the way his father's used to, but if you looked him in the eye you could see that something wasn't right. He seemed to be looking through the world, rather than at it. For him, the world was like a pane of glass. You couldn't guess what lay beyond the glass, though. Sometimes people stood in front of him and his gaze seemed to be saying, *You're not there. You don't exist*. They felt like ghosts all of a sudden. He even did it to me now and then. There were times when I felt that his eyes had stopped just behind my eyes, inside my mind, and that they were reading what was written there, a story I had never told, a secret nobody had guessed – the truth. And then I'd have to remind myself of what he was: a simpleton, an idiot, a fool – with only me to care for him, only me to trust. Only one truth counted any more, and that was this: we would never cause each other harm.

While at work I left Mazey with my father. Mazey's silent staring didn't disturb my father in the least. If anything, it suited him; he'd never been one to use words when silence would do just as well. He thought Mazey needed something to occupy him, though. Hunting through a drawer of odds and ends, he found an old pen-knife with a dark, bone handle and three blades of differing sizes. He gave it to the boy, began to teach him how to whittle. Mazey caught on quickly – so quickly, in fact, that my father claimed his own carpentering skills had skipped a generation; he saw himself in Mazey, which made the task of looking after him much easier, more of a pleasure. Mazey had a natural talent, he said, and it was a shame he was simple because he could have been a fine craftsman. What Mazey actually produced were strange, smooth shapes that didn't look like anything, but somehow this seemed right: he was carving what was in his mind. And he would be absorbed for hours, sitting on the ground with that old blunt knife and a few off-cuts from whatever piece of furniture his grandfather happened to be working on. In those days I finished late at the hotel. Walking along the track towards our house, I'd see the stubborn bulk of it, down in the hollow, the whole place in darkness. The only light would be coming from the barn, and as I crossed the yard I'd see the two of them still bent over bits of wood, their figures shadowy, seeming to sway inside the dirty yellow tent of light shed by the hurricane lamp that hung from a beam above their heads.

Something else Mazey did was go off on his own. He'd touch his grandfather on the shoulder or pull at his sleeve, and he'd point away from the house, into the trees. Then he'd be gone. Once, when he was four, I found him on the road that led into the village. Four years old and he was halfway to the bridge! At first it worried me. But as the years went by, I got used to it; that curiosity or restlessness, it was part of his character. By the time he was six or seven, he would often be gone for the entire day. At nightfall he'd walk in through the kitchen door and, dragging a chair over to the sink, he'd climb up on to it and drink from the cold tap. So far as I could tell, he kept out of the village – almost as if he remembered how it had turned against him once.

The closest he would go was Miss Poppel's place, which was on the edge of the village, across the road from the hotel. It was her front garden that attracted him. It had grown since I was a child. A jungle of broken machinery and appliances: vacuum-cleaners, bits of tractors, bicycle-wheels, refrigerators, ovens, ploughs. Salenko, the local mechanic, donated car-parts, the same way a butcher might give you free bones if you had a dog. She was especially fond of exhaust-pipes, which made excellent wind-chimes, she said. She must have had at least a dozen sets of wind-chimes hanging up outside her house. There were the exhaust-pipes, of course, but there were also hub caps, tin cans, even bottles (strictly for light summer breezes). Mazey's favourite was the one that had been there the longest, the one made out of door-hinges. Though it took a strong wind to stir them into sound, he was just as happy sitting beneath the crab-apple tree and watching them twist silently on their lengths of copper wire. He could sit there for hours. And Miss Poppel would bring him a glass of fresh goat's milk or a slice of something she had baked that day. She had promised him that the wind-chimes would be his when she was dead. She was going to mention them specifically in her will.

When I passed Miss Poppel's house after work, Mazey would often appear from behind some rusting piece of metal and we'd walk home together. I'd tell him what kind of day I'd had; I'd tell him stories, too, like how much Uncle Karl had drunk, or how long Aunt Eva had stayed in the sulphur water. It was like talking to myself, really, because he never said anything; I couldn't even be sure that he was listening.

On one such evening, when he was six or seven, I happened to mention the chimes. Gusts of wind had been rattling the doors and windows of the hotel all afternoon; I hadn't heard the chimes myself, but I'd imagined Mazey in Miss Poppel's garden, entranced. As usual, though, I left no room for him to speak. I'd already started telling him how Eva's cigarettes had blown into the pool, so I almost missed it.

'They were singing.'

I stopped in my tracks. Mazey walked on a few steps and then turned round and looked at me.

'Did you say something?' I said.

'They were singing.'

I began to laugh out loud, right there in the middle of the road. He didn't seem to understand what all the fuss was about. In his head, perhaps, he'd been talking for years.

That night, after I'd put Mazey to bed, I told my father what had happened. My father was cleaning his pipe, chipping at the inside of the bowl with a knife and tapping the scrapings on to the top of the stove. He listened to me, but didn't stop what he was doing. He waited until I'd finished, then he spoke.

'I never heard him say anything.'

'I didn't either,' I said, 'not until today.'

My father was silent for a while, packing tobacco into his pipe. He tamped the tobacco down, then held a lit match above it and bent the flame by sucking hard on the stem of the pipe. When he'd got the smoke moving in clouds towards the ceiling he looked at me. 'Maybe it's only you he'll talk to.'

Towards the end of the month I saw some evidence of this. I passed Miss Poppel's house on my way home, but there was no sign of Mazey. I thought nothing of it; he wasn't there every day and, anyway, I was later than usual that evening. But just before I reached the bridge, I heard chanting coming from a field on my right.

I stepped into the ditch. There was still some light in the sky, and through the bushes I could see several children from the village gathered in the field. They seemed to be playing some kind of game. One of them – the leader, presumably – had his right elbow in his left palm and a cigarette between his fingers. There was a cartwheel propped against a tree, and a boy had been tied to it. I couldn't see his face. I could only see the other children taunting him and their leader pacing up and down, taking quick drags from his cigarette.

'Now,' the leader was saying, 'you're going to talk.'

'He ain't going to talk,' said one of the others.

'He'll talk.' Smiling, the leader passed his cigarette to the boy who stood beside him. 'Do his face.'

The boy who was tied to the wheel strained sideways, and it was then that I saw the blond hair falling across his forehead.

I fought my way through the bushes and ran across the field, shouting. The children stood still for a moment, staring at me, then the leader threw his cigarette away, not looking where it landed, and they scattered. I knelt down in front of Mazey and undid the string they'd bound him with. As soon as he was free, he took his right arm in his left hand and cradled it. He looked out across the field with his mouth stretched wide.

'Did they hurt you?'

When he didn't answer me, I gently took his shirt-sleeve and rolled it up. There were three round burns in a cluster on the inside of his arm, just below the elbow. I drew him close to me. I could feel his heart beating and his breath coming faster than usual. It may sound strange, but I was proud of him then. He talked – but only to me. He wouldn't talk to anyone else. Not even if he was tortured.

He moved in my arms and I loosened my hold on him. He walked a few steps to where the cigarette lay in the grass, a thin spiral of blue smoke rising defiantly into the air. With no expression on his face, he put his shoe on the cigarette and crushed it out.

Of course I couldn't protect him every moment of the day, but I had the feeling, as we walked home that evening, that I'd left him on his own for too long. I ought to be spending more time with him – but what about my work? And if I gave up work, where would the money come from? Maybe, in the back of my mind, I was already beginning to think of taking a husband.

The hotel was frequented not only by strangers but by local people as well and, during the evening, the small bar at the back was one of the few places in the area where you could have a quiet drink. Peter Kroner wasn't a stranger exactly, but he wasn't a local either. He came from a village some distance to the east. He was the foreman at a limestone quarry (Edwin Bock worked for him, among others). His family owned a small vineyard, too, producing a red wine that was fruity and sweet. The wine was popular, and Karl made a point of keeping half a dozen bottles in stock. That was Kroner's excuse (he seemed, even then, like a man who needed excuses). He would call in for a drink on his way home from work, even though the hotel wasn't on his way home at all, and his first words as he walked through the door were always the same: 'So how's it selling?' He didn't expect a reply. He didn't care if it was selling or not. He almost never drank his father's wine; he said it disagreed with him. It was one of the things I liked him for: though he was still living with his parents, he treated them with a healthy disrespect – or so it seemed to me. He was eleven years older than I was, and still unmarried. He had soft black hair and skin that didn't take a razor well. Whenever I looked at him, he looked away, which I found flattering. It surprised me that I was flattered, but I was.

He began to come into the bar at lunchtime.

'Don't you ever do any work?' I asked him once, and instantly regretted it because it gave him just the kind of opening he needed.

'Can't seem to concentrate,' he muttered.

His eyes all jittery, his face looking grazed.

Axel was standing at my elbow suddenly, behind the bar, and he was grinning. 'Why don't you dance with him?'

Dance with him? There wasn't even any music.

'I don't know,' and Kroner twisted his glass of whisky on its base, 'it's just that I keep thinking about you.'

Dance with him.

'I could be married,' I said, 'for all you know.'

'You're not married. I asked.'

'I'm twenty-six years old. If I'm not married yet, there must be something wrong with me.'

'Not that I can see.'

Exasperated now, I said, 'I've got a child.'

'I know,' and Kroner grinned, 'but he isn't yours, is he?'

'I love him like he's mine.'

Kroner's eyes moved across my face, first one way, then the other, not stopping anywhere, just sliding over it. Afterwards he looked into his drink again.

'Then I'll love him, too,' he said in a quiet voice, and nodded to himself. 'I'll love him, too.'

Two months later I was wearing a pale-yellow dress down to the floor and he was wearing a dark-blue suit, and there was confetti on his shoulders and in his hair – tiny pale-blue horseshoes, tiny silver bells. His father's sweet red wine flowed all afternoon and on into the evening. Dr Holbek recited a poem in our honour. He called it 'A Connubial Epiphany'. We hardly knew what the title meant, let alone the poem, but we both applauded loudly at the end. There was a five-piece band, and we were in each other's arms. Round and round we went, until my heels blistered.

'There,' I said to Axel, who was watching from a castle on the far side of the world. 'I'm dancing with him. Are you satisfied?'

I never wanted Peter Kroner's children – that wasn't the point of the marriage – but he took one from me anyway (if you can have a man put his seed in you and call it taking; I think you can). It was a baby girl and, just after she was born, he came into the bedroom with an armful of pink roses. There were twenty-six of them, and they'd travelled all the way from the city, he said, by special courier.

'I'm so proud of you.' His grazed face blurred and I felt his lips on my cheek.

As far as I was concerned, it was like a robber going back to the bank he'd stolen from and congratulating it. I didn't say anything, though. I couldn't. The smell of the roses sickened me, their heavy sweetness thickening the air. I had to ask the midwife to stand them by the open window. Kroner didn't notice. He was holding his baby daughter in both hands and his face had softened like a saint's.

'Black hair,' he said, 'just like her dad.'

I had given birth at my father's house, which was where we were living then. Kroner wasn't happy about it – his parents' house was bigger – but I'd insisted, not so much for my own sake as for Mazey's. I didn't want him to be uprooted from the only place he knew.

It was a hot summer. Every day Kroner would drive over to the quarry, and I would stay in the house and sit by the window and think of the stream all dried up at the bottom of the field and the willow's branches trailing in the mud. In my head everything was numb. I didn't feel much for the child. When it lay in my arms and I looked down at its raw, puckered skin, it wasn't love I felt, or even fondness. I'd loved once and I wasn't about to be tricked into loving again – especially not by a pink, twitching thing with someone else's hair. And besides, after loving Axel and then Mazey, there didn't seem to be anything left over. It was so different from Mazey, too. I remembered how envious Eva had been, and now I understood. This new child cried all the time. There was so much strength in its tiny, swollen body. I heard the crying not with my ears, but my nerves; I felt like wood under a blunt saw, splintering. I'd find myself staring into her mouth, the hard curve of her tongue, dark-red, it was, almost purple-black at times, and then I'd want to hurt her.

I couldn't get over the feeling that I'd been robbed, somehow, or cheated. Partly it was Kroner himself: the joy he took in the child, the holy face he had when he looked down at her, the lightness in his step – I was sickened by it just as I'd been sickened by the flowers. There were days when he seemed to be looking at me with a kind of crafty pleasure, as if he'd slipped something past me. He'd married me. I'd had his child. He'd got his own way all along, and I was too exhausted to do anything about it.

I was just settling into my chair on the back porch one morning when I heard the sound of an engine in low gear. I couldn't think who might be visiting – I didn't have many friends – and though I didn't feel like company, I was curious to see whose car appeared in the clearing. It was Karl's, but Eva was driving and she was alone. I watched her open the door. She was wearing a loose blue dress and a pair of bedroom slippers. As she turned towards the house, I saw the bruising on her cheek and around her eye, and then I knew why she had come.

We sat on the porch all morning drinking sweet black coffee. I smoked one of her cigarettes, my first for more than a year, which made the world glass over. She noticed the cushions I'd arranged beneath me.

'Does it still hurt?'

I nodded.

'After I had Thomas,' she said, 'they sewed me up too tight. They had to cut me open again.'

'Eva.'

'Sorry.' She threw her cigarette into the yard.

She told me Karl had started drinking in the mornings. He had a few before he went out, and by the time he came home at night he was so loud the roof seemed to jump right off the house. The children were frightened. Even the guests were frightened. She tried to smile, but it hurt. I watched her carefully. Her left eye looked like the letter e if you typed it on the hotel typewriter and then went back and typed another e on top of it. She was still talking about Karl. She wondered if I could speak to him. He was my brother, after all. She couldn't think who else to ask.

I didn't think it was right of Karl, hitting her like that, but at the same time, knowing him as I did, I could see how she might have driven him to it. Her hair was dry and split, and her skin was turning spongy. There was a slackness about her, a lack of energy, that I knew would infuriate him. He would want to take hold of her and shake her. Wring her out.

'There's no point me talking to him,' I said.

'Why not?'

'He doesn't listen to me. He never has.'

Sighing, Eva lit another cigarette. She looked greedy when she smoked; it was the way her lips reached out for the filter, as if they couldn't wait to draw the smoke from it.

'What about your husband?' she said.

That evening I spoke to Kroner. He knew Karl through his father and the wine business. I persuaded him to have a drink with Karl, though I told him I didn't think it would do much good.

'Just try,' I said. 'For Eva's sake.'

Three nights later the door burst open and Kroner stood in the middle of the room, his face more grazed than usual, his clothes dishevelled. He was shouting.

'He broke my tooth. He broke my fucking tooth.'

The baby started crying.

Kroner touched one hand against his mouth, then took it away and looked at it. 'Your family,' he shouted. 'Your *fucking* family – '

'My father's in the next room – '

'You, your brother, your crazy fucking child . . .' He was circling the room, first one way, then the other. He kept touching his mouth and looking at his hand. There wasn't much to see. 'I don't know why I got into this. I don't have the first idea . . .'

I looked at the baby's hard, curved tongue. I thought of feeding her, but her blunt gums hurt my breasts.

'I don't – I just don't have the *first fucking idea* – '

'Nor do I,' I said in a quiet voice.

He heard me, though, and suddenly his hands flew up into the air and his face creased above his eyebrows, through his chin. 'Don't say that, Edith.'

I stared at the window. It had begun to rain.

'I didn't mean it,' Kroner was saying. 'He hit me, that's all. Your brother.'

'Let's have a look at it.'

He knelt on the floor and lifted his lip. He showed me the tooth.

'It's chipped,' I told him, 'nothing more. It'll give you character.'

He looked up at me and the way he looked then, just for a moment, even with the child crying and the rain crawling down the window, I knew why I'd allowed it all to happen.

Winter lasted longer than usual that year, and even in April we had sleet driving almost horizontally across the land, the wind tearing out of the north-east and cutting through your clothes as if they weren't there. One morning that month I came back from the village to find both Kroner and Mazey gone. They rarely went anywhere together; I couldn't think where they might be. But the moment I noticed tyre tracks in the yard I guessed.

It was afternoon before Kroner returned, and he returned alone.

He was trying to keep his eyes steady as he stepped down out of the truck and saw me waiting outside the back door. He did a poor imitation of a man with right on his side.

'Well,' he said, 'I did it.'

'Did what?'

'The boy . . .' He stood in the mud, one hand outstretched, as if the truth was self-evident.

It was – but I wasn't about to put it into words for him. I shifted his child higher in my arms. The inside of my head was scorched, charred; I couldn't have spoken if I'd wanted to.

'I thought we agreed,' he said, taking one step towards me. And then, bristling, 'I've done you a favour and that's all the thanks I get?'

I turned and ran into the barn and snatched a skinning knife down from the wall. Then out into the yard again, the child still in my arms.

Kroner was standing where I'd left him, but all his righteousness, and all the indignation that had followed it, had fled. Just those small, square hands spread in the air and his chin at an angle, justifying. Like most men, he could be hypnotised by sudden, unexpected movement.

My head was black inside, all black. I held the knife just below my jaw, which was the same height as Kroner's heart.

'Give me the keys to the truck.'

His Adam's apple plunged, then climbed again. 'Not with the child here, Edith. Not with the – '

'*Give me the keys.*'

He reached into his pocket. Took the keys out, handed them to me. His eyes were still running backwards and forwards between the aimed blade and my face.

I pushed the child at him and left.

I drove the forty-five kilometres with the knife lying beside me on the seat. It was a cold day, with snow at the edges of the road. Everything was grey: the sky, the trees, the fields. I saw a fire burning in the land behind a house. I couldn't believe how orange it was; it was the only real colour anywhere.

Kroner had talked to me the week before, when Mazey and my father were asleep. I was tired that night; I couldn't remember much of what he'd said. He never could say things straight out, anyway. He had to come at you round corners. The long and the short of it was, he'd tried to love the boy; he'd tried, and failed. I thought he should try harder.

Kroner shook his head. 'He doesn't belong with us, not now we've got a child of our own.'

'Where do you think he belongs? With the Poppels?' I laughed scornfully.

'We've got our own family now. It's just not natural.'

'Nobody said it was natural. It's how it is, that's all.'

Kroner shook his head again. I hadn't listened. I hadn't understood. And so he'd been forced to act without me, on my behalf.

That was the trouble with Kroner. He thought he was the clever one. He thought he could get his way. Well, we'd see about that. We'd see. I gripped the steering-wheel so hard, my hands ached for three days afterwards, as if I'd been strangling guinea fowl all afternoon, or scything grass.

The institution was a big building, and it took me almost half an hour to find Mazey. He was in a long room on the second floor. It was something like a church in there, only the smell was different. They'd strapped him to a metal bed, with nothing underneath him but a dark-green rubber sheet. He was almost naked, just a gown on him that was unfastened at the sides, and it was cold in that room, so cold that my breath showed in the air like cigarette smoke. I didn't bother unfastening the belts. I just worked the skinning knife under the leather and sawed until it frayed and snapped. First one wrist, then the other. Then his ankles. I put his clothes back on, and led him out of the room and down the stairs. There were three men in white overalls who stopped talking when they saw us. We walked right through them and they didn't move. It was something in my eyes, maybe. Or maybe it was the knife that I was holding upright in my fist.

He sat beside me in the truck and watched the trees go by. His right hand opened and closed on his bare leg. He didn't seem upset by what had happened. It had happened in the world where his body was, but his mind was somewhere else. There was a gap between the two that most people didn't have: his body might be in pain, but his mind would be too far away to notice or remember. I asked him if he was hungry. He looked at me with eyes that were the same colour as the weather; he didn't say anything, though. I stopped at a roadside café and bought him a sausage and some chips on a paper plate. He ate slowly, his head turned sideways, one finger on the window. Sometimes it hurt me just to look at him. There were things that were going to happen and I would never even know.

He only spoke once during the drive, and that was when we passed a house that had a crab-apple tree in front of it. I thought I heard him murmur the word 'singing'.

I turned to him. 'You mean chimes? The wind-chimes?'

He didn't answer. His head was resting against the seat, and his hands, closed into soft fists, were pressed against his thighs.

'We'll be home soon.' I took one hand off the wheel and pushed his hair back from his forehead. 'I wouldn't leave you in a place like that. I wouldn't leave you there.'

It was dusk when we drove into the clearing. A light was on in the barn – my father, working late. He'd taken to spending most of his time in the barn since Kroner had moved in; he even had a bed out there. The house was in darkness. Just the kitchen window glowing, and the sky still pale above. Those yellow panes of glass looked welcoming, but a welcome was the last thing I expected. There was a man in that room, and three hours ago I'd held a knife to him.

Kroner was sitting by the stove with a newspaper spread on his knees. He was pretending to read, but I knew he wasn't taking in a single word. The baby was lying on a blanket on the table, crying.

'Baby needs feeding,' he said.

Some of the fury that had carried me forty-five kilometres across the county still remained. I took Mazey by the shoulder and stood him in front of Kroner. At last Kroner looked up from the paper, his eyes jumping from my face to my hand and back again.

'See that man?' I was pointing at Kroner, but looking at Mazey.

Mazey nodded.

'That man is not your father,' I said. 'Do you understand?'

According to Eva, Karl had started drinking two years after he'd got married and he'd been drinking ever since, so when I drove to the town one morning I wasn't surprised to see his car parked outside a small bar near the railway crossing. What surprised me was what happened next. I was supposed to be buying shoes for Karin that day. Instead, I parked my car next to his and walked into the bar.

It was a fine September day outside, but inside it could have been any time of year at all. Or any year. The air was half smoke, half dust. Men sat alone, their faces propped against their hands. High up, where the walls turned yellow, a deer's head was mounted on a wooden shield. It had both its antlers, but only one of its glass eyes. Above the bar there was a faded poster of a girl in red shorts and a bikini top. She was advertising tyres. The door to the toilets was ajar and I could smell the disinfectant.

I took the stool next to Karl's. He didn't notice me – or, if he did, he gave no sign of it. His glass was almost empty, its tall sides laced with froth. He must have drunk it fast. I bought him another and put it in front of him. I bought myself one, too. When he looked round, there was a slow, knowing smile on his face. I didn't think he was pleased to see me particularly. I was simply somebody he recognised.

'Nice place you found,' I said.

He grunted.

I raised my glass. 'Your health.'

His shoulders shook once or twice, but if he was laughing, he kept the sound of it inside.

That was the way it began, the two of us just sitting there. The silence was my father's silence: you didn't open your mouth until you had something to say – and even then, sometimes, you didn't. But when an hour had gone and I still hadn't left, when I ordered more drinks instead of leaving (using the money set aside for Karin's shoes), he began to talk. It was mostly to himself, though I must've been the trigger for it. He was at his wits' end. There was a business to run, the family as well, and all Eva did was sit in that fucking rock-pool and read from the Apocalypse. Recently she'd started claiming that their guests were agents of the devil, sent to lead her into temptation. Sometimes she told them the hotel was full. Or else she hid bowls of sulphur water underneath their beds, and the smell was so terrible, they always left the next morning. She already smelled bad enough herself. Like hell, in fact. He'd stood it for years, but he didn't know how much longer he could last. He couldn't even bring himself to touch her any more. It was hard to believe he'd had two children by her.

'Are you going to leave her?'

'Maybe. I don't know. It's Tom and Anna . . .'

I nodded.

'Sometimes I try and wait it out,' he said. 'Mostly that's what I do. It'll get better, that's what I'm thinking. But it doesn't. And if anyone tries to talk to me about it – ' He broke off, shook his head. 'Like that time I hit your husband.'

I didn't say anything.

'That time he came to see me. I shouldn't have done it. I shouldn't have hit him.'

'Ah, fuck it,' I said. 'It doesn't matter.' I drank some beer. When Karl looked at me, I shrugged and said, 'He's a coward.'

I wasn't only thinking about the way he drove Mazey to the institution when I wasn't looking. It was everything that had happened since. At first he tried to separate Mazey from the family by legal means. He wouldn't allow Mazey to use his name. Mazey was a Hekmann, he said, not a Kroner, and he had a piece of paper from the lawyer's office to prove it.

'Fine,' I said. 'In that case, I'm a Hekmann, too.'

From that time on I used my maiden name, even though we were still married and living in the same house. Even though I didn't have a piece of paper from the lawyer's office. But for Kroner that was just the beginning. He wanted Mazey gone, and practised untold cruelties behind my back, hoping to drive him away. He was sly, as always. He hurt Mazey in ways that made it look as if the boy had done it himself. The bruises, the lacerations, the burns – they could have been accidents. Once, Mazey came home smelling of urine and I thought he must have wet himself – he did that sometimes – but I could smell it on his face and hair, and I became suspicious. I couldn't prove anything, though. Later I heard rumours that Kroner and a couple of his men from the quarry had chained Mazey to a fence and then they all undid their trousers and pissed on him. That kind of treatment didn't work with Mazey. He knew no other life – why would it make him leave? Added to which, he didn't understand things that other people took for granted. If you put him in front of a television it was quite possible that he'd use it as a mirror. Kroner never understood that. Someone told me that Kroner had taken Mazey to the bridge one time and pointed out along the road and said, 'Get out of here. Go on, get.' Mazey just stared at Kroner's finger, the way a cat might, and then followed him home.

I nodded to myself. 'A coward's all he is. And what you were saying about Eva, well, the same goes for Kroner.'

Karl looked at me across the rim of his glass, but I didn't want to talk about my husband any more. There were nights when I could feel he was ready and he tried to put it into me, but it had been a long time since I wanted him – in fact, maybe I never had. His white belly lowered over me, his flesh so soft I lost my fingers in it. The way his skin flushed in a wide red collar round his neck. I only had to think of Axel lying by the stream before the sun came up, the colour of his skin in the morning light, the clean wood smell of it . . .

And anyway, I knew what his game was, as surely as if he'd been wearing a stocking over his head and carrying a sawn-off shot-gun.

He'd stolen from my body once, and I wasn't about to let that happen again. I still dreamed about the roses sometimes, all twenty-six of them, and I always woke up feeling sick.

'No one in our family knows how to marry,' Karl said.

'Maybe Felix got it right,' I said. 'He didn't even try.'

Suddenly I looked at Karl, my brother, and I smiled. I'd just realised. This was the first time we had ever talked.

But there was a moment, later, when everything spread out sideways like melted glass, and Karl turned to me and said, 'You know, I never did like you very much.'

At first I laughed, treating it as a joke, but his face didn't change. And suddenly I wasn't drunk any more. Something like that, it sobers you from one moment to the next. In a way, though, I'd known it was coming. By sitting on the empty stool, I'd asked for it. The truth behind those years of silence.

'I just never did.' He was still looking at me with his three-day growth of beard and his sudden, drunken clarity. 'Know why?'

'You're going to tell me, aren't you.'

'Oh yeah. I'm going to tell you.' He turned on his stool so eagerly, so clumsily, I had to smile.

'You smile,' he said. 'But underneath, you're not smiling.'

'Oh?' I said. 'And what am I doing,' I said, 'underneath?'

'You never let anything out, do you. You fucking *never*,' and his hand closed in a tight fist as he fought to explain himself, '*you never* give anything away.'

I was beginning to think I'd made a mistake by walking into the bar. I wished I'd driven right past it. The shoe shop seemed a far better place to be.

'Maybe that's why you look the way you do,' he said.

I asked him what he meant.

'Our mother, she was beautiful. That's why she left – '

'You remember that?'

'Karin's got something of her, in a way. But you – ' He looked down at the bar and shook his head. 'Me, all right, I get drunk,' he said, 'I make a fool of myself, I knock people down, sometimes I spend a couple of nights in prison cooling off – but I'm not dangerous.' He leaned closer to me, one finger lifted, pointing. 'It's you. You're the one who's dangerous.'

'Sure,' I said. 'People are terrified.'

But what he was saying tied a string around my heart and pulled it tight. I'd always wondered if anyone knew. If anyone had guessed.

'I'm right, aren't I. Aren't I.'

I was hoping he'd drink enough to forget what he'd said. At the same time I knew it came from deep down, years back. Being drunk was not the source of it. That was just a way of gaining access. And besides, I'd never believed what people said about being so drunk they couldn't remember anything. Still, I bought him another beer. Just in case it was true.

'You don't hit anyone or go to prison,' Karl said. 'You just sit there, behind those spectacles of yours, and you could kill us all, one by one, and you wouldn't feel a thing.' He reached out for my glasses, but I swayed back on my stool. 'Ah,' and he waved a hand past my face, disgusted now, and drank.

I lit a cigarette.

'You'd do it, wouldn't you,' he muttered. 'Maybe you did it already. Maybe you already killed someone.'

'Like who?'

'See? You're doing it right now. That's it, right there. The look I'm talking about.' And he pointed right into my face with a finger that drew unsteady circles, like the shapes flies make in the air. 'Like who?' he said, imitating me. 'Like who?'

I pushed his hand away so hard, he almost fell backwards off his stool. He was right. I could've killed him. Right there and then. The anger bursting through me like the rush of hot pus from an abscess.

'I got to you.' He sat there, chuckling. 'You might as well admit it. I got to you.'

'Yeah, Karl,' I said. 'You got to me.'

You stupid son of a bitch.

It was all bluff. Curiosity and bluff. He was no threat to me at all. No threat to anyone. I used the mirror behind the bar to look at him. His damp face, the lids of his eyes inflamed.

'Karl,' I said, 'you're so fucking drunk, I could pour you into a bottle and put a cork on it.'

'You'd like that, wouldn't you.'

'Anything,' I said, 'to shut you up.'

I ordered a whisky, to clean the taste of beer from my mouth. I stared at the girl on the poster. I found myself wondering what my mother had looked like. No one had ever told me. I'd never even seen a photograph. That could be her, for all I knew, in those red shorts. It was six o'clock and the bar was beginning to fill up with men from the nearby building site. I would have to be going.

As I climbed down off the stool, Karl took hold of my sleeve. 'Tell me something,' he said. 'Axel's boy. Why'd you do that?'

'Do what?'

'Why'd you take him in?'

I shook myself free. 'I'm tired of your questions, Karl. I'm going home.'

'Home?' He stared into the forest of green and brown bottles on the shelf above the bar. 'Yeah, there's always that.'

Outside, it was dark. The street-lights bounced. I'd thought the fresh air would clear my head. It only made things worse. Now I had to drive.

The car didn't seem to want to move. I had to press down hard on the accelerator. After a few minutes I smelled burning. The hand-brake was still on.

I drove slowly, seeing double. Luckily, the roads were empty.

Then, three kilometres from home, I misjudged a bend. I'd known it all my life, but it seemed sharper than usual that evening and before I could do anything the car was sliding sideways into a field. I got out. Water seeped in over the top of my shoes. I found a fence-post and wedged it underneath the wheels. But when I tried to reverse back on to the road, the wheels spun and the wood just fell apart. I looked around. The trees kept gliding away from me, away from me. The sky was made of dots – millions of tiny, busy dots. It didn't seem very likely that anyone would come along. That was why I'd chosen the route in the first place. I was going to have to walk.

The evening was cool and dry, no sign of any rain. Still. Three kilometres. I spat into the hedgerow, my saliva thick with alcohol. Something Karl said to my father on the day of the accident came back to me. *When was the last time you noticed anything?* The words spread through me and went on spreading, like something that had spilled out of a bottle. I had the sudden, uneasy feeling that Karl knew more than he was telling. He had asked me why I'd taken Axel's child, but he already knew the answer. He just wanted me to admit it to him. He wanted to hear me say that it was out of love. A new love, but distilled from a much older one, and all the stronger for it. On the other hand, did it really matter if he knew? He was hardly going to go round telling people. But the secret was his, and he had to carry it. Perhaps that was the source of his disgust with me, the reason for his silence.

At last I turned down the track that led to our house. There was a light mist rising in the hollow; the clearing looked mysterious. As I passed the barn, I called out to my father. He was putting the finishing touches to a miniature chest of drawers, which Dr Holbek would keep his poems in. I pushed too hard on the kitchen door and it crashed against the wall, dislodging something in the room. Kroner looked up from his evening paper.

'I didn't hear the car,' he said.

I had to laugh. 'That's because there wasn't one.'

'But you went out in it.'

'It broke down. I left it in a field.' I sank into a chair, exhausted suddenly.

'You're drunk,' Kroner said.

He was right. When I looked at him, his whole body kept jerking sideways. 'Is Mazey back yet?'

'I haven't seen him.'

The door opened and Karin walked into the room. She looked at me with eyes that seemed too big for her face.

'Did you get my shoes?' she asked.

I shook my head. 'They didn't have your size.'

The following spring, Karl moved his family away from the village altogether. He'd taken a job as a supermarket manager in an industrial town down south. At first Eva didn't want to leave, but Karl quoted Revelation 3:8 – *Behold I have set before thee an open door, and no man can shut it: for thou hast a little strength, and hast kept my word, and hast not denied my name* – and she went peacefully after that. They rented a small house in the suburbs. Yellow, with brown shutters. Eva sent us a picture later that year. It was the only time we heard from them, apart from a card at Christmas. In some ways, knowing what he knew, I was relieved to have him gone.

They'd asked us to run the hotel for them, though as Karl had told me in the bar, there was nothing much to run. (A glance at the register confirmed this: only thirteen guests in the previous nine months.) It was mostly a question of living there, maintaining it. Kroner was overjoyed. At last we'd have some privacy, he said, some room. He also seemed to think it was romantic, moving into the place where 'we first met and fell in love', as he put it. He talked about 'a brand-new start'. If what I'd wanted was a man with the ability to fool himself, I couldn't have done better than Peter Kroner. Did he think I didn't know about the cruelties that he'd inflicted on Mazey? Did he expect me to forget?

The week before the move, he tried to persuade me to leave Mazey behind. He said Mazey would be happier out at the house. He could sit there whittling all day. No one would bother him. And he'd be company for my father. I stared at Kroner in disbelief. Crafty as ever, brazen, too: he was even using my own arguments against me. I wouldn't hear of it, of course. Mazey was my son. He could visit his grandfather all he wanted, but he would live with us.

Mazey was seventeen now, the same age Axel was when he died. He was taller than Axel, though, and longer-limbed. His mouth was wide. To people who didn't know him, he might appear to be grinning – but if they looked him in the eyes they realised their mistake. He'd lost none of his restlessness: 'I'm going out,' he'd say (he always told me, and only me, beforehand; it was strange how certain fragments of normal behaviour had lodged in him), and then he'd put on his dun-coloured jacket and his cap, and he'd be gone for hours – days, sometimes. I tried not to worry. Now that he was grown, people in the village left him alone. They knew who he was and, more importantly, they remembered what he'd been, and there was a residue of wariness, if not fear, even after fifteen years. The streets he walked along emptied before him. The landscape cleared as he moved across it. Somehow I doubted that he noticed, though, and my heart went out to him in his ignorance. I was often curious about the time he spent away from me, but if I asked him where he'd been, his answers were usually gruff and one word long. *Walking* or, *Around*. In some ways, he was typical for his age: the secrecy, the awkwardness, the resistance to questioning – they were all part of adolescence. I was just his mother. I didn't need to know.

We'd been living at the hotel for about six months when a police van pulled up outside one afternoon. I was by myself that day; Kroner had taken Karin with him to the quarry, and Mazey had gone out two nights before and hadn't returned. I opened the front door and stood on the porch. The policeman was already standing at the foot of the steps. I recognised him as the constable from the next village. He looked down into his hat, which he was holding in both hands, then squinted up at me. 'Mrs Kroner?'

I grunted. I no longer used the name.

'It's your son. He's in hospital.'

As we drove towards the town, he told me that Mazey had been found lying in a ditch. His right leg had been broken in two places. They thought he'd been knocked down by a car. It was hard to be sure, of course, because he wouldn't talk to anyone.

'He hardly ever talks,' I said. 'He's backward.'

'I know. They didn't realise. They thought it was shock.'

When we reached the hospital, I was taken to see the doctor. He wore half-moon glasses with thin gold rims. His lips were too dark, almost purple; it made me think of Felix, when we woke up on that winter morning and he was dead. The doctor explained that the double fracture had not, in itself, been too severe, though it had been complicated by the length of time that had elapsed before the leg received medical attention. It was possible the patient would walk with a limp for the rest of his life.

'Are you in the habit of letting your son wander the countryside at night?' He peered at me over his glasses. 'You're aware that he's retarded?'

'This wasn't an accident,' I said. 'It was deliberate.'

The doctor began to ask me something else, but I interrupted. 'I'd like to see him now. Alone.'

Lying in his ward, Mazey looked unshaven and exhausted. His leg was in plaster, all the way from the top of his thigh to his ankle, and it was being supported by a system of ropes and pulleys. I sat beside the bed and put my hand on his.

'Are you all right, Mazey?'

His eyes lifted, fixed on me.

'It doesn't hurt too much?' I said.

He shook his head, two tiny movements. Right, then left. Then still again. He was glad to see me. I could tell.

I gripped his hand. 'You'll be out of here in no time,' I said, 'don't worry.'

When I got back to the hotel, Kroner and Karin were eating supper at the kitchen table – just bread and cheese, a glass of milk. I knew they'd stopped talking as soon as they heard the front door open. You can always tell when people have just stopped talking: they seem to be acting suddenly – and they're not actors so it doesn't feel natural. I walked across the dark, empty dining-room and into the light of the kitchen. Kroner asked me where I'd been.

'I've been with Mazey.' I took off my coat and hung it behind the door. 'Didn't you hear what happened?'

No, he hadn't heard.

'Someone knocked him down with a car. He was lying in a ditch for twenty-four hours with a broken leg.' I was watching Kroner carefully now. 'Do you know anything about it?'

No, he didn't. He was studying his sandwich, as if he couldn't quite decide what angle to approach it from.

'Look at me.'

His eyes lifted to my face for a moment, then slid away. 'I just told you, Edith. I don't know anything about it. You tell me that there's been some kind of accident. Well, it's the first I heard of it. All right?' He took a deep breath and blew the air out noisily. 'Jesus Christ.'

I stared at him. 'You didn't do it?'

'No.'

The lights in the kitchen flickered, but stayed on.

'Is he dead?' Karin asked.

She lifted her glass of milk to her mouth with both hands and drank from it. Nine years old, with dark-blue eyes and brown hair curling down on to her shoulders. She felt less like mine than ever.

'No,' I said. 'He's not dead.'

'Old Miss Poppel's dead. She – '

'*We're not talking about Old Miss Poppel.*'

Kroner put his sandwich down, only half-eaten. 'There's no need to shout at her.'

I went over to the sink, ran the tap and rinsed my hands in the warm water. I noticed my reflection in the window.

'So you don't know anything?' I said, with my back to the room. 'It's not another of your little games?'

I heard Kroner's chair scrape backwards and saw his reflection rise behind my own.

'Karin,' he said. 'I think it's time you went to bed.'

I stared at my face, then at his. Then I stared into the blackness that was beyond us both. There's no such thing as an accident, I whispered to myself. There's no such thing.

One night, when the moon was almost full and Kroner was asleep, I crept into Karin's room and woke her up. I put my mouth close to her ear. Told her to get dressed.

'Is it an adventure?' she asked me.

I nodded. 'It's a secret, too.'

I took her by the hand and led her down the stairs. Standing in the passageway outside the dining-room, I could hear Kroner snoring in his bed one floor above. I opened the side door and we walked out into the gravel car-park. Then down the steps, towards the pool. Karin was wide awake now, and too filled with wonder at being out at night to say a word. We moved past the fir trees at the back of the hotel, over some rocks and along a narrow path, into the shadow of the woods. It was half an hour to the main road. I looked at Karin, walking beside me. 'You're not tired, are you?'

She shook her head. 'Where are we going?'

I smiled mysteriously. 'You'll see.' In my right hand I had a bucket and every time it swung, the moon broke into a thousand pieces.

I'd spent the afternoon smashing empty beer bottles and pickle jars behind the shed where the pool equipment and the gardening tools were kept. Everyone was out except for Mazey, who was upstairs, listening to his chimes. (Miss Poppel had been as good as her word: *The wind-chimes that hang from the crab-apple tree in my front garden, I hereby bequeath to Mazey Hekmann.*) Even if he heard me, though, it didn't matter. He was hardly going to tell anyone.

When we reached the main road, we crouched down in a shallow ditch. 'This is the place,' I whispered.

Karin looked at me. It wasn't anywhere she knew.

I showed her how the road sloped upwards, dipped, sloped upwards once again, then curved to the left and vanished behind some trees.

'From here we can see them coming.'

'Who?' she said. 'Who's coming?' Her eyes had widened. Maybe she thought it was Holy Jesus, or the Three Wise Men. Christmas was only a few weeks off.

But I didn't answer. I put one finger to my lips and watched the road. Minutes passed. Then I touched her shoulder, pointed to the west. There was a beam of light in the distance. At first it looked like a triangle, long and golden, lying on its side. But as the car came accelerating round the bend, the triangle turned into circles, two circles, also gold. They were so bright that we had shadows, even though the car was still at least a kilometre away. I tipped the bucket, shook some broken glass on to my hand. I waited until the car was hidden in the dip, then stood up and threw the glass across the road. I ducked down again, one hand braced on my knee.

It was almost frightening – the size of it, the speed, the sudden noise. I saw glass glitter underneath its tyres. But nothing happened. The car hurtled over it and on. Its tail-lights were snuffed out. It was gone.

'Church-goers,' I muttered.

I reached for the bucket, and looked round at Karin. She was kneeling beside me, biting her bottom lip.

'Now it's your turn.'

I shook the bucket as if it was a game and she could choose any piece she wanted and maybe win a prize. She hesitated, though. The trees above us shifted in the wind.

'Don't you love your brother?' I whispered.

Her eyes looked into mine.

'Your brother, Mazey. Don't you love him?'

'Yes, I do.'

'Come on, then. Cup those hands of yours.'

I trickled glass out of the bucket. Her hands were so small, even when they were joined together. I hoped it would be enough.

'Careful,' I said. 'Don't cut yourself.'

No sooner had I set the bucket down than I heard the sound of an engine again. It came and went in the silence, the way mosquitoes do.

Headlights were searching the darkness on the bend. I waited until they disappeared, then took Karin's arm.

'Now, girl. Do it now.'

I watched her step out into the road, lightly, almost on tiptoe, as though she was afraid the surface might give way beneath her. She stood still for a moment, then she flung both hands upwards into the air. She might have been releasing something she had caught – an insect, or a butterfly. The glass bounced prettily. But it held her there too long. She'd forgotten all about the car. And now the headlights were rising above the level of the road and bearing down on her, two circles merging into one fierce glare. I reached out, seized her arm and pulled her down into the ditch.

The car howled past us. The hot diesel blast of it.

I heard a tyre blow. As I lifted my head, I saw the car swerve. Then it was rolling, the metal spitting sparks. It hit a tree, bounced off it, turned over half a dozen times. Then it was lying motionless, on its side, two hundred metres down the road.

I stood up. Kicking most of the glass into the ditch, I walked towards the car. One of the headlights pointed into the undergrowth, as if it was trying to show us something. I could smell burnt rubber. Nothing was moving.

Two people were inside. The man wore a suit and a pale hat. His mouth was open. One of his teeth had a green jewel in it; the rest were glistening with blood. There was a woman, too, but she was harder to make out. She was beneath the man, all folded up in what was now the bottom of the car. One of her shoes had fallen off and I could see her stockinged foot, the underside of it. She had high arches. I thought she might be a dancer.

'Trying to kill my son,' I said.

I took Karin's hand and looked down through the windscreen at the ungainly tangle of their bodies.

'Murderers,' I said.

Two days later, at the breakfast table, I read a report of the accident in the local paper. The two occupants of the car were named as J. Swanzy, also known as Emerald Joe, on account of the gemstone he wore in his front tooth, and his companion, Kamilla Esztergom, the singer. Both were killed outright. Police were calling it a case of reckless driving, since the levels of alcohol in the blood of both the deceased had been well in excess of the legal limit.

I touched the names with the tip of my finger. Emerald Joe. Kamilla (the singer!). Had they been talking when the car hit that patch of glass? And, if so, what about? What had their lives been like? I couldn't even begin to imagine. I'd never met people who wore emeralds in their teeth. They reminded me of the stories Felix used to tell. I thought of Mazey, who would walk with a limp until he was dead. Mazey in the ditch, alone, in pain. I brought my eyes back into focus. Only then did I see the misprint: instead of *reckless*, they'd written *wreckless*. What had happened had happened – but, at the same time, somehow, it had not. All the accounts were balanced, all grudges cancelled out.

One year I took Mazey to the lake. I wanted to show him the place where I had found him, and I was also curious to see it again for myself. There was nowhere to park on that particular bend in the road, so we drove past it, leaving the car on a farm-track half a kilometre further on, then walked back. Mazey had recovered full use of his leg. From time to time he would reach down and touch it, just above the knee, and there was a slight unevenness to his walk. You wouldn't have called it a limp, though.

'Your leg's mended pretty well,' I said, 'hasn't it?'

He looked at the leg. I did, too. We looked up again, both at the same time, which made me smile.

'That doctor,' I said. 'He was just trying to frighten me.'

I had the sudden feeling I weighed nothing. I could have floated up into the trees.

Nothing had changed on the road, not in twenty years. As I walked along, I had a thought. What if time wasn't a straight line at all? What if it was more like the wire on a telephone, with loops in it? You seemed to be going forwards, but actually you were going round and back on yourself. There were moments in your life that were far apart, but, at the same time, they almost coincided.

The damage to the tree was old, though. When I bent down, I could see it clearly, a black oblong scar in the wood where the truck had caught it. I took Mazey's hand and we began to scramble down the slope. The trees had healed. Otherwise everything was identical. It was even the same kind of day – halfway through autumn, leaves falling, blue sky high up between the branches . . .

We reached the lake. There was nothing to mark the place; the shrine everyone had talked about had never been built. I bent down at the water's edge, as I'd bent down twenty years before, and dipped my hand in it. I tasted the water. Not the slightest trace of sulphur. Had I imagined it that day? Or was it just that everything had rearranged itself for those few hours? Was it part of the pattern of surprise? I looked around, puzzled by how little I felt; I was almost disappointed. I noticed Mazey tasting the water, as I had done. He put the tips of his fingers in his mouth, then took them out again. His face didn't alter.

Suddenly I wasn't sure why I'd brought him or what I wanted him to understand. At first, I just talked around it, anything I could think of. I told him a story I'd been told by Felix. It had happened early in the century, when the hotel was at the height of its popularity. A wealthy shipping magnate and his wife came to stay for a few days. One afternoon they went for an excursion on the lake. Their boat sank and everybody drowned. It was a tragedy, of course, but it was also a mystery: the bodies of the shipping magnate and his wife were never found. The company mounted a search with teams of expert divers, underwater specialists, but the lake defeated them. It was just too deep, too cold. The bodies simply disappeared.

I pointed eastwards, out across the water. 'They're still down there somewhere.'

The best part of the story was the end – and, knowing Felix, it was almost certainly untrue. Out boating on the lake once, while still a boy, he looked down into the water and saw something glinting. A long way down, it was. A long, long way. *What did you see?* I asked him, my eyes all wide. *What was it?* He claimed it was the diamond on the finger of the shipping magnate's wife. I begged him to take me out on the lake. Begged him to show me the diamond ring on the dead woman's hand. But Felix, in his later years, was frightened of deep water. Also, he wasn't sure he could remember his precise position on the lake. And besides, he said, the sun would have to be shining at the right angle or you wouldn't see a thing.

I looked across at Mazey. Squatting on his heels, he was whittling another of his unidentifiable shapes. I wondered if he'd been listening. You never could tell with him. Sometimes he'd say something later, though – six months later, or a year – and you'd realise that he'd heard every word. I sat beside him, among the leaves, just watching him. The sun warmed my back. I was glad we'd come.

Before we left, I took hold of his shoulder and looked into his eyes. I thought I'd found the words at last.

'You see this place?' I said. 'Right here?' I dipped my hand in the water, took it out and shook it. 'This is where you became my son.'

A cool spring day. Several years had passed. I must have been forty-two or thereabouts. Though I was still married to Peter Kroner, I saw less of him than I used to. His father had died, and he was running the vineyard now, as well as the quarry. Sometimes he'd go drinking, though, and when he came home he'd try and put his hands on me, sweet nothings catching on the tooth that Karl had broken for him, but deep down he knew it was no good and before too long he'd be swaying round the bedroom with his black hair sticking up and his face all red and he'd be calling me foul names.

'Sticks and stones,' I'd say. 'Sticks and stones.'

Karin had just celebrated her fifteenth birthday. I remembered what Karl had said about her inheriting my mother's looks. The hotel phone was always ringing, and whenever we drove into the town together I could feel the eyes of men on her like postage stamps that were already licked and looking for an envelope. I thought there might be trouble and I mentioned it to Kroner, but he just looked at me in utter scorn and said, 'What would you know about it?' I noticed Mazey looking at her, too, with the same damp look, but I wasn't going to mention it again.

And then, a cool spring day – March, I think it was . . .

As soon as I saw Karin from the window, standing in the car-park with her dress sticking to her and her hair pasted flat against her neck, I knew what had happened, I just knew, and I felt my heart sink down, like a cow or an ox when it's been shot, the way their legs just crumple, go from under them.

I walked down the stairs and out through the side entrance. The car-park was empty that day. We had no guests. I listened to my shoes on the gravel as I walked towards her. I could see Miss Poppel's house, still unsold, the front garden piled with machinery, abandoned wind-chimes jangling. Further down the street the sun was out, but where we were, it was shadows and a chill wind.

I said her name, but she didn't look at me. I said her name again. This time she twitched as if I'd pulled on something that was attached to her. She was looking at the ground. Water dripped from the hem of her dress. It drew a black circle round her on the gravel. Seemed to be sealing her off.

'What is it, Karin? What happened?' Though I knew.

Her head moved one way, then the other; she might have been disagreeing with what I'd said. Her eyes rolled upwards, skywards, then she turned and walked past me, back into the house. I followed her through the door and up the stairs. She was already half-undressed when I reached her bedroom. I saw a bruise on her thigh, just below her hip. There were other bruises on her elbow and her knee. On the inside of her upper arm there were four ghostly mauve-blue fingerprints. She bundled her clothes into a sodden ball and put them on the floor in the corner, then she climbed into bed and pulled the blanket up to her chin. She lay on her back, a chalkiness about her lips and her teeth moving behind them. It was three o'clock in the afternoon.

I put my hand on her shoulder, and she flinched.

'Tell me what happened,' I said.

'Don't – don't let him in here.'

'Who? Mazey?'

She closed her eyes tight shut.

'Don't let him in,' she whispered.

Outside her room, I stood with my hands wedged under my arms, uncertain what to do. She didn't seem to be hurt, which was something; I didn't want to involve the doctor. If it was Mazey who'd done it – and I was sure it was – I would take the necessary action myself. I didn't want any strangers interfering. I didn't want him taken away from me either; I couldn't stand the thought of him in an institution. I went downstairs. I made Karin a glass of warm milk with sugar in it and I took it to her. She was sleeping, so I left it on the table beside her bed. Then I sat in the kitchen, waiting for Mazey to return.

I saw him through the window as he came up out of the trees, his hair pale against the dark green of the foliage, his shoulders slightly rounded, his arms hanging loosely at his sides. There was nothing in his face to suggest that anything had happened – but then, I hadn't expected there to be. He walked into the kitchen, stooped over the sink and, scooping a handful of water from the cold tap, brought it to his mouth. It was almost always the first thing he did when he got home, no matter how long he'd been away. It seemed odd to think of him as a creature of habit, but that was what he was.

'Mazey?'

He turned round.

'You did something, didn't you?'

He stared at me, the tap still running behind him, the water dripping off his chin.

'Do you know what you've done?'

He began to shuffle on the floor. The first time he shuffled like that, it was like nothing I'd ever seen before. It reminded me of what a cat does when it covers up its mess.

'Well?'

'I – I did something.' He wasn't confessing exactly, but it wasn't a question either.

'It was bad what you did, Mazey. It was really bad.'

He turned back to the sink again. He cupped his hand under the running water and drank. But not because he was thirsty.

'Mazey,' and I took him by the arm, 'you can't do things like that. If you do things like that, people will come and take you away.' I shook him hard. 'You remember that place Kroner took you to? That place I had to come and fetch you from?'

His grey eyes fixed on my face, and he nodded.

'If you do things like that, they'll take you back again and this time it'll be for ever. I won't be able to do a thing about it. Not a thing.'

'You can fetch me.'

I shook my head. 'Not this time, Mazey.'

'You can fetch me. With the knife.' He was grinning.

I couldn't explain it to him. It was strange. He could operate my father's lathe. He could even drive a truck. But there were things you couldn't make him understand. Simple things, like the fact that we get older. Like the fact we die. Like God. And, who knows, maybe it was better that way, not understanding something that's beyond our understanding anyway. He had his own way of thinking, which he sometimes made available to me. Sometimes.

I did the only thing I could think of: I put him in the car and drove out to my father's house. I told him to take his wind-chimes with him; I thought they might be some consolation.

There were dark clouds to the west of us, a great curving bank of blackness in the sky, a kind of overhang, but the wind was coming out of the north and I thought the storm would pass us by. I drove over the bridge, loose boards drumming under the wheels. It was only four-thirty in the afternoon, but it felt later; I even had to switch the headlights on. We turned on to the track, two ruts with a strip of grass down the middle, grass that was long enough to brush against the underside of the car.

I parked in the yard. From where I was sitting I could see my father in the barn. For almost three years he'd been working on a dovecote. It was going to be a replica of the Leaning Tower, in Italy. He'd got the idea from one of Axel's magazines. He'd torn the page out and pinned it to the wall above his tool-rack. But every time he got the angle right, the tower fell over. And it didn't even have any doves inside it yet. Sometimes he thought he should have been less ambitious – but it was for Karin; only something out of the ordinary would do. I decided not to tell him what Mazey had done, at least for the time being. It wouldn't be hard. He'd never had too much curiosity, even about his own family; and now that he was in his late seventies and partly deaf, he had good reason to dispense with it altogether. I opened the door and got out of the car.

When I drove away an hour later, Mazey wasn't with me. I'd chained him to the truck, the truck that Axel had crashed in all those years ago (it was almost unrecognisable now, most of its paint stripped by the weather, and brambles coiling over the radiator grille and through the broken windscreen like snakes around a skull). Mazey didn't seem to mind being made a prisoner. He didn't seem to notice any loss of freedom. I'd hung his string of door-hinges from the roof of the goat shed. If he stood up, he could touch them. Or he could sit with his back against a tyre and whittle at his bits of wood. I told my father to put him in the barn if the temperature dropped – but I insisted on the chain at all times, as much for Mazey's safety as for Karin's. I wanted to keep him out of sight. There was no concealing the truth from Kroner and, when he found out, it was quite likely he would want to wreak some kind of vengeance.

I pulled into the hotel car-park. Kroner's van was there. I sat behind the wheel and stared at it. It had KRONER CONSTRUCTION painted on the side. A new business he'd started up, which tied in with the quarry. Suddenly I wanted to laugh. Those reliable blue letters. I didn't know what I was going to say. I could've sat in the car all night and I still wouldn't have known.

I found him in the kitchen. He was wearing his work-boots and overalls. He said he'd been up to Karin's room. The door was locked; she wouldn't answer. He wanted to know what was wrong. I explained it as best I could. It was only a few words. I felt it should have taken longer, somehow, but I couldn't think of anything else. I hadn't been there when it happened. Nobody had told me much.

He sat still for a moment, then he reached out slowly for the broom that was leaning against the wall. He stood up and began to break the kitchen windows, one by one. When he'd broken all the windows, he started on the crockery. Then it was the glasses, the vases, the new electric clock. There was a determined look on his face. Sometimes he blinked. At one point he turned and looked at me, as if trying to decide what I was made of, whether I would smash. Though he was breathing hard, his head was motionless; blood ran from several small cuts on his face and arms. I stepped backwards, towards the door. Still looking at me, he hurled the broom sideways. It landed among the saucepans, knocked them to the floor. There was a movement behind me, and Karin pushed past me, into the room. She went to her father and carefully laid her cheek against his chest. He looked down at her. He seemed surprised to see her there. It was almost as if he'd forgotten she existed. Then his eyes closed.

'I'm all right,' she murmured. 'Really. I'm all right.'

His chest heaved; tears poured down his face.

She kept on murmuring to him. 'I'm all right, Dad. I'm all right. Really . . .'

Maybe she was. But he wasn't. That evening, while I was taping newspaper over the broken windows, Karin ran into the kitchen.

'It's Dad,' she panted. 'Something's happening to Dad.'

She took me out to the front of the hotel. The light from the doorway made a kind of V-shape on the grass. Kroner was lying in the darkness just beyond it, his boots lit up, the rest of him invisible. I hurried over. His arms were at strange angles to his body, and they were bent at the elbows; he could have been practising semaphore, communicating with someone in the sky. I felt for the pulse in his wrist. It was faint, irregular, but it was there. I told Karin to stay with him, then I ran to the phone and called Holbek.

In ten minutes the doctor was kneeling on the grass beside us. Kroner's eyes were open, and saliva was spilling from one side of his mouth. The doctor examined him briefly, then asked if he could use the phone. As I followed him into the hallway to show him where it was, he turned to me.

'He's had a stroke. I'm going to call an ambulance.'

When I saw Kroner the next morning, in the hospital, he looked as if he'd aged twenty years. I thought the shock must have done it, the way earthquakes are said to. *His hair went white overnight*. Close up, though, I realised I'd got it wrong; it was just that he was still covered with limestone dust from the quarry. His eyes were open, but he didn't seem to know us. He was still very weak, the Sister said. We weren't allowed to stay for long.

The doctor told me that the stroke had been a major one. A blood vessel in Kroner's brain had ruptured, resulting in a haemorrhage. It meant one side of his body would be paralysed. It also meant he'd lost the power of speech – temporarily, at least. He would be kept under observation for the next few days. Before too long, however, he'd be sent home, where he'd be in my charge. The doctor wanted to know if I understood the implications of this. I said I did (it was like Mazey, only worse; it was almost funny). According to the doctor, Kroner would have to begin again, from the beginning, like a child. To walk, to talk. To tie a shoelace. Drive a car. This would be more difficult, he thought, because they'd detected a stubborn streak in the patient, an unwillingness to return from where he was.

'We can only do so much. In the end, it's up to him.'

Three weeks later Kroner had another stroke. It was less significant, the doctor said, but the date of his release was postponed indefinitely. He stayed in hospital all summer. Two or three afternoons a week I would drive down there, usually alone (the sight of Karin seemed to upset him; once he even wet himself). If the weather was fine, they lifted him into a bath chair and let me push him through the grounds. These days I hardly recognised him. The left half of his face had slipped, and one of the nurses had put a side-parting in his hair and brushed it flat. He looked like a different person. Nobody I knew, though. Sometimes, as I wheeled him round, I found myself believing it: we were strangers, and I was just being neighbourly, doing a good deed. Other days I pitied him, the state he was in, but at the same time I could see the justice of it. What he'd done to Mazey, him and his people up at the quarry, while I was weighed down with his child – or afterwards, when the child was born and my mind was nothing but a misted-over pane of glass. Sometimes the men who seem the most respectable and decent are the worst. There are whole parts of them kept secret. But he'd drunk deep from his own medicine, and the taste of it had altered him for ever.

I was on my way to visit him once when a hub-cap came loose and ran on ahead of the car. I watched it leave the road in a straight line, bouncing across uneven ground, confident but ludicrous. I thought no more about it until I parked outside the hospital. But then I saw the wheel, and I stood there in the sunshine, staring at it. You never know how strong somebody is, and if they're against you, how long the struggle will last. Looking at the wheel, black instead of silver, blind, somehow, I knew it was over. Kroner had come to the end of the cruelty that was in him, and it hadn't worked. There were straps to hold him upright in his chair. I remember fingering the leather that afternoon and thinking back: that drive across the county years before, the knife glinting on the seat beside me . . . There'd be no need for knives, not any more.

I thought of Kroner's love for me, which I'd spurned. I thought of how he'd lavished it on his little girl instead, his daughter. I thought of how my child had ruined his.

And the truth was worse than any of us knew.

It was while he was in the hospital that we found out she was pregnant.

That summer Karin ran away. She was gone for almost a week and when she came back, she was riding in the front seat of a fast, steel-blue car with number-plates I didn't recognise. The man behind the wheel had unusual, bright-orange hair.

'Chromanski's the name,' he said, shaking my hand.

He told me where he was from – a large town, about two hours to the west of us. He said he was a lawyer. I thought he was rather young to be a lawyer, but I chose not to question it. He'd met Karin in the lobby of the Hotel Europa one night, while he was having a drink with two associates.

He took me aside. 'Your daughter's beautiful. Unfortunately, I'm already engaged to be married.' He looked up, saw Karin through the window. She was sitting on the porch, twisting a strand of hair around her index finger. 'And besides,' he said, with a smile that was faintly conspiratorial, 'she's under age, isn't she?'

'And pregnant,' I said.

That put a new expression on his face.

But he seemed honest enough: he hadn't taken advantage of her, and he'd driven her all the way home, a distance of more than a hundred kilometres. I thanked him for going to such trouble. Trouble's the word, he said, grinning, and I thought he could well be right about that. Karin was still sitting on the porch when Chromanski left. He smiled at her as he walked away across the grass. She watched him turn his steel-blue car round as if her last chance of happiness was locked in the boot.

Later that day, she told me she'd gone to the town to find a father for her child. Each morning she sat in the lobby of the largest hotel, the Europa, and waited for the right man to appear. Her plan was to let the man make love to her, and then pretend the child was his. Her condition didn't show yet. She'd studied herself from every angle in the mirror. There was a slight curve to her belly, but nothing a man would notice. At last, one evening, she met Alexander Chromanski. He was a little drunk. Her eyes were beautiful, he told her. Brown and silver, like loose change. 'Not worth much then,' she replied, her bitterness surprising her. 'On the contrary,' he said. *On the contrary*. Those were his exact words. She'd never met anyone who spoke that way, and it seemed beautiful to her, at least as beautiful as her eyes were to him. She thought he must be the man she'd been looking for.

'You were going to deceive him,' I said.

She shook her head. 'He would've been happy.'

I moved to the window. 'Sly,' I said, 'just like your father.'

She joined me, staring at the place where Chromanski's car had been. 'Did he say anything to you?'

'Nothing much. He said he was engaged.'

'And what did you tell him?'

'The truth.'

After that, Karin didn't want to see anyone. I arranged for her to live at my father's house outside the village. On the same day I freed Mazey from his chains and brought him home to the hotel. He moved into my old room on the first floor, at the back. I screwed a hook into the ceiling near the window and hung his wind-chimes from it. The weeks went by. Then, towards the end of June, Karin asked for me. She was worried about the brown line that ran from her belly-button to the triangle of new dark hair between her legs. I told her it was normal. She couldn't get used to it, she said. It was as if someone had been drawing on her in the night. Her body was not her own. She said she'd thought of throwing herself off the roof of the Hotel Europa. If she got three lines in the paper she'd be satisfied. Then she looked at me, and I could tell from her eyes that she hadn't forgotten Emerald Joe and that singer, Esztergom. She wasn't threatening me, though. She didn't have that kind of nature. Later, she lay on her bed and wept at the thought of her death, the smallness of the article, her own insignificance. I knew she wouldn't do it – her vanity would prevent her – but, at the same time, it was too late to dream of husbands.

When Kroner was discharged, in September of that year, I moved him into the room next to Mazey's. I saw that his broken tooth had blackened; it must have happened gradually, over the last few months, but I felt as if I'd only just noticed. He had partial use of the left side of his body, and he could make noises that were almost words (they were like words with all the hard sounds taken out), which was the best that could be expected. He spent his days upstairs in a wheelchair. I had run a piece of string out of his window, down the outside wall and in through the back door, and I'd attached a bell to the end of it; if he needed something, he could pull the string with his good hand.

One day I was standing in the kitchen by myself when a cup dropped from my hands. It landed on the floor and didn't break, it just rolled about, and suddenly I found that I was laughing. I didn't know why I was laughing, but it was very funny and I couldn't stop. I laughed so hard, my stomach ached, and I didn't even know the cause of it. If anyone had seen me then, they would have thought I'd lost my mind. But maybe that wouldn't have been such a surprise, not when you looked at the rest of the family.

The baby, a girl, was born in the early hours of a December morning. Outside, it was dark and cold, sleet falling silently, slanting behind the black glass of the bedroom window. It was an easy birth. The contractions started just after midnight. By dawn both mother and child were sleeping peacefully.

During the first few days Karin couldn't seem to decide what she felt about the baby. One moment she'd be bending over it, holding it against her breast and soothing it, the way any mother would; then she'd remember who the father was and how the baby had been conceived, and she'd push it away. At the end of the month, when the time came for the baby to be christened, she told me I could call it whatever I liked. *Call it whatever you like* – this was exactly what I'd said to Kroner sixteen years before. Some families are condemned to repeat themselves, it seems, old tragedies giving birth to new ones. I suggested Nina, after my father's mother. When Karin heard the name, she laughed harshly and said, 'Why? Was she born of a half-wit, too?' The next time I looked at her, her cheek had reddened where I'd slapped it.

She was still frightened of Mazey and what he might do. She wouldn't eat at the same table or sleep under the same roof. Under no circumstances would she let him touch the baby. She carried on living at my father's house, partly to avoid Mazey, but also, I thought, because she felt embarrassed and ashamed. Everyone in the village had heard that she'd had a baby, but no one knew who the father was. Rumours started flying. People don't like to be left out, and that's one way of getting revenge. There was a lot of mocking talk about a virgin birth. Not that my father noticed. He was almost eighty by then, so silent and so withdrawn that it seemed possible that Mazey's inability to speak wasn't a defect at all but a trait, inherited from him, along with a love of whittling. And besides, he'd always liked having Karin there. Apart from anything else, she could keep an eye on his progress with the dovecote. He was experimenting with lead weights, using them as ballast in the base of the tower. He only hoped he'd live long enough to finish it.

When she told him that the baby girl was going to be christened Nina, after his own mother, he turned away from her, his eyes watering, a man whose life had been empty of consideration for so long that he could now be moved by it. Of course he knew she wasn't happy, but he chose to ignore it. He understood about forgetting; he'd done it himself half a century before. In the evenings they sat together on the porch, the sun setting behind the trees, bats flickering in the dark air of the yard. I don't know what they talked about, or even if they talked at all, but they seemed to find solace in each other's company. She wanted to distance herself from what had happened – her baby was reminder enough; she didn't need any more reminding than that – and staying in the woods outside the village was distance of a sort, though Mazey would still appear from time to time. The house had been his home for most of his life, and was embedded in his memory. When he went walking, it was a station on his way, just as Miss Poppel's garden used to be. So Karin lived in an almost permanent state of dread. If a twig snapped, for example, or the leaves rustled, or if there were footsteps on the track, she'd call her grandfather, or else she'd snatch her baby up and run back into the house. In her dreams the man with orange hair would come and take her away in his fast car. But the man with orange hair did not come. Jan Salenko came instead. Jan Salenko, the mechanic's son.

Something I noticed early on was Mazey's quiet obsession with the child. He had never showed much interest in Karin when she was born; he'd been too busy with his wind-chimes and his pen-knife. With Nina it was different. Whenever he found himself in the same room, which wasn't often, his eyes didn't stray from her, not for a moment. He didn't try and touch her. If anything, he kept away, standing against the wall or over by the window. He seemed content just so long as he could watch. I wondered if there might be a part of him that understood he'd fathered her.

Once, while Karin was visiting the doctor, she left Nina in my care and I let Mazey pick her up. Perhaps it was a mistake, but somehow I couldn't refuse him. He took the baby in his hands as if she was made of glass and held her in a shaft of sunlight. When Nina blinked, he touched her eyelashes gently with his fingers, and he had a way of clicking his tongue that seemed to fascinate her. Later, though, she started crying, and that frightened him. I didn't see it in his eyes, but it was there, I felt it, his panic bent the air between us, and then I saw him put his hand over her face. If I hadn't taken Nina away from him, he would've smothered her. I didn't mention it to Karin when she came home.

There was another time. I was driving back towards the village one evening in April when I saw a girl running along the road ahead of me. She was wearing a nightdress and she had nothing on her feet. Only as I passed the girl did I realise she was my daughter. I stopped the car. Karin clung to the open window, panting.

'Nina's gone. He's taken her.'

I reached across and pushed the door open. 'Come on, get in. We can't have people seeing you like this.'

She sat beside me in the car. Her face was orange in the light of the setting sun. Black, too, where she had tried to wipe away the tears. 'If he does anything to her – '

'He won't do anything,' I said. 'He loves her.' Though I remembered that huge hand of his descending, and all of a sudden I wasn't sure.

'Love? What does someone like him know about love?'

'Haven't you noticed the way he looks at her?'

Karin turned to me. 'You never did care about me, did you? You always cared about him more.' When I didn't answer her, she said, 'I think you wanted this to happen.'

I wasn't certain what she meant by that. We crossed the narrow bridge into the village.

'I think maybe you even planned it,' she said.

I shook my head. 'You're all worked up about nothing.'

When we reached the hotel, Karin opened the door and ran into the house. There was no sign of Mazey in any of the rooms. Then, through the kitchen window, I heard a child's laughter.

'Did you hear that?' I said.

Karin was already disappearing through the back door. I followed her across the car-park and down the steps to the pool. At first I couldn't see anything. It was a cool evening, and steam rose off the water in white, swirling clouds. Then the shape of a man emerged: Mazey. He was holding Nina over the water. Dipping her feet in it, lifting her clear, then dipping her feet again. She was laughing.

I watched as Karin ran round the edge of the pool. Mazey was watching her as well, with Nina still suspended in mid-air. I thought for a moment that he might drop her in alarm. But then Karin snatched her from him and turned away, muttering into her hair. Mazey had surrendered the baby with such calmness, such a lack of comprehension that Karin appeared to be the one who was in the wrong. Her violence seemed exaggerated. Her relief, too. Suddenly, she annoyed me.

'You see?' I said. 'I told you there was nothing to worry about.'

Mazey straightened up and stepped away from the pool. From his trouser pocket he brought out the old blunt pen-knife my father had given him. He felt in the other pocket, found a piece of dowel. Then he sat down on the terrace, his long legs sticking out in front of him, his big shoes pointing at the sky, and, bending his head, began to whittle. He didn't expect anything in particular from life; he'd be happy with whatever he was given. I wanted to take his head and hold it close against me, but I knew this would only have infuriated Karin, who thought he was guilty and who was standing at the bottom of the steps, staring at him, her mouth drawn tight, her eyes accusing.

Not long afterwards – in May or June, it would have been – she went south with the Salenko boy. I never knew exactly where.

There was nothing memorable about Jan Salenko – nothing, that is, except his memory: he won a village competition when he was eight, and all the children used to tease him about it. I'd noticed him watching Karin for years, his eyes full of her as we crossed the street or drove by in the car, but he wasn't the only one, and he was shy, too, so I didn't think it would come to anything. I suppose she must have become aware of how he felt and then realised he could be of use to her – especially when she found out that he wasn't frightened off by the mysterious arrival of a child. There's not much a man won't do when he's besotted. Nobody suspected an elopement, though, not even me.

Strangely, it was Mazey who felt the loss most keenly. In fact, he seemed to be expressing it for all of us. Like a lightning conductor, he drew all the bad feelings down upon himself. He wouldn't eat. He wouldn't sleep. He wouldn't even listen to his wind-chimes any more. There were nights when he walked through the hotel opening every door to every room, every cupboard, every drawer. In the morning it always looked as if we'd been broken into. I asked him what was wrong, but he wouldn't speak to me at all. Not one word.

My father came to visit me one evening. It was rare to see him in the village, even rarer to see him upset. He stood in front of me with his face lowered and the muscles shifting in his jaw. He told me that he'd been working in the barn as usual, building a linen chest for the Minkels family, when he heard sounds coming from the house. Thinking it might be someone who was up to no good, he took his gun off the wall and went to have a look. The whole place had been turned upside-down. Cupboards had been opened, drawers pulled out and tipped on to the floor, curtains torn off their rails. It looked as though a hurricane had just passed through. A movement in the window caught his eye. Something outside, in the yard.

'Mazey,' I said.

My father's long jaw swung towards me. I'd startled him. Yes, it was Mazey. He called to the boy, who was moving in the shadows at the edge of the clearing where he could not be seen. He called again. Mazey stepped out into the sunlight, blinking.

He walked up to Mazey, and Mazey just watched him coming with that empty face of his. Mazey was sweating, and there was blood trickling from a cut on his wrist.

My father pointed at the house. 'Was it you?'

Mazey took a step backwards. The shade on his face like a birthmark, the blood sliding silently between his knuckles.

'Why did you do it?'

He held Mazey's gaze until he felt the edges of his vision blackening. But Mazey was the first to turn away. He walked into the trees, the light and shadow dappling his back, and my father noticed once again how Mazey moved in straight lines, ignoring paths and bridleways. As the crow flies, he remembered thinking to himself. He watched Mazey fade into the gloom of the wood and found that he could breathe more easily.

'Sometimes I look into that boy's eyes,' my father said, 'and I feel like I'm in quicksand and I'm – '

'It's the baby,' I said.

'The baby?'

'Nina.'

Later that night, when Mazey returned home, I took him into the kitchen and sat him down at the table. I reached for the first-aid tin. The cut wasn't serious, but I wanted an excuse to keep him close to me while I talked to him. I had to explain that Nina was gone and wouldn't be coming back, and I had to do this in a way that didn't make it seem as if it was his fault. I had to find an explanation that would break the bond between them, that would persuade him to let her go. I poured a few drops of iodine on to a ball of cotton-wool and began to clean the cut with it. His arm flinched and I heard the air being drawn in through his teeth, but his face didn't register any pain.

'The baby,' I said.

He nodded. 'Hiding.'

'No. She's not hiding. She's gone.'

He looked at me.

As I dried the skin around the cut, I told him that Karin had taken Nina away. He wanted to know where to. I explained that, when a woman had a baby, the baby came from inside her. From here, I said, and placed one hand over my stomach. He bent down and put his face close to my hand, watching it, as though it was about to change into something else. I wondered how to go on. I decided it would be simpler not to mention fathers. When a woman had a baby, I said, the baby belonged to her. She could take her baby away with her, if she wanted to. She could take her baby anywhere she wanted. It was *her baby*. He didn't say anything. I tore off a piece of gauze and taped it over the cut. Nina had come from inside Karin, I said. Nina was Karin's baby. And Karin had taken Nina away with her. They were gone, maybe for ever.

'That's what's happened,' I said. 'That's why you can't find them.'

I looked up. Mazey had placed his right hand on his stomach and he was staring down at it.

'There's no point looking in cupboards,' I went on, 'or in drawers. You won't find her there. Do you understand?'

But he didn't answer. He was still staring at his hand.

During the autumn of that year, stories began to circulate. At first people thought there was a bear on the rampage, despite the fact that no bears had been seen in our part of the world for more than a hundred years. Next they thought it was a pack of wolves. Then somebody remembered the circus that had passed through the region that summer. They remembered trailers with no windows, their side walls painted with ferocious beasts and scenes of carnage and mutilation. Supposing one of the animals had escaped from its cage and was now roaming the countryside? It had to be some kind of wild animal, something exotic. Because dogs and chickens were being killed. Not just killed either, but torn apart. But not eaten. Just ripped open and left there, gaping, on the ground. Nobody had seen anything, of course. The stories took a darker twist. There was talk of pagan rituals and devil worship. An article appeared in the local paper: WHO COULD DO SUCH A THING? For a while, suspicion fell on a young couple who had moved into a woodsman's cottage on a lonely stretch of river north-west of the village. They had dark eyes and dark hair, and the girl wore unusual jewellery. It was enough to keep the fires of rumour stoked up high.

I noticed that Mazey had become restless, as if the talk had affected him as well. I didn't want to chain him up again, but at the same time I was worried about him wandering too far. After all, what if there was some truth to the rumours? What if he tangled with a wild animal or fell into the clutches of a Satanic cult? I couldn't warn him; he wouldn't be able to understand the kind of danger I was talking about. Maybe I could follow him, though. Then, if he got into trouble, I could help. It was an idea. And hadn't I always been curious about where he went?

I waited on the porch, sitting in a rocking-chair and smoking cigarettes to pass the time. I had a small knapsack on my lap. It had some food in it, and a box of cartridges. Kroner's rifle leaned against the wall behind me. There was a wind that night, and the trees on the far side of the road roared like a furnace with the door open. I could see the silhouette of Miss Poppel's house, still uninhabited. I could hear the dull clank of the exhaust-pipes as they swung from the crab-apple tree. I thought of the birthday present I'd given Mazey. It was a tape of his wind-chimes. I'd recorded them one day when he was out. He kept the tape in his pocket at all times, along with his pen-knife; they were his prized possessions. We always played it if we drove somewhere together in the car.

I'd been sitting there for almost an hour when I heard footsteps in the house behind me. We didn't have any guests that night. With Karin gone and Kroner confined to a wheelchair, it could only mean one thing. I put my cigarette out under my shoe, then I sat back and kept quite still.

The front door opened and Mazey appeared on the porch. He was wearing a long coat; his head was bare. He closed the door quietly, one hand on the handle, the other flat against the wood, so he could feel the lock catch. It was surprising to see what care he put into it. I watched him move down the steps and over the grass. He was heading away from the village, making for the bridge. I waited until he was hidden by the trees before I rose out of my chair. When I reached the road I could see him on the bend in front of me, a tall figure, stoop-shouldered, with hair that was so pale, it was hard to tell if it was fair or grey. He seemed at one with the night and the empty road and the fast clouds high above. He seemed at home.

At the bridge I felt exposed: only one lane each way and thin metal railings on either side. I hid behind an upright while he crossed ahead of me. Thick, silver water below. I watched a duck land and blacken it. Mazey turned his head at the noise, but it was just a reflex; he didn't stop to look. Once he was over the river, I had to break into a run to catch up. Me, a forty-five-year-old woman, running . . .

I chose to walk in the grass at the edge of the road, close to the tree-line. Then, if he did happen to turn round, he wouldn't see me. But I was struck by his purpose, his concentration. He didn't look behind him, not even once. He didn't hesitate at all, or dawdle, or meander. Sometimes his head moved from side to side, but I presumed he was just checking his bearings. He had the air of someone who knew exactly where he was going. I was reminded of something Eva had said once, before the sulphur got into her brain and ate everything intelligent. *He looks like he could walk all day and all night, too. Like he could walk for ever.* Then she'd thought for a moment. *He looks like he could walk from this world right into the next.*

I'd fallen into a rhythm, I was hypnotised by it, so I almost missed his sudden plunge into the trees. I had to break into a run again. Up the grass bank, across the road and down the bank on the other side, keeping my eyes locked on the place where he had been. I parted low branches, ducked into the undergrowth. The trees closed over me.

In the forest everything was black and silver. Mostly black, though. I stood still, just inside it, listening. I heard the crack of dead wood, bracken hissing. It had to be him. I began to move forwards, following the noise. Something caught on my cheek and tore the skin.

At last I saw a path.

It was quiet now, except for my own feet in the leaves. I walked on, further into the forest. It was quiet, but not peaceful. Once I saw a man's head float between two trees. Mazey? But it was too high off the ground, even for him. It must have been a bird. Or a piece of pale bark. Or just the fall of moonlight.

All of a sudden, there was a thrashing in the undergrowth ahead of me and to my right. It sounded like horses being ridden in a stream. It sounded wet. A scream lifted out of the darkness. One high note held for three or four seconds. Then it cut out. Darkness poured back into the space it left. Darkness pushing at me, almost too thick to breathe. The scream wasn't human. But it was pain. It was definitely pain. I gripped the rifle hard. Shock had dropped me into a kind of crouch and I was panting.

I forced myself to go on again, along the path. Towards the scream. I kept low and I whispered to myself, it didn't matter what, just words, any words. I felt the ground with my foot each time I took a step. I thought of a mother rolling up her sleeve and dipping her elbow in a tub of water, testing it for temperature. Not my mother, though. Someone else's. And all the time I scanned the forest that massed in front of me. Trees jumped sideways. Moonlight was fog, then snow, then water. Darkness bellied like a black sail with the wind behind it.

Then I saw him.

He was below me. There was a glade, a shallow bowl among the trees. A steep bank rose on the far side of it, casting a shadow. The earth had eroded there, and I could see a tangle of exposed roots. The path I was on circled the edge of the glade, keeping some distance above it.

I stood still, one hand braced against a tree. He was sitting on his haunches with his back to me and, just for a moment, I had the impression that he was washing clothes. I took two silent steps and stopped beside another, larger tree. I could see one side of his face now – half of it, anyway: an ear, part of his cheek, the tip of his nose. In the moonlight his skin shone like bone. He was crouched over something. An animal of some kind. Not a dog or a cat. Larger than that. A deer, perhaps. He seemed to have his hands inside it. His arms were black to the elbow. Though in daylight, I realised, they wouldn't be black. They'd be red.

That scream, it must have been the animal.

WHO COULD DO SUCH A THING?

Whether I made a noise as I stood there, or whether he just sensed my presence, I couldn't be sure, but suddenly he was looking over his shoulder, with his head angled in my direction. He didn't move for at least a minute. I knew he was looking at me, but I didn't think he knew who I was; I didn't think he recognised me. And yet I found I couldn't move. I was hardly even breathing.

At last he stood up. He began to walk towards me. He didn't hurry, though. His arms didn't swing at all, or even bend; they just hung at his sides like dead weights. He came up out of the glade in one straight line and for the first time in minutes I was aware of the wind moving in the trees above my head.

He stopped in front of me. I noticed something I'd never noticed before. The colour of his eyes wasn't a colour at all, not even grey. It was just empty, drained. Or perhaps this was another trick, something moonlight did.

He was staring at me.

I could see dark patches on his clothes and his arms. I could smell the blood. I wasn't frightened of him, and yet I knew I had to speak first.

'It's very late.'

I used my strictest voice with him.

'You should be in bed.'

His face didn't alter.

'No baby,' he said.

He had looked in the hotel. He had looked in his grandfather's house as well. He had looked high and low – behind doors, under beds, in drawers. Then, one night, his mother had explained where babies came from. A hand placed over her stomach. *In here*. And if they came from there, they could go back again. They could hide in there. And so he began to look for the baby in living things. All those dogs and chickens slaughtered and torn open. He was looking for Nina, that was all. He wouldn't rest until he found her.

I lifted the rifle until it was pointing at his head. He didn't move. Moonlight down one side of his face, his eyes still searching mine. *Pull the trigger*. *Pull it*. I felt my finger tighten. Because I wasn't sure what else I could do. There was the institution, of course. I could go to Kroner in his wheelchair and I could say, 'You were right about the boy.' *Kroner*. The tension in my finger eased. I lowered the rifle, looked at it. It was Kroner's rifle. There was his name, etched into the stock. And he was channelling his thoughts through it. I couldn't believe I'd listened. His mind like cardboard when it's been rained on. His brain all soggy. *And I had listened*.

On the way back to the hotel, I threw the rifle into the bushes. If we were broken into, I'd use a hammer to defend myself. A kitchen knife. The broom.

At seven-thirty the next morning I went into Kroner's room and drew the curtains. He was awake. One eye clear and blinking, the other sloppy.

I put my face close to his. 'You think that's going to work, do you? You really think that's going to work?'

His mouth fell sideways like an ice-cream melting. 'Dssh – '

'I suppose you were going to make his death look like an accident,' I said, 'or was it suicide you were thinking of?'

' – Nnnnsshh – Nnnnsshh – '

I picked his glass up from the bedside table and held it above his face. I tilted it very slowly until the water trickled down the outside of the glass, off the end and down, in one thin stream, on to his forehead, into his eyes.

'Now look what you made me do,' I said.

He was moving his head from side to side. Some of the water had gathered in the worry lines. Interesting. Some of it had slid into his ears. I reached for a cloth and dabbed his face with it. Then I sat down on the edge of the bed.

'I'm going to tell you something about accidents.' I stared at the ceiling for a moment, as if I didn't know quite where to begin. But I did, of course. I knew exactly. 'You remember my brother and his wife? They had that terrible accident. The one where their truck went off the road and down that steep slope and they both died – '

He was making his usual soggy sounds. I could tell he was listening, though. His one good eye was fixed on me.

'It wasn't an accident at all,' I said. 'I killed them.'

I watched the eye move round in its socket, trying to escape. There was nowhere for it to go.

'I borrowed one of my father's hacksaws and cut through a track-rod. I only sawed into it a bit. I didn't have much time, you see.' I smiled to myself. 'It's the kind of thing that might not have worked. Not when I wanted it to, anyway.' I paused again. 'I was lucky, I suppose.'

I looked down at him once more.

'Yes, that's right, it was me,' I said when I saw the look in his eye. 'I did it.'

Outside, it was bright and cool. When I drove into the clearing with Mazey, my father was sitting on the back porch cleaning his rifle. This didn't strike me as a coincidence at all. It was more like part of what had happened. The fever lifts. You return to normal. Something's run its course. In daylight the idea of shooting Mazey seemed far-fetched and desperate, the light wind of someone else's madness blowing through my head.

I said good morning to my father.

He looked up from his gun, his eyes pale, a crop of silver stubble on his cheeks and chin. 'Any word of Karin?'

I shook my head. I reached into the back of the car and lifted a small battery-operated cassette machine off the seat. It was Kroner's – he'd bought it just before his stroke; he liked new gadgets – but he would have no further use for it. I carried it across the yard and stood it on the bonnet of the truck. I asked Mazey for his tape. He handed it to me. I put it in the cassette machine, then I pressed the button that said PLAY. My father looked from me to Mazey and back again.

'We have to chain him up,' I said, 'like before.'

This time my father's eyes rested on Mazey for longer. Mazey didn't notice. As usual, he was hypnotised by the cassette machine; he still hadn't got used to the idea that you could hear the wind-chimes even though they were nowhere to be seen. My father studied him for a few moments, then looked down at the gun that lay across his lap.

'You know where it is,' he muttered.

I left Mazey in the yard while I walked into the barn. I found the padlocks and the chain on a shelf next to my father's rack of tools. As I turned away, I noticed the Leaning Tower of Pisa in the corner, propped against the wall, unwanted now, and gathering dust. It seemed a pity he had never finished it. It could have been his masterpiece. I'd always looked forward to the day when doves were roosting in those little arches. Outside in the yard, I ran one end of the chain around Mazey's ankle and fastened it with a padlock. Then I took the other end and hooked it through the truck's front bumper. Mazey stood still the whole time, his eyes fixed on the cassette machine. The fact that he was being chained to the truck again made no impression on him. Somehow it would have been easier if he had kicked and screamed. I'd never forgotten that drive back from the institution when he was eight, and how eerily untouched he seemed, and how remote.

My father laid his rifle on a piece of cloth and, rising to his feet, walked slowly towards us. He touched Mazey on the shoulder. 'Do you have your knife?'

Mazey nodded.

'Show it to me.'

Mazey took the knife from his trouser pocket and held it out to my father on the flat of his hand. There was blood on the knife, and I knew what blood it was, but my father didn't remark on it. He snapped one blade out, then the other. Tested both blades with the side of his thumb.

'I thought so,' he muttered. 'Blunt.'

He turned on his heel and walked away from us. I watched him vanish into the darkness of the barn. We waited in the yard, Mazey and I, both facing in different directions. After a while I heard the rasp of a grindstone.

When my father stepped out into the sunlight, he was carrying two or three blocks of wood. He'd cleaned the blood off the knife, and the edges of the blades were bright silver, thinner than before. He handed the knife and the wood to Mazey.

'Let's see what you can do with those.'

I drank a glass of water in the kitchen. Out on the porch I said goodbye to my father. He nodded. The gun lay on the cloth in front of him, each piece ready to be oiled. It would be hours before he reassembled it. As I drove away, I saw Mazey in the rear-view mirror. He was sitting on the ground beside the truck, with his head bent, whittling.

All summer Mazey was kept chained to the truck outside my father's house. All summer he carved the blocks of wood my father gave him. This time it was different, though. No strange, smooth shapes. Nothing you had to puzzle over, or guess at.

All summer he carved babies.

Babies sitting up, babies lying down. Babies on their backs or on their stomachs. Babies sleeping, laughing, kicking, crying (he even carved the tears). My father tried to persuade him to turn his hand to something else, but he wouldn't. Or couldn't. Each new block of wood that he was given became another baby, as if that was the only shape the wood contained, as if that was all it could ever be.

One morning in August I sat beside him. I remember counting them. There were thirty-seven – some life-size, others no bigger than your thumb. He put down his knife and picked up a block of wood that was as yet untouched. He held it in the palm of one hand and placed his other hand on top of it, and then he looked at me.

'Baby,' he said. 'In here.'

Many years later, on a warm September morning, a letter arrived. I turned it over in my hands, examined the writing on the envelope. I didn't recognise it. The postmark was a city in the north-west; I didn't know anyone who lived there. When I tore the letter open, a photograph fell out and landed on the floor. I bent down, picked it up. There were two people in the picture, a man and a girl. I didn't recognise either of them. I looked at the envelope again to make sure it was addressed to me. There my name was, on the front. I took the picture out to the porch and stood in the sunlight, studying it. The girl was embracing the man, her right arm passing across his chest, her two hands joining on his left shoulder. Now I thought about it, she looked something like my daughter, Karin. I'd only seen Karin once since she left. It was Kroner she came for – which was just as well because he died a few weeks afterwards. She stayed for less than an hour. She was rude. I turned my attention to the man again and suddenly everything fell into place. It was Jan Salenko, twenty years on. He'd thickened, the way men do, but there was the same strangely grateful look to him, as if he didn't deserve to be in the picture. My eyes drifted back to the girl. I thought of that cold December night and the baby I'd delivered. I'd even named her. Nina.

Jan Salenko had written a long letter, telling me that he and Karin were separating, a separation that would end, he supposed, in divorce. He poured out his feelings to me – all his misery, his longing, his regret. I thought it odd to be receiving news that was so personal when I hardly knew the man. After all, they'd married in secret, against my will. For the past twenty years I hadn't even had an address for them. But I knew enough to have told him, even at the beginning, that it wouldn't last. That much was obvious to anyone. In fact, it was astonishing that it had lasted as long as it had. What did he expect from me now? Sympathy? I read on. Towards the end of the letter he mentioned his daughter. At least he still had her, he wrote. Nina lived in the capital now, but they saw each other every two or three months. They got on well. He was enclosing a picture of the two of them, taken a few weeks back.

After I'd finished the letter, I studied the photograph again. She wasn't a bad-looking girl, though she didn't have the fine features of her mother. She looked more like me: headstrong, spirited, but plain. There was also something of Mazey in her – the nose, the upper lip. A Hekmann, not a Kroner. I didn't answer the letter. There was no point. What would I have said? I left it on a shelf in the kitchen, wedged between two glass jars. I forgot it was even there.

Mazey came to me one morning. At forty-three, the shine in his hair had gone and there were thin lines around his mouth, but otherwise he hadn't aged at all. I've often noticed how backward people look younger than they really are, as if their flesh is somehow backward, too; Mazey could easily have passed for twenty-eight or -nine. He stood in the kitchen that day, and the fingers of his left hand curled and uncurled against his leg. I asked him what was wrong. He wouldn't say. In his right hand he was holding Jan Salenko's photograph.

'Reading my letters now, are you?'

He held the picture up in front of me. 'The baby,' he said. 'Where's the baby?'

It took me a few moments, then I understood. He thought the girl in the picture was Karin. And if Karin was there, the baby ought to be there as well – even after all these years. I told him that it wasn't Karin he was looking at but Nina, her daughter. He was looking at the baby, I told him, only the baby had grown up. I could see he didn't believe me. He had never understood change, especially when it was slow. I took him outside. I picked up an acorn off the ground and then I showed him the oak tree it had come from. I told him the tree had been an acorn once. It was the same with the picture, I said. The girl used to be a baby. He just stared at me as if I was making the whole thing up. He was convinced that the girl in the picture had hidden the baby, and he wanted to know where it was. I tried to explain it to him again, but he turned away from me. He stood in the car-park, staring at the photograph, his left hand curling and uncurling against his leg.

My father had died at around that time, of old age. There were only a few of us at the funeral; he'd lived so long that most of the people who knew him were already gone. My father had two suits, which he kept for Sundays. He was buried in one of them, and I dressed Mazey in the other. At the graveside I stood with Mazey's arm in mine and watched the box drop into the ground. My father had carved the symbols of his trade on the lid – a hammer, a saw, a handful of nails; I remember thinking that the nails must have taken him a while. I felt Mazey remove his arm from mine and looked to see what he was doing. He'd opened one of the blades on his pen-knife and he was testing it against his thumb, the way my father had taught him. When he disappeared shortly after the funeral, I thought I understood: my father's death had awakened an old restlessness in him.

But he disappeared every month, returning in clothes that were filthy, often torn and sometimes even spotted with blood. After a year or so, the length of time that he was gone began to grow. Sometimes he would be away for as long as a week. I was worried that he might walk out one day and not come back at all. It was only by chance that I found out where he was going. I was emptying his pockets so I could wash his clothes when I found a ticket stub. It was a tram ticket, and it had the city's name on it. He'd been going to the capital, more than six hundred kilometres away. Sometimes I found money in his pockets, too, money he hadn't had on him when he set out. Sometimes there were stains in his underwear, which alarmed me. When I asked him what he did there, in the city, he became sullen and wouldn't answer. The only way to find out would be to follow him again. Though I was afraid of what I might discover, I felt I had no choice; it was part of my responsibility to him.

The next time he told me he was going out, I was ready. I'd prepared some food and a change of clothing, and I'd made arrangements with Martha, the hired help, to run the place while I was away. I felt like a fool, though, because I was back two hours later. Mazey had hitched a lift on the main road; I'd stood there helplessly while he disappeared into the distance in some stranger's car. It was at least a month before he left again. This time I borrowed an estate car from one of our neighbours (Mazey would have recognised our truck). I sat behind the wheel and watched him walk away from the house. It was a bright, cold October day. A clear blue sky, dead leaves clattering across the ground.

He walked until he reached a junction a couple of kilometres west of the village, then he turned to the south, along a road that led towards the motorway. After another quarter of an hour, he found a grass verge that was to his liking and began to wait. I had to hide the car behind a tree because that section of the road was straight and whenever he heard the sound of an engine he looked in my direction. He kept his thumb stuck out in the air, I noticed, even when there was nothing coming. It was the middle of the morning before someone stopped for him. I didn't recognise the car; it wasn't anyone we knew. I followed the car for an hour and a half. It dropped him at a service station about one hundred and twenty kilometres south-west of the village. There were toilets, petrol pumps. There was a café-restaurant with a red-and-white-striped awning. I parked in the shadow of a removal van and watched Mazey as he walked into the restaurant. He bought a soft drink, then he went and stood next to a man who was sitting at the counter. I saw the man shake his head. I found that my mouth was hanging open. I suppose I'd never imagined Mazey speaking to anyone apart from me. I felt a sudden jealousy of all these strangers. I watched him move along the counter, stopping at the shoulder of every driver. He knew the procedure; obviously he had done it many times before. The way he approached the men, the way he nodded when they turned him down. The way he drank from his Styrofoam cup and then crushed it when it was empty and tossed it in the bin. I'd lost him. I wondered when exactly this had happened.

He was offered a lift by a tall fat man who drove an oil tanker. This was a relief. I'd been dreading something fast; the estate I'd borrowed was a rickety thing, more than ten years old. The tanker would be no problem, though. Also it was silver, which made it impossible to lose in traffic. We travelled south, through flat grey land. It was country I'd never seen before. There were almost no trees. Morning became afternoon and the bright sky clouded over. It began to drizzle.

At last, towards dusk, the driver stopped for something to eat. I parked almost parallel with the tanker, but slightly behind it. From where I was sitting I could see Mazey's shoulder and his forearm. I watched him climb down out of the cab, his face in profile against the cold sodium lights. He followed the driver into the cafeteria and bought a sandwich. I went to the toilets while I had the chance. There was an attendant eating peanuts out of a tin and watching a black-and-white TV. On the way out I dropped a few small coins into a Tupperware container, but she didn't even look at me. I hurried to the car. Just then Mazey left the cafeteria. He didn't go back to the tanker. Instead, he wandered around the car-park. At one point he walked right towards me and I had to duck down, hide under the dashboard. This is madness, I thought, crouching on the floor among sweet-wrappers, dirty tissues, bits of mud from other people's shoes. I should go home.

When I lifted my head and peered through the bottom half of the windscreen, I saw Mazey hoisting himself up into the tanker's cab.

Over in the cafeteria the driver was just finishing his meal. He wiped his mouth on the back of his wrist, then put on a dark-blue wool hat. I had the feeling he was going to be driving through the night.

I was right. It was two-thirty in the morning before he stopped again, this time in a rest-area. There were no facilities; it was just a section of unmarked road that curved off the motorway and joined it again two hundred metres further on. I parked beyond the tanker, at the far end of the curve, and adjusted my wing-mirror so I could see the tanker from where I was sitting. The drizzle had eased. A rain-mist now. Tiny particles of water drifting in the dark air, floating rather than falling. I got out of the car to stretch my legs. There wasn't much traffic any more, but if something did go past, it made a sound like someone drawing curtains.

I climbed a grass bank behind the car, and then I walked along the top of it, through some newly planted saplings, until I could look down into the oil tanker's cab. The driver was still sitting at the wheel. His head was leaning against the window and his eyes were closed. At first I thought he was asleep. But then his mouth opened and his chest swelled, as if he'd just breathed in. It was only then that I saw Mazey. He had his back to me and his head was on the driver's lap. I could only see his hair, the collar of his shirt and his right elbow. I took a step backwards, turned away. I was thinking of Axel as I stumbled among the saplings. Thinking of the branches of the willow tree, the stream flowing beneath us, his tea-coloured summer skin. It had poisoned us, the pleasure we had taken in each other. It had poisoned all the earth around us, all the air. It had poisoned most of the lives that came after us. They never knew the source of it. They never knew it came from that one tree, on that first morning. Before anybody woke. When I reached my car I suddenly doubled over and vomited a frothy yellow liquid on to the ground. I couldn't think what I'd eaten to produce such a colour. Trembling, I got into the front seat. I wanted to wash my mouth out. All I could find was a bottle of distilled water, which my neighbour used for topping up the battery.

I hardly slept that night. Every time a lorry started up, my eyes snapped open and I wiped the condensation off the window and looked into the wing-mirror. But the silver tanker never moved. Not until eight in the morning, when the door on the driver's side slammed shut. The tall fat man spat twice, then turned and climbed the grass bank. He stood among the saplings for a while, just looking out across the landscape, before unbuttoning his trousers. His urine smoked in the cold morning air.

At ten o'clock Mazey was dropped at another service station on the motorway. He stood shivering among the petrol pumps, his hands in his pockets. I watched the tanker pull away without him. I was glad to see the back of it. But because I'd followed it for so many hours, I went on seeing it long after it was gone: a silver disc with banks of tail-lights under it, black mud flaps, giant tyres. I watched Mazey walk from car to car, bending down to speak to each driver, as if he was selling something. Though I was cold, a kind of heat rose through me as it occurred to me that maybe that was exactly what he was doing. The money in his pockets – how else had he got hold of it?

It took him another two lifts to complete his journey. It was a wet day, rain angling across the motorway, but I was grateful for the weather: the cars Mazey travelled in drove slowly, and I was even less likely to be noticed. The last car was a pale-green saloon, which put him down on the outskirts of the city, not far from the main bus terminal. He stood on the pavement for a moment, his mouth set in a straight line as he looked around him. Then he began to walk. I parked, making a note of the name of the street, then followed him on foot. The temperature had dropped into single figures; fog cloaked the tops of the buildings. Mazey walked the same way he walked when he was in the village, as though unaware of his surroundings, as though people were ghosts. His shoulders were drawn in towards his chest and his fists were pushed right to the bottom of his pockets. He only had a thin coat to cover him. It was one of Kroner's coats – too short in the arm, threadbare, too, not even waterproof. His shoes were worn down at the heels so they tilted sideways and inwards; they moved sloppily on his feet, like moored boats. I saw him as someone who didn't know him, and it shamed me that I hadn't clothed him better.

The rain slackened off. Finally it stopped altogether. Mazey was examining the buildings now. We were nearing his destination. I didn't like the area. The streets were wide and derelict. The apartment blocks were many storeys high, their windows curtained with rags or sheets of newspaper or plain brown cardboard. The shops had all been fortified with metal grilles. They sold newspapers, chewing-gum, cigarettes. Fruit that was almost rotten. Fridges and televisions that wouldn't have looked out of place on Miss Poppel's front lawn. There was a bar on almost every corner. They had metal grilles as well. I didn't see too many people – just tramps, drunks, old women with dogs. Mazey began to fit. His threadbare coat, his worn-down shoes. Is this where he belongs? I wondered. At the end of an alleyway I saw the slick grey surface of a canal.

He stopped in front of a building, looked up, then he pushed through the door and vanished inside. I crossed the road towards it. Through the cracked glass panel in the door I could see a hallway, a row of brown metal letter-boxes along one wall, a narrow flight of stairs. I opened the door, let it swing shut behind me. Then I stood there, listening. I heard Mazey's footsteps somewhere above me. I heard him knock on a door. I climbed the stairs quickly, then stopped again and listened. He knocked again. I couldn't see him, but it sounded as though he was on the floor above. The door opened and I heard a voice that wasn't his. The door closed. I climbed to the next floor. There were only four doors on the landing and I put my ear to each one of them in turn. When I'd worked out which apartment he had entered, I climbed one more flight of stairs and then I sat down on a step and waited.

The building was quiet. Just somebody scraping the bottom of a saucepan with a spoon. And one half of an argument – the woman's voice. I was sitting by a window. I could see rooftops, factory smoke. And, in the distance, a strip of dull green, which was where the city ended. I hadn't realised I was so high up. The street must have been built on a hill.

Flies nuzzling the chalky glass.

It was always Axel that I saw, with his eyes narrowed against the sunlight, and the stream running below us, and I couldn't believe the beauty of those moments forty years before had led to this. A staircase in a dismal, run-down building. A street whose name I didn't even know. What did I have in mind? I no longer knew.

More than an hour passed.

The door to the apartment opened and, looking down between the metal banisters, I saw the top of Mazey's head. He was leaving. He was alone. I heard his footsteps fade, the front door shut. From my window I could see him walking back along the street.

After sitting still for so long, it was an effort to move. My knees were cold and stiff; I had to rub the life back into them. At last I stood up. I went back down the stairs and knocked on the apartment door.

A man's voice called out. 'Erik? Is that you?'

I knocked again.

The door opened, on a chain. I saw a man who could have been my age. He wore a green sun-visor and his grey hair was cropped close to his head.

'Yes?'

'There was someone here,' I said. 'Just now.'

'So?'

'He's my son.'

'That's funny,' the man said, 'because he's my son, too.'

I stared at him through the narrow gap. There was a cut on the bridge of his nose, the kind of cut Karl used to get when he drank too much and then fell over.

'Could I come in, please?'

The man studied me for a few moments, then he closed the door. I was about to knock again when I heard him unlatch the chain. This time the door opened wide. The man bent slightly from the waist, and his right hand drifted away from his body. It was a gesture of welcome, but he was mocking me with it.

I walked past him. There were only two rooms. The first was a kitchen. Under the window was a bath that had a wooden board on top of it. The floor was dark-green linoleum. My shoes stuck to it.

The second room wasn't much larger than the first. There were three single beds in there, each bed pushed against a different wall. All the surfaces were covered with ashtrays, bottles, glasses. Someone had pinned a playing card to the fireplace – the Jack of Hearts. A man sprawled on one of the beds, his head and shoulders propped against the wall, a leather cap wedged on to his curly black hair. He wore a diamond stud in his left ear. Dirt had collected round it.

'Who are you?' I said.

The man yawned and looked out of the window. I heard his jawbone creak.

'I think you're the one who should be answering questions,' said the man who'd let me in. He was standing beside me now. Light filtered through his visor, and the upper half of his face had a sickly green tint to it. He smelled of cheap deodorant.

'I want to know what my son was doing here.'

'He's been coming here for a while now.'

I turned and looked at him.

'Two years. Maybe three.' The man unscrewed the top off a bottle and drank from it. 'The first year he only came here twice. Then it got more regular.'

'This place is filthy,' I said.

'That doesn't bother Erik,' the man said.

'That's right,' said the man on the bed, still looking out of the window. 'Erik doesn't seem to mind at all. In fact, I'd go so far as to say that Erik doesn't even notice.' He held his hand out for the bottle.

'Erik's not exactly clean himself,' said the man with the visor.

'Erik shits his pants.' The man on the bed drank from the bottle, then he looked at the man who was standing just behind me. They both laughed.

'Erik?' I said.

'That's his name,' said the man with the visor.

'His name's Mazey. His name's always been Mazey, ever since he was born.'

There was a moment's silence in the room.

'Well, it's Erik when he's here,' said the man with the visor.

'And what's your name?' I asked him.

'Not Erik.'

'His name's Ackal,' said the man on the bed.

'And that's Moler,' said the man with the visor. 'M-O-L-E-R.'

They both laughed again.

I sat down on one of the beds. Suddenly I could have closed my eyes and slept. Even on that bare, stained mattress, among strangers.

'You look like you could use a drink.'

The man in the visor gave me a glass and poured some of the clear liquid from his bottle into it.

'What is it?' I asked him.

'Vodka.'

There were flies' legs floating on the surface. They looked like Chinese writing. I drank half the vodka, wincing at the taste. Then I drank the rest. Was I called something different now? What was my name?

Edith? Is that you?

The man in the visor stood at the window, grey light beyond him. He told me how he'd found Erik sleeping on a park bench one morning. When he sat down next to Erik, Erik showed him a photograph. It wasn't anyone he recognised. He thought Erik might be hungry so he took him back to his apartment. They'd lived in a different building then. He heated up some old tomato soup, with macaroni. Erik ate as if he hadn't eaten in days. He stayed with them that night, and the next night, too, and then he left. He didn't say goodbye or thank you. In fact, it was only after Erik had gone that they realised he hadn't really spoken to them at all. They didn't think they'd see him again. Well, at least he hadn't stolen anything. But three months later, Erik was back.

They talked about him sometimes when he wasn't there. They saw that he had a different way of doing things to most people. He didn't need words, for instance. That was fine. Time didn't mean much to him either. If you gave Erik a clock, he'd sit with it for hours. He'd watch the second-hand go round. Or else he'd put it to his ear and listen to it, the way people used to listen to transistor radios. They could deal with that. They thought Erik needed a home, though. So they adopted him. The man with the visor, Ackal, picked up the bottle and drank from it. He'd adopted Erik legally, he said. He had the documents somewhere. He gestured at a battered metal filing cabinet in the corner of the room. The air moved glassily behind his hand. I thought I might pass out.

'You can't do that,' I muttered.

'I already did.' He was almost gloating, his mouth all crooked.

'But he's my son. I've taken care of him since he was six months old.' And then I said something I never in my life imagined I would say. Think, maybe. But not say. 'He's all I've got.'

I saw the two men exchange a glance.

'If he's really your son,' the man in the visor said, 'then how come the poor bastard was sleeping on a park bench all night, cold and hungry?'

'He's forty-three years old,' I said. 'What am I supposed to do? Tie him up in the yard?'

That silenced them.

Then I said, 'I just never realised he'd go so far.'

All the time I'd been talking to Ackal, the other man, the one called Moler, had been staring at me lazily from his bed, lifting a hand every now and then to examine his fingernails or adjust his leather cap. Now he spoke to me.

'Erik's a man with a mission.'

I stared at him.

'It's something to do with the photograph,' he said. 'It's of a girl. Seems like he's looking for her. Sometimes we take the piss, saying she's his girlfriend, but he doesn't like it when we do that.' He laughed. 'He doesn't like it, does he, Ackal?'

Suddenly I realised which photograph it was that he was talking about. I saw Mazey in the kitchen, with his hand curling and uncurling. *Where's the baby?*

'I don't know anything about that.' I stood up. 'I should be going.'

'Will we be seeing you again?' Ackal grinned unpleasantly.

'Yes,' said Moler, looking out of the window, 'you simply must drop by.'

'I don't think so,' I said.

I walked to the door and opened it. Ackal followed me.

'Don't worry,' he said. 'He turns up here, he's always in good hands.' His chuckle wasn't reassuring, but then it wasn't supposed to be.

Over his shoulder I saw the man in the leather cap. He was yawning. I had the peculiar sense of never having set foot in that room at all. Of never having even entered the apartment. The man in the visor had his hand on the door. I saw him clearly for the first time. His dim round face. Small eyes. A mouth like an owl's.

'Does he ever talk to you?' I asked.

'Erik?' he said. 'No.'

'Not ever?'

'No.'

I nodded and, looking down, I smiled to myself.

'Hey, what do you – '

But I'd already turned away. I was already walking down the stairs.

'Hey!' The man in the visor was shouting. 'What the fuck do you mean by that?'

I didn't answer. I didn't even look round. I just kept walking down the stairs. And out through the front door, and back along the street. The weather had changed. The sky was a sandstone colour now, thin silver sunlight reaching through the clouds. I passed the shops with their metal grilles. I passed the tall apartment blocks. The city moved around me, whispering, like a conspiracy. I could imagine walking for days, and finding nothing familiar, recognising no one. I was astonished when I saw my neighbour's car, astonished when the key I took out of my pocket opened the door. It shouldn't have been that easy.

Driving home took thirteen hours. In the middle of the night I stopped at the edge of the road and slept for forty-five minutes. In my dream I was driving and Mazey was beside me, dozing. I saw his long nose, his slightly drooping upper lip, his blond hair falling across his forehead. There were no knives anywhere. I was happy.

When I woke up, my heart jumped. I was behind the wheel, exactly as I'd dreamed I was. It took me a while to realise that the car wasn't moving and I wasn't going to crash. I rolled the window down. Breathed the cold night air. Then I turned the key in the ignition and drove on. I was still tired, though. My eyes kept trying to close and when I forced them open it felt as if they were revolving in their sockets. All I could find on the radio was static – the noise trains make in tunnels. I had to smoke cigarettes to stay awake.

At dawn I stopped again. I slept for an hour. Waking, I saw a stork standing on one leg in the fast lane. For a moment I just stared at it. That it could be there, in that unlikely place, and look so unconcerned. But I didn't want a car to run it down. I reached for the door handle, thinking I'd shout or clap my hands, do something that would scare it off. The sound of the door opening was enough. It lifted into the air, legs dangling like bits of a broken deck-chair. The first few wing-beats were ungainly, but by the time it cleared the trees, it had achieved a kind of grace.

A few kilometres south of the village I shifted on the seat and felt something in my coat pocket – a small glass, cold and faintly sticky. I held it up above the steering-wheel so I could look at it. It was the glass I'd drunk vodka from. I must have put it in my pocket without thinking. I could still see the room. It was pale-yellow, and there were beds in it. I could see the man with the diamond pellet in his ear. I could see the other man, too, the upper half of his face bathed in a deep green shadow. They were like someone else's memories. But the vodka glass was proof of what had happened, it was evidence, and I wasn't sure I wanted any. I felt as if the glass had been planted.

The next day Mazey came home. He walked in through the back door, as usual. He ran the cold tap, cupped a hand under it and bent his head. In that moment, standing in the kitchen and watching him drink, I realised I would never follow him again. There was nothing more I needed to know – in fact, maybe I already knew too much. I'd tried to guide him, keep him safe, but I'd reached the limits of my power, my influence. He'd invented a kind of freedom for himself.

I remembered the articles they ran in the paper all those years ago. WHO COULD DO SUCH A THING? I could never quite understand why nobody found out about him, why he was never caught. I thought I knew why now. It had to be something to do with the way his mind worked. There were reasons behind the things he did, but they weren't reasons anyone else would think of. What was a reason for him would be madness for them. He lived in a different dimension. That difference was what protected him.

'How are you, Mazey?' I said to him.

Still bent over the sink, he looked at me sideways, the water splashing down into his hand and overflowing. He seemed to be waiting for me to say something else.

'It's all right,' I said. 'Just drink.'

SILVER SKIN

She had talked almost continuously, for hours. As I listened to her, as I filled with unease, foreboding and even, in the end, with dread, she seemed, ironically, to grow accustomed to me, she began to feel comfortable, and her visits to the kitchen became more frequent, less disguised. She didn't get drunk, though. She didn't slur her words or lose her thread.

By the time we climbed the stairs, the birds were singing.

I spent the entire day in bed. Dreams of black lakes, crashed cars. People maimed, contorted, splashed with blood. Once, I saw Emerald Joe slumped in the corner of the room, his arms and legs all jumbled up, his jewelled tooth shining.

I was afraid to sleep, afraid to be awake. Each time I dozed, I woke again like someone who'd just touched an electric fence: bolt upright, soaked in sweat – my nerve-ends charred, my brain a grate containing nothing but a white-hot emptiness.

Then, towards evening, I washed and dressed. I was scrupulous. I invested every movement, every detail of the process, with my fullest concentration – from the first soaping of my face to the final lacing of a boot. It must have taken me an hour. Before I went downstairs I called Munck. I wasn't sure why. Perhaps it was simply a way of clearing my mind, of breathing different air. I wanted someone to talk to – someone who wasn't Edith Hekmann. Munck wasn't his usual self, though. He seemed both guarded and inquisitive. I realised it had been at least two weeks since I'd spoken to him.

'Where are you calling from?' He had to shout; it was a bad line. 'I've been trying to reach you. I tried the Kosminsky, but they told me you'd left. In the middle of the night.'

'That's true. I had to leave.'

'It seems suspicious,' Munck said, 'in the circumstances.'

I laughed. 'Not to me.'

His tone sharpened. 'What can I tell my superiors?'

'Tell them I'm out of town for a few days. Tell them it's personal.'

Munck didn't say anything.

'I'm sorry,' I said. 'That's the best I can do.'

I promised to call him as soon as I returned. Then I put the phone down. I heard the clock strike seven in the hall below. I took a deep breath and began to make my way towards the staircase.

When I took my place at the table in the dining-room I was surprised to find myself alone. I asked Martha where Mrs Hekmann was.

'I haven't seen her,' Martha said.

'Is she ill?'

'Not so far as I know.'

I thought she was probably still recovering. Not everyone was used to staying awake all night.

Martha put a plate of boiled beef and cabbage in front of me. I ate slowly, but I couldn't finish it. I had no appetite. And anyway, the food tasted of nothing.

The pale-pink lampshade, the dismal paintings.

I shivered as a draught moved past my back.

While I was drinking my coffee, the door to the dining-room opened behind me. I heard shoes on the bare boards. It wasn't Martha; she was busy in the kitchen.

'Mrs Hekmann?'

There was no answer. I knew it was her, though. And then I

remembered what she was. A murderer. A *murderer*. It seemed absurd, exaggerated. I didn't know how to think about it. It was like trying to picture a million people, or describe the face of God. In my nervousness I knocked a fork off the table. As I was bending down to pick it up, her shoes moved past me, into the room. I heard a cork spring from a bottle. She'd opened it right in front of me. She'd abandoned all pretence.

'Would you like a drink?' she asked.

I stared at her. 'Yes – thank you. That would be nice.'

What had induced this sudden change in her? I looked for some clue in her appearance, but there was nothing. She was wearing a calf-length skirt, a cardigan, a pair of sturdy shoes. I couldn't read her face at all.

She handed me a glass. I thanked her. She sat in her usual place.

'Now,' she said quietly, 'who are you, exactly?'

It took me a moment to reply. I'd been expecting the usual question. How was your meal? What did you think of the boiled beef?

Who are you?

'It's in the register – '

'That's not what I mean.' Her voice sliced through mine. It was a tone I hadn't heard her use before.

She set her glass down on the table.

'My son,' she said. 'He's come back. You remember I told you about my son. Mazey.'

'Yes. You told me.' I wasn't likely to forget.

'I've been talking to him,' she said.

She took a cigarette out of the open packet at her elbow and lit it. I just looked at her. I waited.

'He had some interesting things to say about you.'

'About me?' I said. 'But I've never – '

'He's seen you before,' and she paused, 'in the city.'

She seemed to be waiting for me to speak, but I couldn't think of anything. I didn't know where this was leading. To steady myself, I concentrated on her cardigan. It was a dull grey-green. Her skirt was brown. Her shoes, they were brown, too.

'You're the police, aren't you,' she said suddenly.

I was staring at her again. Police? What was she talking about?

'You're some kind of detective. Aren't you. I was wondering when you'd come.'

'Mrs Hekmann,' I said, 'I don't – '

'*Don't lie to me.*' Ash dropped from her cigarette and shattered on the tablecloth. 'It's no use lying, not now. That phone-call you made, for instance. Who were you speaking to?'

She didn't give me time to answer. 'It was the police, wasn't it. Your colleagues.' Her voice was level, but only just. 'That was clever of them, sending me a cripple. Oh, that was clever. They knew it would catch me unawares, arouse my sympathy. Send in the blind man. It always works.' She crushed her cigarette out on a plate, and with it she seemed to be crushing any need for ambiguity or restraint. 'You walk into my house, you accept my hospitality, and all the time – ' Her chair scraped backwards and she stood up. 'You betrayed me, Mr Blom. You betrayed my trust.'

She walked away across the room. When she reached the window, she stopped. The handle creaked as she opened it. 'It's snowing,' she said. 'You probably hadn't realised.'

I shook my head. Her cardigan had brown buttons on it. I counted them. One, two, three, four – and there was one missing, at the bottom. They were unusual buttons; they looked like hazelnuts.

'I know your kind,' she said.

'My kind?' My voice sounded weak.

She stood with her back to the window, the snow blowing past her, into the room. I watched it settle on the floor and melt. I was shivering.

'Your kind,' she said. 'I've seen your kind on television.'

'You – you really think I'm a policeman?'

'I know you are.'

'What is it I'm supposed to be investigating?'

'My granddaughter. Nina Salenko.'

I stared at Edith Hekmann's grey-green cardigan. There was a loose thread near one of the cuffs. If she didn't mend it soon, the whole sleeve would probably unravel. I thought I should point it out to her. 'You've got – '

'You were seen,' she said. 'Mazey saw you. You were together.'

I could hear Munck's voice. *About the man in the station . . . tall, apparently . . . pale hair . . . staring . . .* Then I remembered what Loots had told me on the night he came into my room. His description of the man he'd noticed in the hotel car-park. Mazey. Mazey Hekmann. I reached for my glass. It wasn't there.

'You're looking for her,' she said, 'aren't you.'

I shook my head again. 'I'm not. Not any more.'

'That's just as well.'

Something rose in my throat and hardened, like a stone. 'Why do you say that?'

'Because she's dead.'

I couldn't swallow; I could barely speak. 'How do you know?'

Edith Hekmann did not reply.

I stood up. A snowflake landed on the tablecloth, white on white. 'I think I'll go to my room now,' I said.

'Oh,' she said. 'Aren't we going to talk tonight?'

I moved towards the door.

'Don't you want to know what happened?' Her voice had softened.

'No,' I said.

'You don't want to know the truth?'

'You shouldn't tell me anything,' I murmured, 'not if I'm a policeman.'

Snow slanted between us and suddenly it was like watching something on an old TV. Any minute now, I was going to lose her completely.

'I trusted you,' she said.

I reached the top of the stairs. Turning right, I walked to the far end of the landing and sat down on the small upholstered chair beside the phone. I thought of calling Munck again, but I couldn't see what good it would do. And anyway, I wouldn't have known what to tell him. I called Loots instead. My fingers kept missing the holes. Three times I dialled the wrong number. The fourth time his uncle answered. I asked him if I could speak to Albert. He put the receiver down. 'Albert?' he shouted. 'Al-bert?' In the background I could hear the sounds of an ordinary household: voices, music, cutlery.

When Loots came to the phone, he asked me how I was. It wasn't a question I felt capable of answering.

'Listen,' I said. 'When are you coming?'

'Tomorrow.' His plan was to leave in the morning, he said. He'd be with me sometime in the early afternoon.

'Can't you come any sooner?'

He was silent for a moment. 'Not really. Not unless I leave right now.'

It was my turn to be silent.

'You want me to leave now?' His voice lifted, as if he couldn't quite believe it.

'I wouldn't ask,' I said, 'not unless it was important.'

'What's wrong? Are you in trouble?'

'Yes, I think I am.'

'I knew there was something about that place – ' He checked himself. 'What kind of trouble?'

'I can't talk, Loots.'

'You can't tell me anything?'

'Please,' I said. 'Just come.'

Back in my room I stood at the wash-basin, leaning on it, with my head lowered. I wondered if Edith Hekmann had listened to that call as well. The porcelain beneath my hands. The coolness of it. The smooth, rounded edges.

Don't you want to know the truth?

All I could see now were the buttons on her cardigan. The four brown buttons. Like hazelnuts. And that sleeve of hers, unravelling, unravelling –

You don't want to know?

Something was coming apart. I didn't dare to lift my head. I couldn't look into the mirror.

I was afraid of what I might see.

Of what I might not see.

During the night I left my room and tiptoed through the darkened house. Halfway down the stairs I heard somebody murmuring. It seemed to be coming from behind the wall. I thought it must be one of the residents – old people having trouble sleeping. The clock struck three as I stepped on to the porch. The snow had stopped. I'd walked out into an odd silence, a padded world.

I crossed the car-park and, passing through the clustered fir trees, started down the stone steps towards the pool. Then, suddenly, I lost my footing. I was rolling, over and over. I had to throw my hands up around my head, to protect it. When I landed at the bottom of the steps, my glasses and my cane were gone.

I lay on my back in the snow. I didn't seem to be hurt. Just shaken. Had I woken anyone? I lay there, listening. All I could hear was the sound of sulphur water tumbling into the pool. I sat up. Rubbed my elbow, then my knee. I'd been lucky. One of these days I was going to break something.

Why had I fallen, though?

I hadn't been careless or impatient – in fact, I was sure I could remember watching my feet sink, one after the other, into the pure, unblemished snow. There was no reason to have fallen, none at all.

I limped to the edge of the pool. I knelt, reached down with one hand. Above the waterline the walls were sharp to the touch, encrusted with mineral deposits; below it, they were smooth, almost velvety, the consistency of dust. A rope had been fastened along the side in even loops, for people to hold on to. Over the years it had petrified, and it was now as hard as china.

The sound of the water, that sulphur smell, the rope's strange texture – all this I could claim to know.

I slowly raised my head.

But what about the things my undiminished senses couldn't help me with? What about the trees on the far side of the valley? What about the stars?

The night before, in the middle of her story, Edith Hekmann had taken me to Mazey's room. She was so insistent, pulling on my sleeve, that I couldn't refuse. It was up the stairs and through the door I'd put my ear to once, the door marked PRIVATE. Then along a cramped passageway, no more than shoulder-wide. Mazey's room was at the end, on the right. She let me go in first. After what I'd heard, I'd been expecting something bizarre, extravagant – if not demented. I was disappointed. It was a room like any other room. A window, a single bed, a chair. A basin in the corner. Taps. A perfectly ordinary room. And Edith Hekmann was just a mother, proudly showing off her child. I found myself thinking of Gabriela, the Gabriela who appeared in my dreams. Always being admired for something, being special, winning.

Almost angrily, I said, 'What am I supposed to be looking at?'

Edith Hekmann laughed. 'Above you.'

I reached up with my left hand. Nothing at first, just air. Then I felt something that was made of wood. It was smooth, carved into a shape. And it moved when I touched it.

At last I made the connection. 'It's a baby.'

I let go of it and it swung sideways. There was a series of small collisions, as wood knocked against wood. Click click CLICK CLICK click click – it reminded me of pool balls on a table, the sound they make when somebody breaks.

'How many are there?' I asked her.

'I never counted.' She came and stood beside me. 'It's years since he made one, but he still looks at them. Still lies there on his bed and looks at them.' She walked past me, into the room. 'He's got talent,' she said, 'don't you think?'

I didn't know if talent was the word. I murmured something.

'Karin took the baby away from him,' she said, 'and once they were gone there was no one who could explain it to him, not even me.' There was a silence. 'She turned him into what he is.'

I was only half-listening, though. I was still looking up into the mass of babies that were hanging from the ceiling . . .

It was a while before I turned to face her. She was standing by the window, looking out into the night. I thought she'd forgotten I was there. But then she spoke again.

'Are you artistic, Mr Blom?'

I was still kneeling at the edge of the pool. I was no longer aware of my heart beating, or the places where I'd hurt myself; I was no longer aware of the cold. I was thinking about the wooden babies twisting on their strings –

A perfectly ordinary room.

There was a feeling now, a feeling that I remembered having in the car-park after I'd been shot. I was falling from a plane, and the plane was flying on without me. It wasn't just separation, abandonment. It was the falling itself. Something giving way, something seeming to expand in front of me. A kind of gap had opened up, and it was widening. I left my screams behind, thin sounds curving into absolute infinity.

My dark glasses, my white cane. Where were they?

I tried to remember the lay-out of the steps. Think. THINK. There were three flights in all. You walked down the first flight, then turned to your right and walked down another one. Then you turned to your left. The last flight was the longest. I must have fallen somewhere near the top of the last flight.

I began with the bottom step, feeling the length and breadth of it, searching the ground on either side as well. It was a laborious process, and my hands were almost numb, but I could think of no other way. It would look odd, I thought, if someone saw me from an upstairs window. It would look like worship, part of some quaint religion.

I found my cane on the seventh step. I sat down and examined it; it seemed undamaged. The glasses would prove more difficult. A wind pushed at the trees near by – a night wind; I could detect no daylight in it yet. Not that it made much difference now. There would no longer be any days or nights for me. There would only be time – continuous, unvarying.

The eighth step yielded nothing. I was cold and tired. What if the glasses had landed some distance away, in the shrubbery?

As I started on the ninth step, my hand discovered something hard and rounded, with a kind of edge around it. I bent my nose to it. Leather.

It was a shoe.

'Mrs Hekmann?'

Wait a minute. It wasn't a woman's shoe. It was too big to be a woman's shoe.

'Who are you?' I said.

I found a second shoe.

'Loots?' I said. 'It's not you, is it?'

No, it couldn't be. Not yet.

'Who are you?'

My son. He's come back.

'Mazey?'

I was standing now. I could feel his breath on my face.

I had no idea what he intended. I had the feeling I should treat him as I would an animal Stay calm. No sudden movements. *Whatever you do, don't run.*

Something was placed against my chest. I was pushed backwards. I staggered down one step, then another. I didn't fall, though. It must have been his hand.

I still had my cane. Supposing I used it as a weapon?

No sooner had the thought occurred to me than the cane was snatched out of my grasp. I heard it leave his hand. The sound it made, the sound a whip makes when it cuts through empty air. I heard it land in water somewhere to my left.

The violence was happening in silence.

Nothing was being said.

'What is it, Mazey? What do you want?'

The hand pushed me backwards once again. I managed not to lose my balance. I had to be somewhere near the bottom now. I reached out with my foot, found level ground.

Words would be no use. He wasn't even going to speak.

Was he trying to frighten me? Probably not. He didn't know what fear was. I remembered what Edith Hekmann had said. *The simple things he doesn't understand. Like we get older.*

Like we die.

I thought she must have told him that I'd wronged her. Now he was trying to get rid of me. He wanted me gone. Was he capable of measuring his own violence, though? Somehow I doubted it. He could kill me and not even be aware of it. He would stoop over my body with a kind of abstract curiosity, not understanding why all the movement had gone out of it.

It was also possible that she'd loosed him on me like a dog.

I walked backwards, trying to determine where he was. But he was moving quietly, if he was moving at all; the snow took every sound and softened it. Suddenly my heel tipped; there was nothing under it. I'd reached the edge of the pool. There was only one way to keep track of him – at least, only one that I could think of. I had to translate each movement he made into a noise. I had to make him visible.

I turned quickly, jumped in.

It was warm, warmer than I'd expected. Almost the same temperature as a bath. I rose to the surface. My head cooled as the night air closed over it. I was out of my depth. I worked the toe of one shoe against the heel of the other. I worried that Mazey might leap in after me, land on top of me. I wouldn't stand a chance then.

At last my feet were free of my shoes. I slipped out of my jacket and swam away from it. I had no sense of where Mazey was. My plunge into the pool must have taken him by surprise. Confused him.

I don't like swimming-pools. The words came to me, but they were strangely meaningless, redundant. Could it be that one fear cancels another? I was making for the middle. I was calm. Moving cautiously through the water, scarcely disturbing it. So I could hear what was happening.

Then, some distance behind me, the water erupted. It was him. It had to be. He'd stood there on the edge and thought about it. Then he'd jumped.

I started swimming faster, away from the noise. Staying afloat was hard, especially in clothes; it was sulphur water, and it didn't support you the way water usually does. I could hear splashing coming from behind me. It didn't sound as if he swam too often. That was a relief. It meant I was in my element, as opposed to his. Unless it was his fury I was hearing . . .

I felt the bottom with my feet; I'd reached the shallow end. I couldn't stop to rest, though. I had to keep moving away from him, around the pool. While I was crouching there, with my head turned in his direction, I noticed that the sounds were weaker than before. They didn't seem to be coming any closer either. It was as if he hadn't moved in the water. And suddenly I realised. All that splashing. Swimming didn't sound like that. But drowning might. Then I understood why he'd hesitated so long before he jumped. He'd never been in the pool before. *He couldn't swim.*

I began to make my way towards him. It was quiet now and I had the feeling I was entering a trap. The silence, I didn't trust it. What if he was waiting for me? I swam more slowly, trying to listen out for him.

I trod water, called his name.

There was no reply.

I wasn't sure if I was imagining it, but I thought I sensed something move beneath the water, something reaching sluggishly for the surface. An arm, maybe. A hand.

I took one deep breath and dived. I touched the bottom of the pool. There was a kind of dust down there, centimetres thick, and soft as velvet. I pushed my fingers through it. But there was nothing else.

I rose to the surface, took some air. Then dived again.

Nothing.

The water was so warm, so dense.

I shifted some distance to my left and dived a third time. The fingers of my right hand touched his teeth. His mouth was open. He'd been lying right below me.

I came up shouting. 'Mrs Hekmann? Mrs Hekmann?'

I dived again and tried to lift him. But he weighed more than I did. I got halfway to the surface, then I had to let him go. I had the feeling I was sweating, even though I was underwater.

It was probably too late anyway. His body was a dead weight: no movement in it, no resistance. I swam until I reached the side of the pool. I clung to the rope that felt like porcelain and began to shout again.

'Mrs Hekmann?'

I just clung to the rope and shouted.

'You must have woken just about everyone in the village,' she said, 'screaming and yelling like that. What's the matter with you? Did you fall in the pool?'

'It's your son,' I said.

'What about him?'

I was sitting on the terrace in wet clothes, my hands wedged under my arms. I could still feel the imprint of his teeth at the end of my fingers.

'What about my son?' she said.

'He's dead.'

'What are you talking about?'

'He's at the bottom of the pool,' I told her. 'He drowned.'

Her voice was in my ear suddenly. 'I could shoot you for saying that.' She stepped back. 'Why would he be in the pool? He can't swim.'

'He jumped in.'

'He wouldn't do that.'

'He wanted – to kill me.' I was shivering. It was hard to speak. 'I jumped in to get away from him. He came after me. I tried to save him, but it was too late.'

She walked away and when she returned she was dragging something along the ground. I thought it was probably one of those long-handled nets that people use for scooping leaves out of a pool. Or it could have been a gardening implement. A hoe, for instance.

'There's nothing there,' she said after a while.

'He's further out,' I said, 'towards the middle.'

The water swirled as she poked at it.

'You'll need some men,' I told her.

'I found a jacket,' she said, 'that's all.'

'It's probably mine.'

She lifted it clear. I heard it dripping, then it landed on the ground beside me with a soft slap.

'There's nothing else,' she said.

'You should get some men,' I said.

But she wasn't listening. She'd started talking, half to herself, I heard the words *child* and *lake*. She was back in her story again, somewhere near the beginning.

Her voice faded, the way stations fade on the radio. Then it came back, stronger than before. I thought she must be pacing up and down beside the pool.

Her life was made up of everything that she could not forget. That wasn't so uncommon. The difference was, she had to rehearse it constantly, as if it hadn't happened yet. She went over it again and again, even though she knew it off by heart.

My teeth were clattering so hard, I couldn't keep my mouth closed. My body ached from being held in one position for too long.

'Get some men,' I said.

One hand on the banisters, I climbed the stairs to the first floor. Though I didn't expect Loots for a while yet, I doubted I'd be able to sleep. All I could think of was the dead man lying in the dust at the bottom of the pool. Martha had fetched two brothers from the village. I hadn't caught their names. One of them ran the grocer's shop. They were out there now, dredging the water for Mazey's body. I wondered how soft his skin would be by the time they brought him up. I wondered whether they would find my shoes.

I felt for the lock and slid my key into it. I needn't have bothered; the door was already open. I walked into my room. I could tell there was someone there. I could tell who it was, too. The smell of smoke gave her away.

'Mrs Hekmann?'

Where was she? I remembered the chair and table by the window. I thought she must be sitting there.

'Did they find him yet?' she said.

I sat down on the edge of the bed. 'I don't know.'

'Maybe he went to the city. He's always doing that – '

'I told you. He's dead.'

'But of course there's no reason for him to go there,' she said, 'not now.'

She was sliding a hard object around on the surface of the table. The ashtray, probably. I doubted if she knew she was doing it. It was like Nina and the beer mats.

Nina . . .

'I've decided to tell you the rest,' Edith Hekmann said.

I shook my head. 'I don't want to hear it.'

'Of course he didn't tell me everything. I'm going to have to make some of it up. But I've got a pretty good idea. The bare bones of it, in any case.' A hollow chuckle.

'You don't have to do that,' I said. 'I just told you.'

'You're not chicken, are you?'

I laughed, but it sounded unconvincing.

'It won't take long,' she said.

And though the room was different, it was just like that other night. She began a long way back, in a place where the story ran smoothly. She set you afloat on it. You drifted. Then, quite suddenly, you were in white water and by then, of course, there was nothing you could do.

She'd found out that Mazey was going to the city and she'd found out why. He had a photograph of Nina, the one Jan Salenko had sent. He thought it was Karin, though. Not that they looked identical. They didn't. But the girl in the photo and the girl in his memory were the same age. For Mazey, that was enough. The two girls were the same girl, and he was determined to find her. He had a question for her. An important question.

The photo never left his hand, not even when it was winter and he wasn't wearing any gloves. His fingers would practically freeze around it. He would walk into a bar or a cheap café or a fast-food restaurant, and he would lay the photo down in front of him and then he would stare at his hand and wait for the life to flow back into it. People in those places, they were always teasing him. *Is that your little sister? Is that your girl? You think I could make it with her? How much?*

And when he didn't say anything, when he just looked at them with eyes that turned them into ghosts, they sometimes said, *What are you staring at? You got some kind of problem?* And he'd come back to the village with a tooth missing, or flakes of dried blood in his ears. Other times they were fascinated by the picture and they bent right over it and studied it close up. *No*, they'd say. *Don't know her. No, I've never seen her.*

He found her by chance. It was a spring evening and he was walking in the streets behind the flower market. She came out of a corner shop and stood on the pavement, looking up into the sky. All the light was up there, above the rooftops; down on the street it was almost dark. He stood beside her, facing her. He waited. At last, sensing his presence, she turned and looked at him. He showed her the photo. She stared at the photo, then at him. Then at the photo again. She asked him who he was. He didn't answer. He was still holding the photo up for her to see.

'Where's the baby?' he said.

She glanced beyond him, waved her arm. A taxi appeared. She opened the door and climbed in. He watched the taxi pull away with her inside it. Why had she left like that? What had he done?

Edith Hekmann's chair creaked as she shifted on it. I was still sitting on the bed. Nina in profile, gliding out of reach. I remembered Kolan talking. *She saw it as an omen.* Then he'd corrected himself. *A warning.* I put my head in my hands. My face was wet.

'People say men don't cry,' Edith Hekmann said, 'but they do. They're always crying.' She paused. 'I think it's a sign of weakness.'

I spoke into my hands. 'I don't give a fuck what you think.'

'My husband used to cry.' She paused again. 'But I already told you that.'

She was still moving that object around. It sounded more like a bottle now. Or maybe it was an ashtray after all. One of those heavy ones. Cut-glass.

'Anyway,' she said.

Each time Mazey was in the city, he went to the corner shop in the hope of seeing her again and getting an answer to his question. He always appeared at sunset, which was when he'd seen her last. He stood and stared at soap-powder, cereal, canned fruit. Sometimes he was in there for over an hour. He never bought anything. Finally the owner became suspicious. Threw him out. But Mazey got it into his head that the girl must be hidden there somewhere. He pushed past the owner, back into the shop. Then he began to look for her, pulling tins and packets off the shelves. The police were called. Mazey spent a night in a prison cell on a charge of disturbing the peace. When they released him, he hitched a ride north, one and a half days in a lorry that was piled high with grit.

Three weeks later he was back again. He stayed with Ackal and Moler in their two-room apartment near the bus station. He lay on the bare mattresses and drank vodka out of dirty glasses. They taught him card games. Teased him about his photograph. During the long hot evenings he watched the corner shop, but the girl did not appear.

It wasn't until December that his luck changed. On his way south he stole a van. He'd been waiting at the service station for hours; nobody had even looked at him. He was cold and tired, and the van had a cassette machine in it. He forced the door. Soon he was driving past the petrol pumps and out on to the motorway. His tape was playing, the tape of Miss Poppel's chimes. He turned it up so loud, he could hear the wind moaning in the background. His mouth widened a fraction, which meant that he was smiling. Later, Ackal asked him if the van was stolen. He nodded. Ackal turned to the man with the jewel in his ear. 'Learns fast, doesn't he.'

One afternoon Mazey was driving through the western suburbs when he saw the girl walk out across the pavement and climb into a car. It wasn't excitement that he felt. It was more like a kind of recognition or contentment: things had fallen into place at last. The car was a gold colour. He followed it. His photo lay on the dashboard, weighed down with a stone.

The girl drove through the city centre and on into what used to be the railway yards. As she passed a low, concrete building she slowed down. The building had a pink flashing sign on it and no windows. She parked just beyond it. He watched her from across the street as she walked up to the black man who was standing by the door. They talked for a moment, then she disappeared inside.

Mazey waited there all evening. It was a wide street, badly lit, with rubbish blowing over it. Just traffic-lights and tramlines. And that sign, of course – *flash, flash, flash*. He stared at it so long, it was printed on the air in front of him, even when he looked away; he had to shake his head like a money box to rid himself of it. Every now and then he got out of the van and walked up and down the pavement, but he never took his eyes off the girl's gold car, not for more than a few seconds. Once, he went up to it and wiped the window with his hand and peered in. There was nothing much to interest him except the objects dangling from the rear-view mirror. He couldn't quite make out what they were – there was too much condensation – but he knew why they were there. He nodded when he saw them. Chimes.

By the time she appeared again, it was after midnight. The black man walked her to her car. He leaned on the top of the open door while she sat behind the wheel. Mazey could hear their voices. Finally the man took a step backwards and her door slammed shut. She sounded the horn as she pulled out into the fitful late-night traffic. She seemed to enjoy driving through orange lights. He often had to drive through red ones to keep up with her. Though she drove like someone who was being followed, she didn't seem to realise he was there.

She stopped on a street that was lined with trees. He watched her climb a flight of steps. A door opened. She was inside the house for almost an hour and when she came out again, there was a man with her. He was wearing a leather jacket. They drove back to the city centre and parked in a side street behind the railway station. The man said goodbye to her and left. Mazey followed the girl into the station. It was the middle of the night, but there were still crowds of people around, some walking in unsteady circles, others asleep on benches. They didn't surprise or upset him at all; he'd often done the same thing himself.

The girl disappeared into the café. He stayed outside, leaning against the hot-drinks machine. He liked the sound it made when someone put their money in, the way it shook and rumbled. He hadn't been there long when a man with dark glasses and a white stick passed by. Mazey didn't know what a blind man was. He'd never seen one before. The dark glasses, the white stick. It worried him, somehow.

It worried him even more when the blind man walked into the café and sat down opposite the girl. The blind man was facing the window. After a while he took his glasses off and wiped his eyes. Was he crying? Mazey pulled back from the window, puzzled. But there was nothing he could do – nothing he could do except go back to the drinks machine and wait. And wait. The hands on the station clock only moved if you didn't look at them.

At last the door of the café opened and the girl came out. She was alone. Mazey took a step towards her, then he stopped. She looked up and saw him standing there, staring at her. Just then, the café door opened again. It was the blind man. He called the girl's name several times. As she turned to speak to him, Mazey drew back into the shadows.

The blind man and the girl left the station together. Mazey followed them. It was snowing now, bitterly cold, and the wind cut through his coat. He reached into his pocket for the vodka Ackal had given him. His hands were numb; after he'd drunk from the bottle, he could hardly screw the top back on. Halfway down the street the blind man swung round and stared at him. The girl, too. Mazey stopped, uncertain what to do. But then they hurried on again. It looked as if they were making for her car. When they reached the car, though, the blind man turned his back on the girl and walked away. Mazey was relieved. The blind man had begun to frighten him.

The girl stood on the pavement, snow sticking to her hair. She shouted something, but it was taken by the wind – and, anyway, the blind man had already disappeared into a building; he couldn't help her. She found her keys and unlocked the door of her car. She didn't notice the van that was parked behind her. From where he was sitting, hands on the steering-wheel, Mazey could see the shape of her head framed in the rear window. He thought of a morning by the stream. The shape of the girl's head on the ground, hair covering her face. And then, when he had finished, she jumped into the water and she stood there, and her dress spread around her on the surface like the green pad of a lily . . .

It took her a while to start the car. But when she drove away, she drove fast. This time he was ready. He followed her to a tall grey house on a street not far from the flower market. Then, as she opened her car door and got out, he walked up to her and hit her with a jack. She slumped against the side of her car as though she had suddenly, and mysteriously, fallen asleep. He lifted her into his arms and –

'You're making this part up,' I said.

'You think so?' Edith Hekmann's voice was sharp. When I didn't answer, she said, 'What about the rest of it? Was that made up?'

'I don't want to hear any more.'

'Yes, you do.' After pausing for a moment, as if to emphasise the truth of what she'd said, she continued:

He lifted the girl into his arms –

I knew what she was doing now. This story was her revenge on me. I was going to hear it whether I liked it or not (and if I didn't like it, maybe that was even better). There was a door in the room, but I would never find it, not until she'd finished talking. I tried not to listen, but her voice got through. Perhaps, after all, she was right. There was a part of me that had to know.

– into his arms and carried her to the van. He opened the door on the passenger side and lowered her on to the seat. But when he closed the door, her head fell sideways, the skin above her eyebrow flattening against the window. He opened the door and she collapsed. He had to push her further along the seat, further in. He closed the door again. This time she stayed sitting up. He looked left and right. There was nobody about. She lived in a quiet area. And besides, it was late. Probably three or four in the morning.

As he turned out of her street he slid his tape into the stereo. There was a calmness then. Snow lay on the windscreens of parked cars. Houses came and went like dreams – bright and strange, but instantly forgotten. He heard a sigh. The girl had woken up. Almost immediately she bent over and was sick on the floor. A hot, bitter smell filled the inside of the van.

He took the route he would have taken if he'd been driving home. He recognised the buildings, the roundabouts, the signs. Everything was comforting, familiar. Even the girl who was in the van with him. Once, though, she opened the window and started shouting. He had to hit her on the head again to keep her quiet. She slept for a long time after that.

She was still quiet when he turned off the road, into a building site. He stopped the van. He put his arms around her and lifted her out through the driver's side. He laid her carefully on the ground. It was a damp, muddy place. A cold wind blowing. Plastic sheets shifted and billowed against the scaffolding. Mazey stared at the photograph in his hand, then he stared at the girl who was lying below him. Somewhere not too far away there was the sound of metal knocking against metal.

When she opened her eyes, he bent down and held her wrist. He meant to be affectionate. But then he remembered that she didn't like him to touch her and he took his hand away.

'Where's the baby?' he said.

'What baby's that?' she said in a faint voice.

'Your baby,' he said.

She frowned slightly. 'I don't have a baby.'

'You have a baby,' he said. 'You hid it.'

She tried to sit up, but he put one hand on her chest and pushed her down.

He asked her again. 'Where's the baby?'

She closed her eyes and would not answer.

He picked up the jack and hit her with it, then he put it on the ground beside her. He undid the buttons on her leather coat and opened it. Grasping her sweater by the hem, he lifted it up over her body until it covered her face. It wouldn't go any further. His hands hovered in the air above her, undecided. He took hold of the vest that she was wearing underneath. Pushed it up over the sweater. Her arms were still trapped in the arms of her coat. They stretched out on either side of her, bent at the elbows; she looked oddly relaxed. He tucked his fingers under the waistband of her skirt and pulled at it until the zip broke. He tugged it down below the level of her hips. Her underpants came with it. Next, he took his pen-knife out. He chose the longest of the three blades and snapped it open. Tested it against his thumb, the way he'd been taught. Placing the tip of the blade in the middle of her rib-cage, just at the point where the two halves joined, he pressed down hard. He cut in a straight line until the blade ran up against her pelvic bone. Blood slid across her belly. He put the pen-knife down and reached inside her. There didn't appear to be anything alive in there –

I didn't recognise the woman at first. She was bathed in radiance and I was walking towards her. I weighed almost nothing. The ground didn't seem firm enough to be the real ground. Her hair wasn't hair at all but light. Her hands reached out eagerly to welcome me.

She showed me some clothes that were dirty and her face was troubled. What should I do? she seemed to be asking. What *can* I do? I didn't know. I, too, was filled with despair.

'Mr Blom?'

A voice was calling me. I didn't want to answer it.

Time passed miraculously fast and suddenly the clothes that she was holding up for me to see were clean and white, and she was smiling. I wanted to rejoice with her.

'Mr Blom?'

'What is it?' I was irritable. 'What?'

I could feel carpet under my left eyebrow. Under my cheekbone as well. And my right hand.

'You passed out.'

It was Edith Hekmann's voice.

'Probably all that talk of blood,' I heard her say. 'Some people faint even at the mention of it.'

I pushed myself up off the floor and sat on the edge of the bed with my head between my knees. She talked on. I didn't have the strength to stop her. After a while I lay back. Then I turned over, on to my side. The blankets were warm beneath me. I felt peculiarly comfortable all of a sudden. Peculiarly well.

– He wrapped her in her leather coat and lifted her and put her in the back of the van. He covered her with a piece of blue tarpaulin. Not far from the van there was an oil-drum filled to the brim with rain-water. He washed his hands and arms in it. He didn't panic; it wasn't in his nature. He just climbed into the van and turned it round and drove out of the building site. The snow eased as he moved north. For a while there was sleet. Then, finally, just rain.

When it was light, he pulled into a petrol station. The man who worked the pumps wanted to talk. First he said something about how early it was. Mazey just nodded. Next he mentioned the weather. Mazey agreed with him. Then, as he walked round the van to put the pump back on its bracket, he said, 'You've got something bleeding in there, mister.'

Mazey looked up from the money he was counting.

'There's something bleeding in the back of your van,' the man said.

'Deer,' said Mazey.

'Making one hell of a mess.'

Mazey nodded.

'Deer, eh?'

'Shot it this morning. Back there.' And Mazey angled his thumb over his shoulder, back along the road.

He paid for the petrol.

'Interesting music,' the man said.

'Yeah,' said Mazey.

Then he drove away.

It was late afternoon when he reached the village. She remembered that she was taking the washing in when he came round the corner of the building. She remembered watching him as he walked towards her. There was nothing nervous or hesitant about him, nothing to suggest that something might be wrong. There never was.

But then he took her by the arm and though his touch was gentle there was a pressure in it.

'What is it, Mazey?'

'The van,' he said.

'What van?'

He led her to the car-park at the side of the hotel and showed her the van. It was pale-blue, with rust around the headlights and the wheel-arches.

'Where did you get it?' she asked him.

'I took it.' He told her the name of the service station. Then he opened the back doors and lifted the tarpaulin.

She reached in quickly, drew the tarpaulin over the body, then glanced behind her. The windows of the inn were black, empty. At that time of day the residents would be sitting in the drawing-room and listening to the news on the radio. Martha would be preparing supper in the kitchen. No one could have seen anything. She bent down, felt for a pulse. Not that there was much chance of that: the injuries were too severe. But she had to make quite certain.

The girl was dead, and had been dead for hours. She wasn't sure whether or not she should feel relieved.

'When did this happen?' she asked.

Mazey stood beside her with his hands in his pockets. He was also looking at the inn, not furtively, though, as she had done, not guiltily at all, but with the complacency of somebody who called it home.

She had to repeat the question.

'Last night,' he said.

'Did anyone see you?'

He shook his head.

She took him by the arm. 'You have to get rid of the van. I don't care how you do it. Just get rid of it. Do you understand?'

'Maybe tomorrow.'

'Now, Mazey. You do it now.'

Only then did he look down at her, a look that stopped just behind her eyes, at the entrance to her brain. It angered her, to think that he might challenge her.

'Right now,' she said.

He stood there for a while longer, frowning. At last he moved past her and opened the door on the driver's side. He ducked sideways for a moment. His music started up – the tape she'd made for him.

'Quieter, Mazey,' she said. 'Quieter.'

He grinned at her and pushed the hair out of his eyes.

She watched him reverse into the road and drive away. That night there was a storm. A month's rain fell in less than twelve hours. Even the church flooded; hymn-books were found in the meadow, swollen to twice their normal size. Mazey did not return.

He was gone for three days.

I heard a car in the distance. Thinking it might be Loots, I swung my legs on to the floor. But the sound didn't grow any louder; instead, it seemed to pass at a tangent to the village.

'Three days it took him,' Edith Hekmann said, 'and when he came back he was on foot.'

I asked her what had happened to the body. She didn't know.

'You've no idea?'

'That's right. I've no idea.' She seemed to relish the fact. She'd tortured me with what she knew, but that wasn't enough. Now she wanted to torture me with what she didn't know as well.

'You're lying,' I said. 'He would've told you.'

'He didn't tell me.' She paused. 'I didn't ask.'

'*You're lying.*'

She laughed. It was only air, almost inaudible, but utterly contemptuous at the same time. I reached out and my hand closed round a lamp. I pulled it hard, snapping the wire, and threw it at her. It hit the wall and shattered.

'You're in a bad way.' Her voice came from the corner of the room.

I didn't say anything.

'You'll never make it in the police,' she said. 'You're not cut out for it. If I was you, I'd start looking for some other kind of work.'

'How many times – ' I began, but she talked over me.

'Those castles in the mountains,' she was saying, 'those battlements. They don't exist.'

I stared at her.

'Don't worry,' she said, 'you're blind. You won't see a thing.'

'What do you mean?'

There was a click made up of two quick sounds, but I didn't have time to identify it because it was followed, almost immediately, by a deafening explosion. I felt bits of something land on me. At first I couldn't imagine what it was. It felt like mud thrown up by the wheels of a passing car. It was solid, and strangely warm. It went cold fast, though. Then I knew.

I couldn't move.

'Mrs Hekmann?'

My voice sounded far away, as if there was a wall between me and what I'd said.

'Mrs Hekmann?'

I listened for a whisper, breathing, anything – but all I could hear was people coming up the stairs. Two people. Both men, by the sound of it. I listened carefully. Yes, two men.

The brothers from the village.

I sat on the steps of the hotel, my suitcase on the porch behind me. I remembered my call to Loots. He'd told me he would drive through the night. He would be with me by dawn, he said, or shortly after – I'd made him promise – but it was after dawn and he hadn't appeared yet. I was sitting on the steps waiting for the sound of his car in the distance. I hoped it wouldn't be much longer.

The police had already been, tyres slurring on the gravel as they braked. I didn't understand what the hurry was. There was nobody to arrest or apprehend. There was hardly even anyone to question. All the crimes had been committed and all the criminals were gone.

'Are you the blind man, sir?'

The policeman was too alert. There was something farcical about it. He was like someone who thought it was the beginning of the story when really it was the end.

'Well?' His voice moved closer, officious now and slightly nasal. 'Are you?'

Don't ever ignore policemen. If there's one thing they can't stand.

I nodded wearily. 'I'm the blind man.'

'We're going to need some kind of statement.'

'It's no good asking me,' I said.

'Oh? Why's that?'

'I didn't see a thing.'

'You were there, though,' the policeman said.

No sense of humour. No sense of humour whatsoever.

I dictated a few sentences for him. I said that I had fallen into the pool and that Mazey Hekmann had drowned while trying to rescue me. When Edith Hekmann learned of her son's death, she had shot herself. The real crimes were hidden between the lines. I was keeping them for Munck. I thought Munck should get the credit. I wanted him to have that street named after him.

I reached for my suitcase, pulled it closer. The old people would be sitting at their tables in the dining-room, waiting for their breakfast to be served. If only Loots would come. I already knew what I was going to say to him. *I'm blind. I realise that now. But still. Don't ever tell me what you look like. I've got my own ideas. You're thin, just as Nina's beautiful. I don't want to hear any different. I don't want to know. You're thin, with red hair. You've got shoulderblades that stick out. Cheekbones, too. You do extraordinary things on bicycles. No, don't laugh. It's what I think. It's true.* Somehow I felt that he would understand. I couldn't wait for him to arrive. I wanted to throw my arms around him, embrace him.

The sun slowly warmed the left side of my face.

To think that I'd entertained the notion of a silver room! I could still imagine it – the walls and ceiling lined with kitchen foil, and bits of wire radiating in all directions – but I knew I'd never build it, not now. I couldn't spend my life in a place like that. Nobody could. And besides, it wouldn't have been going far enough. After all, what would happen when I left the room? Everything I'd been trying to avoid would be waiting for me just outside the door. No, a silver room would never have sufficed. I'd have needed more protection than that. A silver suit, perhaps, like something an astronaut might wear. A helmet, too. But why stop there? In the end I would have been forced to take the idea to its logical conclusion. Silver skin.

I took a deep breath and let the air ease out of me. The smell of the countryside in winter. Wood fires and muddy fields. Snow.

At last I heard the car. It crept, soft-tyred, along the road and parked outside the inn. I stood up, stretched. A door opened. Footsteps across the grass, keys bouncing on a hand.

Loots.

'About time,' I said.

The footsteps stopped. A shadow fell across me. 'There you are.'

I stared. Because it wasn't Loots' voice. It was Visser's.

'We've been looking for you everywhere.'

I stepped backwards, stumbled, almost tripped. What I felt was partly surprise – I'd been expecting someone else – and partly trepidation, which was the legacy of all the hallucinations. But there was nothing to be frightened of, I told myself. There was nothing to fear. Visser was my doctor. And excellent he was, too, by all accounts. He would only have my best interests at heart.

'How are you, Martin?'

'You know, you were right,' I said. 'You were right all along.'

There was a silence, one of Visser's famous silences, but I knew that, if I'd been granted a moment's vision, if I could have seen him, just for an instant, standing there in his overcoat (if indeed he wore an overcoat!), he would've been smiling down at me, with pride.

At the same time, though, now that he was here, in the village, it was hard to rule out the possibility that he might simply have discontinued the experiment. Just kind of disconnected me. Brought the whole thing to an end. Out of pity. Believing, finally, that I'd had enough.

It was possible, surely.

After all, on the far side of the moon, there are intelligent life-forms who are keeping us under constant observation.

And there is always somebody behind you, with a gun.